Where had the simple life gone? Days I'd only have to worry about Keats playing around behind my back, my mother loose with her credit card in some shopping center, Delia's soft smile lying lovingly into my naïve eyes, small, everyday occurrences in the life of a growing boy? Not homicide, suicide, and now litigiousness in preppy-dom.

I could hear the chapel bells tolling.

"Lauren? I have to go now, but before I do—I'm sorry all this has had to happen."

"Some of it didn't *have* to happen. Damn him! If he wasn't dead, I'd—"

I could hear the sob.

"There're still some unanswered questions," I said.

"FELL?" she said threateningly.

"Okay," I said. "Okay."

ALSO BY M. E. KERR:

FELL BACK

Edgar Allan Poe Award Finalist
(Mystery Writers of America)
Books for the Teen Age (The New York Public Library)

FELL

Best Books for Young Adults (ALA)
Booklist *Books for Youth Editors' Choices*
Books for the Teen Age (The New York Public Library)

LITTLE LITTLE

School Library Journal *Best Books*
Golden Kite Award (SCBWI)
Books for the Teen Age (The New York Public Library)

GENTLEHANDS

Best of the Best Books (ALA)
School Library Journal *Best Book*
Christopher Award
Outstanding Children's Books of the Year
   (The New York Times)
Books for the Teen Age (The New York Public Library)

IF I LOVE YOU, AM I TRAPPED FOREVER?

Outstanding Children's Books of the Year
   (The New York Times)
Child Study Association's Children's Books of the Year
Book World's *Children's Spring Book Festival*
   Honor Book

DINKY HOCKER SHOOTS SMACK!

Best of the Best Books (ALA)
Notable Children's Book (ALA)
School Library Journal *Best Book*
Children's Books of the Year (Library of Congress)

PRAISE FOR THE FELL TRILOGY

"[The John Fell books] are clearly becoming the best YA mystery series around."
—DONALD R. GALLO, *THE ALAN REVIEW*

"Not since GENTLEHANDS has Kerr so poignantly combined a story of romance, mystery, and wit with serious implications of class conflict and personal betrayal." —ALA *BOOKLIST*

"The plot is well constructed, and the characterization is superb. Kerr's breezy style smacks with vitality and realistic humor."
—*SCHOOL LIBRARY JOURNAL*

"Will enthrall both Kerr's fans and new readers."
—*PUBLISHERS WEEKLY*

"Kerr manages an almost perfect balance of dry wit and suspense, with Fell standing squarely as a likable, well-balanced hero in a world more than slightly off-kilter. . . . Readers will be hooked."
—*VOYA*

"As pithy and as rhythmically involving as the sharply witty shadow dance that constitutes the plot." —*KIRKUS REVIEWS*

"The writing has vitality and substance."
—*THE BULLETIN OF THE CENTER FOR CHILDREN'S BOOKS*

THE BOOKS OF FELL

M. E. KERR

fell

fell back

fell down

HarperTrophy®
An Imprint of HarperCollinsPublishers

Harper Trophy® is a registered trademark of
HarperCollins Publishers Inc.

The Books of Fell
Copyright © 2001 by M. E. Kerr
Fell copyright © 1987 by M. E. Kerr
Fell Back copyright © 1989 by M. E. Kerr
Fell Down copyright © 1991 by M. E. Kerr

Library of Congress Cataloging-in-Publication Data
Kerr, M. E.
    The books of Fell / M. E. Kerr.— 1st Harper Trophy ed.
        p.   cm.
    Contents: Fell — Fell back — Fell down.
    Summary: A young man from the wrong side of the tracks, John Fell investigates
spies, drug dealers, murders, and a decades-old disappearance case, all of which are
connected to his exclusive prep school's mysterious club, Sevens.
    ISBN 0-06-447263-9 (pbk.)
    1. Young adult fiction, American. [1. Boarding schools—Fiction. 2. Schools—
Fiction. 3. Secret societies—Fiction. 4. Mystery and detective stories.] I. Kerr,
M. E. Fell. II. Kerr, M. E. Fell back. III. Kerr, M. E. Fell down. IV. Title.
PZ7.K46825 Bo 2001   2001016840
[Fic]—dc21   CIP
                                                                            AC

Typography by Karin Paprocki
❖
First Harper Trophy edition, 2001
Visit us on the World Wide Web!
www.harperteen.com

CONTENTS

THE
BOOKS
OF FELL

fell

SMILES WE LEFT BEHIND US

part 1

chapter | 1

On the night of the Senior Prom, I was stood up by Helen J. Keating—"Keats" they called her in Seaville, New York.

This isn't a story about Keats and me, and it isn't about that humiliating event in my seventeenth year. But Keats is a part of the story, and that humiliation was responsible for everything that happened to change my life . . . and even my name.

The Keatings lived on Dune Road, at the top of a hill in a palatial home. Adieu, they had named it, and it looked down on Seaville as surely as they did. It was the last house Keats's father would ever build—his good-bye to his profession. He was an architect of some renown, and certainly Adieu was an architect's dream. It was anyone's dream—who wouldn't like living in that place?

But to me Adieu meant good-bye in another way, from the moment I first saw Keats up there. It meant hello and good-bye. It meant good-bye, you can never have that girl. Say hello; then say adieu.

What does your father do? was the second question I was ever asked by Keats's father. The first one was How are you? Mr. Keating didn't wait for an answer. He didn't care how I was. He cared what my father did.

I said, "My father was a detective."

"Was?" he said. "Is he dead?"

"Yes, sir. He died six months ago."

"I'm sorry to hear that, Fell. That's your name, isn't it?"

"Yes. John Fell."

I would have liked to say (and Mr. Keating would have liked to hear me say), But, Mr. Keating, sir, I am heir to a fortune and descended from William the Conqueror, bound for Harvard University when I graduate from high school, a Christian, a Republican, an honor student.

If I could have said those things, he wouldn't have heard me anyway, for his plump behind was turned by then, and he was slapping his arm around Quint Blade, Keats's football star boyfriend. All of them up at Adieu that day would be seniors in the fall. I would be a junior.

I had been invited to that pool party by a fluke. I had waited on Keats in Plain and Fancy, the gourmet food shop where I had a part-time job. She'd wandered in there one afternoon after school to buy truffles with almonds in them, a quart of Häagen-Dazs coffee ice cream, and fresh everything from cherries to strawberries—a shopping bag filled with goodies and charged to her father's Diner's Club account.

"Aren't you the new boy at school?" she asked me.

"Sort of new. I've been here a year," I told her. But I *was* new to her and her crowd. I was new to any crowd in Seaville. (And the less said about my old crowd in Brooklyn, the better.) That was when she invited me to Adieu.

In between that party up at Adieu and her Senior Prom, we fell in love, blown away by the kind of passion that made Dante write about Beatrice, Tristram hunger for Isolde, and my father's last client dog the steps of his young, unfaithful wife, who sneaked off to roadhouses where the jukebox roared and men drank beer from the neck of the bottle.

My father died sitting outside one of those

places, waiting for something to report back to his anxious client. My father was always waiting outside someplace. A detective's life is not really filled with car chases and flying bullets. It is almost never what you see on TV. It is waiting with a thermos of coffee, and an extra pair of shoes in the backseat of your car, in case you're somewhere all day on your feet.

I had inherited his patience and his determination . . . and I would need them to be Helen J. Keating's lover. Love is never enough when there are parents whose dream for their only daughter does not include someone whose father had a heart attack in a 1977 Dodge Dart while waiting for a roundheels to leave a bar with someone she'd picked up inside. It does not include someone whose mother has gone over her $1000 limit on every charge card in her purse. (The morning of the Senior Prom, I'd found a Born to Shop decal in a store next to the florist, bought it, and attached it to the back of my mother's rusting white Volkswagen.)

Keats's mother we could handle. She was most famous in Seaville for her book reviews in *The Seaville Star*. She'd once reviewed a book called *Coke Is Not It!*, about kids who put themselves through college dealing drugs, with this lead paragraph: *If anyone's child is using pot or cocaine, I have yet to meet the parents, and I pride myself on getting out and about in my community. So who is to believe this author with her alarmist Henny-Penny warnings?*

That was Mrs. Keating . . . a tiny, smiling woman, suntanned in winter from visits to Palm Beach, forever warning Keats "Don't tell Daddy!" when she allowed us to go places and do things Mr. Keating would have denied us.

Once Mr. Keating got the idea that Keats and I were captured by a chemistry between us that compelled us to head for the dunes, or the game room in the basement of Adieu, or the backseat of the old Dodge I'd inherited from my father, he began to put his foot down. But Mr. Keating traveled as a consultant and a lecturer, and his foot was often miles away from Seaville, New York.

One day in late May we felt the full weight of that foot when he arrived unexpectedly at Adieu. Mrs. Keating was off at a Ladies' Village Improvement Society meeting, dealing with a way to prevent Dutch elm disease in the trees that lined Main Street. Keats and I were up in her yellow-and-white bedroom, listening to old tapes of Van Halen and Phil Collins, the rain pouring down outside. We'd just come from school, drenched, enough of our clothes drying over the backs of yellow chairs for Mr. Keating to see red.

"The Senior Prom is out of the question for you two!" Mr. Keating shouted. "Helen, the only way you'll get to it is to get yourself another date!"

It was Mrs. Keating who finally said, "All right! All right! All *right*! Go to the prom! I haven't the heart to say no! But don't tell Daddy!"

So with Daddy away, I went to Pittman Florist the day of the prom and ordered a white orchid sent to Keats. Across the card I wrote three words my father's last client had had embroidered across half a dozen silk nightgowns he'd given his young bride for a wedding gift: *Thine until death!*

When the box arrived at noon, Keats called me. "Oh, Fell! Thine until death! No one's ever written anything so romantic to me! I can't wait until tonight! Don't come at eight, come at five to."

"I'll be there at quarter to."

"No, come at twenty to."

We were always doing that, making our dates earlier and earlier, unable to wait.

I rented a white dinner jacket and black tuxedo pants. I bought a red boutonniere, and put a shine I could see my face in on a pair of my father's old black wing tips.

Maybe Keats and I were just narcissists, in love with our own reflections. We looked enough alike to be brother and sister. Both of us had blond hair and deep blue eyes, though Keats claimed mine were really purple. She'd say, "I'm in love with a boy with purple eyes." Keats had shoulder-length hair, a long thin nose, and skinny long legs, and she always wore Obsession.

The rich don't live right on the road. They live up, back, and behind. From the time you enter the property at Adieu, you have a good three minutes before you see anything but trees. Once you see the house, you have another three minutes before you pull up to it. So on prom night I had six minutes to anticipate seeing Keats. Six minutes to gloat over the idea that I, a lowly junior, had beaten out Quint Blade in the contest for Keats. Six minutes to imagine my white orchid pinned to her, and that smile of hers that lights up rooms already aglow.

Now, looking back, I don't think anyone in Seaville, including my mother, ever thought Keats and I would make it through a year. We were a golden couple without a cheering section. No one was for us but us.

The Keatings didn't call Eaton a butler, but that's what he came off as, even though he doubled as caretaker. He wore an ordinary dark business suit when he answered the door.

"Good evening, Eaton!" I said jovially. Eaton could smile. I'd seen him smile. But he couldn't smile at me, or wouldn't, not even that night, when he must have known what I was walking into.

Foster, the black poodle, was sniffing my pants leg as though I were a suspicious character.

I'd never won the dog over, either.

"Mr. Fell," Eaton said, "Miss Keating left you this note and this package."

The note was one of those little white cards, folded over. Inside, her handwriting, with the circles over the i's:

Daddy came back right before dinner.
He's forcing me to go into New York City
with him and Mother. I tried to call you.
I'm destroyed over it, Fell!
Thine until death, and after, and after that!
K.

I looked up at Eaton, who had no expression.

I didn't want to have an expression, either, for him to take any satisfaction in, so I turned to go. I wondered if I could still walk now that my heart had fallen down into my shoes.

But Eaton was not finished.

"You have another message, Mr. Fell."

He handed me a small business card with raised print. On the front: *Lawrence O. Keating.* On the back, in a large, firm hand: *You are no longer welcome at Adieu! This ends it, Fell! L.O.K.*

Foster punctuated the message with an angry bark.

I went outside in a blur, clutching the small, gift-wrapped package. My father used to tell me never be ashamed of your tears, only be ashamed when you don't have any and the occasion calls for tears.

He would have been proud of me that night.

By the time I opened the gift from Keats—a purple silk bow tie—there were tears rolling down my face.

I shoved the tie back into its tissue and threw the box on the seat beside me. I took off with a lurch that kicked up the gravel in the driveway. I began to pick up speed as I headed down toward Dune Road.

Adieu is flanked by Beauregard on one side and Fernwood Manor on the other. All three driveways lead down to Dune Road.

The car I didn't see was coming from Fernwood Manor.

It was a dark-blue Mitsubishi I'd seen going in and out of there before. But I'd never come as close to it as I did that night—I rammed right into its back end. Then I sat there with my horn stuck, waiting for doom to descend.

That was how I met Woodrow Pingree.

chapter | 2

One day Keats and I watched them, through the elephant grass, on a dune out behind Adieu.

"Who are they?" I asked her.

"Woodrow and Fern Pingree," Keats said. "They live at Fernwood Manor. *Woodrow* and Fern. Fernwood. Get it? Isn't that really gross, calling their house after their two first names?"

"At least it's in English," I said. "The Penningtons aren't French, and neither are you. So what's this Beauregard and Adieu? I think *that's* really gross."

"You just don't like Daddy," Keats laughed.

"Why didn't he just call it Good-bye? What's this Adieu crap?"

"Adieu sounds classier."

"It sounds more pretentious," I said.

She put her hand gently across my mouth and said, "Hush, Fell! Don't start in on Daddy. Let's watch the Pingrees instead."

Woodrow Pingree had the muscles of someone who worked out regularly. From the neck down he looked like a man in his late thirties. Above the neck he was around fifty, white-haired, the cut close-cropped like someone in the military. He had a red hue to his face that my father's high blood pressure used to bring to his.

Woodrow Pingree was coming out of the water, even though it was a cold May afternoon, so chilly Keats and I were bundled up in sweaters. Fern Pingree was sitting back near the dunes, sketching.

"He's always going in in weather like this," said Keats. "I've never seen her go in, not even in summer."

"Is she drawing him, do you think?"

"I know she's not. She only paints the ocean. I saw an exhibit of hers at the Stiles Gallery. There are never any people in her ocean scenes, and get this!— she doesn't sign her name. She draws a teensy-weensy fern where the artist's name would be."

Fern Pingree looked much younger than Woodrow Pingree. When my father had that last client with the much younger wife, he'd tell me some men imagine that a new young wife will give them back their youth. I'd say, but what's in it for the new young wife? Money, usually, he'd say. He'd say those young women don't want to wait for a young man to make it, so they grab some old geezer who believes one of them when she says he's sexy, he's fascinating, he dresses too old for how she sees him. Oh, the crap they hand a poor guy you wouldn't believe!

Fern Pingree had inky black hair pulled back behind her head. She was wearing white-framed dark glasses. She was dressed in a white jogging suit with a red down vest and a pair of those shiny olive Bean boots. She had her sketch pad propped up on her knees, but the moment she saw Woodrow Pingree coming toward her, she put it aside. She grabbed a white towel-cloth robe, got to her feet, and ran to meet him, reaching up to put the robe over his wet shoulders.

"His first wife died about eight years ago," said Keats. "That place never had a name until Fern came into his life."

"I don't think I'd name a place anything, either," I said.

"I don't think you'll have a place to name," said Keats. "What do chefs make a year? About twenty thousand?"

"I won't be just a chef. I'll own the place," I said.

"Oh, you'll *own* the place! Will the place be a Burger King, or a McDonald's?"

We were giving each other little pushes, clowning around until we heard Mr. Keating's voice bellowing out over the bullhorn.

"HELEN? I WANT YOU!"

"I want you, too, Helen," I said.

The first time old man Keating ever pulled that on us, we'd jumped as if someone were shooting at us. We'd been stretched out in the dunes and his voice had come booming over that thing like the wrath of God, ready to punish us for all we were about to do.

That afternoon, the Pingrees heard Mr. Keating's voice, too, and glanced up in our direction so that for a moment we were looking at them and they were looking at us.

"Damn Daddy!" Keats said. "That's really humiliating! I know he's watching us through binoculars, too."

"Let's give him something to look at!" I said, and I tried to grab her, but she pulled away. "I have to live with Daddy, Fell! You don't!"

I gave a little wave to the Pingrees as we stood up, but they didn't wave back.

"They don't encourage neighborly behavior," said Keats. "They don't even wave when they come out of their driveway the same time we come out of ours. Daddy says it's just as well. He doesn't want to know his neighbors, either."

"He knows the Penningtons."

"That's different. They're old money, and Skye Pennington is in my crowd. We don't know anything about the Pingrees."

I tried to take her hand, but she was thinking of Daddy with his binoculars out. The very thought of Daddy's watching us touch each other stopped Keats cold.

"We don't even know what Woodrow Pingree does for a living," said Keats.

"Ah!" I said. "The all-important question! What

do you do for a living? What does your father do for a living?"

Keats let that one go by. "But they have this weird kid. He's not a kid, really, he's about your age." I was exactly one year younger than Keats, but in high school a senior is a senior and a junior is not a kid, really, he's about my age.

Keats said, "This kid goes to a military school down south somewhere. Daddy really hates him."

"He must have something admirable about him if Daddy hates him," I said.

"Last Thanksgiving Daddy was jogging down on the beach and this kid jumped out of the dunes and pointed a gun right at Daddy. When he pulled the trigger, a black balloon sailed out of the mouthpiece with BOOM! BOOM! written on it in white. Daddy almost had a heart attack before he saw that it wasn't a real gun. So Daddy called Woodrow Pingree, and do you know what that man said?"

"What?"

"He said, 'I'm sorry, but Ping loves tricks,' and then he laughed like it was funny."

"I think it's kind of funny myself."

Keats said what she always said. "You just don't like Daddy."

That was the only time I even thought about the Pingrees, until the night I drove into the back of their dark-blue Mitsubishi.

chapter | 3

"ou look like you're going someplace special,"
said Woodrow Pingree, after he lifted the hood
of my Dodge and made the horn stop blowing.

"I was. I'm not now." I'd gotten out to face him.

He lit a Viceroy and shoved the little white
Bic lighter back into the pocket of his sports
coat. "This shouldn't take long. We just need to
exchange some insurance information. You can
probably still make it."

"I changed my mind," I said. "I'm not going
where I was going."

He laughed as though I'd said something
funny and told me he didn't think he was going
where he was going, either.

"So follow me up to the house," he said. "We
might as well be comfortable while we're writing
down all the information."

I got back behind the wheel and waited for
him to go up the driveway first. I had a melon-
sized dent in my right front fender, but I figured
I was ahead because he didn't seem at all angry
about his back fender. At least this would help
take my mind off Keats, who was probably a total
wreck because she had to miss her Senior Prom.
Things like that were important to Keats. She

made a big deal over everything from Easter to Valentine's Day. She loved ceremonies, traditions, rituals . . . and the Senior Prom was a once-in-a-lifetime thing. It'd kill Keats not to show up there.

Fernwood Manor didn't look like much of a manor, not like Beauregard or Adieu. There were only two stories. It was built of stone and shingle, with only one chimney. There was a hedge out front, and some trees in tubs. There was a metal jockey holding out a steel ring.

Woodrow Pingree was smoking, no hands, as he got out of the Mitsubishi in the circular driveway. He took another look at the damage I'd done, then gave me as much of a smile as he could and still hold the Viceroy between his lips.

We started walking toward the front door.

"What's your name?" he asked me.

I told him. I told him that I knew his. I'd seen him go swimming one cold day in May.

"Was that you up there in the dunes? Were you with the Pennington girl or the Keating girl?"

"Helen Keating," I said.

"I tell my boy it's a shame. Two beautiful girls within walking distance and he won't even bother to go over and introduce himself."

He held the door open for me, and we walked down this black-and-white tile floor, with a living room to the right, and a dining room the other way.

"Woody?" Mrs. Pingree was sitting on a white wicker chair in the center of the living room. She was an audience of one, facing this kid in a black top hat, who was standing behind a card table with a cloth covering it. He had on a black turtleneck sweater and black pants, and there was a black cape with a red lining over his shoulders. He had a wand in one hand. His glasses were about a half inch thick.

"It's all right, sweetheart! This young man ran into my car down at the bottom of the hill. Don't let me stop the show! We'll have a talk in my study."

He was sort of leaning into the room, without inviting me to go that way.

Mrs. Pingree had her white-framed dark glasses pushed back on her head. She was a tiny woman. I thought she looked a little like Yoko Ono, John Lennon's widow, without the oriental eyes. I guessed she was in her thirties.

"Then you're not going out, Woody?" she said.

"No, I'll be here."

He led me through the dining room toward another room.

"My son's going off to a summer camp for budding magicians in a few weeks," he said. "When he gets there, he has to put on a show. So he's practicing. Do you like magic?"

"Only sort of." I really didn't like it at all. I

thought only real yo-yos did.

"I think my wife only sort of likes it, too, but she tries to humor Ping. He's a nice boy, but he's like America was in 1491. No one discovered it yet." He chuckled at his own joke and led me into his study.

There were a lot of framed photographs lining the walls. There was a large desk, with French doors behind it leading out to a terrace.

He pointed to a leather armchair beside his desk and said to make myself comfortable. He said he was going to call "the Institute" and let them know he wasn't going to be there after all.

He punched out a number, then said to me, "I work at Brutt Institute in Bellhaven. Do you know the place?"

I shook my head no. I only knew that Bellhaven was down in Nassau County.

"No reason why you should," he said. "I'm a physicist. Do you like science?"

"It's my worst subject."

"Are you flunking it?"

"No, not flunking. But anything to do with science and I go down into the B's."

"So. You're mostly an A student," he said. And when I nodded, he added, "Like my son."

Someone answered the phone at that point. Pingree said, "Something's come up. I won't be by. No, nothing to worry about."

He put down the receiver. "I didn't have anything important scheduled. I've seen every one of my son's tricks again and again, so . . . " He let his voice trail off. "Did you bring in your insurance card?"

I got it out of the pocket of my white dinner jacket.

"After telling you to bring yours in I forgot to bring in mine," he said. "I'd better get it, so we can write down all the information. You want a Tab?"

"Do you have Coke?"

"Just Tab. My wife's always on a diet."

"Okay. Tab. Thanks."

He stood up. "You look like you were on your way to a dance. Are you sure you don't want to go?"

I told him my date got sick.

He stubbed out the cigarette he'd just lit and said he'd be right back.

I sat there for a while, glancing through a yearbook that was on the end of his desk. It was from The Valley Academy. The motto of The Valley Academy was *Ne Pas Subir.* Don't submit.

There were things written across photographs of boys in uniform.

Ping,
Next time you make something disappear,
make sure it's you. Steve.

And,

*I just told Brown he was the most
obnoxious boy in roll call, but I'd forgotten
about you, Pingree! George.*

And,

*Don't let me catch you in the dark,
if you come back next year, Nerdo! Al.*

It was more of the same all through Woodrow
Pingree, Jr.'s, yearbook. I wondered why any kid
would bring it home to let his folks see. I wouldn't
have.

I got up and walked to the French doors. I
could see the lights of Adieu across the way. It
seemed as though every light in the place was on.
I wondered if Eaton was throwing a party over
there while the Keatings were in New York City.

I opened the door to get more of a view just as
Mr. Pingree returned with two Tabs on a tray, carrying his insurance card between his teeth.

I took the tray from his hands.

"That's a good idea," he said, nodding toward
the terrace. "Let's sit out there."

After we went outside, he sat there writing out
names and numbers he copied from our insurance
cards. I stood, fascinated by the clear view of

Adieu. Even the driveway lights were on. You could hear the ocean over the dunes.

Finally, Mr. Pingree tore a sheet of paper in half, handed me a piece of it, and said all the information I needed was there.

"I know now isn't a good time," he said, "but I'd like you to meet my boy sometime. He needs a buddy."

"I saw his yearbook in there," I said.

"He's through at Valley now. Are you a sophomore?"

"I'm going to be a senior."

"At Seaville High?"

"Probably not. My mother wants to move back to Brooklyn."

"So you're not from here?"

"No. Brooklyn."

"How long have you been out here?"

I told him, all the while staring over at Adieu. For someone who didn't even wave at his neighbors, he seemed really interested in a complete stranger. He asked a lot of questions. I found myself rattling on about my father's heart attack, my kid sister, my mother's job at Dressed to Kill—I even told him about the Born to Shop decal I'd stuck on the back of my mother's Volkswagen that morning.

He laughed hard at that.

I said, "I guess all women could use one of those decals for their bumpers."

"My first wife would have clobbered you for that remark," he said. "She was a feminist. She hated it when you tried to say females were this way or they were that way. She'd say that was sexist, and I'd say well, when the day comes when we don't know who's going to have the baby, the male or the female, we can stop talking about the differences between us."

I kind of liked him. But I couldn't give him my full attention, sit down and sip my Tab and shoot the bull with him, as he seemed to want me to do. I couldn't get Keats off my mind. I kept thinking of her on her way into New York City while her whole class was pouring out of cars right that minute, heading into the Seaville High gym, the band playing, all the girls wearing flowers.

"This dance you were going to, was it over at the high school?"

"The Senior Prom," I said.

He winced and said, "Ouch!"

"It's not so bad for me. It wasn't my prom. It was hers."

"The Keating girl's?"

"Yes."

"Still . . ." he said. "You wouldn't go stag?"

"I don't really hang out with any senior but her."

"Who do you hang out with? You have your own crowd?"

"I don't hang out that much."

"Oh. A loner. Like my son."

I said, "Well . . . " with a noncommittal shrug. I wasn't a loner, but the crowd I'd hung out with my last year in Brooklyn was filled with fast trackers. They were the kind my father'd take in off the streets and book, days he used to still walk a beat.

Pingree was a chain-smoker. He'd light one Viceroy after the other. He'd drop the spent butts into a seashell ashtray on the wrought-iron table in front of him.

He had very light sea-colored eyes. Around his neck he wore a scarf the same color, tucked into a white shirt.

I thought of the purple silk bow tie Keats had bought to match my eyes.

I watched Adieu.

"I didn't go to a high school," Pingree said. "I went to Gardner School. Did you ever hear of it?"

"No, sir." I was watching a car go up the driveway over at Adieu.

"It's a fine old school. My father went there and his father before him. Now, Ping will enter there as a junior."

I knew the car. It was Quint Blade's silver Porsche.

"Pingrees have always gone to Gardner," said Woodrow Pingree.

Then I saw Keats.

I saw her walk out the front door of Adieu with Mr. Keating.

I watched Quint Blade get out of the Porsche and go around and open the passenger door for Keats. He had on a light-blue dinner jacket, with black tuxedo pants and a white ruffled shirt. Keats was in a long white gown, with gold slippers. She had a white cape over her shoulders. She had my white orchid.

"Those Gardner years were my happiest years," Mr. Pingree was saying.

I murmured, "*Ummm hmmm.*"

"I still know all four verses to the school song," he said.

I had the feeling he was almost ready to sing them.

I watched Keats's father wave from the front steps as the silver Porsche pulled away.

I had to sit down or sink to my knees.

"Someday," said Pingree, "maybe I'll tell you about that school."

I figured he was this lonely man, with a young wife and a ditsy kid—a man who'd planned to drive down into another county to check in at his office just for something to do.

Then I came along. Someone to talk to—never mind what I'd done to his Mitsubishi, this fellow needed someone to talk to.

When I visited my grandfather at his nursing home, he'd always try to get me to stay another hour. He'd say things like, "Someday I'll tell you what happened the first day your father ever walked a beat." William the Conqueror might not be in my background, but there were a lot of cops.

I'd ask my grandfather to tell me about it, and his eyes would light up. He'd say, "You want to hear about it *now*?"

But this man across from me was no relation. I couldn't rise to the occasion and do him any favors.

I kept thinking she'd called Quint Blade and he'd come running.

I swallowed my Tab, chug-a-lug.

"I have to go," I said.

"So soon?" Pingree said.

"So soon?" my grandfather would always say. "When is your father coming, Johnny?"

He's not, Granddad. He had a heart attack, remember?

Pingree got up when I did.

"I'll walk you out," he said.

The TV was on and my five-year-old sister was asleep on the rug in front of it, her paper doll and a bag of Chips Ahoy! beside her.

"Wake up, Jazzy," I said.

"Is it tomorrow?"

"No. It's still tonight."

"What are you doing home?"

"I got jilted."

"What's jilted?"

"Stood up. Keats went to the dance with someone else."

Jazzy sat up and rubbed her eyes. She checked to be sure the paper doll was there. She never made a move without the paper doll. She called the doll Georgette.

"Is Mommy home?" she said.

"No, Mommy doesn't seem to be home," I said. That teed me off, too. Our mother was supposed to be home by eight-thirty on Saturday nights. The store where she worked on Main Street closed at eight in the summer.

I'd felt bad enough leaving Jazzy alone at seven-thirty, when I'd left to go to Adieu. Mom said she'd be all right by herself for forty-five minutes. Mrs. Fiedler was right next door.

"I bet you didn't have any dinner," I said.

"Georgette had fwogs' legs," she said, caressing the doll.

"Say frogs," I said. "You're old enough now to say frog, not fwog." Then I leaned down and patted her blond curls, to make up for snapping at her. "I'll make you an omelet," I said.

"I don't want an omelet. I want your beef Borgan."

"My beef Bourguignon takes five hours to cook," I said. "I'll make you a cheese-and-tomato omelet."

"With bacon," Jazzy said.

"All right, with bacon. But it'll take longer."

I took off my white coat and undid my black silk tie.

"Can Georgette have your red rose, Johnny?" Jazzy asked.

"Tell her to help herself. I can't use it."

"Did you have a fight with Keats?"

"No, we didn't fight. Her father doesn't like me."

"I like you, Johnny."

"I know. I like you, too."

I went into the kitchen and started getting stuff out of the refrigerator.

Jazzy came in after me in a few minutes, carrying Georgette and the two shoeboxes that contained Georgette's wardrobe. Jazzy made all Georgette's clothes. In one shoebox the clothes

fell |

were shabby: torn dresses, sweaters with holes in them, and tattered shorts and slacks. In the other shoebox there were short dresses, long dresses, hats, and fancy high-heeled shoes. Those clothes in that shoebox were trimmed with lace, decorated with real, tiny buttons, and colored with the brightest shades in Jazzy's crayon collection.

Jazzy's game was to have Georgette discover that her real parents were millionaires. She would dress Georgette in her poor clothes and serve her macaroni, or shredded wheat, or a few raisins. Then Georgette's real family would come by to claim her, and she'd be dressed in her other clothes and sit down to "fwogs'" legs or champagne and caviar.

When we lived in Brooklyn, my mother had a part-time job at The Gleeful Gourmet. She'd bring home some new delicacy for us to sample nearly every night: guacamole, cold lobster mousse, artichoke hearts with mushroom sauce— things we'd never tasted before. Sometimes my mother'd make salads for the place, or hors d'oeuvres or desserts, and I'd help her. That was when I discovered that I liked to cook, and that I was good at it.

My father'd retired from the force by then. He was doing private investigating. I'd fix him the food he'd take on stakeouts, surprise him with things like deviled meatballs, Chinese chicken wings, or stuffed grape leaves.

When we moved out to Seaville, after his first heart attack, we were talking seriously about opening a place like Plain and Fancy, where I'd gotten my part-time job.

What we hadn't counted on was the high rents for stores in a resort area. The stores in Seaville cost from a thousand to two thousand a month.

Since my father's death, all Mom talked about was getting back to Brooklyn and opening something there.

I was just flipping the omelet over when my mother's Volkswagen pulled into the driveway, with the Born to Shop decal still fixed to the back fender. I figured she hadn't noticed it yet.

I told her that I'd been stood up, leaving out the encounter with Pingree because I didn't want to get her on my back about the dent in the Dodge just yet.

"Would you mind making one of those for me, too?" she asked. "I'm really beat! We had three customers come in at five minutes to eight. I said, 'We're closing at eight,' and one of them said, 'We won't be long.' What time is it now?"

"Quarter to ten," I said. "That's too long to leave Jazzy alone."

"Mrs. Fiedler was coming over every twenty minutes, Johnny."

"Mommy? Georgette had fwogs', frrr-ogs' legs for dinner!"

"That's nice, honey. I know it's too long to leave her, but I couldn't walk out on a thousand-dollar sale, and I called Mrs. Fiedler to be sure she was home and could check on Jazzy. A thousand dollars in an hour and a half, and only two of them were buying! I don't know where people get their money! Do they rob banks?"

"They put it all on credit cards," I said. "You know how that goes, Mom."

"Don't start on me tonight, Johnny!" she said. "Just because your fancy girlfriend stood you up, don't take it out on me!"

"Keats's father doesn't like Johnny," Jazzy said.

"Johnny should stick with his own kind if he doesn't want to be treated like a doormat," Mom said.

I passed Jazzy her omelet. "What's my own kind? Dad always said it was the wrong kind."

"It was! But that's over. We moved out here so you could meet just your average kind of kid. Can't you settle for your average kind? And now I hate it out here!"

"I hate it out here, too," Jazzy said.

"Jasmine, eat your omelet your brother was nice enough to make for you."

"Do you want cheese and bacon and tomato in

your omelet, too?" I asked my mother.

"I'd eat ants and grasshoppers and spiders in my omelet at this point!"

Jazzy began to giggle.

Mom put her arms around her. "At least someone thinks I'm funny."

Mom did look tired, but she was still a good-looking woman, even after nine and a half hours behind the counter at Dressed to Kill. We were all blonds in our family, although my mother's hair was veering toward orange because of something she was using to "highlight" the color. My deep-blue eyes had come from my mother. Jazzy'd gotten her pug nose.

"How did your girlfriend get Quint Blade over there so fast?" My mother asked what I'd been asking myself ever since I left Fernwood Manor. Don't tell me Quint Blade didn't have a date for his Senior Prom?"

"Maybe there are two jilted people with broken hearts tonight," I said. "Me, and Quint Blade's original date."

"Or just maybe she never intended to go with you at all!" my mother said.

"Mom, Keats was all excited this morning when the orchid arrived. She bought me a purple silk bow tie."

"I'd like to give her a purple fat lip!" my mother said.

"I'd like to give her a purple punch in the eye!" Jazzy said.

"Do you want your omelet firm or runny?" I asked.

"Runny," my mother said.

"Runny out the door and give Keats a purple kick in the pants," said Jazzy.

"Jazzy, *eat!*" my mother said. "So how did you find out that Quint Blade took Keats to the prom?" My mother sat with her elbows on the kitchen table, waiting for an answer.

I began to tell her about my run-in with Woodrow Pingree and somewhere near the end of the story, speak of the devil, the telephone rang.

"John Fell?" said Mr. Pingree. "What are you doing for dinner tomorrow night? Would you like to come here?"

chapter | 5

*S*unday morning I took Jazzy to St. Luke's, where she went to Sunday school and I went to church.

When we got back, Mom was standing in the kitchen, holding the phone's arm out with her left hand, muffling the receiver with her right. "It's Herself!" Mom said. "She's been calling you all morning."

We had our dinner at one o'clock on Sundays. I watched Mom pull a ham out of the oven while I spoke with Keats.

"I have to tell you something, Fell."

"I already know."

"How can you already know when you don't know what I'm going to say?"

"You're going to say you went to the prom with Quint Blade."

"God, I hate this town!" Keats said. "You can't even turn around in this town without everyone talking about it!"

"I'm going to be over your way tonight," I said. "Why don't we arrange a secret meeting on the beach?"

Behind me, Mom said, "Don't let her treat you like some backdoor Johnny."

"What did your mother just say?" Keats asked.

"She said I was a backdoor Johnny."

"Oh, Fell! She's mad at me, too, I suppose."

"Why don't we meet clandestinely?" I asked. Keats once wrote a poem that began "Clandestine skies beckon me," which kicked off a long harangue from her English teacher, who said skies couldn't be clandestine.

"A clandestine meeting," she said, "under a clandestine sky. Shall we do something terribly clandestine?"

"Yes," I said.

"I'm glad you're not furious, Fell."

"I'm furious. I'm just holding it in."

"What do you mean you're going to be over my way?"

"I've got a date."

"You're stabbing me right through the heart, Fell. Last night wasn't my fault."

"Meet me down on the beach at nine o'clock."

Keats laughed. "That's not a very big date if you can get away by nine."

"Meet me down near Beauregard," I said.

"I love you, Fell."

"We'll talk about it."

When I hung up, Mom said she thought there was something fishy about that dinner invitation from Woodrow Pingree.

"I think he thinks I'll make a good companion for his son."

"What's wrong with his son that he needs a companion?"

"I think he's this loner or something."

"So are you. That's like the blind leading the blind," she said. "What's in it for you? Are you just going there so you can be within panting distance of Adieu?"

"No," I said. "I'm just curious."

"That killed the cat, and it killed your father, too."

"At least he was being paid for it."

"Paid to sit around, stand around, hang around—that was no life. Tell Jazzy she's to set the table. How was the new minister's sermon?"

"Jazzy?" I shouted into the living room. "Set the table! The new minister is one of those guys who makes you feel good about something you shouldn't feel good about," I said.

St. Luke's had just tossed out Reverend Shorr. In his place they'd hired Jack Klinger. He was a new, dynamic, Yuppie preacher who'd given a sermon the week before in favor of opening the North Shore Nuclear Plant, the one that a lot of people claimed wasn't safe to operate. He'd called his talk *Let Go, Let God!* He'd said faith was all about that: trusting. But I kept thinking, let go and meet God a few decades before you'd planned to.

This morning's sermon had been billed out front on the sermon board this way: *I Talk of*

Dreams/Shakespeare, Romeo and Juliet/Rev. J. J. Klinger, DD.

"What did he make you feel good about that you shouldn't feel good about?" my mother asked.

"It wasn't me he made feel good. It was all the people going to shrinks. All the people paying out a fortune to headshrinkers. Reverend Klinger said sometimes it's worth it."

"I'd like a headshrinker to help me figure out why we ever moved out here," said my mother.

"Reverend Klinger said shrinks help you discover what your dreams mean, the same way Daniel, in the Bible, helped Nebuchadnezzar find out what *his* dream meant."

"Never mind Nebuchadnezzar, why did I pick someplace to live where I can't make more than six dollars an hour?"

"*I* can tell you the answer to that," I said. "You don't need a shrink. You just didn't do any research on living in a resort area."

"Don't blame everything on me, Johnny. Your father wanted to make this move, too."

"You talked him into it," I said.

"Well, we're not going to stay."

"You keep saying that, but we never talk about how we're going to move back to Brooklyn, without an apartment to move into."

"Get Jazzy away from the TV and in here to set the table," my mother said.

She wasn't good at facing things, or making plans, until the last minute.

I was best at facing and planning clandestine meetings.

chapter 6

Pingree's son answered the door.

He had these little pins for eyes behind thick swirls of glass, a kid about my age and height, with light-brown hair combed forward so that he looked as if he had bangs.

Without a hello or how are you, he pointed down at the black-and-white tile floor as I stepped inside. There was an ace of hearts there.

"I can change the face of that card," he announced.

I just looked at him. He had on a pair of faded blue jeans, a black tank top, a heavy military belt, and tan Top-Siders. My mother'd said, "Dress up when you go there for dinner. Don't always be locked into the Teenage Look—they're probably fancy-schmancy." So I had on a dark suit, white shirt, and blue-and-white striped tie.

"With your permission?" he said.

"Okay." I shrugged.

He stepped on the card, took his foot away, and there was a five of spades.

I didn't know how he did it. The thing was, I didn't care. I didn't warm up to kids who said things like "with your permission?" I had as much curiosity about stunts like that as I had about Icelandic breakdancing.

He had this big, triumphant grin on his face. It reminded me somehow of Jazzy's smile when she was being toilet trained and could make it through a whole day without dumping in her Pampers.

I managed to mumble something congratulatory before I said, "I'm John Fell."

"Everyone calls me Ping."

"Everyone but my family calls me Fell."

His father appeared then. "All right, we'll call you Fell, too." He grabbed my hand in one of those viselike grips that's macho enough to knock your socks off. "Come into the living room, Fell!"

He had on the same sea-colored scarf that matched his eyes, tucked into another shirt as white as his brushcut hair.

He stooped over to pick up the playing card.

"Ping? Hand over the other one, or you'll wonder where it went someday."

"You're not supposed to give away the trick, Dad."

"Oh, Fell could figure out that trick, easily."

I couldn't have. I watched while Ping lifted his left Top-Sider and bent over to take the ace of hearts off the bottom. So there'd been one card on top of the other. Ping'd fixed some adhesive to the bottom of his shoe, stepped on the ace of hearts, and left the five of spades there.

I hated having to be around anyone who made me feel sorry for him, or embarrassed by him. Right away I felt both ways about Woodrow Pingree, Jr.

We went into the living room and sat down. My mother would have called it "a tasteful room." It wasn't at all like any living room the Fells had ever occupied. In the Fells' living rooms you took your chances when you sat down. A pair of Jazzy's scissors or my mother's knitting needles could jab your butt. Our living rooms whispered clutter, clutter, clutter: old dog-eared magazines lying around under chairs, tabletops weighed down with books, soda cans, loose change, empty Lorna Doone boxes, crayons. We looked like an indoor yard sale.

The Pingrees' living room looked like something Macy's or Bloomingdale's had set up in its furniture department to show off its finest pieces. There wasn't anything out of place. There wasn't too much of anything in place. It was white and clean and modern.

"Is that gum off your shoes, Ping? Fern'll have your head if any of it gets on the rugs."

"It's off, Dad."

Ping removed his thick glasses and blew on them, then cleaned them with the bottom of his tank top.

I thought of a time way back in Brooklyn when

my father'd found a pair of thick glasses smashed on the ground, beside the body of a man everyone thought had jumped out a window. My father'd said the minute he saw those glasses he'd known it wasn't a suicide. "Do you know why, Johnny?" I didn't. "Because," my father'd explained, "people who wear glasses and jump out of windows take their glasses off before they jump. They either leave them behind or put them in their pockets, but they don't ever jump with them on. So someone pushed that fellow."

Things like that interested me a lot more than magic tricks.

But I was in for an evening of magic tricks.

After Ping put his glasses back on he sat forward in an armchair and asked me, "What's half of twelve?"

"Six."

"Do you want me to prove it's seven?"

"It's up to you." That was as close as I could come to telling him I didn't know any way to stop him.

Apparently, Pingree didn't know how to stop him, either. Maybe Pingree didn't care that his kid was like some performing bear, compulsively going through his routine come hell or high water.

Pingree had returned the ace of hearts and the five of spades to a deck of playing cards. He was shuffling the cards quietly in his large hands, leaning back against the white couch, smoking. He was watching his son get out eight oven matches, which his son arranged on a table beside his chair.

Ping formed a Roman numeral twelve (XII), using four matches to make the X and four to make the II.

"Twelve. Right?" Ping looked over at me.

"Right."

Then Ping removed the four bottom matches, and what was left was VII.

Pingree said, "Bravo, son. Bravo."

There was more of the same before Mrs. Pingree called us into the dining room: card tricks, rope tricks, a handkerchief that turned into a rose, coin tricks, and the final trick, before we all sat down to a rib roast.

For this trick Ping borrowed his father's lit cigarette. There were four place cards made out of heavy paper, with nothing written on them, on the table.

"We have to see where everyone's sitting," said Ping.

He picked up the first card and touched the cigarette to it.

WOODROW PINGREE SR. burned itself out of the paper.

Then he made the rest of our names appear on the remaining place cards.

(Later, Mr. Pingree would let it slip that Ping

had drawn out our names on the place cards with potassium nitrate. Again Ping would protest that it wasn't fair to give away "trade secrets.")

And so, we sat down to dinner.

Appearances are deceptive. My father used to tell me that that cliché, like so many others, was one you could rely on. What you know by looking at someone is zilch. I don't think I've learned that lesson yet. I certainly hadn't learned it by the time I went to Fernwood Manor for dinner.

There was something very different about Mrs. Pingree, other than the fact that she was a magician of sorts, too. Her talent was turning a prime cut of roast beef into leather. But it wasn't her cooking that interested me, beyond the first hard bite into the catastrophe she served with overdone asparagus and underdone new potatoes. It wasn't anything as simple as the fact that she could use a Julia Child cookbook.

"Skim milk masquerades as cream," I used to sing joyfully when I acted in Gilbert and Sullivan's *H.M.S. Pinafore* one year. It never dawned on me that cream could masquerade as skim milk just as easily.

Fern Pingree had a way of being present without being there—not so you'd notice, anyway. She behaved as though her purpose was to serve us, listen to us, and not watch us. She watched what was in front of her. She sat with lowered eyes, her very black hair held back behind her head with a piece of white net tied in a bow. She had olive skin, small hands, and a gentle, whispering voice. She seemed to be some female from another country, an Eastern one, where females did not participate equally with men.

No one tried to draw her into the conversation.

Second only to being with someone who makes you feel sorry for him or embarrassed by him, I hated being in a group with someone who was ignored. No one directed any conversation to her, or sought out her eyes, or even glanced her way.

The conversation began with some questions directed at me by Mr. Pingree. The usual. What subjects I liked in school, family stuff, how we'd come to live in Seaville . . . and I threw Keats's name in a couple of times. I didn't have the heart to mention that I loved to cook, not with what was on the plate in front of me.

Mrs. Pingree didn't ask me anything. She seemed to be part of the conspiracy to keep her out of things. I couldn't be sure if she preferred it that way, or just deferred to the male Pingrees.

I waited for her to say something about the dinner, the way my mother would have—"Oh, *no*, I think I overdid the roast!"—some little acknowledgment that she knew what we were eating wasn't wonderful. . . . Nothing.

Now and then I'd get a whiff of this sweet gardenia scent coming from her, almost as if to remind me she was still there. There was little else to remind me. I caught occasional glimpses of her out of the corner of my eye.

The conversation turned to a dream that Ping kept having.

Like the yearbook from The Valley Academy, which I wouldn't have brought home, with all the bummers written across the other cadets' faces, the conversation was one I wouldn't have had with my father, not in front of a guest.

When Ping told the dream he put down his fork and gestured with these stubby fingers. "There are stairs going up to a tower. I don't want to go up them." He glanced at me. "I have a fear of heights, Fell! I have a phobia about heights!"

His father was looking down at his dinner, chewing, holding both a fork and a knife while he ate.

Ping continued. "But I must go up those stairs. Halfway up, a jack-in-the box pops out at me and hands me a card. D.D.H. are the initials on it."

"What's that supposed to mean?" Pingree asked.

"I'll tell you! I turn the card over, and written there is *Don't. Dare. Hope!*"

Ping leaned toward his father. "You see, the

tower is the one at Gardner School. I don't want to go up in it. The jack-in-the box is telling me not to hope that I won't have to. The dream is about my not wanting to go to Gardner, Dad!"

There was a long silence.

I can't stand a silence like that. I'll start to babble about anything to fill it.

What I said was, "At church this morning, the minister preached a sermon on dreams. He said shrinks are as good as Daniel was at helping Nebuchadnezzar figure out what his dream meant."

"I know what mine means," Ping said. "And so does Dad."

That was when Fern Pingree finally spoke up.

"Dreams don't have meanings!" she said flatly. She was looking up now, meeting all of our eyes as she continued. "Dreams are just mental noise. They're neurological junk the brain is discarding. Dreams are the trash bag of the brain!"

I never expected anything like that to come out of her mouth.

"I don't happen to believe that, Fern," said Ping.

"It doesn't matter what you happen to believe. Those are the facts!"

"Why does the dream come again and again, if it's just junk the brain's getting rid of? Why the same dream again and again?"

"Because," said Mrs. Pingree, "recurring

dreams are those that wake the dreamer and cause him to learn instead of unlearn them. A recurring dream is a kind of neurological flypaper."

"Well, Freud would say you were wrong, Fern," Ping said.

"Not if Freud were still alive. A lot has been learned about the brain since Freud was around."

"You always have an answer for everything," Ping said sullenly.

Mr. Pingree said, "And we always have a solution." He did something I thought was peculiar then. He put down his knife and fork long enough to reach across and grip Ping's arm. "We always have a solution," he repeated.

Mrs. Pingree, in a white cotton jumpsuit, stood up and got the salad from across the room. "Do you like salad on that plate or a separate plate, Fell?" she asked me, and without waiting for an answer, added, "Daniel tricked Nebuchadnezzar, Fell. He wanted power over the Babylonians!"

I didn't have an answer to that.

"I'll take the salad on this plate," I said.

She stood in front of an enormous oil painting on the wall. It was the most barren landscape I'd ever seen. There wasn't anyone in the picture. It was a painting of this field of weeds on dried earth, with an abandoned barracks far off in it, weathered and worn. Above everything was this burning yellow sun that looked hot enough to make an iguana pant. At the bottom left was a parched white cow's skull. At the bottom right, a minuscule fern where the signature of the painter would have been.

"Isn't that one of your paintings, Mrs. Pingree?" I asked her.

"One of my early ones," she replied. "I did it long before I started at the Institute. Since I've been at Brutt, I've only painted the ocean."

She glanced over her shoulder at her strange landscape.

She said, "I call that one *Smiles We Left Behind Us.*"

That was just spacey enough for me to grin, but Mrs. Pingree wasn't smiling.

No one was.

"I didn't know you worked at the Institute, too," I said. "What do you do there?"

Mr. Pingree said, "She's my boss, Fell."

It was Mr. Pingree who walked me down to my car after dinner.

"My son doesn't want to go to Gardner," he said.

I wondered why he thought I gave a damn what his son wanted, and why I'd even been asked to Fernwood Manor for dinner in the first place.

"Anyone would give his right arm to go to Gardner," he continued. "It's a wonderful school! But it's in Pennsylvania, this little town filled with ragweed, hell on Ping's asthma, and then there's

The Tower. A very tall one. New boys are made to go up in it. My son has a phobia about heights, as he mentioned."

I was already imagining how Keats and I would make up. We wouldn't stay down on the beach, not with me in my dark suit, and not in the cold night air that was beginning to blow off the sea.

No. I'd park my car behind Beauregard. We'd go there to make up. Keats and I had nicknamed the backseat of my Dodge "The Magnet."

Pingree said, "If you had the chance to go away to an excellent prep school, wouldn't you jump at it, Fell?"

"I suppose so."

"Of course you would. But Ping has his reasons. They're valid."

We stood by my Dodge.

Pingree said, "Come back, won't you, Fell?"

"Thanks," I said.

Thanks wasn't yes.

There was a moon rising with the wind and I thought of the way Keats sometimes touched my lips with her fingers, smiling promises.

D.D.H., I laughed as I got into the Dodge and drove away from Fernwood Manor.

Keats had the kind of face that told you right away what her mood was, and that night in the moonlight it said down.

"What's the matter?" I said.

"Mother's reviewing this book by this poet named Lorine Niedecker, and I read one of her poems and I feel awful, Fell."

"Well, get over it," I said. "It's just a poem."

"You know what she wrote? She wrote, *Time is white, mosquitoes bite, I've spent my life on nothing,*" Keats said. "That's exactly how I feel, Fell."

"You haven't spent your life yet."

"I've spent eighteen years of it. On nothing."

"Thanks," I said.

"I didn't say on no one. I said on nothing. I'm going to be this terrible failure, Fell. I can feel it in my bones."

We started walking along the wet sand, Keats barefoot with her jeans rolled up, a cold wind coming off the ocean that made me shiver. Keats just had a sweatshirt on. She was never cold, even in winter in below-zero weather. I always was.

"You have to *try* something first, before you can be a failure," I said. "One step at a time."

"I don't even know what to try. I want to *be* someone, but I know I'll end up like Lorine Niedecker."

"At least she's published."

"She's dead, Fell. And no one ever heard of her but my mother and some other reviewers who got the book free in the mail, so they'd write something about it."

"Keats," I said, "I didn't come down here to talk about Lorine Niedecker. How did Quint Blade get over to your house so fast last night? Why did you lie in your note?"

Silence, except for the sound of the waves hitting the beach and a plane passing above us among the stars.

"Well?" I said.

"I don't like myself for any of that," said Keats. "If I liked myself for doing something like that I'd have made it more foolproof. You found me out right away. I probably wanted to be found out."

"You didn't want to be found out," I said. "So don't make it into something deep. I probably wouldn't have known if I hadn't run into your neighbor's car last night."

I told her about it. I told her how I'd seen her get into the silver Porsche from the terrace of Fernwood Manor.

"I would rather be anyone but me, Fell," she said. "Daddy didn't come home last night. He got home the night before."

"Great!"

"He'd come out on the jitney with Quint Blade. Quint told him Tracy Corrigan had come down with the flu and he didn't have a prom date. So Daddy said . . ."

I cut her off. "Daddy said, 'Why, you can take my daughter. My daughter will be happy to stand Fell up.'"

"No, that's not what Daddy said and you know it! Daddy didn't even know we had a date! I couldn't get Mother in hot water by telling him we had a date, could I? So Daddy just told Quint to call me, and Quint called me."

"You knew you weren't going with me when you called to thank me for the orchid," I said.

"I wanted you to be happy for as long as you could, Fell."

"Then out, out, brief candle."

"Something like that. Only I kept you lit all day, right up to the last minute."

I slipped my arm around her waist. "You're not spending your life on nothing. You're spending it on deceit and manipulation."

"I don't *like* it."

"I don't much like it, either."

"I didn't have a good time at the prom."

"Tell the truth," I said.

"It wasn't a rotten evening or anything like

that, but I missed you, Fell."

"Well, at least my white orchid got to the prom."

"It wasn't yours once you sent it to me. You always do that, Fell. You call my gold bracelet your gold bracelet, and you call the ring you gave me your ring."

"Sorry," I said. We walked along with the ocean spray hitting our faces. "How come *I'm* the one saying I'm sorry tonight?"

"I'm sorry, too," Keats said. "Quint had four teensy little brown orchids on a branch for my wrist, but I hate wrist corsages! I decided to wear the white orchid."

"You have a hard life, Keats," I said. "Decision after decision to make."

"Don't. I'm really down," she said. "Daddy hates you."

"Well, I don't exactly love Daddy, either."

"I think he's going to send me to tennis camp, Fell."

"What do you mean he's going to *send* you to tennis camp? You're not ten years old! He can't send you somewhere you don't want to go."

"That's just it," said Keats. "I do want to go."

"This could be our last summer!" I said. "Do you want to spend our last summer in tennis camp?"

"Daddy says he doesn't want me to see you, anyway."

"So we'll sneak around."

"I don't want to spend the whole summer before I go away to college sneaking around!"

"Keats," I said, "I'm cold."

"Where's your car?"

"In back of Beauregard."

"I'm afraid if we get into The Magnet we'll just fight."

"We won't fight," I said.

"We'll just start talking about everything and fight."

"We won't talk about everything."

"Do you promise?"

"I promise."

"What will we talk about if we don't start talking about all this?"

"We won't talk."

I was turning her around, and she was almost following.

She stopped. "What will we talk about on the way?"

"The Pingrees," I said.

"Oh, hey," she said, "I forgot to tell you something." She was going with me back toward Beauregard then. "Mr. Pingree actually spoke to Daddy today, right down here . . . and it was about you, Fell."

"What do you mean?"

"Out of the blue," Keats said. "Daddy was down here letting Foster run, and Mr. Pingree said hello, and then Mr. Pingree said he was thinking of hiring you and he wondered what Daddy thought of you."

"Hiring me for what?"

"He didn't say. He just said he knew you dated me and he wondered what Daddy thought of you."

"So what did Daddy say?"

"Daddy would never blacken your name, you know that. Daddy's always said you might be right for some other girl, you're just not right for me."

"So what did Daddy say?"

"Daddy said we used to date, but we don't date anymore. See? We're starting to talk about it."

"No, we're not starting to talk about it! What else did Daddy tell Pingree?"

"Daddy just said you'd probably be a good worker. That's all. Daddy said we weren't dating anymore and you'd probably be a good worker. He said the conversation didn't last two minutes."

"I wish you'd told me this!"

"How could I tell you? It only happened this afternoon."

"Why didn't you tell me a few minutes ago, when I told you about running into Pingree's Mitsubishi?"

"It slipped my mind, Fell! I'm depressed tonight! I don't have any real goals!"

"Never mind all that!" I said. "Don't start in on all that again!"

"What does Mr. Pingree want you to do, Fell?"

"It beats me!"

"I think that's why Daddy just suggested tennis camp. He doesn't want me around with you working right next door."

"I *have* a job," I said, "at Plain and Fancy."

"Then what does Woodrow Pingree want to hire you for?" Keats asked.

"It's the first time I heard about it," I said.

"Didn't he mention it at dinner?"

"No. Maybe he changed his mind."

"Maybe you picked up the wrong fork or something." Keats bumped against me playfully, more like her other self.

I laughed. "I guess he got turned off when I drank out of my finger bowl."

"You know what Daddy said?" Keats asked. "Promise not to get mad?"

I put my thumbs in the corners of my mouth, screwed my features into a monster face, and said, "Do I look mad, my girl?"

"Daddy said maybe their cook quit."

"Oh, Daddy's a riot!" I said.

"I knew you'd get mad."

"For Daddy's information, there are chefs, there are restaurant *owners* who make just as much as Daddy ever made!"

"See? We're doing it, Fell," Keats said. "That's what I mean. We can't stop talking about it all!"

"Yes, we can!" I said. "C'mon!" I grabbed her hand and we began to run until the lights from Adieu and Fernwood Manor were back in the distance.

At the end of June, Keats went off to Four Winds, a tennis camp in Connecticut. She said we could do our sneaking around up there, and some weekends I drove up to Greenwich and we did.

Four Winds also had a theater program. Keats couldn't resist any kind of dramatics, whether they were her own or Tennessee Williams's.

"You've got to come up a week from next Saturday," she said. "I'm going to be in *Cat on a Hot Tin Roof*."

"I'd rather come on a weekend you're not in a show," I said. "You're too hyper at showtime."

"I'm only in this damn thing to impress *you*, Fell!"

I was getting the eye from Keith Cadman, the owner of Plain and Fancy. It was a Friday, late in the afternoon, and the weekend animals were arriving in their Audis and BMWs. The line at the cheese counter was all the way up to desserts.

"I'll be there," I said. "I'm already impressed, though, or didn't you notice?"

"I noticed, but I can't get enough. I'm inse- cure. Speaking of which, I had a terrible dream that you were dating Skye Pennington, and I could see you through Daddy's binoculars in her bedroom at Beauregard."

"Dreams are just mental noise," I said. "They're neurological junk the brain is discarding."

"FELL!" Cadman yelled. "Get back on the floor!"

"I need my ego boosted, Fell," said Keats.

"I specialize in boosts to the id," I said.

"Because you're a dirty-minded high school boy," she said, "getting your kicks with an older woman. Hurry, Fell! I need any kind of boost you can give me! I miss you!"

"Miss you, too," I said.

I hustled back to the floor to wrestle with the wheels of brie and the crocks of goat cheese. I was trying to look at my watch without Cadman seeing me do it. He was already p.o.'d with me for baking a couple of their famous White Raisin Dream cakes and forgetting the raisins. I'd frosted them and renamed them "Remembering Helen," in Keats's honor.

"What the hell does that mean?" he barked at me when he showed up that noon. "First you leave out the raisins, then you stick that pink guck on them and name them *that!*"

But they'd been selling all morning and were almost gone by the time Cadman was simmering down.

"People like kinky names on things," I told him.

"I'm running this place, Fell."

"If we renamed the Black Walnut cake something like 'Smiles We Left Behind Us,' we'd sell that out, too."

"We're not in show biz here, Fell."

The Pingrees were still on my mind, way into July. I wondered if I'd ever know what Woodrow Pingree had wanted from me that night in June. I doubted it. I suspected that it had to do with Ping. I figured that he'd changed his mind when he'd noticed that magic tricks didn't really thrill me.

I sold a lot of brie and a lot of blue cheese dip, all the while looking forward to a date I might have that night. I wasn't dating Skye Pennington, but I was going to try dating. Keats was, too—I'd bet anything on it. Four Winds was coed. I knew Keats. She was up to something at that place on weekends I wasn't there. Neither one of us formed our A-one relationships with the same sex.

My "maybe" date that night was with a summer girl named Delia Tremble. She was always coming into Plain and Fancy to buy the latest fads for the woman she worked for: fiddlehead ferns, or sun-dried tomatoes, or green peppercorns. She'd always wait for me to help her: pitch-black hair spilling down her back, dark eyes, a sexy body—Tremble was right. I'd go up to her and she'd start grinning and looking all over my face while she talked to me. She said she was hired to take care of these twin kids who were always with her.

After about ten days of convincing myself I needed a dark lady in my life, I asked her if she liked going to movies. She said no, they had a VCR where she worked, but she liked to dance outdoors. I told her I knew where they did that, and she said if she could get off that Friday she'd like to go. I was going to call her at nine-thirty, after she got the kids to bed.

She gave me the address where I could pick her up. It was an address south of Montauk Highway, meaning it was near the ocean, like Adieu was— and Beauregard, and Fernwood Manor.

My mother said, "Aren't you ever going to get out of that neighborhood? Maybe you should get a job in Kmart so you can meet your own kind."

"She's my kind," I said. "She's just an au pair there. She's your average person you're always talking about."

"Don't get too attached to her," Mom said. "We're not staying out here."

It was the summer of my discontent, as Shakespeare put it once about Richard the Third's winter. Keats was away doing God knows what besides playing tennis and acting in plays. Even if I got really turned on by Delia Tremble, she'd said she lived in New Jersey . . . a long way from

Seaville, or Brooklyn. Fall was right around the corner, and where would I be then?

Lately Mom was saying your fate is already set; you just lean into it. The Mysterious Mr. X had told her that. He was this customer who came into Dressed to Kill, bought things like ninety-dollar pants in about two minutes, didn't even try them on, then stayed to chat with Mom for an hour at a time.

"Is he flirting with you?" I asked her.

"If he is," she said, "he's a glutton for punishment, because all I ever talk about is you and Dad and Jazzy."

At about two minutes to six, Cadman rang the chimes that meant everyone out. I began to undo my apron strings. I was planning to use my employees' discount to get a Droste Dark Chocolate Apple for Delia Tremble. I walked up toward the candy and heard a voice call, "Fell!"

He was standing by the coffee grinder, holding a bag of French Roast beans. He had on yellow linen pants, that scarf he seemed to love, a yellow cotton shirt, and rope sandals. He was smoking, even though there were No Smoking signs up. After I said hello, I started to take the package from his hands to pour into the grinder.

"No, thanks, Fell," Mr. Pingree said. "We have a Toshiba at home that does that. . . . How are you fixed for dinner?"

"I usually just go home. I might have a date later, too."

"I'm going to take a drive out to Lunch now, for some steamers. Does that interest you?"

Lunch was a place on Montauk Highway, just outside of Amagansett. It was a ten-minute drive. They had the best of everything there, from fish and chips to homemade pies and cakes. It was just a little shack, nowhere you'd spend a long time at, and you didn't need to be dressed up. You could sit outside and eat, too.

I hadn't had steamers yet all season.

Pingree said, "Ping's in camp and Fern's in New York City."

That clinched it for me. I said, "Why not?"

When I called Mom to tell her, she said, "Aren't you supposed to call your new girlfriend tonight for a date?"

"Mom, I'm old enough to keep track of my own calendar."

"Well, excuse me!" She said it the way the comedian Steve Martin used to say, "Well, excuu-uuuuse *me!*"

"I'll be home later to change my clothes, anyway," I said.

"Good, because I have a surprise for you. I opened a charge account at Westway today."

"Oh, Mom."

"Don't oh, Mom, me. We need some things.

They had a sale on corn poppers. I got one, and I got a Micro-Go-Round, a Little Leaguer top for Jazzy, and something for you."

"To wear?" I asked, hoping the answer was no.

"To wear on your date, if you have one."

I didn't like her to buy me clothes. She'd get me stuff like a "spring knit top" made in Korea. I'd wash it a few times and it'd tear if I opened an envelope while I was wearing it.

I told her I'd see her later, and to be sure the Mysterious Mr. X was out of the bedroom by then. She said, "That ends my ever telling you a single thing about my customers! Your mind is warped!"

"Did you get your dent fixed, Fell?" Pingree asked me as we went out to his Mitsubishi. I said I had. I could see his dent was still there.

He said, "I reported it but I haven't had time to take it in and leave it there. I've been away. I drove Ping to Tannen's—that's the camp for kids who are budding magicians. Then I flew out to Las Vegas for a while. You see, I like cards, too, but I like to play cards, not do tricks with them."

"I don't like either very much," I said.

We got into the Mitsubishi. "What *do* you like, Fell?"

"I like to cook. Someday I'd like to own a restaurant."

"That takes money."

"Yeah, that takes money."

"Well, don't sound so discouraged. There are ways to get money."

I watched him light a cigarette and thought about his saying "get" instead of "make." Just listen carefully, my father used to say, and people will tell you all they don't want you to know about themselves.

"At least you weren't born rich, Fell," said Pingree.

"For sure."

"You're ahead of the game if you weren't born rich," he said. "We had a certain amount of money when I was a boy. Then we lost it. It's harder to get over something like that than it is to get over being poor."

"I suppose that's true."

"It is, Fell. Most of your big entrepreneurs never had a dime. That's what drove them. But people like me—we grew up with the mistaken idea that we're entitled to it."

"I see what you mean."

"You see what I mean, Fell? Then we get sent off to someplace like Gardner."

Back on that, I thought.

All roads lead to Gardner.

chapter | 9

ou see, Ping's in an unusual and enviable position," Mr. Pingree said. "He'll actually get paid to
go to Gardner."

I was pigging out on the steamers. There wasn't
a speck of sand in them. They were little and juicy,
and the butter was real butter and warm.

"Who pays him?" I said. I ate the tails, too.
Keats said you weren't supposed to eat the tails,
and it was really gross to see someone do it, but I
always ate them. Once Keats said what do they
taste like? They couldn't be good. I told her they
tasted like rubber erasers at the ends of pencils.
They tasted like good rubber erasers at the ends
of pencils.

Pingree said, "Ping's grandfather left twenty
thousand in his will. Ten thousand goes to Ping
when he finishes his junior year at Gardner. The
other ten is his when he graduates."

"Neat!" I said.

Mom hired this kid to take my grandfather out
of the nursing home one afternoon a week, to get
him a good meal in a luncheonette called Little
Joe's. They made things like macaroni and cheese,
meat loaf, franks and beans—it was a mom-and-
pop place near Carroll Gardens in Brooklyn. This

kid would sit across from my grandfather and let him talk while the kid ate as if there were no tomorrow. I felt like that kid.

"Ping isn't impressed with money," Pingree continued. "Two things that always kept my wheels oiled don't even make Ping's spin: love and money. He hasn't any interest in either."

Out in the parking lot near the dunes, gulls were circling overhead, waiting for customers to toss out corners of clam rolls, or potato chips.

"Money and love," Pingree said. "They'll both make you and they'll both break you."

"For sure," I said.

"You at your age," Pingree snickered, "you can't even see the tip of the iceberg yet."

I tore off some bread from a thick slice, to soak up some of the clam juice left in the shells.

Pingree said, "The person you think you'll love all your life when you're your age, when you're my age you'll either feel sorry for, or trapped by, or bitter over if you marry her. Possibly all three. I married my high school sweetheart, only I was in prep school, of course, and she went to boarding school."

I got a fresh napkin out of the metal container on the table, and wadded up the old, wet one.

"After Ping's mother died," Pingree went on, "I married my Fern. I think poor Ping suffered because I loved her so much. He was little, getting over his mother's death still, and I'd fallen for Fern like someone your age falls. I was besotted. Do you know that word?" He didn't wait for my answer. "That's a good word," he said. "Besotted . . . I owe Ping something for that. Do you want more butter?"

"Sure. Thanks."

He signaled to the waitress, pointing at the small green dish between us with a quarter inch of melted butter in it.

He wasn't eating much. My grandfather'd eat like a bird at Little Joe's, but the kid who took him there ate a couple of entrees and a couple of desserts. He never said anything.

My grandfather'd complain, "That kid sits like a dummy, like a dummy who's been starved." I didn't like feeling like the starved dummy.

So I spoke up.

"If you could have love or money, but not both, which would you rather have, Mr. Pingree?"

"You can call me Woody."

I wasn't so sure I could. He was a lot older than my father'd been when he died. He was older than most of my teachers at school.

"That's a good question, Fell," he said.

It was a fantastic July evening, white clouds floating around in the sky like big pillows. We were sitting on the outside porch, under a red-and-white-striped awning. You could hear the ocean just over the dunes.

Pingree said, "I'd choose love if I could trust it. I'd choose money if I could hang on to it."

"But which?"

He thought about it. I'll give him that. He frowned and passed one hand over his white hair, looking up from his clams.

"If I have to choose, I'll choose money," he finally said. "I understand it better, and I need it more."

There were a couple of kids racing by, waiting for their parents to finish eating, and their mothers were screaming at them, "Don't run!"

"I'm going to tell you something, Fell, and it may shock you."

What shocked me was what I saw driving into the parking lot: a battered white Volkswagen with a Born to Shop decal on the rear bumper.

I didn't believe it, but there they were. Mom must have left the house about two minutes after I'd mentioned steamers on the phone. That was probably all she needed to hear to start her mouth watering.

The Fells were seafood lovers. Summer nights back in Brooklyn we'd pile into the Dodge and drive out to Lundy's for the Shore Dinner at the drop of a hat.

I looked back at Pingree. He'd put down his clam fork to light a cigarette.

"You were about to shock me," I said.

He took a drag on the cigarette. He said, "My son hates Fern no matter how she tries to please him. He thinks she was responsible for his mother's death. You see, we all worked at the Institute together: Ping's mother, Fern, and I. We were all close friends."

"What *is* the Institute, Mr. Pingree? What kind of work do you do there?"

He shrugged. "Research, mostly. For the government. Classified, so it rarely gets publicized. I think that disappoints Fern, too. She's blooming in a bowl. But that's another story."

"How did Ping's mother die?" I didn't have any choice but to call her that. Pingree couldn't seem to say her name.

"It was a boating accident. Ping's mother knew boats. Fern didn't. Still doesn't. Hates the water now. Anyway, they were out in my old boat together. Ping's mother fell overboard. Fern didn't even know how to steer the damn thing or turn it around. Before she could do anything, Ping's mother drowned. She was a good swimmer"— Pingree took a suck from his cigarette—"so my guess is she hit her head when she went over, and knocked herself out."

At that point, the three of them were heading into Lunch. My mother. Jazzy. Georgette.

Here was Pingree talking to me man-to-man;

here was my mother headed in to call me Johnny and say things like "Don't talk with your mouth full."

"So Ping and Fern don't get along too well," Pingree said. "My son is laughed at. I know that. It's my fault. He wants to be a magician because that's all he thinks he can change: one card into another, a handkerchief into a rose . . . Poor Ping. I want him to know he isn't trapped and that his life can be changed, too."

Jazzy'd even brought along the fancy clothes shoebox, easy to distinguish from the poor clothes one because there were red and silver sequins pasted on it.

"I have certain plans I'm going to keep from Fern."

"Like what?"

I kept my head down as though that would stop Mom from seeing me. That was ostrich thinking: Bury your head in the sand and no one's supposed to be able to see the rest of you.

"I'm going to find a way Ping won't have to go to Gardner, without Fern knowing anything about it."

"That'll be a neat trick."

My mother was inside then, telling her hostess there was her son, out on the terrace. I saw her pointing in my direction, saw the hostess step back to let Jazzy and my mother pass.

"That will indeed be a very neat trick," Pingree said. "And, Fell?"

"Yes?"

"Keep it under your hat. Can I trust you to do that?"

"Absolutely!"

Then my mother appeared on the porch, calling out, "Johnny? Look what the cat just dragged in!"

"Us!" Jazzy squealed. "We want screamers!"

"Oh, migosh," I said to Pingree. "This is embarrassing. My whole family's just shown up."

"Quite all right," he said. He looked toward my mother and Jazzy, heading our way. My mother liked to wear white in summer. She was in a white pants suit, with a white plastic bracelet. She had on white plastic earrings and white beads.

Jazzy had on her new Little Leaguer top, with red pants and red sneakers.

"Don't tell me *you're* Woodrow Pingree!" my mother exclaimed when she got to our table.

Pingree rose and stuck out his hand, the cigarette hanging on his lips.

"So we meet again," Pingree said.

"This is the mysterious Mr. X!" my mother said. She said to Pingree, "This is my son, Johnny . . . the one I told you all about . . . and all along you've known each other!"

"All along," Pingree said.

"You knew he was my son," said Mom.

"Yes, I knew."

Jazzy put Georgette down on the table, still dressed in her rags.

chapter | 10

t was nine o'clock.

I said, "I'm going to call my date and tell her I can't make it."

"I wish you'd keep your date, Fell," Pingree said.

"I don't know. I just don't know."

My mother was saying the same thing—"I don't know"—over and over. But it wasn't as if she were considering an idea that didn't appeal to her. There was that little light in her eyes, the sort that comes there at the prospect of a new store opening nearby, inviting the public to open charge accounts.

Pingree had suggested we all go back to our house. He'd waited until my mother put Jazzy to bed to drop the bomb. The saucer my mother'd given him for an ashtray was overflowing with butts. There was a smokey haze above the room. My mother got up to open another window and put on some lights. We'd been sitting in the living room listening while it got dark out.

I didn't know how I could go on a date and act normal after someone had just offered to pay me twenty thousand dollars to become his son for two years.

"Let me get this straight," my mother said. "Johnny goes to this Gardner School as your son."

"Yes. My son's already been accepted there. I've already paid his tuition."

"Everyone at Gardner will know Johnny as your son."

"Exactly. Johnny will be Ping there." Pingree shook up a cigarette from the Viceroy package. He picked his lighter up from the table. "Gardner is in a very small town in Bucks County, Pennsylvania. The boys come from all over the United States, about seventy in all. Most of them rich kids. About fifty are old boys and twenty new ones." He lit the cigarette. "None from around here. I checked. None from Brooklyn. A lot of them are legacies, as Ping is. Their fathers and their grandfathers have all gone to Gardner."

My mother sat down on the leather hassock near the armchair where Pingree was sitting. He had his legs stretched out in front of him, relaxed, no hint in his voice or his posture that my mother's sudden arrival at Lunch had thrown him. He said it had. He said he hadn't counted on making this proposal quite yet. Then, with a shrug, he said so what if it was a little premature? We'd all need the extra time.

"Johnny will be Ping at Gardner," said my

mother, "and Ping will go off to this school in Switzerland."

"L'Ecole la Coeur. Yes. Ping will be John Fell there."

"But what about my school transcripts?" I said.

"We'll have them forwarded to Switzerland. As I told you, Ping will skip a year. Gladly. Ping hates school. And you'll repeat a year. You'll enter Gardner as a junior."

"I don't know," my mother said for about the fortieth time.

I said, "And I'm supposed to say I won a Brutt scholarship to go overseas to prep school?"

"That's the easiest part. Fern and I are on the search committee for those scholarships. We give several a year to worthy students. They study in France, Italy—all over the place. I usually do the interviewing and Fern okays my choices. Fern already likes you. She's for it. She thinks I was looking you over for the scholarship."

Mom said, "But she doesn't know Ping's going there in Johnny's place."

"No."

"But won't she write him, call him?"

"She's never called him. They aren't that close. She may write him once or twice. Johnny will forward the letters to Ping. Ping will send his to Johnny to mail. Ping rarely uses the telephone. But if he wants to call, Fern will think he's calling from Gardner."

I said, "But what if Keats wants to call me, Mr. Pingree?"

"Woody."

"Woody. What if Keats decides to call me? She *could*."

"Tell her L'Ecole la Coeur discourages transatlantic calls. That's all. You can call her, if you have to. She'll think you're in Switzerland. *But*"—Pingree dropped an ash into the saucer—"I'd cool this thing with the Keating girl. It's cooling anyway, isn't it? Her father led me to believe it was."

"She's the least of it!" said Mom.

"Mom, she's not the least of it."

"She is where I'm concerned. She's never treated you like anything but a toy."

"Well, that may change," Pingree said. "Girls treating you like a toy may change once you've had some Gardner polish. You'll come out of there a man."

"What am I now?"

"A boy," my mother said.

Pingree glanced down at his Rolex. "A boy with a date soon. I have to run along. You keep your date, Fell. We'll talk more about all this. . . . But how does it strike you, Mrs. Fell?"

Mom turned her palms up. "I wish I could

understand why you can't just tell your wife you don't want your son to go to Gardner. He isn't even her son!"

"There are a lot of reasons I can't," said Pingree. "You have to know my wife, know a lot about her background, things I'm not privileged to reveal. People are complex, Mrs. Fell. And sometimes it comes down to little things, too, like the fact that my wife would hate to have Ping give up that twenty thousand left for him in the will. My wife is very parsimonious."

"Par-si-what?"

"Parsimonious, Mom. The opposite of what you are. Careful with a buck."

Mom shot me a look. Pingree smiled. He said, "Yes. Fern is careful with a buck. She's also convinced that I've spoiled Ping. She talked me into sending him off to this military school he hated."

"If you ask me," Mom said, "you've let her push you around."

"Agreed," said Pingree. "The heart has its reasons."

"Isn't she going to find out anyway, someday? She'll wonder where the twenty thousand went, won't she? And you have to pay Ping's tuition in Switzerland?"

"Only half. The scholarship takes care of the rest. I have the money set aside to cover all that, Mrs. Fell . . . and if she finds out someday, well"—

Pingree shrugged—"I'll handle it then."

"What about vacations?" I asked.

"What about them? You'll come home at Christmas, spring break, and summers, as Ping will."

"They'll probably speak French at that school in Switzerland," I said. "People will expect me to rattle off French."

"They speak English and French at L'Ecole la Coeur. But after Gardner," said Pingree, "you'll be able to rattle off French. You'll get a first-rate education, far better than Ping will get at that country club he's going to. But Ping can't wait to get away."

"And he knows I'll get the twenty thousand?"

"He knows you'll get ten thousand at the end of your junior year, and ten when you graduate, yes. Ping doesn't give a hoot about money. But the Gardner diploma will be in his name—*I* care about that, strangely enough. Our family has always come out of Gardner."

"And I'll have this diploma from a country club."

"A diploma that will surely impress all your customers in your fancy restaurant one day." Pingree smiled at me. Then he stood up. "It's time for your date, isn't it?"

"I have to call her," I said.

Mom said, "You've given us a lot to think about."

"We'll work things out," said Pingree. "When you decide, if it's a go-ahead, we'll start by getting Fell's passport."

"Is Ping going to use my passport? We don't look at all alike."

"No. Ping will travel with his own passport. You won't use yours. We'll work out all the details, don't worry."

Mom said, "What an opportunity it would be for you, Johnny!"

I just couldn't believe the offer was for real.

"Remember what I told you when I first came into Dressed to Kill?" Pingree said to Mom. "Your fate is set. Just lean into it."

"I hope those pants fit," Mom said.

"They're too young for me, Mrs. Fell. I didn't go in your store for pants."

Mom walked him toward the door. "I thought you were this lonely man, just interested in hearing about my family."

"I *was* interested in all you had to say about Fell."

chapter | 11

I t was close to ten o'clock when I got down to the place where Delia Tremble was an au pair.

On the phone she'd told me it wouldn't be much of a date. The family she worked for went out, so she couldn't leave. She said she was tired, too, and hungry, and there wasn't anything in the house but eggs.

I said I didn't feel like much of a date, anyway. I was tired, too, and I could do fantastic things with eggs.

It was a big stone house near the ocean, the kind with the front facing the dunes. When I walked in the door, the kitchen was right there on the left. Delia Tremble steered me that way.

"I ate about five, with the kids," she said. "Then the Stileses had lobster, which I hate, and now I feel like something sweet and there's only eggs."

"Is there bread?"

"Yes, a whole loaf."

"How about French toast?"

"Can you make it? I love it!"

I watched while she cleared away a cup of coffee and an ashtray from the butcher block table. She was wearing skintight jeans and spiked heels, with a white cotton sweater. Her earrings were tiny gold hoops and she wore several gold rings.

She looked back at me and smiled. "Do you really know how to make French toast, because I can hardly cook?"

"I like that." I smiled and began rolling up the sleeves of my plaid shirt.

"What? That I can hardly cook?"

"Yeah, because I really like to."

"Be my guest." She laughed, pointing to the stove.

She got a carton of eggs out of the refrigerator and slid a loaf of bread down the counter. She was tall; with her high heels, as tall as I was. Her hair was very black and very long, touching her shoulders.

"I'll need a bowl and a frying pan. I hope you have milk and butter."

"I'm glad you came, Fell. I wasn't looking forward to it, but now I'm glad you came."

"The way to a woman's heart is through her stomach."

"Usually not." She laughed again, and I looked at her waistline and figured she was telling the truth. She didn't look like someone who lived to eat. She looked like someone who lived to dance or play tennis or swim. She had a good tan. She almost had dimples when she smiled. Very long black eyelashes, a straight nose, and straight white teeth.

I beat the eggs and milk, and added a little salt and sugar.

"I can't believe you're doing this," she said. "It seems strange to have someone you don't even know walk in and just start making you French toast."

"Everything that's happening to me lately seems strange," I said.

"Do you want to talk about it?" I heard her scratch a match, and smelled a fresh cigarette.

"No, I don't want to talk about it."

"Is this how we're going to begin? With you keeping secrets from me?"

"Yes," I said. "Tell me about Delia Tremble." I put the slices of bread into the liquid.

"I look younger than I am. I never tell my age. I like serious guys who are good talkers."

"What do you like to talk about?" I put some heat on under the frying pan and dropped in some oil and some butter.

"I like the way people talk on planes," she said. "They just start in telling you about themselves."

"Do you know why that is? It's because people on planes don't have the scenery people on buses and trains have to distract them."

"Is that true?"

"My father used to be a detective. He said

you could travel more unnoticed on a train. People don't look at you as closely."

"I never thought of that, Fell."

"Okay," I said, "we're on a plane. Start talking." I raised the heat and waited for the frying pan to get hot.

"When I first noticed you in Plain and Fancy I figured you for one of these prep school kids. A preppy. I figured you came from money."

"Were you wrong!"

"Do you go to high school?"

"Umm hmm." I dropped the bread into the pan. "I'll need some paper towels in a minute. Were you after my money?"

"Maybe." I liked her laugh. "I liked the way you moved, too. I figured you'd be a good dancer."

"And that we could dance outdoors. That's what you said you wanted. To dance outdoors. Why outdoors?"

"Because I smoke," she said. "People are really getting to hate us smokers."

"So that's why," I said, and she came up behind me and reached around me to put down some paper towels.

"Did you ever smoke? Do you drink?" she asked.

"I used to do both," I said. "Name it, I did it."

"I'm glad you don't drink now. I don't really like men who do."

I noticed the "men." Keats still said "boys."

I said, "Do you go to boarding school or high school?"

"I graduated from high school."

"Oh," I said, "an older woman."

"Not that much older than you are. I was ahead of everyone."

"Are you going to college?"

"I want to travel. I haven't been many places. Have you been many places, Fell?"

"Not many at all."

"Oh, Fell, it looks good!"

I dropped the fried bread on the paper towels. "Jam, or maple syrup?"

"Maple syrup," she said. "I'll get it from the cupboard. Will you go to high school again next year?"

"Maybe," I said. "Or maybe I'll go away to school. I might get a scholarship. I might go to Switzerland."

"I want to hear all about it!"

"I'm not going to talk about it. It's bad luck to talk about something that hasn't come through yet."

She had out plates and I put the French toast on them.

She said, "Let's take this into the living room. If the twins wake up, I can hear them better from in there."

I followed her, carrying some forks and napkins she handed me.

"Are you a happy type, Fell?"

"What do you mean?"

"Just what I said. Are you a sad type or a happy type?"

I watched her bend over to put the plates down on the marble coffee table in front of this long, beige sofa. I saw the movement of her breasts under her white sweater.

"Right now I'm a happy type," I said.

"When were you last sad?"

"The last time? When my father died."

"That makes sense."

"And you?"

We sat down side by side on the sofa.

"Sometimes I get a melancholy feeling out here, so close to the ocean, not really connected with anyone in Seaville. I think the beach brings out a sadness in you, if you're alone. But it never stays with me. It comes and goes."

"Now you know me, so you're not alone anymore."

"Now I do." She took a taste of the French toast. "You're a good cook, aren't you, Fell?"

"Yes."

"And what else about you?"

I put up one hand. "Don't rush us."

She looked over at me. She wasn't smiling.

"Oh, Fell, I like that you said that. That's the best thing you've said all night. Do you mean it?"

"I do." I did. I wanted to take my time with her. I liked the way she looked, and I liked her style. She was easier than Keats, wiser, less manic-depressive. I liked what she'd said about being at the beach alone, and the sadness it brought out in you. Keats wouldn't have had the good sense to figure that out. She always made any sadness into something she was doing wrong, into failing and spending her life on nothing.

"We should have some music on, I guess," Delia Tremble said.

"We don't need it."

"What do you like?"

"Everything, but I don't know anything about classical stuff."

"I don't either. I like Whitney Houston. I like songs I can hear the lyrics in more than I like hard rock, and I don't like heavy metal."

She was telling me the names of singers and songs she liked when I happened to look across the room and see this painting of the ocean. Down in the lower right was the familiar fern.

I waited until she was finished talking. Then I said, "This family you work for . . ."

"The Stileses."

"Did they buy that painting?"

"Mrs. Stiles owns the Stiles Gallery in town.

One of her artists did that."

"Fern Pingree," I said.

"Do you know her?"

"Not well."

"How come you know her, Fell?"

I told her that I had dated a girl who lived next door to the Pingrees.

"What does she say about this Fern Pingree?"

"She doesn't know her."

"I'd be curious about her."

"Would be or are?"

"You listen too carefully sometimes, Fell. I would be, if I lived around here. She'd be someone I'd be curious about if I lived in Seaville."

"Why?"

"Look at that painting."

I looked again. It was an angry-looking ocean, with another sun above it that looked hot enough to fry eggs on the sand. There was a haze over the whole scene, the kind of whiteness that comes over a beach on a sizzling day when the sun just breaks through the clouds.

"Do you know what she named that painting?" Delia Tremble asked. "*Arizona Darkness*. Figure that one out!"

We both laughed.

Delia leaned back against the couch cushions. We were silent for a while. You could hear the sounds of the sea off in the distance. Delia was twirling a strand of her black hair around her finger.

"Fell? If you could have one wish now, what would it be?"

"That I could see you tomorrow."

She smiled at me. "Not tomorrow. They're having company. But maybe Monday night."

"And what would you wish for?"

"What would I wish for?" She thought about it for a while. "I want to get away. I want to travel."

Then we heard the Stileses arriving, heard Mrs. Stiles say, "Something smells good!"

"I told you it wouldn't be much of a date, Fell," Delia Tremble said.

I said quickly, "If you'd like to travel, how about traveling out to the Surf Club with me Monday night? You can dance outdoors there."

She said okay.

'm all for the idea [Mom had written]. *You'll get a good education, money to use for college or a restaurant, and don't you think your father would want you to go? I've thought and thought and I vote yes! Jazzy and I are at church. Meat loaf for dinner is cooling, don't put in fridge. . . . I think you should tell Mr. Pingree you'll do it, before he changes his mind!*

But I wanted to think about it, and talk more about it, and figure out how the whole scheme would work.

"All right," Pingree said, "but don't take too long to decide. If I can't get you to take the offer, I'll have to think of someone else."

Pingree watched me through a cloud of his own cigarette smoke.

We were sitting out on the front porch of the Frog Pond, having Sunday breakfast. He'd called early and I had said I'd meet him at ten. I couldn't sleep late, anyway. I usually liked to, when Mom took Jazzy to church and I didn't have to get up, but I couldn't. I woke up thinking about going to Gardner as Ping, and I laughed aloud at the idea. I thought of the way kids back in Brooklyn would say "Farrrr out!"

I kept thinking about Delia Tremble when I first woke up, too. I kept remembering the look in her dark eyes when she talked about sadness. I even got out of bed, pulled on my shorts, and tried to reach Keats at Four Winds. I guess I was guilty because I'd awakened thinking of someone else. Finally. After a year!

But Keats wasn't around. They rang that cow bell of theirs and shouted, "Keats! Keats! Keats!" She wasn't around. The girl who answered the phone asked me if I was Quint. I said yeah, Quint. She said someone just told her Keats was on her way to my motel; she'd left about ten minutes ago.

"You seem distracted this morning, Fell," Pingree said. "Or are you just a sad type?"

I remembered Delia asking me if I was a happy type or a sad type.

"You ought to know the answer to that. You've done enough research on me."

"All right. You're not yourself this morning. Why?"

"I can't imagine going through two years answering to the name Ping."

"You don't have to answer to that name. You can be Woodrow, Woody. My middle name is

Thompson. You can be Thompson, Tom."

"Just kidding," I said.

"I don't like Ping, either. No one ever called *me* that."

There was a young couple behind Pingree who looked as if they'd just left a bedroom somewhere and it was too soon, because they couldn't stop touching each other. I remembered what that was like back last year when Keats and I would go anyplace. We couldn't keep our hands off each other. What was the word Pingree'd used to describe falling in love? He'd said he was besotted. I'd looked it up later in my Webster's. It meant mentally stupefied, silly, foolish.

Pingree looked around to see what I was looking at. He shook his head as though he knew what that was like, too.

He gave me a wistful smile. "Do you miss Keats?"

"I miss her. But I don't think she misses me. I might take your advice. I might cool it with Keats." I'd already decided not to go up to Four Winds for the play. Let Quint Blade go.

"Good!" he said. "Cool it."

"Not because I'm taking you up on your offer."

"All right. It's probably still a good idea."

"I can't trust her."

"Can she trust you?"

"I don't know, after last night."

"I forgot about last night. How did it go?"

"Fine."

"You liked her?"

"She was easy to talk to. She likes to talk."

I watched the couple kiss. Everyone out on the porch was watching them. The waitress was standing there with orange juice on a tray, grinning, waiting for room to put the juice down in front of them. I counted to five, slowly. They were still at it.

Pingree said, "Let me tell you about this club at Gardner."

"Another thing," I interrupted him. "What if I get a thing for Delia Tremble?"

"If it's 'a thing,' it won't matter, will it?"

"You know what I mean. What if I fall for Delia Tremble?"

"Write her. That's what you'd do anyway, isn't it? She's not from Seaville, is she?"

"No."

"Well then?"

"But I'd want to see her."

Pingree stabbed some bacon with his fork. "You can't have everything you want. You can have a lot, but not everything. No one can ever have everything!"

I looked out at this fat pigeon waddling around

on the green lawn, and bit into my English muffin. I said, "What club were you going to tell me about?"

"It's called Sevens. It's a secret club at Gardner. It's *the* club."

"Like a fraternity?"

"No. No. It's not like anything you've ever heard about. They have their own rules, their own privileges. They control The Tower there."

"Why do they call it Sevens?"

"No one knows."

"What do you mean, no one knows? Someone must know."

"Members of Sevens know what it means, of course. My grandfather knew. He was the only member from our family."

"Did he tell you anything about it?"

"Never! If you get into Sevens you never tell the reason you got in, or the meaning of the name, or anything about Sevens. You're set apart when you get into Sevens . . . some say for life."

"You didn't make it, and your father didn't?"

"Just my grandfather."

"Why are you mentioning it this morning?"

"There's something else I didn't tell you about my grandfather's will," he said. He finished his bacon and eggs, pushed his plate back, and lit a cigarette. "If you make Sevens, you automatically get another ten thousand dollars. You get it instantly."

"You didn't think I'd make it, so you didn't mention it before, hmmm?" I couldn't eat any more. I tossed the rest of the muffin out toward the fat pigeon on the lawn.

Pingree began to speak extra clearly, as though he wanted what he was saying to really sink in.

"No one knows why a boy qualifies for Sevens. There's no type. Anyone can be in Sevens, but few are. Only about five or six a year. One year there was no one tapped for Sevens."

"This club really impresses you, doesn't it? You're not just talking about it because of the extra ten thousand, are you?"

"Yes, I guess it does really impress me, Fell. I like solutions to things. I could never solve that one—what makes a Sevens."

"If I were to go to Gardner, and if I got in, I'd tell you."

"Oh, no. No one's ever been told."

"But I think that stuff is crap! I don't care about secret clubs!"

"Gardner will teach you about tradition. Tradition isn't a bad thing, Fell. Sometimes it's the only continuity."

"I don't mean tradition. I like tradition, too."

I did. So had my dad. Christmas used to be this big production when he was alive, starting with the tree trimming on Christmas Eve. He always made Christmas breakfast, too. "It's snobbery I don't like. It's people thinking they're better than other people just because they're in some stupid club."

"I see."

He stirred his coffee. We both checked out the lovers. They were still at it. Pingree met my eyes and we grinned.

Then Pingree said, "I wish I'd been more like you when I was growing up. I was all caught up in what it meant to be a Pingree, what was expected of me. My father drilled that into me. I've done a lot of bad things to Ping, but I'll never do that to him. I'm surprised Fern isn't more sympathetic in this regard. She hates snobbery, too, but she's dead set on Ping's going to Gardner. Ping can't conquer that phobia of his. We've tried hypnotism, everything. I think Fern thinks he's faking it."

I said, "I saw *Arizona Darkness* last night."

He looked across at me. "That belongs to the Stileses."

"Delia Tremble's their au pair."

"Ah! For the twins."

"Yes. We wondered why your wife named

something *Arizona Darkness* that's this ocean under this hot sun?"

"She chooses very unusual titles for her paintings. I think that one had to do with Jerome, Arizona. Oh, they all do, really."

"What does Jerome, Arizona, have to do with your wife?"

Pingree ground out his cigarette in the ashtray. "Her grandfather was there in World War Two, long before she was born. They had one of those internment camps there for Japanese-Americans. Our version of concentration camps. We didn't gas them the way the Germans did the Jews. Didn't work them. But we confined them. They were our prisoners. Only Japanese-Americans were put through that. Fern can't forget it."

I remembered watching a program about it on TV.

"I didn't even know she was Japanese."

"Her father is. Not her mother. Her mother's Irish-American."

I was remembering the barracks in the field, in the painting she called *Smiles We Left Behind Us.*

"Then came Hiroshima, another shattering blow to Asians. And Vietnam. Fern has a very melancholy nature as a result. I fall in love with very melancholy women. My first wife was the same way."

I liked him. I wasn't sure why. Maybe because he never talked down to me.

He called for the check.

"There's so little time," he said. "You know that, don't you, Fell?"

On the way to the Surf Club Monday night, Delia Tremble said she wanted a frozen custard. I stopped at Frosty's, and she passed two dollars to me and said, "Get yourself one, too, Hunk!"

I took the money.

I said, "This doesn't mean you can have your way with me later."

She had that lilting laugh I'd grown to love in just forty-eight hours. The sky was deep blue with an orange ball up in it, and a thousand stars. We were headed down to the club to dance outside under them. She smelled of roses, or she reminded me of how roses smell. I didn't know which.

When I came back with two chocolate frozen custards dripping down my fingers, she said, "Why do you carry a gun?"

"Why do you snoop into my glove compartment?"

"You go first," she said.

"It's my dad's gun."

It was his .38 Smith & Wesson, never loaded, with ivory butt plates and an owl carved into it, the eyes made of two real rubies. Years ago some Mafia character'd given it to him as thanks for following his wife around.

She said, "But he's dead, you said."

I got behind the wheel. "I can't throw it out or turn it in."

"So you keep it in your car?"

"My dad did, too. He said you should never keep a gun in the house. A lot of accidents with guns happen in policemen's houses, did you know that?"

"No." She was licking the frozen custard off the side of the cone. It was sexy the way she did that.

"A lot of homicides happen in policemen's homes, too," I said. "Their guns are always there." I put a napkin around the bottom of my cone. It wasn't going to do any good. It was a hot night. I was glad to be with her.

"Now your turn," I said. "What were you looking for in my glove compartment?"

"Any evidence I could find of you."

"Why?"

"I'm curious about you."

"Are you glad I'm not the preppy you thought I was?"

"I like preppies."

"What do you like about them?"

"I like the ones who go to all-male schools."

"Why them?"

"They're starved for women, so they're eager

to please and shyer, but they have more dignity than other guys." She bit into the tip of the chocolate custard. "I like all three traits."

"You like eager to please, shy, and dignified?"

"Yes. Are you any of those?"

"I'm eager to please, and I'm dignified."

"I'll make you shy," she said.

I laughed painfully. "It's worth a try." I managed to sound my idea of suave. Maybe not hers. I started the car.

"Could you ever use that gun?"

"I could. I know how to shoot. I learned to shoot when I was thirteen."

"Guns scare me," she said, "but they fascinate me, too. This is awful. When I saw that gun in there, it turned me on."

"*This* is awful," I said. "It turns me on that it turned you on."

We both laughed. I took her left hand with my right.

I wished I had a convertible. We should have been speeding down toward the sea in a convertible. I'd never had that kind of thought with Keats. I suppose that was because there was only one thing I could do with Keats that Daddy and she hadn't already done, including speed along Ocean Road in a little blue Benz, top down. But with Delia Tremble I felt there were things I could show her, maybe not then and there, but there was the feeling she hadn't seen it all. She'd already said she hadn't been many places. Keats had been to Europe three times, India, the Orient, even China. I couldn't begin to name all the islands in the Caribbean she'd carried her tube of Bain de Soleil down to and come back bronze from.

Delia let go of my hand and reached into her pocket for a cigarette. I pushed in the lighter. She had on a bright-blue cotton blazer with the sleeves rolled up, over a dress with big blue and white flowers all over it. The same hoop earrings; the same gold rings. She had white low-heeled sandals on, so she was shorter than I was this time.

I had on some khaki stone-washed pants that Keats had given me last summer. It seemed like way back last summer with Delia beside me and something new starting. Something good.

When the lighter popped out, I held it up for her.

"Thanks," she said. "Fell? Do you miss anyone now?"

"No. Do you?"

"Not now. Thanks for taking me dancing, Fell."

I couldn't remember any girl ever thanking me for taking her somewhere, on the way there.

She shifted her cigarette to her right hand and held my right hand again.

I looked over at her. I decided to try out my father's old imitation of Humphrey Bogart. I sucked down my lower lip and said, "This is just the beginning of our travels, kid."

"Don't," she said.

"Don't what?"

"Do the Bogie bit. I don't like bits. I always think men pull that stuff when they're afraid to show any emotion."

So *there*, Dad.

I said, "Why shouldn't we be afraid to show emotion? Show emotion and die."

"No. That's see Naples. See Naples and die." She laughed. "Show emotion and take your chances."

Delia Tremble was a real good dancer. When you danced with her, people watched. Not you. Her. Some people watched her and danced. A few couples stopped to watch her.

She had all sorts of moves, and she'd heard every song whether it was a hard rock disco song or the softer kind that came rarely and only at the end of a set. She did things with herself that were graceful and hot and new to me. New to a lot of us. What I liked was she didn't dance for them, and she didn't dance for herself like some girls do. Some girls dance in a way you could go down to the corner and back and they wouldn't know you'd been gone. Delia danced for me, and with me, smiling at me, her eyes always coming back to me.

We danced out on the big deck, without sitting down, for about an hour.

Then we went into the bar, got some cherry Cokes, and took them outside to the little deck and talked for another hour.

She told me she was from Atlantic City. Her father had once managed a big hotel there when Atlantic City was still pretty much a summer resort.

"When I was a kid," she said, "I used to wait for winter, when all the tourists would be gone. Then my mom and my sisters and I could move into one of the big suites that looked out on the ocean. That's why the ocean here affects me so. It reminds me of when I was little."

A red-faced, crew-cut older guy began playing piano on the little deck.

Delia said, "Let's dance here. On the lawn. It's slow. We can take off our shoes. It's wet on the grass."

We did.

I knew the song the fellow began singing. It was an old, old Billy Joel one, from before he'd met Christie Brinkley. It was one he wrote to his first wife about not changing, and it used to get Mom mad. It said he didn't need clever conversation, he wanted her to stay the way she was. Mom would say, "Stay dumb, huh? Is that the message, Billy Joel?"

But it sounded really romantic with this old saloon singer doing it. He sounded as if he were an inch away from having lung cancer. He was smoking, no hands, the way Pingree often did. He was singing "Don't go changing."

We were dancing out there on the wet grass by ourselves, in the dark. I kissed her near the end of the song. She kissed me back.

I think we both felt changed, never mind don't go changing, because we didn't smile or joke as we walked back toward the deck. You could cut the tension with a knife. It was sex. It was this great physical thirst that had come over us, and that we knew was coming, but weren't sure what to do with after its arrival.

We sat down on the steps and picked up our cherry Cokes.

Delia said, "I have a chance to go around the world in the fall. On a ship. I'm going to take it."

"Will you be an au pair?"

"Not for the Stileses."

"Did you just decide?"

"Not *just*. About a month ago. I wasn't sure I wanted to go away for such a long time."

"How long?"

"A year at least."

I let out a low whistle instead of a wail.

"I wanted to tell you," she said. "I was going to wait to tell you, but now I think you should know."

"A year?"

"Yes."

She put her hand over mine. "I feel things, too, Fell. The way you dance."

"The way *I* dance," I said.

She took her hand away and reached for a cigarette.

"Thanks for not being mean about my smoking, too."

I smelled her light up. She smoked those long brown Mores.

I finally said, "I might go away myself."

"Really? Where?"

"I told you. Switzerland. Prep school."

"Oh, Fell, you'd be a preppy after all."

"Don't laugh."

"I'm not. I told you. I like that."

"I like you," I said, "and I think I know what you're saying."

"What am I saying?"

"You're saying we both feel something. *But.*" I took her hand and brought it up to my lips, and let my tongue play lightly between her fingers. Then I put her hand back. "You're saying we can't help feeling it, but we can't expect to make anything out of it. Nothing permanent for now."

"Nothing permanent. Exactly. Because I'll be away a long time."

"I will be, too," I said.

I decided then and there to go to Gardner.

We danced an hour longer. I never danced that way before with anyone, never felt that way with anyone while I was dancing.

Then we drove down to the beach. We were still there when the sun started coming up.

Tuesday was her day off.

I said, "Come home with me. I'll make us breakfast. You can meet my mother and Jazzy."

She ran her finger down my lips, then pressed them together with it. "Hush, Fell."

She had the collar of the blue blazer turned up and my aqua sweater wrapped around her neck like a scarf.

For once, I wasn't at all cold.

"I don't want to meet your family, or get to know your friends. I don't want ties. I don't want us to be a couple."

"What are we then?" I wasn't whining around as I used to with Keats. I was asking her to see what she'd come up with, after what had just happened between us.

"We're what we are, Fell." She smiled. She looked sleepy. "We don't have to define it or label it . . . and I want our memories to be just of the two of us."

I kept trying to keep myself from making some kind of wisecrack, or doing a Bogie imitation, or all the other jazz. She'd taught me that.

She took my hand. "I like what we are," she said. "It's good enough, isn't it?"

"It's better than that," I said.

We left the beach, and I dropped her off at the Stileses'.

When I got home, I called Woodrow Pingree and told him I'd decided to do it.

"You won't be sorry, Fell," he said.

fell

ARIZONA DARKNESS

part | 2

chapter | 14

The first thing I found out was that no one going to Gardner School ever called it that. They called it The Hill. The school sat on a hill in the middle of farm country. That was all I saw, once I got off the train at Trenton, New Jersey, and into the school bus. Ten of us new boys were bound for the little town of Cottersville, Pennsylvania.

There we were met by a dozen fellows in light-blue blazers and navy-blue pants. All the blazers had gold 7's over the blue-and-white Gardner insignias. The group formed a seven around us and sang the Gardner song.

Others will fill our places,
Dressed in the old light blue.
We'll recollect our races.
We'll to the flag be true.
And youth will still be in our faces
When we cheer for a Gardner crew . . .
And youth will still be in our faces
When we cheer for a Gardner crew!

A fellow behind me said, "Now we have to plant trees."

"We have to what?"

"We each have to plant a tree. It's the first thing you do when you get here, even before you get your room assigned. You get a little evergreen handed to you. You have to give it a name."

"What kind of a name?"

"Any name. A name. By the way, I'm Sidney Dibble. Dib."

"I'm Thompson Pingree. Tom."

He was the basketball player type, all legs and arms, skinny, so tall I had to look way up at him. He was blond like me. He had on a tan suit with a beige T-shirt and Reeboks.

I'd worn the only suit that had been mine in my other life: the dark-blue one. I felt like Georgette after her real family had come to claim her. Pingree had driven me into New York City one August afternoon and taken me to Brooks Brothers. I had a whole trunkful of new stuff.

I asked Dib if he was sure about this tree thing. That was one detail Pingree'd left out. Dib said he was positive. His brother'd just graduated from Gardner. Dib said he was the world's foremost authority on Gardner—"Except when it comes to Sevens," he added.

The words weren't even out of his mouth a half second before a member of Sevens began barking orders at us. He was a tall skinhead, with vintage thrift-shop zoot-suit pants, and two earrings in his left ear. He had on a pair of black Converse sneakers.

"My name is Creery! Leave your luggage on the ground! It will be in your room when you get there! We will now walk back to Gardner Woods for the tree-planting ceremony! Think of a name for your tree on the way. Whatever you wish to call it. After you have planted your tree, you will line up to receive your room assignments in The Tower!"

"Who's the punk rocker?" I asked Dib. "I thought Sevens was this exclusive club?"

"He just told you. His name is Cyril Creery."

"And *he's* a Sevens?"

"There's no predicting who'll make Sevens. But he's easy. It's a guy named Lasher you don't want on your case . . . unless *you* make Sevens. Then he can't touch you. Creery and Lasher hate each other. When Creery first got here, Lasher hated the sight of him. Creery had hair then. Purple hair. Lasher was out to get him. You know, Creery's the kind that named his tree Up Yours! Lasher would have made his life hell here, but Creery made Sevens."

"Don't the other members have a say in who makes Sevens?"

"I don't know how it works. No one does."

"Maybe you need three blackballs, like in a fraternity."

"Nobody knows," Dib said.

Besides the ten of us who'd gotten off the train in Trenton, there were ten other new boys already at The Hill. Now there were twenty of us walking to Gardner Woods.

There we found twenty holes in two rows, with twenty shovels beside them, and twenty mounds of dirt.

There was a line forming to receive the evergreens.

"You tell Creery the name of your tree, then stick it in the ground and throw the dirt over it," Dib said. "I'm going to name mine after my dog, Thor."

"Are all those trees in the background from classes ahead of us?"

"You've got it. What are you naming yours?"

"I'm not sure yet."

"You better have a name ready when we get up there."

I thought of naming mine Delia. But that wouldn't have been the way we'd agreed to be. Nothing permanent. A tree was pretty permanent. I thought of all the names people called their houses down on Dune Road in Seaville. I thought of Adieu. I thought of Keats's saying on Labor Day, "Daddy says you can come here as long as you've come to say good-bye." I told her she could tell Daddy to shove it! Keats said, "Oh, my, my, my. Aren't we arrogant now that we're going abroad to school. Do you kiss arrogantly now, too?" I didn't kiss her good-bye arrogantly, but I did try to get something simulating emotion into it. Nothing. Delia'd have laughed. She'd have said, "What did you think, Fell, that you could forget me?" She was already gone by the time Keats came back from Four Winds. But Delia was never going to be gone.

I said to Dib, "I may name mine Adieu."

"Oh, oui?" He laughed.

I thought of how I'd razzed Keats because Adieu had sounded pretentious. Why not just good-bye? I'd said. Why the French?

"No, not Adieu," I said. "Good-bye."

"Your tree's going to be called Good-bye?"

"It's as good as Thor, isn't it?"

"Sure. Call it anything. You know this guy

Lasher I told you about? My brother says he puts on this big act. He wants to be a playwright. He writes these plays with characters in them named Death and Destruction, like he thinks he's profound, but it's all a lot of bullticky crap! I mean, he's a vegetarian, and he works out, and he's this big hypochondriac, but he's always playing with nooses and pretending he's being called to the grave. Well, he named his tree Suicide."

"I'm going to call mine Good-bye."

Good-bye to John Fell and his life, but not good-bye to Delia Tremble. We were going to write. "Promise," she'd said, "and if you don't like to write letters, or if you think you probably won't write me once you get there, tell me right now. I don't want false expectations."

I said I'd write. I promised.

Keats'd said, "Are we going to write ever?"

"I don't know," I'd said.

"Do you know you've changed since June? I'm going to think you've met someone else."

I couldn't tell her about it.

I was afraid I'd jinx it if I told anyone about Delia. "Jinx *what*?" my mother'd said. "She's going away for a year and all July and August you never knew when you were going to see her."

"Men! Plant your trees!" Creery shouted after we'd all been given an evergreen.

Men? The last time I'd ever been in on a tree

planting was back in grade school in Brooklyn one Arbor Day. We'd all sung "This Land Is Your Land!" and walked around this little cherry tree holding hands.

Something about being one of ten boys in line with silver shovels and our holes already dug for us, with ten of the same behind us, reminded me of third grade.

But later, what happened in The Tower, didn't.

He said Sevens were always called by their last names, so I would call him Lasher. Everyone else on The Hill, except for faculty, was called by their first name. Good, I thought! No Pingree.

He said I'd been assigned to him. I was in his group. If I ever needed anything, I'd ask him if I could have it.

He had very thick glasses, like Ping's. He had thick, coal-black hair like Delia's, but his was cut very short. He had one of those almost beards—stubble, really—and a stubble mustache. A smile that tipped to one side.

How much older than me? A year maybe. Maybe my age. Seventeen. But I was sixteen at Gardner School. I wasn't a Gemini anymore, either. I was a horny Scorpio. Don't ask me how Ping could be a Scorpio with all the sex appeal of a can opener, but he was. So was I, now.

Lasher said, "What'd you name your tree?"

"Good-bye."

"Good-bye's its name or are you a smartass?"

"That's its name."

We were way up in The Tower. We had to go up one at a time, alphabetically. One hundred and twenty steps. The stairs were stone ones on the outside. Even if you didn't have a fear of heights it wasn't a climb that set your heart to singing.

In the top of The Tower was this one stone-walled room, lit by a single candle on the table. Lasher sat at the table. There was nowhere for me to sit. I stood. Lasher had on a white tank top under his blazer.

"Thompson, I want to tell you something. Don't screw up! You've been assigned to me. I hate having scumbags who come here and can't take it or can't make it! I happen to hate legacies, too—types like Creery, whose father *and* grandfather went here, and miraculously all got to be Sevens! I happen to love this place . . . *and* Sevens! It's a privilege to be here, not a right! Act like you wanted to come here more than you wanted to get laid the first time, and we'll get along."

"I'll do that."

"You have gotten yourself laid by now, haven't you?"

"Yes, I have."

"Good. I won't have to cart you out to Willing

Wanda's to get laid. I don't like virgins under my charge. Virgins are vulnerable. I don't like vulnerable scumbags under my charge! *Latet anguis in herba,* Thompson! Do you know your Latin?"

"I don't know what that means."

"It's from Virgil. It means the snake hides in the grass. It's my motto."

"Okay," I said.

I could see that the gold buttons on his blazer had little 7's on them.

Then he said, "Seven Seas: the Arctic and the Antarctic. North and South Pacific. North and South Atlantic. The Indian Ocean."

I didn't know what that meant. I stood there.

"If a Sevens meets you he might ask you to name seven things that go together. If you can't think of seven things that go together, he might ask you to clean all the toilets in Hull House, where you'll be living. He might ask you to do anything, if you can't come up with seven things, and you'll have to do it!"

"All right," I said. "I'll find seven things for an answer."

"Find a lot of seven things. You can't repeat."

"All right."

"Your roommate is sixteen. He's from New Hope, Pennsylvania. He's a legacy, too."

"Okay," I said.

Lasher took off his thick glasses while he continued and talked with his eyes shut, as though he was bored out of his gourd but he had to get through this.

"Your roommate is a virgin. Your roommate called me sir all through his interview. Your roommate named his tree after his puppy dog. He lets people call him Dib, a boy's nickname. He's obviously still on Pablum, so grow him up, Thompson, because your roommate's a vulnerable scumbag who doesn't realize *latet anguis*—finish it, Thompson!" He opened his eyes and looked up at me.

"In the grass . . . *in herba*."

So I was rooming with Sidney Dibble.

Lasher gave me this smile that was as beautiful as he was, without those thick glasses.

"Welcome to The Hill!" Lasher said.

chapter 15

John Fell
L'Ecole la Coeur
C H–1092 Rolle
Lake Geneva
Switzerland

Dear F
     E
       L

        L [I liked the way she wrote my name falling down], *I'll never forget our last dinner at The Frog Pond, remember? You were so sunburned you couldn't lean back in your chair. I liked it because you had to lean toward me.*

I know we said we wouldn't write about ordinary happenings—my idea, because I want our memories to be of what we shared together, but I want to know certain things about you . . . if you like where you are . . .if you are glad you made the choice to go to Switzerland. . . . You must tell me those things. . . . Tell me a thought you haven't told anyone. I won't tell you about life on this ship, except to say one port is like the next, and I think of you. I remember once you combed your hair after we were down on the beach. You put the

comb in your back pocket, looked over at me and
said, "Do I look all right?" I love it that you gave
me that unguarded moment. "Do I look all right?"
you asked me. . . . I don't write long letters,

F
  E
    L
     L

but I think long thoughts. Love, Delia.

The envelope Ping had sent it in was addressed to W. Thompson Pingree, Gardner School, Cottersville, Pennsylvania, U.S.A.

There were two letters from my mother inside. Even she had to write to me in Switzerland, where Ping would forward her mail. Pingree had insisted.

There was also a note from Ping.

Your French is improving, but you are
avoiding all courses in computer science.
How am I doing?
Have I been up in The Tower yet?

I was rereading my mail in Hull House on a Sunday morning in October, anxious to get a letter off to Delia before "my father" arrived. It was Pingree's first visit. He was going to chapel with me.

"Just think," Dib said behind me, "right now,

in that luxurious clubhouse in the bottom of The Tower, there's the aroma of rib roast cooking for the Sevens to enjoy after chapel! They'll have rib roast, mashed potatoes. We'll be lucky to have chicken again. They've got it made, haven't they?"

"One thing I'm sick of," I said, "is everyone's obsession with the Sevens! God, who are they that everyone runs around in awe of them?"

"Wouldn't you like to be one?"

"Only because of all their privileges."

"And their meals."

"That's part of their privileges."

"They're like another race," Dib said. "The Master Race."

Dib was munching on some Black Crows. He was always eating. Eating stuff like Hostess Ding Dongs, M&M's, Fruit Bars, and Sno-Caps. Dib was like most kids who'd rather eat Whoppers at Burger King than duckling à l'orange at the best French restaurant. He thought frozen Lean Cuisine was gourmet food, and a box of Sara Lee double chocolate layer cake was a better dessert than fresh-made key lime pie. It wasn't just the food Sevens were privileged to have, that we weren't that got to Dib. It was the whole aura of Sevens, and it got to everyone. Everyone at Gardner envied them, watched them, gossiped about them, and wished they were part of them.

The night before, Lasher had taken Dib out to

Willing Wanda's for Dib's sexual initiation.

When he came back, Dib said, "Did you ever hear an old song called 'Is That All There Is?'"

"Yes. Some woman named Peggy Lee made a record of it. My mom loved it."

"In it, this kid sees a fire and says is that all there is to a fire?"

"Right."

"That's how I felt about what went on at Willing Wanda's."

"You'll feel more when you're in love."

"I hope so. I'd rather eat a box of Mallomars or dig into a plate of Chicken McNuggets."

"Chicken McNuggets," I said, and I put two fingers down my throat and retched.

Dib was working on his paper for the New Boys Competition. There were always rumors about how one got tapped for Sevens, and one of them was that the N.B.C. had something to do with it. All new students were required to write a paper by the last day of October. The theme that year was "They All Chose America." You could choose any group that'd immigrated. Dib was doing the Irish. I got the bright idea to do Japanese-Americans, and to call mine "Arizona Darkness."

I had only the title and some books from the library about President Roosevelt's executive order 9066, which sent 150,000 Japanese Americans to concentration camps back in World War Two. They were given less than forty-eight hours to gather their possessions together for evacuation. Although there were three times as many Americans of Italian descent living on the West Coast, they weren't affected. Neither were German Americans. Only Japanese.

I wanted to answer Delia's letter before I worked on that.

Dib said, "Name some famous Irish-Americans."

"How about the Kennedys?"

"I've got them."

"I want to write a letter before my father gets here," I said, "so don't talk to me, okay?"

"Dear Delia," Dib said, "how are things in Switzerland?"

He thought that's where she was, and that was why I got mail from Switzerland. I let him think it.

Dear Delia [I wrote],
 Last week in Classics we read Aeschylus's account of Clytemnestra's welcoming Agamemnon home from the Trojan War. She asked him to walk the last few yards on a purple carpet of great value. He didn't want to do it. He said it was too valuable to walk on. But she insisted. Then he went inside the palace and she murdered him in his bath. . . . I thought of when a girl I loved gave me a purple bow tie, then stood me up for the

*Senior Prom. . . . I got an A+ for the paper I wrote
about it.*

*I thought, I'm glad she's in my past. I'm glad
there's Delia.*

*A secret thought. Oscar Wilde once wrote he
who expects nothing will never be disappointed.
I don't expect anything from you, Delia. Will you
ever disappoint me?*

*I'm not sorry about choosing to come to L'Ecole
la Coeur. So far, so good. That night at the Frog
Pond? My back wasn't that sunburned. I wanted to
lean into you.*

  Love, F
     E
      L
       L

I addressed the letter c/o The Worldwide
Tours Group, Goodship Cruise, San Francisco,
California, for forwarding. Then I put that letter
into an envelope addressed to John Fell at
L'Ecole la Coeur. Ping would mail it for me.

Just as I was finishing, the buzzer rang three
short, one long, my signal.

"Your dad's here," said Dib.

I hadn't seen or talked to Pingree since early
September. I never called him, though I'd memorized his phone number in case of emergency. He

didn't even want me to write it in my address book. That was just one of his rules, along with others like no photographs of myself at Gardner ever. He said to take sick the day they scheduled class pictures for the yearbook. Avoid all cameras!

I wore the new tan gabardine suit he'd bought me. He had on a dark, vested, pin-striped one.

"What a day!" he said. It was warm and the sun was out. "I'm glad to see you, my boy! I'm glad you're doing so well!"

I walked along beside him, down the path toward chapel.

"I haven't gone below A since I've been here, so it must agree with me. I'm not repeating that much, either. It's harder here than it was in public school."

"Your monthly report was excellent, Fell! That paper you did for classics, what did you call it? The one you got an A+ on?"

"'The Purple Carpet.' Did they mention that?"

"Dr. Skinner reported that you have a flair for composition. I even showed it to Fern, because of the carpet business. That would be like Ping, you know. He was always intrigued by magic carpets. *The Arabian Nights.* It sounded like Ping."

"It didn't have anything to do with *The Arabian Nights*," I said.

"It doesn't matter. Fern thought it did. She said, 'You see, I was right. He got past all that

Tower business.'" Pingree chuckled. He clapped his arm around my shoulder, an inch of ash dropping off his cigarette. "It's working out. You're doing fine!"

"And Ping?"

"He loves it over there! When I spoke to him last night on the telephone, I said, 'Complain a little more. You don't sound like yourself.'"

In chapel, the Gardner choir sang:

> *And youth will still be in our faces*
> *When we cheer for a Gardner crew.*
> *Yes, youth will still be in our faces*
> *We'll remain to Gardner true!*

Pingree wiped tears from his eyes.

After, Pingree said, "I can't stay for Sunday dinner. I don't want to get involved up here, anyway. But good Lord, it takes me back to walk around this place!"

"How are things in Seaville?"

"The same. Is your mother happy in Brooklyn?"

"They still can't find a decent apartment. But she says it's so good to be a subway ride from Macy's again she doesn't care."

We both chuckled, and then he stopped as he saw The Tower.

"Ah! The Tower!"

"Do you want to walk over there?" I asked him. "My roommate says they're cooking rib roast down in the Sevens's clubhouse for Sunday dinner."

"Yes, their Sunday dinners are always the envy of everyone. Steak Wednesday nights, so they say. The inside of that clubhouse is supposed to be very elegant! No, I'll just admire it from a distance, as I always did."

We started walking along again.

"What did you name your tree?" I asked him.

"My tree. I almost forgot about planting that tree."

"That was one thing you didn't warn me about."

"I completely forgot. You plant it, you forget it. I named mine Sara. That was my first wife's name."

"You knew her way back then?"

"Oh yes. Way back then." He lit another cigarette. "She went to Miss Tyler's in Princeton. You would have liked her. She was always questioning what it all meant. What we were put on this earth for, all that sort of thing. She was a philosophy major. She was my first melancholy baby. Do you know that song?"

"No."

"You don't know 'Melancholy Baby'?"

"No, I don't."

"I can't believe they don't still sing it."

"Maybe they do. I don't know it. I guess Delia's a melancholy baby, too. She doesn't sound like she loves the trip she's on."

"Ah, yes. Delia."

"We write," I said.

"Well, good."

"She's going around the world. Did I tell you that?"

"Yes, you did. Do you really love this Delia, Fell?"

"I don't know."

"That's good, that you don't know."

"Why is it good?"

"Love is such an interference. When it happens to you, you let your guard down. You should never let your guard down."

"I guess you're right," I said. I don't know what he was thinking of, but I was thinking of Keats, and how she'd treated me once she could take me for granted. . . . I still hadn't written to Keats.

"You know, Fell—I should call you Thompson around here, or Tom—I've grown very fond of you."

"Thanks," I said. "I like you, too."

"I'm going to travel next month, and I got worried over the idea what if something happens to me? Where would that leave you? So I've already transferred the first ten thousand to a savings account for you. Here's your book."

"Aren't you afraid I'll skip out on you now that I have the money?" I laughed.

"No. I trust you. I know you won't touch it until your year is over. Your allowance is sufficient, isn't it?"

"Yes, and I have some extra from selling the Dodge."

I took a look at the bank book. It was from the Union Trust Company in Brooklyn Heights. John T. Fell. The T. was for Theodore, my grandfather's name. When I'd gone to the nursing home to tell him that I was going away to school in Switzerland, that I'd won a Brutt scholarship to go there, he'd said, "I was named after Theodore Roosevelt, Johnny. Did I ever tell you why?" I was in a hurry. I had to tell him yes, he'd told me why. I still felt lousy about that.

Pingree said, "I was going to put the money in trust for you, in your mother's name."

"I'm glad you didn't. MasterCard would get their hands on it, or Visa, or some collection agency. My mother owes all over the place."

"I realize that. And you're a big boy. We have to trust each other, don't we, Fell?"

"Yes, we do," I agreed. "I'm working hard on the French, too. By Christmas I'll *sound* like I've been going to L'Ecole la Coeur."

"I'm not worried about you," he said. He let the cigarette drop from his mouth, stepped on it, and said, "Walk me down to my car. I love this place, you know. I was happiest right here."

November. I was out in front of Hull House one afternoon reading a letter from Keats. Even if it hadn't been written to me, and wasn't signed, I would have known it was Keats's, right away.

Dear Fell,

Here's a poem I translated for Spanish, written by Pedro Calderon de La Barca (1600–1681).

And what is life but frenzy?
And what is it but fancy?
A shadow, mere fiction,
for its greatest good is small,
and life itself a dream,
and dreams are only dreams.

Doesn't that make you really depressed, Fell? So why am I writing you? It won't help my mood to remember that you caught me out in everything, from going to the prom with Quint to his coming to Four Winds that weekend . . . and you never forgave me. I don't blame you. . . . But I was in Seaville last weekend to see Seaville High play Northport (I'll always go back for that game). They lost, which was depressing, too. They only won two games the whole season!

Oh, Fell, I'm never going to be supportive of anyone. I'm always going to need it and never be able to give it, which makes me practically worthless!

One thing I did do when I was home, went to the Stiles Gallery. Maybe just because I'd heard you dated their summer au pair and hoped she'd show up there, so I could get a look at her.

Fell, I'm not over you yet, although I gave you every indication I was. I dream of your smell. The scent awakens me like a ghost tickling my nose with a thread from its sheet.

Also, Mrs. Pingree's work was on display. "Early Works," they were called. *Smiles We Left Behind Us* was there, just as peculiar as you'd described it, but even more weird was the painting of seaweed. Just this orange seaweed under green water. Well, that is not the shock. She called it Sara. It is really strange, Mummy says, because when the first Mrs. Pingree died (her name was Sara!), there were rumors Fern Pingree pushed her overboard. She couldn't swim. She drowned. . . . Seaweed . . . Sara . . . How about that for weird? It's 10X weirder than anything going on in my life, which is at a depressing standstill. Is yours?

Do you speak French fluently now? I saw *L'Ecole la Coeur* advertised in the back of Town and Country. *Très chic! Je t'adore! Toujours,*
     Keats.

Then from behind me someone shouted, "SEVENS!"

I whirled around. It was Lasher glaring down at me through those thick glasses. I thought of Ping's glasses, and I thought of that suicide back in Brooklyn who my father said wasn't a suicide, because his glasses were smashed beside his body.

I was supposed to answer with seven things that went together.

"Grammar," I said, trying to remember all the seven sciences, "Logic, Arithmetic, Music, Geometry, Astronomy, and . . . and . . ."

"And?" Lasher said. "Are you naming the seven medieval sciences?"

"Yes."

"Well, what have you left out?"

"I don't know."

"You left out Rhetoric, Thompson!"

Lasher had on an old tweed topcoat, with the collar up. He had his stubble beard with his stubble mustache. I wished my father'd lived to see stubble get to be an in thing. My father used to come home from all-night jobs unshaved, complaining that he looked like some bum.

"Okay," I said. "The seven names of God. El, Elohim—"

Lasher cut me off. "No second chances, Thompson!"

He came around to face me, his hands sunk in his pockets. The wind blew back his thick black hair. I could never see his eyes. The leaves were off the trees above us. It was a blustery, late-fall afternoon. I was cold in just a yellow turtleneck sweater and tan cords.

"I want you to go to The Tower after your dinner tonight," said Lasher, "and place a lighted candle on every step. You'll find the candles and their ceramic holders in a carton outside the Sevens clubhouse. Do you understand, Thompson?"

"What about study hall?"

"Just tell the proctor you're on a Sevens assignment. Get your ass there by seven-thirty. Seven-thirty, sharp, scumbag!"

"All right."

"You go all the way to the top. Then press the clubhouse bell so we can all come out and admire your handiwork before you blow them all out on your way back down."

"All right."

"Stupid!" Lasher growled as he walked away. "You left out Rhetoric!"

It was a Wednesday. We always had a test at the start of French on Thursday mornings. I usually studied hard on Wednesday nights. I wouldn't that Wednesday night. Not after one hundred and twenty steps.

"He's really a sadist," Dib said. "I have a theory about why he is."

"Why is he?"

Dib was eating a Baby Ruth, getting ready for dinner. Our room in Hull House looked as if burglars had just left it. Dib never closed a door he opened, or picked up anything he took off. We never had room inspections. No one ever got on our backs about whether or not the beds were made. The only tyranny at Gardner was Sevens.

"He's mean because God gave him that one flaw," Dib said. "His eyesight. That's the real snake in the grass."

"He ought to get contact lenses. His eyes are real pretty."

"He can't wear them. He gets allergic to anything in his eyes. Creery says if Lasher didn't have to wear those glasses you could shave him, put a dress on him, and ask him to go out on a date."

"Except he wouldn't go out with Creery," I said. "Creery's too much of a stonehead."

"Creery says he's mean because both his parents are shrinks, and shrinks' kids are always messes. Sevens is his real family—that's why he makes so much of it. He's been in Sevens since he was fourteen."

"Maybe he's mean because his family shipped him out when he was so young."

"Or maybe," said Dib, "his family shipped him

out when he was so young because he was mean."

The dinner bell rang and we went downstairs and walked across the commons together.

"I'd be a little scared to go up in The Tower by myself after dark," Dib said.

"I'm not looking forward to it."

"You should have packed your gun."

"I never carry it or load it."

"Yeah. Guns scare the hell out of me, too."

"I know a girl who got turned on by the sight of that gun."

"Delia?"

"Yeah, Delia."

"Why don't you have a picture of her?"

"We never took any."

"Ask her for one. I'd like to see this Trembling Delia."

"I've asked her and asked her."

In my last letter to her, I underlined my request in red. When she answered it, she wrote:

Oh, don't tell me you've forgotten how I look,

> F
>   E
>   L
>   L

That was all. I shook the envelope to be sure she hadn't put a photograph inside. She hadn't.

I sometimes thought if I hadn't been assigned

to Dib for a roommate, I'd walk everywhere alone at Gardner. I wasn't good at making friends with kids whose smiles and clothes and walks shouted money, prep school, connections, tennis!

Dib and I were two of a kind that way. He didn't make friends easily, either. His father wasn't a captain of industry. His father was the great-grandson of one. He drank a lot and raised orchids and a brand of wrinkle-faced dogs called Chinese Shar-Peis. Dib's brother had gone from Gardner to a seminary, to become a priest.

Dib said his mother was strange, too. She went to séances and hunted ducks they raised on their farm for her to hunt.

He'd asked me once if my family was strange. He'd said your father didn't look it, in chapel. What you know about someone from looking at him is zilch, I'd said, but I'd played down my family. I'd just said they were both physicists. I'd said my mother painted.

On the way to dinner that night he asked me how come a physicist had a gun like that?

My one slip. The gun. I'd told Dib my father'd given it to me.

"He's a collector," I said.

"I hope you're not from Mafia," Dib said. "That gun looked like something the Godfather'd pack. Are you sure your real name isn't Pingratti?"

I laughed hard and felt my knees go weak.

"No. My real name's not Pingratti," I said.

After dinner I told the proctor I had a Sevens assignment.

"In that case . . ." He shrugged. You could get away with anything at Gardner if Sevens said so.

I walked over to The Tower. The campus lights were on.

I could smell steak. We'd had Spanish rice and beets for dinner.

I could see inside the Sevens clubhouse, where the curtains fell apart in one window near the bottom of the steps.

I looked in.

It was like some kind of movie set in there. MGM filming King Arthur's Court, only the knights were all in light-blue blazers and black top hats. It looked like a convention of chimney sweeps.

There were enough silver candelabras set out on the long dinner table to make Liberace look chintzy. There were four waiters running around in white jackets. I could see floor-to-ceiling bookcases all around the room, and a roaring fire inside a walk-in stone fireplace.

I could see Creery in there with a hand-painted palm tree tie around the neck of one of those formal shirts usually worn under tuxedo jackets. He looked like his old goofy self, the top hat covering his shaved head, two razor-blade earrings dangling from his left earlobe.

I got to work.

I pulled over the carton near the stairs, and began my ascent. I had to drag the carton up with me. There were oven matches inside, and the ceramic holders were tall enough to keep the candles from blowing out in the wind.

I thought about Mom and Jazzy, wishing I could get to Brooklyn for Thanksgiving. I used to always make the stuffing, a corn-bread one with sausage and mushrooms. I longed to cook again. Mom had a job as a hostess in a restaurant down near the World Trade Center in New York City. She was looking for something in catering or fancy food. She'd written that she made just enough money to last the month, unless she bought something. She'd write *Ha! Ha!* after one of her jokes. She'd put it in parentheses. Sometimes she'd write *(Sob!) . . . I miss you (Sob!)*. She said Jazzy was working on costumes for Georgette, since soon Georgette was going to discover her real parents were Rumanian royalty. *(She pronounces it "Woomanian." She thinks they dress in furs and crowns.)*

Sometimes in his sleep, Dib would whimper and cry, "Mommy? Are you there?" He'd get me thinking. Are you there, Mommy? Jazzy? Georgette?

I thought of Delia, too. Delia with the slow

smile and long kisses, dancing on the wet grass to "Don't go changing."

I thought of Keats going to the Stiles Gallery, and I thought of a lot of orange seaweed in green water, called *Sara*.

When I was at the top of The Tower, I looked down at all the candles, and I remembered once when the Stileses went out, we'd let the candles burn down in their living room, Delia and I, while we held each other on the long, beige sofa.

It was the first time I'd told her I loved her.

"Don't make me say I love you, Fell."

"Who said you had to say it?"

"I thought you'd expect it because you said it."

"I did, but I'm not going to stay awake nights if you don't say it." I stayed awake a lot of nights because she didn't say it. I knew I would when I said I wasn't going to stay awake nights if she didn't say it.

Just as I was about to go inside the room at the top of The Tower to ring the clubhouse bell, I heard Lasher's voice behind me. I jumped. He held me with his hand around my neck.

"Thompson, look down there at the ground and tell me if it makes you want to jump."

"No, I don't want to jump." My heart was racing. How'd he get up there?

"I named my tree Suicide, Thompson."

"I heard you did. If you want to jump, let go of

me first." He held me near the edge of the wall, and I thought, He's crazy. I'm up here by myself with this maniac.

Then Creery's voice came like a sweet release. "Knock it *off*, Lasher!"

Lasher let go of me.

Creery had a lantern flashlight. He was shutting a gate in the little stone-walled room behind us. It was the first time I knew anything about an inside elevator in The Tower.

Creery pushed the clubhouse bell.

It rang out in the windy night. There was a moon overhead, with clouds passing through its face—now you see it, now you don't. Below us, there were shouts as the Sevens poured out of their clubhouse.

Creery put the lantern on the table. He picked up a bullhorn and walked out to where we were.

I thought of sunny days in summer by the ocean when Daddy shouted through his bullhorn, "HELEN? I WANT YOU!"

"SEVENS!" Creery shouted.

Then the Sevens shouted up in thinner voices: "Wisdom! Understanding! Counsel! Power! Knowledge! Righteousness! Godly fear!"

Creery led the singing.

The time will come as the years go by,
When my heart will thrill

While they sang the song, I remembered something my father'd once said, that anything that is too stupid to be spoken is sung. But it was then that Lasher stopped singing and started talking while they sang, grabbing my shoulders with his hands; behind him, Creery's razorblade earrings bobbed as he sang and shook his head up and down.

Lasher was calling me Pingree.

"You made Sevens, Pingree!"

Creery said, "Congratulations, Pingree!"

> *And the Sevens who came*
> *With their bold cry,*
> *WELCOME TO SEVENS!*

Lasher and Creery had turned me around so I stood looking down at the candles in the wind, with the moon shifting above us, the sounds of their singing, the lights of Gardner scattered over The Hill.

> *Remember the cry.*
> *WELCOME TO SEVENS!*

Below, with their top hats flying into the night, they shouted seven times: "PINGREE! PINGREE! PINGREE! PINGREE! PIN-

GREE! PINGREE! PINGREE!"

Then Creery said, "We'll take the elevator down to our clubhouse, Pingree."

"Sevens don't walk when they don't have to," Lasher said. Then he smiled at me. "Surprised you, didn't we, Pingree?"

chapter | 17

Thursday night at dinner, Gardner's headmaster, J. T. Skinner, announced that the winner of the N.B.C. competition was me . . . for "Arizona Darkness."

I got a handshake and a gold plaque. Then everyone in the dining room stood and applauded.

"You're really stepping in it!" Dib said after lights out.

Well, W. Thompson Pingree was. For sure. It didn't seem like John Fell's luck. My father used to say, "Even in heaven you'll find the wrong people to hang out with, Johnny; you head for trouble like a paper clip toward a magnet." I hoped he was "up there" looking down on me, marveling. I knew I was marveling.

"I'm not trying to find out anything secret about Sevens from you," Dib continued, "but . . ."

"Good! Because I couldn't tell you anything, anyway. I don't have a clue why I got in!"

"But," Dib persisted, "don't you think it's got something to do with the N.B.C. essay?"

"What could it have to do with that? The richest boy in the whole state of Florida got into Sevens, too, right? His essay didn't even place, didn't even get Honorable Mention." That was true. Monte Kidder was the kid who was dragged out of his bed by the Sevens over in Parker House, some five hours after I got in.

"Right." Dib sounded dejected. "Right. And that guy that sings the solos in chapel, and sounds like a castrato his voice is so high, he got in, too."

"Outerbridge," I said.

"Yeah, Outerbridge."

Outerbridge, Kidder, and Pingree.

We were the only three to make Sevens. We were as different from each other as Sean Penn, Mr. T, and Emmanuel Lewis.

All of us were tapped for Sevens on Wednesday night. All of us were told we'd be initiated into the mysteries of Sevens in seven days, at seven o'clock, in the clubhouse under The Tower.

"It just doesn't add up," Dib said.

"Go to sleep," I said. "I'm going to sleep it off, like it was all a big binge."

That night my brain discarded some neurological junk. I dreamed Lasher pushed me off The Tower and I discovered I could fly. So could Delia. She flapped her arms like slender silver wings, and we glided along in sunny blue skies. "Don't fall!" she called to me, and I saw

F
  E
    L
      L

spelled out as she always wrote my name in letters, going down.

I cabled John Fell the news at L'Ecole la Coeur, and waited for an answer of any kind. Congratulations? Good work, W. Thompson Pingree!? The bonus for Sevens is in the bank, as promised? Something . . . I figured Ping'd find a way to get the news to his father.

Days passed.

Even though I didn't yet know the mysteries of Sevens, I was already basking in its reflected glory. Faculty smiled. J. T. Skinner called out, "Ah! The man of the hour! Hel-lo, there!" Kids whose smiles and clothes and walks shouted money, prep school, connections, tennis, also shouted "Pingree! How're you doing?" Creery gave me a wink, passing me on the commons. Lasher clasped his hands together above his head in a gesture of victory.

In a letter to Delia, I wrote:

I got into a club here that's special, but it makes me melancholy, too, the way champagne tastes flat when you drink it without the one you want there, there. . . . The roses don't smell. The music's too loud. I want to breathe in the smoke of your cigarette, and hear you tell me that you like my French toast. Delia, send a picture. Send a photograph. Send a snapshot.

I'll settle for a pencil sketch. I need a fix!

I even wrote to Keats.

You are going at happiness all wrong. Don't go back to your old high school for football games, or into galleries featuring orange seaweed called Sara. Don't tell boys you once stood up you can smell them in your dreams, and stop translating Spanish poems that say what is life but frenzy? Don't analyze feelings of worthlessness; there's no gain in it.

F

E

L

L

On the weekend, I broke all the rules and called Mom. I signed out and went down into Cottersville with my pockets full of change at dinnertime, and found a phone booth on the corner.

When Jazzy answered, I said, "This is the King of Rumania. We have reason to believe our little princess was taken from us years ago by someone at this number."

"Johnny? Where are you?"

"Switzerland, honey! Can't you hear the skiers swooshing down the mountain right behind me?"

"I wish you was here, Johnny!"

"I wish I were, too, Jazzy!"

"Mommy! Johnny's calling from Switzerland!"

When Mom came on, I said, "I know I'm not supposed to be doing this."

"I'm glad you did, sweetheart!"

"I miss you, Mom. I made Sevens!"

"That snob club?"

"I don't know that it's such a snob club," I said. Oh, it didn't take much to blow me the other way, did it?

"Johnny! You'll get more money!"

"Yeah! But remember, Mom, money can't buy happiness."

"Anyone who says that doesn't know where to shop!"

"I won an essay contest, too, Mom!"

"I'm proud of you, Johnny. . . . Are you happy?"

"I think so. I'm a little confused."

"Me, too. Happy but a little confused. You know how much I owe MasterCard? They just gave me fifteen hundred dollars more credit! I'm going to buy you something to celebrate all your good news!"

"Nothing to wear, Mom, *please*," I said.

When I hung up, the lights were bright up on The Hill. The little town of Cottersville was pretty dead. I walked around until I found a soda shop that had an hour to go before closing. I parked myself at the counter and ordered a Western on toast with mustard, and a vanilla soda without ice cream. I longed for the old egg creams I used to buy in Brooklyn. The soda wasn't even close.

I saw a copy of *The Cottersville Compass* on a rack by the door, and bought myself a copy for fifty cents.

I turned the pages slowly while I ate, and came to my own photograph on page six. I was shaking hands with Dr. Skinner, the night he gave me the gold plaque.

I hadn't even been aware of a camera in the dining room, but someone had been there with one, because there I was in all my glory, smiling up at the headmaster in my Brooks Brothers navy blazer with the gray pants.

Under my photograph was

> **W. Thompson Pingree wins**
> **essay contest for new boys.**

Under that was my essay.

ARIZONA DARKNESS

Picture rows of tar-papered buildings surrounded by barbed wire fences, set down in an empty wasteland blown by swirling dust and whistling winds. . . .

I remembered Pingree's saying to me, "Don't *ever* let anyone take your picture!"

I began to panic. The picture. The essay. And her title: *Arizona Darkness*.

The Cottersville Compass was only a weekly with a small circulation, but I knew from so many of my father's cases how things could begin to unravel through little slips.

I decided to do something risky. I'd call Fernwood Manor, hoping Pingree would answer. If *she* answered, I'd hang up and try to think of another tack. But if he answered, I'd just say, "I need to talk to you! Can you call me tonight in an hour or so?"

I got more change from the girl behind the counter. I recognized Billy Joel's voice singing on the radio and it made me think of Delia. I wished that summer had never ended.

I left half the toasted Western behind. There was too much mustard on it, anyway. I put a few bills down to cover my check, and went back out into the street to find the phone booth again.

I dialed 516, then Pingree's number, which I knew by heart, and put in a lot of change when the operator told me the charges.

I got an answering machine.

It was Fern Pingree's voice.

"You've reached 555-2455. We are not able to answer the phone just now. At the sound of the beep, please leave your message. If this is you, Woody, there's an emergency. Come here or call the Institute. Woody, if this is you, there's an emergency."

Four days went by. Still no word from Pingree. Nothing from John Fell in Switzerland, either.

I knew Pingree was planning to travel in late November. He'd told me that when he'd presented me with the bank book. But it was only the second week in the month. I couldn't figure out what kind of an emergency would prompt his wife to leave that message on the phone answering machine, or why she wouldn't know where he was.

I made myself stop thinking about it. There were too many projects to finish before Christmas vacation. I had a paper due on the cosmological theory of the big bang, for science. I had to finish an analysis of Euripedes' plays for classics. For French, we were supposed to compose a Christmas poem called "La Paix." There was a major Latin test scheduled for the first week in December.

Then there was the move from Hull House into Sevens House, which was to be completed before the Sevens's dinner.

I'd finished that late Wednesday afternoon, with Dib's help.

I asked Dib to walk partway to The Tower with me that night. After I left the Sevens's clubhouse, at the end of the dinner, I'd be going straight over to Sevens House. I'd be a bona fide member then, an object of awe and envy for the rest of my days at Gardner.

"You look a little down for someone who's lucked out all over the place," Dib said.

"Did you see anyone with a camera at the N.B.C. dinner?"

"Just Mr. Parish, Gardner's P.R. man. Why?"

"I wonder if he'll take pictures at this dinner?"

"Nobody goes inside that clubhouse but Sevens members and the help. Is that all you've got to worry about now, whether someone's going to get your shining hour on film?"

"I don't want my shining hour on film."

"No, not much. I never saw anyone primp the way you just did."

I'd showered, shaved, cut my nails, cleaned under what was left, and refrained from dousing myself with Aramis. I'd remembered what Cadman, the owner of Plain and Fancy, used to say about wearing cologne or after-shave to sit-down dinners. Don't. It ruined the smell of the food.

It was raining out, wanting to snow. Dib was holding the umbrella. He was in the oldest clothes he could find. I was in rust cotton trousers with a thin navy stripe, the navy blazer, a white shirt, a polka dot tie, and just-shined black loafers.

I slung one arm around Dib's shoulders. "This isn't going to change that much between us. We're still going to see a lot of each other, Dib."

"Sure. In classes. Study hall."

"Movies. We'll go to movies."

"They've got a VCR in Sevens House with a screen the size of the side of a house."

"I'm not going to get stuck up, Dib."

"You say now."

"I'll say later, too."

"Later we'll see what you say."

I stopped him halfway along the commons.

"I don't want you to go the rest of the way with me."

"I understand," he said, as though the reason were him.

"I just don't want the Sevens to think I brought someone along for courage."

"You did," Dib said.

"Yeah, but they don't have to know I did."

I gave his arm a light punch. "Okay, scumbag, from now on stay out of my way."

"Very funny," he said sadly. He wasn't taking it well. I was. I didn't like moving out on him, but I was champing at the bit to hear about the mysteries, get a good meal, and go directly to Boardwalk . . . or heaven . . . or whatever you wanted to nickname Sevens House. The beds over there were bigger and firmer than those in Hull House. There were thick rugs on the floors, fireplaces in some of the rooms; only two shared a bathroom. Lights out was when you wanted lights out, and your room was cleaned, your bed made, by a maid.

"Okay, Dibble," I said. "I'll be around, pal."

"Me, too, Thompson. Don't you want the umbrella? I don't need it in these clothes."

"I don't want to look all fresh like the blushing bride," I said. "A little wet'll be good."

But it was starting to come down hard and cold. I ran the rest of the way to The Tower.

Lionel Schwartz presided over the dinner that night in the Sevens clubhouse.

He was known around campus as the Lion. He was in all the school plays, a good-looking senior, the type who wore bow ties and leather patches on his sports coat, and had permission from home to smoke a pipe he could never keep lit.

The room was filled with candles; even the chandelier above our heads held candles. The Sevens seemed to be candle freaks. They all had on their top hats and their light-blue blazers with the 7's on the pockets. There was a fire going. Creery sat across from me, grinning at me.

We were served filet mignon, baked potato with sour cream, fresh green beans, salad, and hot rolls.

Creery said, "Over in the dining room, this would be a menu for an alumni banquet, or for the boys who don't get to go home for Christmas. We eat like this all the time here."

I smiled, but I felt my first pang of guilt at being among the elite. I wondered how I'd gotten in—and if I could stick it out.

They even served artichoke curries to Lasher and Outerbridge, the two vegetarians.

We all gulped down dinner and sat waiting for dessert.

Schwartz banged his fork against a crystal goblet for silence, then stood up and began: "There are seven days in creation, seven days in the week, seven graces, seven divisions in the Lord's Prayer, and seven ages in the life of man."

"SEVENS!" the old members chorused.

The three of us—Outerbridge, Kidder, and I—looked at each other questioningly, trying to figure out what we had in common.

I was sure I saw Kidder's lip curl with distaste at the thought that we had anything in common. He thought he was Mel Gibson. He almost was, take away ten or twelve years. He had his own red Mercedes. He'd had a date once with Molly Ringwald, and her photograph was on his desk. He began sentences, "It's my sense that . . ." or "Correct me if I'm wrong, but . . ." as though he were addressing a committee. They said Kidder had a boat, as long as the front of Saks Fifth Avenue, moored in Key West.

And Outerbridge? Not nearly as charismatic. More asthmatic. Known for his beautiful sister, Cynthia, a Bryn Mawr freshman. He was a vegetarian. A near soprano who excelled at singing hymns such as "Lead, Kindly Light" in chapel. A redhead. A mad, crazy giggler in movies, the type you turned around to stare and hiss at, because he laughed through the next lines of the joke.

Schwartz looked down the long table toward us. "What I'm going to tell you now, no Sevens has ever told an outsider. You are on your honor *never* to reveal the reason for your selection in Sevens! Repeat after me: So be it, solemnly sworn!"

"So be it," we three said, "solemnly sworn."

"It is in the highest tradition of Gardner," said Schwartz, "that you did nothing to earn this distinction, that nothing you *are* earned it for you, that nothing your family is secured this high honor for you!

"Gardner has never stressed background over accomplishment, physical appearance over mental prowess, anything over anything, or anyone over anyone. We are all equal, and yet . . ."

Schwartz paused for a long few seconds.

"And yet . . ." he paused again, and looked hard at us: Outerbridge, Kidder, and me. "Gardner would be remiss not to point out one great lesson in life. Gardner prepares you for life, and in preparing you, points out that you are never truly prepared. For an unexpected circumstance can change your fortune . . . *pffft*"—a brush of his fingers through the air—"like that! Chance is something out of your control!"

Then all the old members said softly, "Mere chance."

"Mere chance made you all Sevens," said Schwartz. "Sevens will make you more, but you did nothing for the privilege. You three new members were chosen as we old ones were, because you named the trees you planted your first day here with seven-letter words.

"Kidder named his Key West. Outerbridge named his Cynthia. And Pingree named his Goodbye. There are seven letters in Gardner, too.

"It is no more complicated than that. . . . It is as whimsical as the fickle finger of Fate. But from this moment on, you are privileged. You can never be expelled from Gardner for any reason! You will always have special privileges! Gardner will become a different experience for you than it is for the others.

"*And*"—another long pause—"when you leave Gardner, you will connect with a national, and in some cases an international, fraternity of Sevens alumni that will help you throughout your life!"

You could hear a pin drop in that room while the three of us took this in.

Then Schwartz said, "Only another Sevens knows that you are here by . . ."

"Mere chance," the old members said.

"And so," Schwartz said, "you have been given a favor by mere chance. Sevens hopes you will accept it with grace, gladness of heart, and thanks to God!"

The old members began to sing:

> When I was a beggar boy,
> And lived in a cellar damp,
> I had not a friend or a toy,
> But that was all changed by mere chance!
> Once I could not sleep in the cold,
> And patches they covered my pants,
> Now I have bags full of gold,
> For that was all changed by mere chance!
> Mere chance, mere chance,
> Mere chance makes us gay,
> Mere chance makes night day,
> But whoever she'll choose,
> She can also make lose,
> Mere chance has her way,
> Mere chance!

They ended with a thunderous "WELCOME TO SEVENS!"

From the ceiling, a square-shaped, enormous silver tray descended slowly. On it were three top hats and three light-blue blazers with three white carnations in the buttonholes.

Through the door from the kitchen, waiters came carrying flaming Cherries Jubilee on silver platters.

I walked slowly back toward Sevens House in a misty rain after. I'd hung back a little so I could walk alone. I felt good. I kept thinking of Pingree's saying, "I was happiest right here." I wasn't happiest, but I *was* happy.

What I liked best about getting into Sevens was that it was really just a fluke. I'd almost called my tree Adieu, which would have meant I'd have missed by two letters.

Schwartz had named his tree after the rock star Madonna, and another guy had called his Cormier, after the man who wrote *The Chocolate War.*

I could live with the reason I'd gotten into Sevens.

When I got inside Sevens House, the house-mother came gliding across to me in a velvet robe that touched the floor, the same color as her blond hair, which was held back in a bun. She looked like some model out of a fashion ad, about to ask me to share the fantasy.

"Are you Woodrow Pingree, Jr., dear?"

"Yes. Only I call myself W. Thompson Pingree.

Thompson, or Tom, for short. And you're?"

Not a day over thirty. Oh, I would confide all my troubles to this one. I would tell her about a Spanish poet who said life was itself a dream, and dreams are only dreams.

"I'm Mrs. Violet. I'm glad I caught you."

"I'm easy to catch, Mrs. Violet."

"You're not, though. I've been waiting and waiting for you, dear. Your mother is here."

"My what?"

"Your mother."

"Not mine."

"Mrs. Pingree. Yes. She's right outside in that big, long white limousine."

"She is?"

"I was hoping she'd see you come in."

"I came up the side path. My *mother*? Mrs. Fern Pingree?"

My heart was hammering under my shirt. I figured Mrs. Violet could see my blazer move in and out.

I looked out the front door and saw a white stretch limo.

"What a beautiful car!" said Mrs. Violet. And with a gentle push at my shoulders, she added, "You'd better hurry, dear. She's been waiting a long time. She wouldn't wait in our little reception area."

So I went back out into the misty, cold night

and walked very slowly down toward the Cadillac.

The back door opened as I approached.

Fern Pingree sat forward in a fur over her shoulders, a white turtleneck sweater, and black leather pants, her small, almond-shaped eyes suddenly very large.

"You!" she said.

I tried to think of what to say. I bent down, peering into the backseat, when hands grabbed me.

They were not her hands.

A man I'd never seen before introduced himself by pulling me the rest of the way inside, holding me by the throat.

He reached back and shut the car door.

"No!" Mrs. Pingree said. "This isn't Ping!"

"This isn't your son?" said the man.

"This is John Fell," she said. "Let go of him. We're not taking him. Where's Ping, Fell?"

"Your son," I managed to choke out, "is in Switzerland." My neck felt as if it'd been in a vise. I moved from my knees to the small jump seat facing Mrs. Pingree and her henchman.

The driver said, "What do we do now?" He didn't bother to turn around when he spoke.

"Where's Woodrow Pingree? Ask him," the henchman said.

"I think I know where Woody is," said Mrs. Pingree. "I think he's also in Switzerland. Right, Fell?"

"I don't know where your husband is."

"Who is this kid?" the driver said.

"It doesn't matter to you," said Mrs. Pingree. "He's no use to us. Both the fish and the bait are in Switzerland. Right, Fell?"

"Ping is," I said. I could smell the sweet gardenia perfume she wore.

"Yes, I'm beginning to get it now. Ping is at L'Ecole la Coeur. He's there as you, and you're here as Ping. Is that how it worked?"

"I'm here as Ping," I admitted.

"And you last saw my husband when?"

"About a month ago."

"Yes," she said. "He went to Atlantic City about a month ago. He must have come here then."

The henchman said, "What do we do now?"

"We say good night to John Fell," said Mrs. Pingree. "Let him out!"

chapter | 19

From *The New York Times*:

BRUTT PHYSICISTS NAMED AS SPIES
SPY RING TIPPED BY CHINESE DEFECTOR

SAN FRANCISCO—Woodrow Thompson Pingree, Sr., 58, surrendered to Federal agents here late yesterday, and was charged with passing United States intelligence secrets to the People's Republic of China.

Clued to the fact the Federal Bureau of Investigation was shadowing and wiretapping him and his wife, Fern, 37, as they plied their trade, Mr. Pingree was reported to be about to flee to Switzerland.

Fern Pingree, still being sought by authorities, is the alleged ringleader of an espionage coterie that passed classified documents for nearly nine years to the Chinese. She is said to have recruited Mr. Pingree sometime after their marriage, while they were both employed at the Brutt Institute in Bellhaven, New York. There, both Pingrees were privy to highly sensitive nuclear research and had top security clearances.

Unbeknownst to Mrs. Pingree, her husband had

enrolled his son by a former marriage, Woodrow Thompson Pingree, Jr., 16, in L'Ecole la Coeur, in Switzerland, under a false name, apparently to put him out of harm's way, and Mrs. Pingree's reach, while he made preparations to leave the country. Apparently long reluctant to continue in the espionage work his wife was committed to, in the last six months Mr. Pingree was liquidating his holdings and disentangling himself from debts incurred by gambling.

The defection last month of Wu Chu-Teng, 63, a double agent from the People's Republic of China, was said to have precipitated the investigation of the Pingrees.

"Come in, Thompson," said J. T. Skinner. "Shut the door after you. There's no point in calling you that anymore. What do you prefer to be called?"

"Fell."

"Of course. By your last name, as all Sevens are called."

The headmaster of Gardner was a lot like his office: big, friendly-looking, immaculate. He even had a manicure. He had a large belly, covered by a vest with brown-and-white checks, and a gold Phi Beta Kappa key. He had on one of those unpressed tweed suits that made him look relaxed and slightly English. He was bald and gray eyed, with a ruddy complexion.

He sat back in a leather swivel chair behind his mahogany desk and pointed to the straight-backed chair in front of his desk. I sat down in it.

Behind him, through his office window, I could see snow coming down from the late-afternoon sky.

"Well, Fell, I've talked with the FBI agents, as you have. We'd better have *our* talk now that some of the smoke has cleared away. You'd better thank your lucky stars that you made Sevens."

"Yes, sir."

"I'm a legacy, you know. When I came to The Hill as a boy, it was my dream to make Sevens. My father was a Sevens."

"I didn't know that, sir."

"He told me not to count on it, and not to think there was anything wrong with me if I didn't make it, but I was still very disappointed. You know how a boy feels—that he can't measure up to his old man."

"Yes, sir."

"If you hadn't made Sevens, you'd be a very disappointed young man, too—assuming that you like it here. Do you?"

"Yes, I do, sir."

"You'd be held reprehensible for enrolling at Gardner under a false identity. I'd probably have to expel you. I can't expel a Sevens. *You* made it. Young

Pingree didn't. So you're under the protection of Sevens. Of course, I could ask you to resign."

"Are you, sir?"

"No, I'm not, Fell."

I watched the snow come down behind him.

He said, "Of course, if the Sevens didn't want you among them, they could make it very uncomfortable for you. There was a case like that a few years back. There was a Sevens member suspected of dealing cocaine. While he was under investigation we couldn't touch him, even though we knew he was guilty. Sevens gave him an immunity from immediate disciplinary measures. But the Sevens made life so unbearable for him that he resigned. That won't happen to you, according to Schwartz. The boys are behind you."

"I'm glad to hear that, sir."

"You have a good record. You won the N.B.C. competition, too. . . . I'm a little curious about that, Fell. I know you're probably tired by now of being questioned, but did the infamous Fern Pingree coach you about life in a Japanese internment camp?"

"No, she didn't, sir. I hardly knew her."

"The newspapers say her grandfather died at Jerome, in Arizona, back in World War Two."

"I didn't see that article. I only saw the write-up in *The Times*."

"I'll give you what I've got there on my desk,

if you're interested. There's a lot more being written about her now in *Time, Newsweek,* and the tabloids."

"I'd like to look at it."

"They still haven't found her."

"I should think she'd have been easy to find in that white stretch Caddy she showed up here in."

"She rented that in Philadelphia. That's where they lost her trail. Oh, they'll find her," he said. "I was just curious what you know about her."

"No more than I told the FBI agents," I said. I'd been grilled by them for hours on the morning after Mrs. Pingree had made her attempt to kidnap Ping. They'd explained that if she'd gotten Ping, Pingree would have kept his mouth shut about anything to do with the espionage operation at Brutt. Now he'd probably cooperate in exchange for immunity or a lighter sentence.

"And Woodrow Pingree," said Dr. Skinner, picking up a gold letter opener to pass from hand to hand while he talked, "what did you think of him?"

"I liked him, sir. It's impossible for me to believe he sold secrets to China. I didn't even know he was a gambler."

"All around he's not casting the best light on Gardner," Skinner said with an ironic chuckle.

"He always said he was happiest here."

"I have no doubt, considering what came later. I looked him up in his yearbook. Want to see?"

He passed across the light blue leather-bound book with THE HILL BOOK, 1944 stamped across it in white.

There was a rubber band holding back page 23.

There was a photograph of this dark-haired kid with a faint smile on his face and bright, earnest eyes.

WOODROW THOMPSON PINGREE
SEWICKLEY, PENNSYLVANIA
"WOODY"

First Prize Westinghouse Science Talent Search '43; Student Council '43; Captain, Baseball '43; Secretary, Current Events Club '43; Upper School Tennis Champion—Singles '43; Highest Average in Form '44; Cum Laude '43, '44; Upper School Tennis Champion— Doubles '44; Science Club President '44; Senior House Prefect '44; Choir '43, '44.

Ambition: To be a good Marine.

Remembered For: Ask Sara!

Slogan: Semper Fidelis!

Future Occupation: Move over, Einstein!

I gave the book back to Skinner.

"You just never know, do you?" Skinner said.

"I think *she* did it to him."

"Nobody does it to you, Fell. You do it to yourself. You have choices. You make your own choices."

"But he was under her spell. Even the papers said she recruited him."

"According to the tabloids, he wasn't under her spell recently." He'd picked up the letter opener again and was playing with it as he talked. "What's the real Ping like?"

"He's interested in magic. He didn't like her, either. There were some rumors that she was responsible for his mother's death."

"I read about that. They were out in a boat together when the first Mrs. Pingree was drowned."

"Where did you read that?"

"It's all in these magazines and papers. Here, take them with you." He leaned forward in his swivel chair and picked them off a pile on his desk. They were all open to the pages with the write-ups on the Pingrees. As he passed them across to me I caught glimpses of Fernwood Manor, Pingree with his arm around Fern Pingree, and one of Pingree with Ping.

I could pick out random sentences.

. . . They never lived ostentatiously—Fern Pingree bought her wardrobe off the rack. . . .

. . . She was an old-school spy, doing it out of conviction, long embittered by old memories of her Japanese grandfather's World War II internment, by

Hiroshima, and by a belief that the United States was anti-Asian in its Vietnam policies, as well. . . .

. . . He was her opposite, the modern spy, convictionless, and only in it for the reported $300,000 paid them over the years, a gambler with vast real estate holdings on Long Island, in Atlantic City, and Nevada, and . . .

Dr. Skinner said, "You'll have time to look at all of that later, Fell."

It was hard for me to stop thumbing through what was on my lap.

"Are the other boys treating you well, Fell?" Skinner asked.

"Very well. They're just full of questions."

. . . reports of a romantic involvement that was also said to have prompted Pingree's withdrawal from his wife's espionage . . .

"You'd be wise to tell the other boys you can't talk about the matter, Fell, and be sure not to talk to any reporters. This isn't the kind of publicity Gardner seeks."

"I realize that, sir. I'll be careful."

"Another thing, Fell. You can't continue as a junior. You'll have to be entered as a senior and make up any back work on your own time."

"Yes, sir."

I'd shifted in the chair so I could turn the copy of *Time* around and see what was on the next page.

That was when I saw her.

"You'll have a lot of homework ahead on your Christmas vacation," said Skinner.

It was Delia, in a raincoat, with a scarf around her long black hair, a cigarette going in one hand, a large satchel over the other arm.

Delia Tremble, 25, questioned in Zurich about her relationship to Pingree, says, "I'll stand by him forever."

"So far," Skinner said, "you haven't made the news, but I suppose they'll get around to it."

"I suppose so," I said.

. . . began two years ago when the pair met in Atlantic City, where Pingree went to gamble. Miss Tremble denies knowing anything about the Brutt operation, but admits she was helping Pingree escape.

Everyone in my family's so strange—I didn't pay much attention to your strangeness. That's how you got away with it," Dib said.

"My strangeness?"

"The gun. I would have thought harder about the gun."

"And what else?"

"Your interest in cooking. Remember, once I asked you who taught you to cook, and you said your mother. Then in another conversation, you said you'd worked in a gourmet shop and gotten your interest in cooking there."

"No one's perfect. But I'm not so different now, am I?"

"You're more popular. First Sevens, then this. You've become a star at The Hill."

"The public is fickle, though, Dib. After Christmas I'll be the senior who can't keep up with his class."

We were on the bus to Trenton, New Jersey. I had a wire from Keats in my pocket.

MUST SEE YOU HOPE YOU CAN COME TO ADIEU
OVER HOLIDAYS ALL IS FORGIVEN DADDY SAYS OR I'LL
DRIVE INTO BROOKLYN DID I SAY I'D ACTUALLY GO

"Anyway," Dib said, "you're not a star in Lasher's eyes, are you?"

"No, not in his." I'd heard he was the only Sevens who voted for my resignation.

"Creery says he calls you Felon behind your back."

"And to my face."

"Maybe he'll lay off Creery for a while and concentrate on you. The new snake in the grass."

"Probably."

"By the way, I overheard a knockdown fight between them while all this upheaval was going on. I'd gone over to Sevens House looking for you. . . . Lasher was accusing Creery of getting help getting into Sevens." Dib looked over at me to get my reaction. "Can you get help?"

"I'm not going to talk about Sevens."

"Lasher shouted at Creery, 'Your father helped you and his helped him!'"

"I don't know anything about it," I said. But I'd wondered about something like that. If Pingree'd been a Sevens, for example, and if Ping had gone to Gardner, would Pingree have told Ping about choosing a seven-letter word for his tree . . . or would he have been honorable and not told him? And I laughed to myself. *Honorable*. Pingree . . . That was like saying *Hot*. Snow.

"Sorry I mentioned it," said Dib, "but your name came up, too."

"How did I get into it?"

"Lasher said, 'You and Pingree don't belong in Sevens! Neither of you got in honestly!' Then it sounded like they were knocking each other around the room, and Lasher was shouting, 'I'll kill you!' I made tracks at that point, scared they'd spill out into the hall."

"Yeah," I said. "He's going to have it in for me. That's the least of my worries right now."

"Fell?" Dib said. "Listen, I never said I was sorry about Delia."

"You didn't have to."

"I didn't know if you wanted to talk about it."

"I didn't. Still don't." I never will want to talk about it, I thought. I'll never be able to talk about it.

"Okay with me," Dib said.

He looked out the window. The farm country was disappearing and the tacky suburbs of Trenton were coming into view. I'd get the train to New York City after we got off the bus.

"But thanks, Dib."

My first night home I made spaghetti à la carbonara for Mom and Jazzy. Georgette was dressed in a long black gown with a gold crown on her head, in my honor. Jazzy had propped her up against a corn flakes box in the kitchen. There was a royal-blue ribbon across her gown saying WELCOME HOME, JOHNNY!

Jazzy was in watching TV while I fried the bacon to go into the spaghetti.

I knew Mom'd been wanting to say something she didn't want Jazzy to hear. I thought it might have to do with Delia.

"There's something on my mind, Johnny."

"I know."

"Do you know what it is?"

"Is it her? Because I don't feel like talking about her yet, Mom."

"No, it isn't about her. You'll have to work that out yourself. It's about the money. It's about the ten thousand dollars Mr. Pingree put in the bank for you."

"What about it? Do you need it to get out of hock?"

"I don't appreciate that crack, Johnny."

"I'm sorry, Mom. I didn't mean to put it so crudely. Do you need it?"

"No, I don't need it. And you don't need it, either."

I dropped some onions in with the bacon.

"I was wondering about that," I said.

"There's nothing to wonder about. I don't care

that the money was left in the grandfather's will—if that story's even true. We've had too much to do already with those people and their money. I think any money that comes from them is bad money! Your father would roll over in his grave, Johnny! They sold our country's secrets to the enemy! Your father fought for this country! He loved this country!"

"I know."

"You can't help the fact your tuition was paid by that man, and you have to go back and graduate. But we don't want that ten thousand dollars!"

"What'll we do with it?"

"Give it to some good cause."

"I'm not a good cause?"

"You know what I mean, Johnny. Your father used to get tears in his eyes when anyone sang 'The Star-Spangled Banner.'"

"Maybe because he couldn't ever remember the words. He'd get as far as 'Oh, say can you see, by the dawn's early light'—then stop cold."

"Can you go any further?"

"Not really."

"Then don't talk, Big Mouth!"

I turned on the heat under the water for the pasta.

Mom said, "I thought you might give me a fight."

"I never won one with you yet."

"We'll figure out something to do with the money."

"Okay."

"Are you planning to see Keats?"

"Probably."

"I knew you'd give in."

"I'm not giving in. She's going to come all the way to Brooklyn."

"Big deal! She doesn't deserve Brooklyn! Brooklyn's too good for her!"

I said, "Tell Jazzy dinner in ten minutes."

"Is that what they teach you at that fancy school? To order your mother around?"

"Please," I added.

"Johnny," she said, "there are nice girls in this world, honey. I don't want you to lose sight of that. Keats and that other one—they're the exceptions. I know you've been hurt but . . ."

"Not by Keats," I said. My damn voice cracked. I couldn't have gone on, anyway. I still couldn't even get Delia's name out. I didn't want Mom to see my eyes start to fill, so I ducked my head around the corner into the living room. I shouted, "Jazzy? Georgette's being whisked away by bandits!"

"Get their license numbers!" Jazzy yelled back.

The next day, I walked down to Carroll Gardens

to visit my grandfather in the nursing home.

"I was named after Theodore Roosevelt," he said when he saw me walk into the room. "Did I ever tell you why?"

"Tell me again," I said. I gave him a kiss and sat down in the chair beside his bed.

"Well, it's a long story," he began.

"Take your time," I said.

So that was how I spent my Christmas vacation. Like my father used to say, "You got your family. You got your health. You got Brooklyn. What else do you need?"

What is there to say about Delia?

From the time she first walked into Plain and Fancy to the time she wrote me letters saying things like *Tell me if you think you made the right decision going to Switzerland,* she was keeping an eye on me for Pingree.

I remembered so many things: the phone call Pingree made that first night I ran into the Mitsubishi, when he said to somebody that he wouldn't be by, that something had come up. The time we'd all gone back to our house after dinner at Lunch, when he kept encouraging me to keep my date with Delia. I remembered him telling me he liked cards, too, but not card tricks: He liked to play cards. And Delia telling me how her life had changed after the gamblers took over her hometown, Atlantic City.

Pingree'd arranged everything, from her job as au pair at the Stileses' to the cruise she went on until he warned her that he was turning himself in. Then she flew to Zurich to be with Ping.

I don't know what Delia knew about Pingree's double life, or even if she knew that he had one.

I don't even know if there really was something in his father's will about money for Ping when he graduated from Gardner, and more money if he made Sevens. I somehow think that all of that was true, but as my mother's fond of pointing out: The man's a liar.

All I really know for sure is that Pingree was planning to leave the country and begin a new life with Delia and Ping. Then a double agent named Wu Chu-Teng changed all that.

Fern Pingree was arrested three days before Christmas in New York City. I saw a picture of her in the paper, with those white-framed dark glasses on, being escorted by two FBI men. She had no comment.

Sometimes I still hear Fern Pingree saying, "Dreams are the trash bag of the brain!" But that hasn't stopped me from going over and over certain dreams. Because I still dream of Delia. She's flying with me through blue summer skies, dancing with me on wet grass, her eyes watching mine the way they used to. And she's telling me again not to make her say she loves me. She never did say that, awake or dreaming.

About two weeks after I returned to Gardner, one cold Wednesday afternoon, there was a crowd gathered down by The Tower. I jogged that way to see what all the excitement was about. There were snowdrifts all around. We'd hit a record for bad weather in January.

"Fell! Hurry, Fell!" Dib shouted at me.

I pushed my way toward him, and before I got to the front of the crowd, Dib said, "It's Lasher! He jumped from the top!"

Someone else said, "He finally did it!"

Dib turned and told me, "He's committed suicide, Fell!"

I stood there beside Dib, looking down at the cold pavement.

Beside Lasher's body, I saw his thick glasses with the panes smashed.

Then, in less time than it takes a paper clip to inch over to a magnet, I said, "No. He didn't kill himself."

Those five words were going to get me into a lot of trouble.

Someday I'll tell you about it.

fell back

chapter | 1

About two weeks after I returned to Gardner, one cold Wednesday afternoon, there was a crowd gathered down by The Tower. I jogged that way to see what all the excitement was about. There were snowdrifts all around. We'd hit a record for bad weather in January.

"Fell. Hurry, Fell!" Dib shouted at me.

I pushed my way toward him, and before I got to the front of the crowd, Dib said, "It's Lasher! He jumped from the top!"

Someone else said, "He finally did it!"

Dib turned and told me, "He's committed suicide, Fell!"

I stood there beside Dib, looking down at the cold pavement.

Beside Lasher's body, I saw his thick glasses with the panes smashed.

Then in less time than it takes a paper clip to inch over to a magnet, I said, "No. He didn't kill himself."

Those five words were going to get me into a lot of trouble.

"No one who knows he is about to get a new Porsche for his birthday kills himself," said Lasher's father.

His sister said, "Oh, come *on*, Daddy! He *gave* his VCR away, his watch, the Mont Blanc pen you bought him for Christmas. He was planning it!"

I watched the snow fall outside my window in Sevens House.

"Why didn't he even leave a note?" Dr. Lasher shook his bald head sadly.

"Because he wasn't in control of himself, Daddy. You saw how he was at Christmas—never smiling, always sleeping."

"He said nothing about suicide, however."

"He said nothing. Period. He wouldn't talk to anyone."

"Paul was often moody and melancholy."

"Not like that, no, never."

"Are you listening, Fell?" Dr. Lasher asked.

I glanced across at him. He bore a faint resemblance to his late son. He had the same bad eyesight, too.

"Yes, sir," I said. "You don't think it was suicide. I heard you."

"I know it was," his daughter said. "I knew him better than anyone."

No one would argue with that. Lauren was Lasher's twin. "Poised" would not describe her adequately. "Conceited" would be going too far. She was somewhere in between. Miss Tyler's School, over in Princeton, New Jersey, specialized in this type. Seventeen . . . but the kind of seventeen who had stopped reading the magazine by the same name at twelve.

She was blue eyed and beautiful. It was that sort of beauty helped a lot by great-looking clothes—a soft, black cashmere suit the same color as her straight shoulder-length hair, and the kind of sophisticated makeup that looked natural until you realized eyes weren't outlined in black, lips weren't glossy, and cheekbones against olive skin did not have pink tones.

She was thin and tall. If she wasn't rich, she looked it. She wasn't poor. Both her parents were

Philadelphia shrinks who cost upward of one hundred dollars an hour.

"We didn't know him at all, apparently," said the doctor.

Just where his blazer buttoned, I could see the bulge of his potbelly, fighting the alligator belt holding it in. He was the blue-blazer (gold buttons), gray-flannel pants type—Bean boots (the kind that lace), a storm coat (with a Burberry lining) tossed on my couch.

Lauren's coat was the female version of his, but her boots were high-heeled ones with fur tops.

"Fell," she said, "unless you have some definite information, you'd save Daddy a lot of agony by simply saying you know less than we do." She was one of those girls who called her father "Daddy," as my old girlfriend, Keats, always did. She treated him the same way Keats treated her father, as though there was no way he'd ever know as much about life as she did, but she was going to be patient with him just the same.

Girls like that can usually wrap Daddy around their little fingers when they want to. Me, too.

I told them what she wanted to hear. "I know less than you do." I was glad to comply. I hadn't asked for this meeting. It was my only free period before lunch, then on to English class and the bad news probably awaiting me on my paper about

Robert Browning. You don't think I understood "Fra Lippo Lippi," do you?

"No, no, no, no," Dr. Lasher said. "We came here to hear what you have to say, no matter how vague and uninformed. I'll listen to hunches at this point."

I told him my major reservation, about Lasher's death being a suicide wasn't a hunch, exactly. My feeling was based on something my dad had told me about suicide: that a person who wore eyeglasses removed them before he jumped from a high place. He left them behind or put them in his pocket. I told him my father'd been a private detective, and a cop before that; it was just something he'd pointed out to me.

Lauren said, "My brother couldn't see his fingers in front of his face without his glasses. He'd have worn them."

"What else?" her father asked me.

I lied. "Nothing." The last thing I wanted was to get involved.

What I had to do was stay out of trouble that term. I'd been in enough last term to hold me for a lifetime, living up to my father's prediction that I'd head for trouble like a paper clip to a magnet: It was my nature.

I'd opened my mouth without thinking when I saw Lasher's body, and his broken glasses beside it. Someone had told Dr. Lasher what I'd said. Maybe even Dib, my best friend on The Hill. Dib had his own reasoning about Lasher's leap from the top of The Tower. When had Lasher screamed? Does someone scream when he's planned to jump . . . or does he scream when he's *pushed*?

"What can you tell me about this fellow named Creery?" Dr. Lasher asked.

Dib had decided Creery'd pushed Lasher. He'd overheard a fight between them just before Christmas vacation. During that fight Lasher had threatened to kill Creery. Dib had theorized Lasher'd tried to do it, and Creery had pushed him while he was defending himself.

Both Lasher and Creery were in The Tower that fatal afternoon.

Lauren jumped in to answer her father's question herself.

She said, "Cyril Creery is just a goofball." She laughed a little, as though there was something really cute about being just a goofball. "Cyr wouldn't harm a fly."

I noticed she was wearing a gold 7 around her neck. Only a member of the secret Sevens could buy one of those. I'd never heard of a Sevens giving one of those to his sister, not even Outerbridge, whose sister, Cynthia, looked like Madonna and sometimes came over from Bryn Mawr to be his date at dances.

Usually Sevens gave these things to their girl-friends, or their mothers, the same as Air Force men did with their wings.

I'd always known that Lasher had a thing about Lauren. He'd brought her name up any chance he could, and her photographs were all over his room.

Often, on weekends, Lasher'd disappear, telling us later he'd gone away with his sister. He'd never say where.

I was remembering that while Lauren sat there sighing, saying in a somewhat exasperated tone, "Cyril and Paul didn't like each other, that's for sure. But Cyril's no killer. Mon Dieu, Daddy."

I thought about someone blithely saying Mon Dieu, Daddy, dangling one great long stockinged leg over another while right that moment in chapel they were festooning the walls with black-and-white-striped mourning cloths for that afternoon's memorial service. Black for sorrow. White for hope. Her brother'd been buried only a few days ago.

"Fell?" said Dr. Lasher. "Is there anything you're not telling me?"

"If you've spoken to Dib, there isn't."

"To whom?"

"Sidney Dibble," said Lauren. "The one we took to breakfast."

I thought so.

"He knows what I know," I said.

Dr. Lasher said, "Tell me about Twilight Truth, Fell."

"We've gone all over that, Daddy."

"I want to hear Fell's version."

I said, "Damon Charles, The Sevens' founder, seemed to have a fondness for twilight. Sevens get married at twilight, and buried at twilight. No one knows why. . . . Then there's Twilight Truth, on the second Wednesday of the month. Any Sevens who feels honor bound to confess he's done something to make him unworthy of the privileges of Sevens leaves a written statement in the top of The Tower. The officer of the day rings the tower bell and reads it over the bullhorn."

"And then?" the doctor asked.

"We come up with an appropriate penalty. If it's serious, we ask him to live and eat at the dorm, or we give him the silent treatment . . . If it's not that serious, we suspend certain privileges. We whistle 'Twilight Time' in his presence . . . Sometimes we whistle that to force Twilight Truth on him, if he doesn't seem likely to step forward on his own."

"So ridiculous!" said Lauren.

"It's just ritual," her father said. "All clubs, including sororities, have their rituals."

"Which is why I'd never join one!" she said.

The doctor passed me something Xeroxed.
"Have you seen this, Fell?"
I hadn't. It was signed by Cyril Creery.

CREERY: That Wednesday afternoon Lasher said he
            left a copy of a letter I'd written up in The
Tower. He said it would be read at Twilight Truth. We
had a fight about it. I punched him. Then I took the elevator up, but of course there was no letter. He was going
crazy—I knew that. We all did. . . . I took the elevator
down and went into Deem Library in The Tower. . . .
About ten minutes later he jumped from the top.

LT. HATCH: Did you think he'd made up a letter, or was
            there a real letter?

CREERY: My father had a stroke two years ago. Ever
            since, my stepbrother's been running our
paint factory.
     Right before Christmas I wrote Lowell a letter.
There was a lot of personal stuff in it. I was talking about
changing my behavior and being more help to him.
     I kept a copy. When Lasher mentioned a letter, nat-
urally I thought of it. I was afraid he'd gone through my
desk and found it. He wasn't above that sort of thing. . . .
I wouldn't have wanted it read over a bullhorn. . . . So I
went up to look, but he was bluffing.

When you came back down and went into the library, who was there?

No one was around that I could see. . . . I'd never kill anyone, not even Paul Lasher. I don't have it in me.

> *Cyril Creery*
> *Cottersville Police Report*

I handed it back to Dr. Lasher.

"I didn't know about a letter," I said, "just that they had a fight."

"There wasn't a letter, apparently," said Lauren.

"It sounds like something Lasher'd do," I said. "They were always baiting each other. Lasher thought Creery was selling drugs. Lasher said you could get any kind of pill you wanted from him. He called his room 'The Drugstore.'"

Lauren said, "But Paul had become so paranoid! He made up lies about everyone. Remember, Daddy? He said Mother hadn't asked him a personal question in five years."

"Both your mother and I neglected Paul."

"Oh, Daddy, I heard her with my own ears. How are you? How's school? How're things at Sevens?"

"Yes," said the doctor. "Very general questions. Hardly personal."

"What was she supposed to say?" said Lauren.

Her father answered, "We both should have said, 'Sit down, Paul. Tell us what's going on in your life.'"

"Stop blaming yourself, Daddy! *Please!*"

The noon bell rang.

"Fell has to eat now," said Lauren. "I'm hungry, too. And Mother's waiting for us."

Maybe a death in the family didn't make Lauren lose her appetite. Mine was missing for weeks after my dad died. So was my mother's. My little sister's. As good a cook as I am, I couldn't even tempt them, and everything from my spaghetti carbonara to my Chinese chicken wings had tears in it.

Dr. Lasher didn't want to leave. "Your mother is with the headmaster," he said. "She's not waiting for us."

Lauren was already putting her long arms down the sleeves of her Burberry.

"What do you know about Rinaldo Velez?" Dr. Lasher asked me.

"Not much. He works in The Tower, waits tables and stuff."

Lauren said, "My brother gave *him* the VCR and the Mont Blanc pen. We think he might have given him his good Gstaad watch, too."

Was there such a thing as a bad Gstaad watch?

"Why?" I said.

I meant why Rinaldo of all people? He was a townie. He'd be someone who'd really value those gifts, of anyone on The Hill—someone unlikely to be able to afford anything like them; but Lasher hadn't ever had a reputation for being friendly, charitable, or even thoughtful. He'd called Rinaldo *"Flaco"* because of how skinny he was. *Flaco*, Lasher'd say, you know I don't eat beef—take this back. *Flaco*, he'd say, this spoon has soap film on it—get me another.

Lauren didn't get my drift. "My brother gave them to him because my brother was preparing to leave this life."

"No," was all Dr. Lasher said.

He didn't say it loudly.

Softly, he said it.

But he did say it emphatically, as though there was no possibility that Lasher was preparing to leave this life.

I felt the same way he did. No . . . no way.

chapter 2

Try reading "Fra Lippo Lippi" and see if you understand it.

This poem by Browning, I'd written on my test paper, *tells a rather disgusting story about the famous martyr St. Laurence, and about the painting Fra Lippo Lippi did of him roasting on a gridiron in 258 A.D.*

After my father became a private detective, my mother started calling him "The Martyr" because of all the hard work he put in on the job.

But my father couldn't hold a candle to St. Laurence, famous for telling the men who had him on a spit over hot coals, "One side is done; now you can do the other side."

The only thing I could really remember the day of the test on Browning's poetry was this fellow getting off that zinger while the Romans were cooking him.

I didn't understand the poem.

John Fell, you don't understand this poem, Mr. Wakoski wrote in red ink across my paper. *It is not about St. Laurence. It's about the monk who painted him. You make it sound as though Fra Lippo Lippi was being roasted. Painting while he sizzled. Neat trick. Reread this poem. It is also a defense of*

*artistic realism. . . . What's wrong with you, Fell?
It's not a hard poem, no more so than "Andrea del
Sarto."*

Einstein's theory of relativity might not be
any harder than Newton's law of gravity either,
but you'd never prove it by me.

I was standing in the hall between classes
reading Wakoski's remarks with a sinking heart,
the D- at the top of my paper making my stomach
turn over.

"Another A+?" Dib asked me.

"Look again," I said. He was already glancing down over my shoulder. He let out a surprised whistle and tried pushing back his blond
hair from his eyes.

I'd roomed with him before I became a
Sevens. We were both blonds, but there the
resemblance ended. He was taller and younger
and he lived on junk food, proving that metabo-
lism may have more to do with weight than calories because Dib was almost a skeleton. If I ate
all the Hostess Ding Dongs and Drake's golden
creme cups he put away in an afternoon, I'd be
ten pounds heavier.

"Browning is hard." Dib tried to make me
feel better.

We started walking along together. I hadn't
seen him in almost a week. When I first got into

Sevens and he didn't, I made a point of looking him up at the dorm nearly every day, to try and let him know things weren't going to be any different.

But things *were*. Once a Hill boy made Sevens, the others treated us differently . . . and I guess we contributed to the change, too, because we were on our honor never to tell the secrets of Sevens, and never, never to let anyone know how we got into the club.

That was the big mystery: How did someone get invited to join Sevens?

I wished I could tell Dib. He would have howled. He was right beside me our first day of school, when all of us had to plant little evergreen trees. That was the first thing you did when you arrived at Gardner School: You got into a line with other new kids, and all of you planted your tree . . . and named it something . . . Anything . . . I remember Dib named his after his dog: Thor.

I named mine "Good-bye," on a whim. My old girlfriend, Keats, lived in a house called Adieu. I'd tease her about the French, tell her it was pretentious. What's wrong with plain old good-bye? I'd ask her . . . It was good enough for me. Good-bye to her, and to Long Island where I'd met her. Good-bye to public high school. Hello to Pennsylvania and preppydom!

Nobody but a member of Sevens knows that what you name your tree is the most important thing you do at Gardner School. If you name it something with seven letters in it, you are automatically a Sevens member.

There's no more to it than that. No one ever makes the connection. Everyone thinks you've done something special, or are someone special, to get asked to join, but it's a fluke. Mere chance, as The Sevens like to sing. And from the moment you are initiated into Sevens, you live in the luxurious Sevens House, and eat in the Sevens clubhouse at the bottom of The Tower . . . You get a lot more privileges, too . . . The other kids resent you, and envy you . . . and like Dib, they can't believe you won't even give them a clue about how you got to be a privileged character overnight.

Dib continued talking about Browning. "The only line he wrote that I ever understood," he said, "is: *Grow old along with me! The best is yet to be.* And I'm not sure I agree with him on that point, either."

"Why don't you think the best is yet to be?"

"Because someone's getting away with murder," he said, "and I don't think anyone gives a damn!"

"You had breakfast with Mr. Lasher. He seems to give a damn."

"He's the only one."

"Are you going to the memorial service?" I was trying to change the subject, I admit. Five more months and I'd be graduated.

"Yeah, I'm going," said Dib. "Shall I save you a seat?"

"I have to sit with The Sevens."

"Sorry I asked." He took a box of Old Crows from his pocket and offered me one.

"Didn't you just eat lunch?"

He popped a couple of the licorice candies into his mouth. "Why don't you want to talk about this, Fell? Did The Sevens say you can't discuss it?"

"Come on, Dib. It's not like that. I'm just trying to keep my nose clean this semester so I can get out of this place."

"But you were the one who started me thinking it wasn't suicide. *You* told *me* the thing about the smashed glasses."

"I wish I never had."

"But you did, Fell. And I told the Lashers."

"Did you tell them he was screaming?"

"I couldn't bring myself to."

"We should have, I suppose. Nothing seemed to faze Lauren. Her eyes glaze over if you even suggest it might not have been suicide. The case is closed where she's concerned."

"And she let Rinaldo keep everything Lasher gave him."

The class bell rang. I was due down the hall for Latin.

Dib said, "The VCR, the pen, et cetera! He got a lot of stuff from Lasher. He's even selling some of it. I wish I could afford the word processor."

"What kind of a word processor is it?" I needed one myself. "Maybe we could go in on it together."

"A Smith-Corona," Dib said. He grimaced and shook his head. "I feel like a vulture. . . . Maybe if I was trying a little harder to find out what exactly happened that day in The Tower, I wouldn't."

"All *right*!" I said. "Can you come to my room tonight, after dinner? We'll talk about it."

Everyone around us was disappearing into classrooms.

"You mean your suite, don't you?" Dib gave one of his sarcastic laughs. "Yeah, I'll come over about eight."

"Eight thirty," I said. "We eat our dinner slower at Sevens. You know how it is: You savor every morsel when you're eating roast turkey with stuffing . . . and mashed potatoes . . . and giblet gravy."

I decided to rub it in. At Main Dining they'd

get something like chili over baked potato. He'd succeeded in making me feel guilty about Lasher's so-called suicide, but he wasn't going to do a number on me with The Sevens.

"Do they have doggie bags over there?" Dib said. "I wouldn't mind a turkey leg."

Second bell.

Then the carillon from chapel, playing "Farewell, old friend, farewell. Rest now, rest."

chapter | 3

I miss you, Mom. Try not to (1) go shopping; (2) open any new charge accounts; (3) worry about me—I'm fine.

I stopped at the end of the letter and crossed out 1, 2, and 3. My mother didn't have a sense of humor about being a spendthrift. She'd take it as criticism. Trying to point anything out to her, such as the fact that every time she used a credit card she was borrowing money at around 19 percent interest, only made her mad . . . decided she was as entitled to her mistakes as I was to mine, even though I'd probably end up paying for my kid sister's college one day, at the rate Mom was dancing through Macy's, Bloomingdale's, Savemart, and Sears.

Don't worry about me. Give Jazzy a big kiss.
Love,
Johnny
P. S. I've ordered you something for your birthday.

Her birthday was at the end of February. She was a Pisces. She liked to remind everyone she was born the same day as Elizabeth Taylor . . . another great shopper.

I didn't know where I was going to get $175, but I'd checked *Gold 7, with necklace* on a Sevens order form and given it to Rinaldo . . . In a week it would be delivered to my room, gift wrapped in the special 7's paper.

Although Mom liked to razz me about being in Sevens, I had an idea she was secretly impressed. We didn't have a lot going on in our life that singled us out from millions of other families who spent too much time watching the boob tube, using credit cards, and reading the gossip about people who went to Paris on the Concorde to have breakfast.

I'd gone over to The Sevens clubhouse before the memorial service to write the letter.

A lot of Sevens did their letter writing there, not just because there was always a fire on cold days in Deem Library and it was quiet, but also because the Sevens stationery was there. It was not supposed to be taken from that room. It was watermarked, cream-colored paper with THE SEVENS in light blue across the top. The stamps on the table were free. There were Parker pens with 7 on them in gold, the old-fashioned kind that took real ink. When you were finished, you just put your letters in the light-blue box marked CORRE-SPONDENCE, and the help got it to the post office.

There were always vases filled with fresh flowers in the library, even in January, and apple or cranberry juice in carafes on the table outside the door.

These little extras were just another reminder that we were special and privileged. Spoiled, my mom said, and you did nothing to deserve it. But that's what I liked about it. How could I feel guilty about things like having fresh sheets every day, and a maid to clean my room, when it all came about by mere chance?

I put my boots back on and got ready to walk down to chapel. It was snowing again, a wet one now, not the kind that sticks—and I walked along thinking about this girl I still loved—how she was out of my life without ever having been in it. I tried to picture her in winter clothes.

My relationships with females are a lot like the snow I was walking in, not the kind that stick.

There'd been Keats, who actually stood me up on the night of her prom, and that was just for starters . . . and then there'd been Delia.

My memories of Delia could melt the snow and turn the winter day into a July night with an orange ball up in the sky, a thousand stars, and the scent of roses, and I could even hear the sounds of that old Billy Joel song we danced to . . . but I wouldn't let myself go back.

Forget Delia, I told myself, and I almost laughed when Kidder gave my arm a punch down near chapel. "Fell?" he said. "Come down from outer space. We need you here on earth. You were just light-years away. What were you thinking about? You walked right past me."

"I was just reviewing the quantum theory," I said, "relating it to blackbody radiation, relativity, and the uncertainty principle." Kidder didn't laugh at my joke.

"You know what I've been thinking about? How much I'm going to miss Lasher around the poker table. Did you ever play with him?"

"I couldn't afford it."

"Yeah, who could?" (Kidder could.) "He was good at cards, anyway."

Kidder had named his tree Key West, where his own little yacht was berthed. He could have been a model for Colgate toothpaste or jockey shorts, if he'd needed the money. He didn't.

We were both wearing our black-and-white-striped mourning bands on our overcoat sleeves. On our heads sat the black top hats Sevens wore outside of the clubhouse only for funerals.

"Look over there," said Kidder, nudging me, nodding toward a black Mercedes with MD license plates. It was stopped in front of the chapel, and I could see Lauren Lasher getting out of it, then her father.

But I think Kidder was calling my attention to the woman already standing on the curb. She was wrapped in mink from shoulders to ankles, sucking one last drag from a cigarette. A tall lady with black hair, black shades, and a face you'd pass on the street, then whirl around to see again.

I suddenly remembered Lasher's face when he wasn't wearing his glasses. He'd had a certain beauty too, broken and bloody last I'd seen it . . . as though he'd landed on the icy pavement headfirst.

Inside, the organist was playing "Just a Song at Twilight" like a dirge. There were red roses everywhere, including one across everyone's hymnal.

We put them in our lapels.

After all the guests had filed in, the organist stopped playing. The Sevens Sextet stood in front of their chairs on the platform, their top hats over their hearts. They sang a cappella, the song played all afternoon on the carillon:

"*Farewell, old friend, farewell.*
Rest now, rest.
You did your best.
Farewell, dear heart, farewell.
Sleep now, sleep.
Your love we keep."

I tried to think of worse things than Lasher dying, which should have been easy since I'd never liked him. I pictured droughts in Africa, and the war-torn Middle East. Still, there were tears right behind my eyes. My mother was the same way at weddings, and whenever bands marched in parades. The floodgates opened.

Next it was Dr. Skinner's turn. He was Gardner's headmaster, a big, bald, roly-poly fellow who always wore a vest so his Phi Beta Kappa key would show.

He was the eulogist.

Finding words to praise Paul Lasher was a challenge to anyone who hadn't played cards with him, but Skinner came up with some. They were mild enough for all of us to keep straight faces. He didn't pour it on. Sevens were always called by their last names, so he stood there fondling his gold key and said Lasher was always a presence on The Hill. He said Lasher loved this place, more perhaps than anyone he'd ever known. He said Lasher was a loyal member of Sevens. He said the song that would be sung next always meant a great deal to Lasher.

Outerbridge appeared then. When he sang his Sunday-morning solos, you were tempted to turn around and see if he was in a dress, his soprano was so high and tremulous. But now he was up in front, the single red rose in one hand, the top hat in the other, across his chest.

He sang the school song.

"Others will fill our places,
Dressed in the old light blue,
We'll recollect our races.
We'll to the flag be true.
And youth will still be in our faces
When we cheer for a Gardner crew.
Yes, youth will still be in our faces,
We'll remain to Gardner true."

I looked around the chapel. All dry eyes except for Lauren and her father. At least I think Lauren was crying. She had a handkerchief to her eyes. The lady in mink wore the black shades, but she didn't seem to be weeping, though her chin was stuck forward in the gesture of someone steeling herself.

Creery was the only Sevens not present. He had spent two nights in the infirmary. There were rumors he couldn't sleep, and others that he slept around the clock. It could be either way with Creery—he was famous for his changing moods. We'd heard that his stepbrother had been summoned from Florida, that Creery was threatening to leave Gardner.

I had last seen him the night of Lasher's death, at the assembly Skinner'd called us to, warning us not to discuss "this accident" with outsiders. He looked like the same old Creery to me: eyes that said no one's home, no one's expected.

As far as I knew, not one soul had signed up to speak at this memorial. The night before, I'd seen the sheet hanging on the Sevens bulletin board, still not a name on it.

I wasn't surprised, then, when Dr. Skinner said a member of the family, Dr. Inge Lasher, would say a few words.

She had the long black mink coat draped over her shoulders, the dark glasses pushed up on her head. She had the kind of eyes you'd think a shrink would have: radar ones, sending out as much as they took in, searching all our faces. They were as dark as brown could get.

The thick German accent was a surprise.

When she said we, it sounded like v. All her v's were w's, her w's v's. There were other things too. *She* vould haf said dere vere udder tings. That's just to give you an example.

Her very short speech turned out to be a minilecture on a new view of adolescent suicide. According to Inge Lasher, her son had a chemical abnormality in his brain.

It has been proven, said she, that young people who suffer from major depression, and attempt suicide or dwell on suicidal plans, secrete less growth hormone than other depressed but nonsuicidal young people or other healthy youngsters.

No one, she insisted, was responsible, or

should feel guilt.

All her speech did for me was make me remember the scream. I'd never heard a scream like it. Not even in the worst splatter films. It was so unlike any everyday human sound, I hadn't known what it was until I'd seen him, what was left of him, crumpled there on the ice.

See what happens when you don't secrete enough growth hormone?

I couldn't buy it.

After she sat down, and before we Sevens gathered at the front to sing our song, Dr. Skinner made an announcement that caused a ripple through the chapel, all heads turning toward the rear when he was finished.

"And now, someone else who knew Lasher would like to read something. Rinaldo Velez . . . Would, you come forward, please, Rinaldo?"

Rinaldo was The Tower jester. Although he had no accent, he affected one when he felt like it, sometimes peppering his conversation with Spanish words like *pijos* (yuppies) and *fachas* (fascists—said, with a grin, of The Sevens). He tried to teach certain Sevens *salsa sensual,* the song-and-dance craze he was master of, but he claimed we had *blanco* hips that didn't swivel, and our hearts weren't beating hot enough inside our bodies.

All last semester he'd belted out *"Ven Devorame Otra Vez"* from the kitchen: *"Come and Devour Me Again."*

He was skinny, and very tall, with silky black hair he slicked back and wore in a short cut.

Although he was a townie, Rinaldo sometimes had a proprietary feeling about Sevens. He stood behind me once in the dining room when we sang, "The Star-Spangled Banner" on Veterans' Day. I'd forgotten the Sevens habit of placing your hand over your heart when you came to the words "at the twilight's last gleaming." Rinaldo reached around and put my arm up across my chest. I glanced over my shoulder at him and he gave me a stern look, the kind a parent would give a thoughtless child.

Had I ever seen him with Lasher anyplace but in the dining room, waiting on him? If I had, I didn't remember it.

Had anyone? Had anyone in Sevens even been asked what their connection was?

I had never seen Rinaldo when he wasn't wearing a white waiter's jacket and a black clip-on tie. I had never seen him look so uncomfortable, either.

There was already perspiration dotting his forehead, where a lick of black hair dangled. His tight, black, two-buttoned double-breasted suit had wide shoulders with the waist nipped. He wore a black mock turtleneck.

His hands were shaking. He tried holding up

the piece of paper he carried, but he could not read it until he'd flattened it on the top of the podium. Then he had to lean over and bend down his head.

His voice carried well, though it quivered and slipped out of its register a few times into a higher one, which made him pause and clear his throat.

No one could doubt that he had written the strange poem himself, though he had nothing to say in the way of introduction.

He just read.

> "Here, he said, these are all for you.
>   I have to leave.
>   And it is true
>   That I did not perceive,
>   The circumstance . . .
>   A backward glance,
>   Then *Hasta la vista*, he said,
>   And he was gone.
>   And he is dead.
> "Here, he said, these are all for you.
>   "Here, this is my good-bye,
>   And that is all.
>   I never really knew you, Paul.
>   But here, let me say so long,
>   Before the Sevens song."

I got up then, along with the other Sevens, and we went to the front of the chapel.

Once again I felt slightly choked up. It had to be something about Rinaldo's poem . . . or maybe just that it was sad someone who hardly knew Lasher was the only one of us to come forward to say good-bye. Not even someone from The Hill . . . And Rinaldo was probably shamed into doing it because Lasher'd given him stuff.

We sang with feeling; the words rang out. Maybe we were all thinking of the same thing: the way Lasher belted out those words:

> . . . *my heart will thrill*
> *At the thought of The Hill*
> *And the Sevens* . . .

like a Marine singing "from the halls of Montezuma," like some newly freed hostage joining in on "God Bless America."

There was a brief silence at the end of our song.

Then, in unison, we said the Sevens farewell. From Tennyson.

> "Twilight . . . and evening bell . . .
> And after that . . . the dark."

The chapel bell tolled seven times.

chapter | 4

Lauren saw me outside the chapel, waved, and beckoned me with her finger.

The campus lights were on. We stood in the cold wet rain that had turned most of the snow to slush. I felt foolish in my top hat; it'd always been a bit too big.

She was carrying her red rose. Over by their Mercedes, I saw Dr. Skinner helping her mother into the front seat.

Her gloved hand held an umbrella over her head. On the other hand, long nails, unpainted but glossy. A ring with a red stone.

"I'll come back to pack Paul's things next week, or the week after," she said. "Does it matter?"

"You know, I'm fairly new here," I told her. "I'm not the one to ask."

"Then why do you act as though you're in charge?"

I hadn't expected that, nor her sharp tone.

"I don't. Why do you think I do?"

"You're the one with all the opinions."

"You came to me and asked for them," I reminded her.

"*I* didn't. I came with Daddy."

She was toying with the gold 7 around her

neck, under her Burberry. She went right on. "We're going to give Rinaldo my brother's clothes. Apparently that's who Paul wanted his things to go to . . . And he can keep everything Paul gave him."

"Why tell me?" I asked her.

"So you don't start any rumors about that, too."

"I didn't start any rumors, Lauren. I made a comment to Dib."

"Which was overheard by a lot of people."

"I blurted it out. I wasn't trying to spread it around."

"I wish you'd tell Cyr you were the one. He thinks it was Rinaldo."

"Why does he care? No one said *he* did it." Not out loud, anyway.

"We don't want all these rumors and bad feelings between you guys. Just let Paul rest in peace."

"Gladly," I said, "but why does Creery care?"

"Because of that fight they had. How would you feel if someone jumped to his death immediately after you'd had a fight with him?"

"They were always fighting, Lauren."

"Still."

"Don't worry about Creery. He'll roll a few joints and forget all about it."

"He claims there's such a thing as The Sevens Revenge."

"That's an old rumor . . . Besides, what did he

do to deserve The Revenge?"

I'd heard of it, of course. It was said that if you told The Sevens secrets, or if you were guilty of Conduct Unforgivable, you were taken to The Tower and a live rat was tied around your neck. Surviving that, you were given the silent treatment until you resigned and left Gardner. There were other versions, each with a rat in it . . . and though The Revenge supposedly had not been performed since 1963, rumors about it were part of Sevens lore. One death was attributed to The Revenge. An automobile accident an alumnus had, while a rat was tied to his ankle, was said to be The Revenge too.

I tried a smile, to lighten things up. I smelled her perfume and thought I knew its name. Obsession. Keats always wore it. Lauren didn't smile back at me. I was getting wet. She made no attempt to share the umbrella.

She said, "*Latet anguis in herba.* Do you know your Latin?"

"I know that Latin. Your brother taught it to me."

She decided to translate it anyway. "The snake hides in the grass."

"It was his motto," I said.

"Sometimes I can see why it was," she said. "Fell, I don't happen to believe in hormonal loss. What I believe is that people who don't know how to care about other people get obsessed with things. Clubs, for example. The way my brother was about Sevens."

I didn't know what she was leading up to, but I couldn't have agreed more. I was always suspicious of guys who got too attached to their schools or their private clubs and fraternities. I figured they were probably getting their first taste of belonging anywhere, that maybe no one had ever made them feel important before.

"I know," I said. "Your brother felt about Sevens the way a Doberman feels about his backyard."

"I don't think it did Paul any good. A club doesn't love back. It can't take the place of people. You get twisted putting all your energy into a club."

"I think so too," I said. I was a little amazed that we could agree on something.

Then she said, "A theory, *theories*, do the same thing when you begin to put all your energy into them."

She wasn't talking about Lasher and Sevens anymore. She was after me.

"People with too many theories about other people don't have real feelings for other people," she said.

"I have both," I told her. I was getting wetter. "If I was carrying that umbrella, you'd be under it, along with all my theories."

"Touché," she said. "Get under for a sec."

While I did, she said, "What I'm going to ask you to do isn't my idea—it's Daddy's. And you might as well know Dr. Skinner said you weren't the ideal person to ask."

"Well? Ask."

"You have too much attitude, Fell."

"I was thinking that about *you* this morning."

"My brother did a lot of writing. Daddy wants to take his best pieces and put them in a memorial book. Would you read through everything and select them?"

"Why does Daddy think I'm the one to do that, and Skinner think I'm not?"

"Daddy likes you. Skinner thinks you're better off not dwelling on Paul's death."

I was too curious to play hard to get, and the wind was pushing the rain down my neck.

Lauren said, "Daddy will pay you, of course."

"All right. I'll give it a try. Where are the manuscripts?"

"They're with Mrs. Violet at Sevens House. Your name is on the package."

"You and Daddy aren't short on confidence."

"Dr. Skinner said *you* were short on cash, so you'd have to get a hundred dollars, at least. Daddy thought that was cheap."

"I have to get a new business manager.

Skinner's not working out at all."

Down by the black Mercedes, Lauren's father called out, "Come on, honey!"

She said, "One other thing: Daddy wants a few pictures of Paul in the memorial book. I'm going through his album, and I'll get some to you."

"Does your father know your brother wrote a lot about death and suicide?"

"Paul used to keep a noose in his room. He'd tell mother it was just in case he felt like having a last swing . . . We were used to Paul."

Lauren's father called her again.

She said, "But now both my parents are into denial."

Inside the Mercedes her mother honked the horn impatiently, three times.

chapter | 5

The Sevens had turkey roast on Friday nights, steak on Wednesdays. Always fresh vegetables, fresh asparagus that night. Don't ask me where they managed to find it the last week of January.

While we ate, the committee for The Charles Dance was announced, and I was on it.

Named for The Sevens' founder, it was a major event at Gardner, held every March on our anniversary. Dorm boys and their dates were invited too. Females wore evening dresses, but all males came in costume as someone named Charles. The ill-omened rulers of England and France were favorites, from Charles II (the Fat) to Charles III (the Simple), but any Charles would do.

In the dining room of The Tower the only art was a lighted portrait labeled *Wife of Damon Charles*. We knew that if Gardner ever went coed, as our trustees were threatening, female Sevens would be outraged that like Lot's wife in the Bible, she had no name of her own. Did The Sevens even know what it was? I doubted it. She was a handsome and regal brunette in a white gown and pearls. Underneath *Wife of Damon Charles* was a quote from Wordsworth:

Her eyes as stars of twilight fair;
Like twilight's, too, her dusky hair.

Before the chocolate cake was served, while
the uniformed waiters cleared the table under
the candlelit chandelier, we all sang our song
together.

"When I was a beggar boy,
And lived in a cellar damp,
I had not a friend or a toy,
But that was all changed by mere chance!
Once I could not sleep in the cold,
And patches they covered my pants,
Now I have bags full of gold,
For that was all changed by mere chance!
Mere chance, mere chance."

Rinaldo made an entrance from the kitchen,
carrying a tray filled with cake on the light-blue
T's-crested plates.

"Mere chance makes us gay,
Mere chance makes night day,
But whoever she'll choose,
She can also make lose.
Mere chance has her way,
Mere chance."

I leaned back in my chair to try and get his attention. I wanted to say I'd see him after dinner. If I didn't move fast on that word processor, someone else would. Maybe now that he'd become heir to so many valuables, he'd let Dib and me pay in installments. Maybe not . . . and maybe he'd charge too much. But I ought to get it settled.

He went right past me, looking straight ahead, ignoring my *"Pssst!"* There was a watch on his wrist, lots of gold and stainless steel. The good Gstaad?

I decided to take a look at his shoes. My dad used to tell me a man's shoes say a lot about him. That was back before everyone was into Reeboks, when shoeshine still meant eager/accountable/ready.

And sure enough, Rinaldo had on black Reeboks.

Suddenly I saw very clearly one white Reebok get between Rinaldo's black ones.

Next, Rinaldo was on the floor.

So was the silver tray and the cake and the china.

The white Reebok had disappeared under the table.

I took a look at its owner. I never had liked that face. It used to remind me of my own back when I was running with fast-track kids in Brooklyn, rebelling against being a cop's son, proving I could get as wrecked as anyone else.

Out of the infirmary, Creery seemed fully recovered. A skinhead last semester, he was letting his hair grow in. He already had a thin tail in back, reaching down toward his neck. There were the same two skull earrings in his right ear, and a silver GUNS N' ROSES pendant around his throat.

At the sound of Rinaldo and the cake plates crashing to the floor, Creery's mouth twitched almost imperceptibly. He did not look over his shoulder to see the damage he had caused.

Since Lasher's death it hadn't been fear of seeing my old self in that face. It was more the feeling that if I did take a good look at it, I'd see Lasher in those eyes of Cyril Creery's. I'd see Lasher

    f

      a

        l

          l

            i

              n

                g . . . the way a certain old girl-friend of mine—Delia—always used to write my name:

    F

      E

        L

          L

chapter | 6

"Did anyone else see Creery trip him?" Dib asked.

"I doubt it. I was the only one looking at Rinaldo's feet."

"Then what happened?"

"Rinaldo picked himself up. He and the other waiters cleaned up the mess, and they brought out more cake. You know The Sevens: The good life always goes right on."

"I don't know The Sevens," said Dib. "I only know you."

"You know what I mean, though. If there's a soul mourning for Lasher, I don't know who that'd be."

Dib was tearing the wrapper from a Milky Way. "How does somebody get into Sevens when no one even likes him?"

I let the question hang there.

Dib said, "Got any instant coffee?"

"Help yourself."

I didn't live in a room—Dib was right when he said that earlier in the day. I lived in a suite. Dib got off the bed and went into the other room, where there was a small refrigerator, a hot plate, a leather couch, a coffee table, some chairs, and a view of The Tower from the window. Private bath on the right.

I stretched out while I listened to an old Talking Heads song and thought about the reason Creery would be gunning for Rinaldo. Because of what Lauren had told me, I supposed. Because Creery thought Rinaldo'd spread the rumor Lasher'd been murdered.

If someone had spread a rumor about me being a kleptomaniac, I wouldn't react unless I'd had a habit of walking out of stores with things hidden in my pockets.

Creery had always looked for a fight with Lasher. He was our resident cynic. He'd named his tree Up Yours. He'd slap his knee and laugh hysterically when Lasher'd speak about Sevens in the same way someone in a cult would drool over their guru. I remember how he cracked up once when Lasher had explained the habit old grads had of meeting for drinks only at hotels and restaurants with seven letters in the names. The Ritz, in Boston. Laurent, in New York. Creery'd almost wet his pants over that one.

Lasher had hated him, too. Everyone in the Sevens House was familiar with the scent of incense wafting from Creery's room, masking the marijuana smell inside. He was not the only pot smoker on The Hill, or in Sevens, but he was the only one who took advantage of the freedom we enjoyed in Sevens House, where there were no proctors or faculty, and Mrs. Violet, our housemother, rarely came above the first floor.

He flouted our self-regulatory system flagrantly. There was always one. Some grumbled about it; most minded their own business.

It was the kind of thing Lasher would lose sleep over.

He'd dog Creery's footsteps, whistling "Twilight Time" and promising to get Creery.

Lasher'd been in Sevens since he was fourteen.

Lasher used to get tears in his eyes when he'd hear the song The Sevens sing to let guys know they're in. The one we sang at the memorial service. Creery'd ride him about it, put his knuckles to his eyelids and mimic him.

I didn't know much about Lasher's life before he got to The Hill, but he'd named his tree Suicide.

Even after he was in the club, he wrote all these plays about Death, and he kept a noose in his suite at Sevens, too. Creery always asked him why he was stalling, why didn't he pee or get off the pot.

Still, it didn't seem like old cool-head Creery to care whether or not there were rumors Lasher'd been murdered. Unless he'd had something to do with the murder.

Dib came back with some Taster's Choice, turned down Talking Heads, and asked me point-blank if I thought Creery was capable of murder.

"My dad used to say anyone's capable of it, but not many are sufficiently provoked at the same time they have a weapon handy. That's why he was against ordinary people having guns around."

"What about being sufficiently provoked by someone while you're at the edge of a cliff . . . or standing on top of that tower?"

"Same thing, I guess."

"What about defending yourself when someone's about to murder you . . . and there you are at the top of that tower?"

"It could have happened that way. . . . I remember the night I got in Sevens: Suddenly Lasher was right behind me at the top of that thing. He said, 'Look down there at the ground and tell me if it makes you want to jump.'"

"You never told me this." There was always a slightly resentful tone when Dib would discover I wasn't reporting back to him the way we used to tell each other everything, anything, before Sevens, when the two of us were new on The Hill.

"He was holding me near the edge of the wall, and I thought, He's crazy. I'm up here by myself with this maniac."

"What did you do, Fell?"

"There's an elevator in The Tower, you know."

"I didn't know."

"Not many people outside of Sevens do. Creery came out of it at that point and told Lasher to knock it off.... Lasher was just trying to scare the hell out of me. All of Sevens knew I was up there with him, but I didn't know they did."

"Fell," Dib said, "Creery killed Lasher. I'm positive of it."

That was when a new voice was added to the conversation. Lionel Schwartz's. You could have said he was the president of Sevens, except president had nine letters in it instead of seven. So Schwartz was our captain.

"Sidney Dibble," he said, "you've got a wild imagination." He was chuckling like a lenient parent who'd just heard his three-year-old say the F word.

We called him The Lion. He wanted to be an actor. He had on a tweed sport coat with leather elbow patches, a red bow tie against a blue-and-white-striped shirt. Dark-brown hair cut short and parted down the center. John Lennon spectacles. He always looked like a lot of planning went into how he looked.

The Lion was the kind of guy you didn't get next to easily. You saw him in all the school plays. You couldn't miss him strutting around campus while everyone called out his name and hoped he'd remember theirs. He had SPECIAL written all over him.

He was also the kind of guy Dib envied and resented. I would have too, if I hadn't made Sevens. But propinquity changes your view of people. In Sevens we knew his mother was a madwoman, in and out of institutions. We'd hear him trying to reason with her on the house phone, reassuring her that the doctor wasn't from the CIA, that the neighbors weren't making bombs, and telling her no, he couldn't come home, not in midterm.

We knew certain Sevens' deepest secrets, guarding them as if they were our own.

But to Dib Lionel Schwartz was arrogant and vain. Worse, he was patronizing. I could feel Dib losing ground facing him down. "There're a lot of unanswered questions," Dib muttered.

"There always are when someone kills himself." Schwartz was still smirking, rocking on his heels with his hands stuck in the pockets of his trousers. He told Dib, "I'd like to talk with Fell, if it's all right with you."

Dib jumped to his feet and said it was fine with him, he'd see me tomorrow.

"How long is the talk going to take?" I asked Schwartz. I figured Dib could sit it out downstairs in our reception room.

But Dib didn't wait for The Lion's answer.

"I've got a paper to write tonight anyway," he said.

He was out of there.

chapter 7

Schwartz sat down in the captain's chair next to my bed.

"Seven," he said to me. So he was there on Sevens business, following the formalities. This ritual was to seal our conversation as confidential. Probably they did it at The Ritz and Laurent, too. Maybe someday years from then I'd be meeting someone, leaning on my cane, my hair white, starting off "Seven."

I came up with seven things that went together, as I was expected to do.

"Pride, Wrath, Envy, Lust, Gluttony, Avarice, Sloth," I said.

"The Seven Deadly Sins. So be it. . . . Fell, you're about to receive an honor."

"I *am*?"

"An old member is asking for our help, and you've been chosen for the assignment."

"I see," I said.

"Were you expecting the Croix de Guerre or something?" he asked. He laughed and swung his legs up on my bed.

"What kind of an assignment?"

"Tutoring. That's part of it."

"I just got a D- in English."

"That's a fluke, isn't it, Fell? After all, you won the New Boys Competition last fall for your essay, and you wrote a rather remarkable paper on Agamemnon's death . . . Dr. Skinner reminded me of all that when I discussed this with him."

"I didn't know Skinner was told Sevens' business."

"He wasn't told very much about the assignment, but I wanted his recommendation because it takes you off campus."

"And he recommended me?"

"He said you could use the money, which amounts to six dollars an hour . . . and he thinks you may have overreacted to Lasher's death, that it would be good for you to be busy."

"Is that also why I'm on the committee for The Charles Dance?"

Schwartz smiled. "No. *I* chose you for that. You haven't been on any of our committees."

Lasher's manuscripts were in the envelope on my desk. As curious as I was, I hadn't had a chance to glance at them.

Dib was going to offer Rinaldo three hundred for the word processor, one fifty apiece. I needed money—Skinner was right. I wasn't sure I needed Skinner telling everyone I needed it.

"This assignment concerns a girl who lives right here in Cottersville," Schwartz began. "Her father's a benefactor of Gardner—a very generous one, particularly to Sevens. Her name is Nina Deem."

"As in Deem Library?"

"Exactly," said Schwartz. "It was donated by the Deem family."

"Does she go to school in Cottersville?"

"Yes. She's a junior at Cottersville High. She'd probably be over in Miss Tyler's, except two years ago her mother died. There aren't any other children. She's all David Deem has. . . . She's a good writer, wants to be a professional, plans to go to Kenyon College. They have a whole writing program there."

"You can't tutor someone in writing. You mean help her with her grammar and her spelling and stuff like that?"

"Help her get back to writing. She's lost interest."

"Because I don't know anything about grammar and spelling. I need help with that myself."

"I *said* help her get back to writing . . . The hidden agenda is more important than the tutoring, anyway."

"What does that mean, the hidden agenda?"

"It means there's another part to the assignment."

He reached inside his sport coat and took out a photograph. He passed it across to me.

"Edward Dragon," he said.

Dragon looked about my age, seventeen. He had a certain clean, American-boy quality, the kind models for Ralph Lauren's clothes have when they're shown in ads riding around in the family jeep with Dad, Sis, and the dog. He wasn't in a jeep, though. The backdrop was almost comical, as though he'd posed for it at a carnival or a fair. Behind him was a fake waterfall, an old mill, and a weeping willow tree.

He was seated on a real bench in front: brown suit, white shirt, and maroon-and-white-striped tie. His hair was the same dark brown, short and straight, slicked back. He was holding a Siamese cat on his lap.

I started to hand it back to Schwartz.

"Keep it," he said. "You'll need to know that face."

"What does he have to do with Nina Deem?"

"I'm coming to that. Last summer Nina enrolled in a writers' workshop held at the Cottersville Community Center. Dragon did, too. The Center isn't far from the Deems' house, and Dragon would walk her home nights after class. He told her he was from Doylestown, and that he was a freshman at Penn State. Told her he was nineteen, and told Mr. Deem he was premed. That really appealed to Deem. He never went to college, never had a profession. You know Sun and Surf?"

"The sporting goods store?"

"That's his."

"How'd he afford to give us a library then?"

"That store's a little gold mine, Fell! Apparently he's a genius when it comes to money. He started from scratch, right out of Gardner. Like a lot of men without a formal education, he's in awe of doctors, lawyers, et cetera. He thought Dragon was the perfect guy to escort his daughter around."

Schwartz took his legs off my bed, crossed them, and tipped back in the chair. "Deem really liked him, too. He trusted him like a son. Nina was under a shrink's care since her mother's death, shutting herself off from the world, depressed, that sort of thing. Dragon got her out and about: tennis, swimming at the club, the movies. He was her first real boyfriend, too. So. . . ." The Lion shrugged his shoulders.

"So they fell in love and were miserable ever after," I said.

Schwartz held up one hand. "Hold your horses, Fell. It's not really a love story, though she was certainly in love. Whatever *he* felt, he was lying to her. He wasn't going to Penn State at all. Then one night late last fall the Cottersville police arrested him. The age on his driver's license was twenty-three. . . . They picked him up for selling cocaine."

"Was she with him?"

"No. Fortunately. It was around midnight. He was in a bar down near the train tracks. It was in the papers. That's how David Deem heard about it . . . Dragon had a smart lawyer, and supposedly it was a first offense. He got off. But Deem told him he was never to see Nina again." Schwartz looked at me. "That's where you come in, Fell. You keep an eye out for him."

"I'm supposed to go there under false pretenses?"

"What other kind of pretenses are there? . . . Didn't your father do something like this for a living?"

"He was a cop and he was a detective. This is different."

"Not that different," Schwartz said. "Fell, this is a Sevens assignment. It's not an unreasonable one. Deem has done a lot for us. Do you think we take and never give back?"

I just sat there.

"This is a nice girl," Schwartz said. "Suppose you had a sister and—"

"I have a sister." She wasn't in first grade yet.

"And suppose she was hanging out with some pusher who'd lied to her and your family?"

"My sister wouldn't hang out with a known pusher." I thought of the day my father'd told me the last thing he ever thought he'd find in his own son's bureau drawer was shit. When he wasn't making out reports and calling pot "a controlled substance," he called it what we did on the street. Shit. He said that was the name for it, all right. He said, What in the name of God are you doing with this, Johnny? . . . What made me so sure Jazzy'd be invulnerable?

Back to Schwartz. "Suppose she fell in love with someone like Dragon and couldn't help herself?"

"Is that the case with Nina Deem?"

"It seems to be. She's promised Deem she won't see Dragon again, but Deem's not taking any chances."

Then he said, "You've had all the benefits of Sevens without any responsibility, Fell. You haven't volunteered once for any service to Sevens."

I sat there. I hated pushers . . . It wasn't that. It was going there as something I wasn't, suckering some girl into trusting me when all the while she couldn't if she tried to see this Dragon.

"You'll be making fifty dollars a week."

Tiny mind that I admit having, it went to Mom's birthday and the gold 7. It went to the word processor Dib and I were hoping to buy from Rinaldo.

"Mostly you'll be a tutor," Schwartz said. "She really wants help getting into Kenyon."

"Have you ever met her?"

"Once. She was a sweet kid. After her mother drowned, I was part of the group Sevens sent to the funeral . . . Let me tell you something, Fell. I think this assignment will be good for you. I think you've overreacted to Lasher's death, too." I started to say something, but he held his hand up again. "Wait. Listen. I think the Fates arrange exits and entrances for us. When I came to The Hill, we'd just committed my mother to someplace. She'd look out her window through bars, with people around her who cawed like crows. My dad was telling me just get on with my education, but I was going to have to do it on a shoestring, we were so broke because of what she'd cost us. I had a scholarship, but I didn't have a dime in my pocket . . . I couldn't get her out of my head. I even named my tree after her, I was so guilty . . . Her name is Mildred."

"Seven letters."

"Exactly. Exits and entrances, Fell. I have a feeling this is an entrance for you."

"Enter the two-faced tutor."

"You'll be helping her, Fell!"

"Her mother drowned?"

"In their pool. This poor kid needs rescuing."

Schwartz was getting up. He knew he'd made the assignment without my even telling him. He'd used all his big guns: his mother, my sister, rescuing some innocent female, what I owed Sevens, the extra money I'd make. He'd shot me down.

"Oh, and Fell? She's a jet crash now, thanks to Dragon. Don't bring up Lasher's suicide. She doesn't need to hear about that sort of thing. You ought to forget it, too."

He reached out and grabbed my hand. "A week from next Wednesday afternoon at four, Fell. Her address is outside on your coffee table. She's expecting you."

The day that I was to go to the Deems' to meet Nina, two strangers showed up on The Hill.

One came early that morning, after breakfast. He was a grief counselor from Philadelphia, there to meet with any students still reacting to Lasher's suicide. He parked his car in the faculty lot and went to the student lounge, where he would be available all day.

His car was a red bi-turbo 425 Maserati, with HEADOC on the license plates.

"Where did they find him?" Dib asked me as we walked to lunch.

"He's a Sevens," I said. "Class of '74."

"That figures," Dib said.

The only meal The Sevens ate in the Gardner dining room was lunch. The other stranger was there, at Dr. Skinner's table. He was tanned from the Miami sun, so Miami in his appearance that he stood out like a cop at a bikers' rally. His face was too young for the mop of white hair, thick and silky, a lock falling across his forehead. He had a white mustache curved down around the corners of his mouth, where there was a cheerful smile with even white teeth, and dimples.

He must have come directly from the airport. White suit, brown silk shirt, red-and-tan-patterned silk tie. He looked like Florida's version of Mark Twain.

Dib passed me the word going around our table.

"He's Creery's stepbrother. Lowell something."

Creery was beside him, wearing his wraparound blue Gargoyle shades, shoveling down tuna melt while Skinner and Lowell something talked.

"They say Creery wants to go back to Florida with him," Dib said.

"Good!"

"Why is it good? Then the whole thing will be forgotten."

"We're not getting anywhere anyway."

"Because your heart isn't in it, Fell! Now you're going to tutor some townie, and that'll end it."

I couldn't tell Dib everything about the Sevens assignment, or even that it *was* an assignment. I'd told him Skinner'd put me on to the job, and Dib decided it was part of the school cover-up.

Dib said, "Even if somebody tells his suspicions to that grief counselor, you don't think a guy with HEADOC on his license plate is going to take it seriously?"

"Here's a joke for you, Dib," I said. "A guy comes into a therapist's office and he says, Doc, I'm a wigwam. No, I'm a teepee. . . . No, I'm a wigwam. No, I'm a teepee. . . . The therapist says to the guy, Relax, you're two tents."

"Very funny, Fell," Dib said. "About as funny as this tuna fish is fresh."

"The point is," I said, "you have to relax. You *are* too tense. We'll just keep our eyes and ears open. We can't do any more than that."

"You haven't even questioned Rinaldo to find out why Lasher'd choose him to give his stuff to."

"He's bringing the word processor to my room after lunch. I'll do it then."

"Make sure the tutorial's in it so we know how to work it."

"I keep it until April, right? Then it's yours."

"But I can practice on it in your room, okay?"

"Okay," I said.

Dib said, "They say Creery is afraid of The Sevens Revenge, Fell. Did you hear anything about that?"

"Of course not. I'd tell you if I had."

"I'm not so sure," said Dib. "Anyway . . . why would he be afraid if he didn't have anything to do with Lasher's death?"

"Good question, Dib. But The Sevens Revenge is a myth."

"Sure, Fell, just a myth."

While we were all eating lunch, Lauren Lasher had come by Sevens House and packed up her brother's things.

She'd left a note on my desk.

Rinaldo will pick up Paul's clothes. How are you coming with the memorial book? Here are two photos, but still looking for a smiling one.

LL

In one snapshot she'd left on my blotter, Lasher looked more like Lauren than he looked like himself. It was a head shot of him in a parka. Without his glasses he was almost beautiful, with thick, coal-black hair and dark, solemn eyes.

In the other photo there was a girl posed beside him in a long evening gown. He was dressed up in aviator's clothes, goggles covering his eyes, "Lindy" stitched over his pocket. He must have been impersonating Charles Lindbergh at the last Charles Dance.

It had taken me a week to get through his manuscripts.

He reminded me of Jazzy during "the terrible twos." My father was working nights then on a warehouse theft case on the Brooklyn docks. He was sleeping in the daytime, or trying to. Jazzy was literally screaming for attention: throwing her food at the walls when we'd put it in front of her, dumping in her pants the minute we'd take her off the potty, anything to keep our attention focused on her. She missed playtime with Daddy.

Lasher was doing a number with Death. He had titles like "The Graveyard Calls My Name" and "Death Be My Lover." His writing had all the organization and lyricism of some little tone-deaf child seated at a piano. He banged and pounded, hit-and-miss.

The only one I liked was one he'd worked and reworked for English. I remembered it from Mr. Wakoski's class last term. It was a play about a heaven where you were ranked according to the age you died: the younger, the better for you. In Lasher's paradise the ones who'd lived to grand old ages were called "The Feebles" and denied wings. The top angels were small babies who'd survived only a day or two.

He'd called it "Only the Young Fly Good."

That one I'd pulled out for the memorial book—grim and ironic as it was, it had humor.

I fastened the photos to it with a paper clip and shoved them in the top drawer.

I had a free study period before I was due down at the Deems'. There was a Latin test coming up, and I got out Cicero and began working my way through one of his senate speeches.

At two o'clock Rinaldo came staggering into my room with the top half of the word processor.

"The typewriter's out in the hall, Fell."

I brought it in while Rinaldo set everything up for me.

"You're getting a bargain," he said. "If I had time to learn it, I'd keep it for myself."

"Have you tried it out?"

"How would I try it out when I don't know how it works? I just know how it's put together, from taking it apart when Lasher gave it to me."

I checked to be sure the tutorial was in it; then I asked Rinaldo, "When did you two become such good friends?"

He gave me an exasperated look. Under his duffel coat he had on his work clothes: the black pants, white shirt, black plastic bow tie.

"We weren't good friends, Fell, and everyone knows it. We weren't friends at all. Are you fishing, is that it?"

"That's it."

"Walk down the hall with me," he said. "I want to show you some things in Lasher's room."

I walked with him while he told me the arrangement he'd made with Dib to pay him for the Smith-Corona.

"If it was disc instead of tape, you'd have paid a lot more," he said. "That model's out-of-date now. Lasher had a new computer ordered."

"A Porsche, a new computer. Why would he—"

Rinaldo didn't let me finish. "I know what you're going to say. Lauren Lasher filled me in on all your theories. They're right up there with her mother's *mierda* about hormones causing suicide."

"*Lack* of hormones," I said.

"Either way."

We were in Lasher's room then.

"Look around this place," Rinaldo said.

There was one lone poster left on the wall: Uncle Sam pointing his finger as he did on recruitment billboards. Under him: *Join the Army. Visit strange and exotic places. Meet fascinating people. And kill them.*

There were dozens of cartons packed with books marked for the Gardner Library. The closets were open and empty. In one corner there was a leather massager recliner, which Rinaldo kicked gently with one foot. "This has a built-in AM/FM/cassette stereo player," he said. "It cost about two thousand dollars."

He pointed to a walnut pants presser by the window. "That's a Corby Pants Press," he said. "Around two hundred and fifty dollars. . . . Want to look in the bedroom a minute?"

"What's there?"

"A Lifecycle," he said. "It has a matrix of sixty-four light displays changing terrain as you ride. It gives you pedaling speed, elapsed time, and calories you're burning. Costs about one thousand five."

"What's your point, Rinaldo?"

"There's no mystery here, Fell," he said. "You wonder why he gave stuff to me. He felt like it. Who would he give it to? No one liked him. Compared to what he had, he gave me a few little peanuts. He did it on impulse, the same way he bought all this like he could buy his happiness. He *pissed* money away, Fell. His family's, his own."

I nodded. "I can see he did."

"Money didn't mean anything. He made a pile of it every weekend down on Playwicky Road, playing cards. You know he had an apartment there? Number six Playwicky. That's where he went weekends he didn't go home. Ask Kidder."

The apartment was news to me. I said, "I believe you."

"Finally they're believing Rinaldo." He moved over to the couch and began sorting through jackets and pants piled there. "I told Creery's stepbrother: *Listen!* Rinaldo does not know zilch about any letter. *Nada!* . . . Look at these clothes, Fell. Where am I going to wear stuff of this kind? Am I going to strut around at a dance looking like some *blanco* preppy? You want to buy anything here?"

"I have to pay you for the word processor,

remember?" I said. "Is that what's bothering Creery? He thinks you have the copy of the letter he wrote?"

"He thinks. His stepbrother thinks. But not anymore. I set them straight this morning. *Hola,* look at this suit, Fell! All this good cashmere and it's cut like a tent!"

"Rinaldo, why do they think *you've* got the copy of the letter?"

"They *thought.* They don't think it now. . . . Because he gave me his things, they thought he gave me his confidences. You ask me, nobody got those."

"Did you hear the fight between Creery and Lasher?"

"All the way in the kitchen! Sure! Lasher said he had the letter and Creery said, Were you going through my things? *Sweat* it, Lasher shouts, and he tries to whistle 'Twilight Time.' Then POW! I heard the smack Creery gave him, too. But they were always at it!"

"Who was in The Tower that afternoon?"

"You think I know? I *said* I was in the kitchen. Most of The Sevens had classes, gym . . . You sure you don't want to buy something here, Fell? I'll give you credit."

"I don't want to wear his clothes," I said. "You wear somebody's clothes, you get their luck, too."

"I never heard that," Rinaldo said. I wasn't

surprised, since I'd just made it up. "Only thing I heard is you give someone shoes, they walk away from you."

He laughed and gave my shoulder a punch. "I gave a girl some of those stilt-heel pumps with no toes? She danced out of my life like a tornado leaving a Kansas barn on the ground in little pieces."

I said, "One danced out of my life the same way, and I hadn't given her anything."

"Maybe that's why," said Rinaldo.

We shut the door behind us, and I went back to put Cicero away and get into my boots and coat.

I checked a Cottersville map to see where Jericho Road was and to figure out my bus route to the Deems'.

I noticed that Playwicky was two streets down from where I was going.

chapter | 9

The Deems lived on Jericho Road in a red brick house that Nina Deem told me she wouldn't mind dying and coming back as.

"Nothing around here gets so much attention," she said, "except Meatloaf."

Maybe she told me this by way of apology for making me take off my boots before I followed her down the hall. Meatloaf, a fat red dachshund, licked my face and hands as I began praying my socks weren't going to smell.

I didn't get a really good look at her until I straightened up and let her lead me along polished wooden floors into the living room.

She was blond, like me, her hair falling to her shoulders, straight and shiny-soft. Green eyes to match the scoop-necked heavy green sweatshirt she wore. She had on jeans and some yellow Nike aqua socks, those shoe-sock things you can even wear into the water. Keats would wear them when we'd go clamming at the bay back on Long Island.

Meatloaf was waddling along behind us and Nina was saying, "Christmas? Dad didn't even let the tree in the house this year. It was out there on the sunporch"—waving her hand toward the long doors—"so we could see it, but the needles wouldn't drop to the floor. I mean, is that obsessive-compulsive or is that obsessive-compulsive? Really."

"We didn't have one," I said.

"One what?" She turned around and looked at me, waiting.

"A Christmas tree."

"Oh," she said, as though she'd forgotten she'd brought up the subject.

"We just had a lot of wreaths," I finished, feeling foolish for going on about it.

"We can sit here on the couch," she said, and Meatloaf took her up on the invitation, so I sat down beside him. We were a dachshund sandwich.

It was a large, comfortable room, lots of armchairs, and tables with flowers in vases, built-in bookcases all around, the same floors you could see your face in, but covered with old Oriental rugs. Big, orange-and-brown pillows to go against all the beige-and-white slipcovers. In front of us a long, low table with a marble top, filled with the latest magazines. A single framed photograph of a blond woman in shorts, carrying a tennis racket. Nina, fifteen years from then.

There was a notebook there, too, with a Flair pen stuck in its center.

"Do I call you John?" she asked.

"Everyone calls me Fell."

"As in fell down, fell apart, fell to pieces?"

"Or fell back on or fell on one's feet—it doesn't all have to be negative."

"Fell in love," she said. "Yeah, I guess there are good ways to fall, too . . . or you wouldn't be here."

"I don't follow you." I looked into her eyes for the first time. She wasn't shy about meeting someone's glance. Just the opposite. She was one of those we'll-see-who's-going-to-look-away-first types. So I looked away and added, "I don't get the part about I wouldn't be here if . . ." and I let my voice trail off. I was beginning badly, mainly because I didn't know what we were really talking about.

She let me know. She said, "If I hadn't fallen in love with Eddie, Dad wouldn't have called you to the rescue."

What was I supposed to say? Eddie? Who's Eddie? I don't know any Eddie?

I didn't say anything.

She said, "It's all right. I need tutoring, too, but Dad's an earhole sometimes. Really."

I had to laugh at the earhole bit. You couldn't say Nina Deem wasn't a lady.

"Everything you heard about Eddie Dragon is a lie!" she said.

"Fine. Let's get to work."

"We will, but remember that. He would never sell cocaine! He wouldn't even smoke pot with me when I asked him to!"

"Okay," I said. "I'm not arguing the point."

"Don't! He was the best thing that ever happened to me. He could no more sell dope than I could. He said it was a sure way to wreck your head."

"He was right about that."

She didn't press the point, I'll give her that. She leaned forward and got the notebook, opened it, and took out the Flair. "What I'm trying to do," she said, "what I want your help with, is this biographical essay I'm writing on Browning. I don't understand him."

"*Robert* Browning?"

"Is there a Walter Browning, a William Browning? Really. I thought you were supposed to be this dynamite writer."

"I'm not a dynamite writer," I said, while my greedy and materialistic mind raced ahead of me whispering gold 7, word processor, six dollars an hour, don't mess it up, don't be an earhole. "I mean, I'm a good enough writer, and I certainly know Robert Browning. I just thought I'd never have to read 'Fra Lippo Lippi' again, ever!"

She laughed. "You won't have to. I'm more interested in his life, and his romance with Elizabeth Barrett."

We were off and running. The air was clear, despite the odor that was now compelling Meatloaf to get all the way down on the floor and investigate my argyles.

When she finished reading aloud what she'd written, she said, "Rate it on a scale of one to ten."

"Eight."

"Why only eight?"

"It's very good, but you can't have sentences like 'Against all odds, these young lovers eloped in 1846'."

"Why can't I?" Nina said, waving her arms in the air, and it was then that I saw it.

A tiny insect, a few inches above her left breast, coming out of her bra.

"You can't," I said, "because they weren't young. Elizabeth Barrett Browning was thirty-nine. He was thirty-four."

It wasn't alive.

"They couldn't have been that old, Fell!"

"They were," I said.

It was a tattoo of a pole-thin black what? With a long tail and deep-blue wings. A beetle.

"I don't believe you!" Nina said. Then she saw where my eyes were rooted.

"All right," she said, "we're not going to get anywhere until you take a good look!"

She grabbed the collar of her sweatshirt and yanked it down. "There! See it?"

"A dragonfly?"

"Good, Fell! A lot of slow wits think it's a mosquito or a beetle."

"Is it a permanent tattoo?"

"Yes. I found out where Eddie got his and I got one just like it. A fellow down in Lambertville does them. Like it?"

"It's an attention-getter, all right."

"Only if you're with guys who look down your blouse," she said. "Let's get back to the Brownings."

She wasn't one to waste her father's money.

At five thirty, the grandfather clock in the hall gave a bong.

"Dad said to ask you to stay for dinner," Nina told me. "We eat at six, so we'll have another half hour if you can do it."

I said I could before I realized it was Wednesday, steak night at Sevens. She tossed back her hair and straightened her posture so the dragonfly disappeared. There was a phone in the hall by the clock, she said, if I wanted to call The Tower. "You won't miss out on the steak, either," she said, "because I had our butcher cut us a thick sirloin . . . The only thing is, I haven't cooked a steak for ages! Dad's cut way back on red meat and I hardly ever eat it."

I jumped in. "I'll cook it!"

"Can you?"

I smiled. "How did you know we have steak on Wednesdays?"

"Dad. He was one of you, remember? . . . He wouldn't ask just anyone from The Hill to rescue me from Eddie. It'd have to be one of the holy Sevens, of course. Really."

"We're not that bad," I said.

"I know. You're a good tutor, Fell. Do me a favor?"

"I charge extra for favors."

"Let Dad think I don't know what you're really doing here—he hates it when I outsmart him."

"We're doing the Brownings so far as I'm concerned," I said. "Time out while I marinate the meat?"

chapter | 10

My first date with Delia, I'd made her French toast. I was thinking about that while I reached up in the cupboard for seasonings to go in the marinade.

I was also thinking about the tattoo, and the look in Nina's eyes when she said Eddie's name.

I was beginning to be sorry for myself because I wasn't connected to anyone. It made me feel like a kid again, this half-assed (half-eared?) preppy who'd have to put his name on the blind-date list for The Charles Dance and hope the girl who got off the bus from Miss Tyler's school didn't have bad breath and think we ought to nuke Nicaragua.

Then I saw something that started me going the other way, and I began to grin while I grabbed it.

"Hey, Nina, where'd this come from?"

It was a bottle of Fox's U-Bet chocolate-flavored syrup. Made in Brooklyn!

"That was my mom's. It's about three years old. She used to order it by the case to make egg creams."

"Which I'd kill for! Do you happen to have any seltzer?"

"There's a cylinder in on the bar. Can you

make an egg cream, Fell?"

"Can Michael Jackson dance?"

"I've tried to make them like she used to, but they don't come out right.

"Just leave everything to me. All I need now is that seltzer and some milk."

I finished marinating the steak while Nina got the cylinder, a carton of milk, and two glasses.

"Was that your mom's picture in on the coffee table?"

"Yes, but it's not good of her. She was beautiful. She was like some exotic hothouse flower daddy'd never let breathe fresh air. He's very overprotective, Fell."

"Sometimes you need protecting, Nina."

"*I* need it?"

"Not you in particular. We all need it sometimes."

"I get too much of it."

"I thought you said you'd like to come back as this house so you'd get some attention."

"That's right. This house gets loving care. I get locked inside with a bodyguard."

"How's this for loving care? Watch me," I said.

She stood there while I spooned an inch of Fox's U-Bet into each glass, adding another inch of milk.

"Is that all the milk you use? I use half a glass."

"That's too much. Now, the trick is to tilt the

glass like so, and spray the seltzer off the spoon."

Soon there was a big chocolaty head.

"See?" I said.

We were right on the verge of clicking our glasses together in a toast I proposed to H. Fox & Company, Brooklyn, New York, when Meatloaf began crooning while he ran from the room as fast as his fat little legs could carry him.

"Dad's home," said Nina.

Dad was your average nice-man type, getting gray at the temples, but keeping himself lean, dressed in a brown suit, a guy who probably wore his necktie from the time he got up until he went to bed. He looked like he'd be at home in an office, a bank, a church, at Rotary, on the golf course, or on his way in first class to some Hilton hotel for a meeting.

If he'd started his business from scratch, as Schwartz had said, he was way past scratch now, and his voice let you know it.

"Nina, before we go in to dinner, I want you to change your top."

I automatically looked down at my own seedy sweater, scruffy jeans, and stockinged feet. Nina said, "Don't worry, Fell. Dad just doesn't like scoop necks."

"I don't have to look at it while I'm eating," Mr. Deem said.

"You don't ever have to look at it," said Nina. She finished the rest of her egg cream and left me in the kitchen with David Deem.

I told him I'd cook the steak, and he mouthed a few sentences about his cholesterol level finally getting down, and his triglyceride staying at about 150.

"You don't have to worry about all that yet, John."

I asked him to call me Fell, and if I should get the steak in right away.

He said Nina usually had the salad washed and waiting in the refrigerator, peeked in there, and nodded. "Yes, go ahead. Mrs. Whipple left us lima beans from last night we'll just heat up."

He got busy behind me, after he dropped the beans into a pan he put on low, but he didn't take his coat off or loosen his tie.

Meatloaf sat up and begged, and Mr. Deem tossed him something and told him to go into his bed.

Then Mr. Deem said, "I'm glad we have a few minutes alone, Fell. . . . If you ever hear anything or see anything that tells you Eddie Dragon is in touch with my daughter, I want you to tell me immediately. You know that, I hope."

Already I knew how hard this situation might become. I liked Nina. I couldn't see myself ratting on her. But I couldn't see myself letting her hang out with a pusher, either.

He went right on without waiting for any comment from me. "He's very clever, don't forget that. He can charm the birds down from the trees, too, so you have to be on your guard. . . . Did you see it?" he asked me.

"See what, sir?"

"The tattoo. You couldn't have missed it."

"I saw it." I liked it. I'd never tell him that, but I wouldn't have minded if Delia'd had something like it to remember me.

"He did that to her," said Deem.

"She said she did it on her own initiative."

He laughed unhappily. "Don't believe it! . . . Now she thinks it's zany and original. But imagine, Fell, years from now when Nina will want to attend a dance, or a dress-up dinner party, or go to the club for a swim: There it will be. He's marked her for life."

"Well, I'm sorry about that," I said.

"Then she talked about him, hmmm, Fell?"

"Not much. Just a little when I noticed the tattoo."

"What did she say?"

I sighed. I wasn't going to be good at this at all. "She just said anything I might hear about him is a lie."

"Ha! *He's* the liar! He's a pro, Fell! He had me believing him, and I've met my share of liars!"

The thought of it made him work the wooden fork and spoon so vigorously, a piece of lettuce flew at my sweater.

I picked it off and popped it into my mouth. "Good dressing," I said. It needed salt and a touch more garlic, but it was surprisingly tasty. A great mustardy tang.

"My wife's recipe. . . . Did I see you two drinking egg creams?"

"Yes, sir."

"That's good. Nina says she can't make one right. They remind her of her mother too much, I think."

"She told me something about that."

"She did? She talked with you about her mother?"

"Not a lot, but a little."

"I'm surprised . . . and delighted. Nina has a lot of trouble talking about her. She took her death very hard. We both did, of course. Nina's so much like Barbara in every way, sometimes I walk into a room, see her, and have to stop and catch my breath. She's Barbara to her bones: the daredevil, the romantic—all the qualities I lack. But Nina could use some of my dull, old common sense, too. She needs to come down to earth."

I was timing the steak. "Mr. Deem? Do you two like your steak rare?"

"Yes, rare. . . . I'm glad you came on the scene,

Fell. I know Nina will win you over, and you may feel disloyal if you have to report anything to me, but just remember this."

He stopped and came around so he could face me.

"If you care anything at all about my daughter, you'll be doing her a very great service keeping Dragon out of her life."

Then his eyes got very wide and he said, "Oh, no!"

"What's wrong, sir?" I thought of cholesterol and triglyceride, of high blood pressure and heart attacks.

He went over to the sink and ran the cold water.

"Are you all right, Mr. Deem?" My own father had died very suddenly of a heart attack.

He grabbed a towel and put a corner of it under the water, turned, and handed it to me. "Your sweater," he said. "There's oil or something on it."

Where the lettuce had hit me.

I grinned with relief and dabbed at the stain.

"We should both have on aprons," he said.

Nina was definitely out to get him at dinner. She was pretending to be reviewing for him what we'd gone over during the tutoring, but she talked far more about Elizabeth Barrett than she did about

Browning, harping on her controlling father.

"Ummm hmmmm," Mr. Deem would respond. "Well, Nina, they were very strict with young ladies in those days."

Nina gave me a triumphant look. Then she said, "Dad, when she met Robert Browning she was practically forty! Her father was *still* telling her what to do!"

"She was ill, wasn't she? Didn't you just say she was ill?"

"He made her think she was! He wanted to keep her home with him!"

"It all turned out all right, didn't it?"

"Yes, because she defied him! She eloped!"

"That's a word we don't use much anymore. Elope."

"Oh, we still use it, Dad. Those who have a reason to use it still use it."

She could have been talking about basket weaving in Madagascar for all the reaction she got out of him. He gave the same bland responses no matter how impassioned Nina became. He sneaked bits of steak to Meatloaf, who was stationed at his feet, under the table.

"The steak is done just right, Fell!" Mr. Deem decided to change the subject.

"Thanks, sir."

"Nina, did you show Fell any of your old stories?"

"I'm throwing them all out," she said. "They were from another time."

"You'll regret it if you do. You might want to remember that time someday, how you felt when you were younger."

"I don't want to remember feeling like this little Goody Two Shoes who raised her umbrella and heard the wind *sough* in the trees. I actually wrote that line, Fell. 'She raised her umbrella and heard the wind sough in the trees.'"

"Sough is a perfectly legitimate word," said her father.

"My future characters aren't going to own umbrellas," Nina said, "or slipcovers or coasters. I'm never going to write about careful people again!"

One thing I'd learned about her: If she *was* a jet crash, she had a certain brave facade about her. I couldn't imagine her letting anyone feel sorry for her. I liked that about her, maybe because I was a little that way myself. We jet crashes had our pride.

I had to be back at The Hill by ten. At eight Mr. Deem walked out on the front porch with me, and we stood a moment in the cold night.

Then he grabbed my hand, and I felt his thumb push against my fingers. I had almost forgotten the Sevens handshake. I let my thumb touch his. It was an awkward gesture that made me feel silly, but he seemed satisfied.

"This is going to work out fine," he told me. "I can tell."

He went back inside and left the light on for me as I headed down the walk.

His Lincoln was there in the driveway.

The license plate read DDD-7.

The wind was soughing in the trees.

could have walked back to The Hill or caught the bus at the comer of Main and Hickory.

I thought of Dib and decided in favor of the bus. I wanted to tell him all that Rinaldo had told me.

But a block before Hickory I turned into Playwicky Road.

While I'd been at the Deems', I'd forgotten Lasher and Creery. For all the luxury at Sevens, I'd missed cooking, and eating a meal in a quiet room where there was a female. I'd missed a living room and a four-legged creature padding around.

I remembered Jazzy dressed up as a question mark in a kindergarten play last Christmas. She'd had to recite some lines from Kipling:

> I keep six honest serving men
> (They taught me all I knew),
> Their names are What and Why and When
> And How and Where and Who.

Temporarily, anyway, I'd parked the six serving men at the curb, and reveled in the idea of being in a real home again.

Playwicky Arms was a row of two-story houses, each with its own twin entrances onto the street. The houses on the winding street were alternately gray and white, with brass lanterns in front and cobblestone sidewalks meeting the city's paved ones.

I wasn't looking for anything in particular, "just looking," as my mother was fond of saying in department stores.

Number 6 was white and in the middle.

Both the top and bottom floors were lighted. I figured Lauren must have gone from Sevens House to here, rather than catch the bus back to Miss Tyler's. Midwinter, during the week, there wasn't regular service to Princeton.

I was only slightly curious about this off-campus pad of Lasher's. It figured that he'd had one, and that only card players knew about it. He wasn't the first fellow from The Sevens to have one, probably just the first one to chance reprimand for poker or blackjack instead of girls.

What interested me more was the idea of surprising Lauren. I was trying to imagine that unflappable face reacting with surprise. It was a little like trying to picture the Mona Lisa throwing her head back to have a good belly laugh.

I enjoyed the idea of telling Dib I'd checked out Playwicky, too. He liked the image of Fell, Boy Detective, far more than he appreciated Fell, member of Sevens. It would go a long way in helping him to stop suspecting I was part of some Sevens cover-up.

I walked up and down the street while I invented these excuses for my own chronic curiosity, and while I practiced what I'd say to Lauren.

Lauren, I can't stay but I finished assembling the memorial book, so can you pick it up tomorrow? I had my own selfish reasons, too. Sevens drew the line at free postage and delivery of packages. We had to get them to the post office ourselves, a chore I could easily postpone for weeks.

There were two bells at number 6, the top one with the name Lewis under it, the bottom one unmarked.

I pushed the bottom one, heard it ring, and waited.

My father used to say he could always feel it when he was being watched. It was a sixth sense. It had saved his life once when all he could see on a street where he was doing surveillance was an empty florist's station wagon with a roof rack carrying a coffin-sized cardboard box, the sort used for wholesale flower deliveries. There was a man with a gun inside the box, aiming at him through a hole. Dad ducked just in time, getting away in a crouch.

I could feel eyes on me from inside. I could see the curtains move in the downstairs front window. I knew there was no gun aimed at me, but some of the same feelings people who point guns have were probably overwhelming Lauren then. She'd say how did you find out about this place, Fell? I'd tell her I was in the neighborhood and number 6 just looked like her. Something about it.

I smiled at the thought and jabbed the bell again.

This time all the lights on the bottom floor went off. So did the one inside the brass lantern.

Plain enough. I walked away.

I went up the street in the opposite direction from where I'd entered it, and stood a moment beside a large oak tree, seeing if the lights would go on again.

I wondered if Lauren had seen that it was me, or if she feared that it was someone who could cause trouble. Maybe over at Miss Tyler's the idea of her crashing in her brother's off-campus card den wouldn't sit so well. It probably wasn't the first time either. A girl like Lauren couldn't have been interested in cards. Boys, more likely . . . Rinaldo'd said to ask Kidder about number 6 Playwicky. What if Kidder, with his Colgate smile, his Polo wardrobe, and his Key West yacht, appealed to Lauren?

My thoughts were chasing in circles while I stood hugging myself to keep warm. I was ready to admit that my imagination was overtaking reality again. Kidder'd played poker there; whatever Lauren had been up to, I'd probably never know.

Staying was pointless, I decided. That was the second the lantern light went on again.

Just for a moment, a man stepped out and looked around.

I'd seen him before.

I'd never seen him barefoot, in an orange kimono, but I'd seen the thick white hair and the white mustache.

Only someone from Miami wouldn't think to pack slippers.

I n Sevens house my mailbox was full. There was a large package from Mom, a letter from Keats, three messages from Dib. *Where are YOU?* was one. Then, *Where ARE you?* Finally, *WHERE are you?*

Mom never sent me stuff unless it was a special occasion. She said that since I'd made Sevens, sending me anything was like carrying coals to Newcastle.

I opened the package on the spot. Little plastic peanuts spilled from the box to the mailroom floor.

There were some bottles of Soho lemon spritzer, a jar of Sarabeth Rosy Cheek Preserves, and a box of David's Cookies. Things I loved and couldn't buy in Cottersville.

There were two white envelopes inside, too.

I opened one and gulped. It was a valentine. It was the thirteenth of February. I'd forgotten Valentine's Day.

I knew the second envelope contained Jazzy's valentine.

I checked my Timex. Nine thirty. If I hurried, I could get over to Deem Library and make some homemade cards before mail pick-up at ten o'clock. At least they'd be postmarked the fourteenth.

Dib could wait a day for my news.

I shoved the package back into my box and headed for The Tower. Under the campus lights along the path, I read what Keats had written across a red heart.

Thanks for your postcard. Why would you read "Fra Lippo Lippi" when you could read Browning's "Confessions"? How about this line, Fell?
"How sad and bad and mad it was—
But then, how it was sweet."
Does that remind you of us? Does anything?
xxxxx.

She was a freshman at Sweet Briar, down in Virginia, where February nights were never as cold and windy as the one I was hurrying through.

I'd call her with Valentine wishes. I couldn't do that with Mom and Jazzy. They liked getting theirs in the mail. Even late was better than none at all.

For a while I had the library to myself. I grabbed some cream-colored Sevens stationery and sat down at a table.

I folded one sheet and drew a heart across the front.

BE MY VALENTINE.

Inside I didn't get any more original.

Two hearts across the second one. Jazzy's name in one; mine in the other.

Only girlfriends inspired me, not my family. For Delia I'd have drawn the Taj Mahal, and written a verse in perfect iambic pentameter promising it to her.

The clock was striking ten when Rinaldo appeared. He wasn't in his usual uniform. I could see why Lasher's clothes hadn't thrilled him. He had on very tight black pegged pants, a black leather vest, a black-and-white silk shirt, and a black leather belt with a silver buckle. Black suede ankle boots . . . Lasher's style had alternated between classic preppy and baggy tramp.

"Closing time, Fell." Rinaldo put down the mail sack he was carrying, unlocked the CORRESPONDENCE box, and reached in for the letters there.

"Can you wait one second? I forgot Valentine's Day."

"Wait how long?"

"One second."

"One second's up." He walked toward me while I scratched the address across an envelope.

"You smell like a magazine, Rinaldo."

"I've got on Giorgio V.I.P. Special Reserve," he said. "You know what the ads say: Maybe one man in a thousand will wear it." He grinned. "That's me."

"Is it part of your inheritance?"

"No. Lasher—what did he wear? Something like Royal Copenhagen. This is sweeter! This gets the girls like honey draws bees. . . . I've got a date, Fell—crank it up."

"I'm done," I said. I handed the envelope to him. "Will it be postmarked the fourteenth?"

He nodded. "I'm dropping it off down there now."

I got up and walked along with him. The Tower clock was hammering out ten. In half an hour the dorm doors would be locked. It wasn't worth trying to get to Dib.

"I was on Playwicky Road tonight," I said, "and I saw something odd."

"Sniffing around?"

"I thought Lauren might be there. Instead, I saw Creery's stepbrother come out of number 6."

Rinaldo snapped off the lights in the library. "I heard he's staying awhile."

"In Lasher's apartment?"

"That I didn't hear."

"You don't think it's odd?"

"Others used that place, Fell. It was for card playing, so why would Lasher's sister be there? . . . You are naive sometimes, you know." He picked up a black leather coat with a yellow quilted lining that was lying on the table outside the door. "Kidder went there. Other Sevens. You think it was a secret? Even you'd heard of the place."

Not until Rinaldo'd told me himself, but I skipped by that saying, "So Sevens arranged it?"

"A Sevens did, probably. Why not? This stepbrother of Creery's needs a place for a few weeks. Why wouldn't it be offered to him? That's what your Sevens is all about, isn't it? Something for nothing."

He snapped the hall lights off as we walked toward the front of The Tower. "Everything isn't suspicious, Fell, the way you think. You've got something on the brain, Fell." He flicked his fingers toward my head and laughed. Then he patted his heart with the same hand. "You need something here to occupy you. You should see what I'm going to occupy in about half an hour."

We went through the front door. Rinaldo had the mail sack over his shoulder. "Now if that little Porsche of Lasher's had been delivered early, maybe Rinaldo'd be heading off for the evening in style."

I gave him a smile. "I wouldn't worry."

"Yes, you would, Fell. Because you worry about everything, I'm learning. What you need is to have a girl."

"This is true," I said.

He feigned a punch at my chin. "You want me to fix you up with a townie?"

"Later," I said.

We waved and took off in opposite directions.

Then I called to him. "Wait, Rinaldo!"

He stopped.

I walked toward him. "Why is Creery's step-brother staying for a few weeks?"

"You don't quit, Fell, do you?" He switched the mailbag to the other shoulder. "He's staying until all this calms down."

"Until all *what* calms down?" I asked him.

"Maybe until *you* calm down, *compadre* . . . I don't know why he's staying. I just know Creery's off the Sevens dinner list until the stepbrother leaves. Two weeks or so, he said."

Rinaldo turned to go. *"Hasta la vista,* Fell!"

I could almost hear Lasher's voice. *Hasta la vista, Flaco!*

"Buena suerte, Rinaldo!"

And the scream from just above us, I could hear. Still.

That night, as I was undressing, I found Jazzy's unopened valentine in my shirt pocket.

There was a picture of a white dog holding a red heart in its paws.

Inside it said, DOGGONE I LOVE YOU!

Jazzy'd printed something at the bottom in her usual style: large, crooked letters.

Johnny? Why is 6 afraid of 7?

There was an arrow pointing to the back of the card.

Turning it over, I thought of number 6 Playwicky Arms, and of Mark Twain's bare feet on the cold stone.

Because, Jazzy had continued, 7 8 9.

chapter | 13

One of the perks that went with keeping my eye on Nina Deem was getting to drive the second car. That's what both Nina and her father called the BMW, as if it had never belonged to anyone in particular, though I knew it'd been her mother's.

Deem had checked out my New York driver's license—he was a careful man. He'd advised me to get a Pennsylvania one, and to ask Dr. Skinner's permission. All done by the third week in February, when Nina talked me into taking her to New Hope for a poetry reading.

The roads were clear, and the sun was out, and even though "Fra Lippo Lippi" had spoiled poetry for me forever, I liked to be behind the wheel.

I needed to get away from The Hill, too.

Late February, at Gardner, you crammed for tests, wrote papers on every subject from the design of the Parthenon to Romanticism's eighteenth-century beginnings, and took your S.A.T.'s over if you were trying to raise your score. I was trying to get mine out of the 500's.

I was also spending too much time working on The Charles Dance for The Sevens.

In between, Dib and I met when we could. And when we did, we fought.

He'd become convinced there was no way we'd ever figure out the true story of Lasher's death, that Sevens had too much power . . . He'd also teamed up with a scruffy group of townies, led by John Horner, a day student known as Little Jack. They drove around Cottersville in an old Mustang, no muffler, black, furry dice hanging from the mirror, six-packs iced in the backseat . . . .

"You've got your gang, I've got mine," he told me.

Neither of us had done anything about learning how to work the Smith-Corona PWP.

Creery's stepbrother was still with us, and Dib bought Rinaldo's explanation that it had been arranged through Sevens for him to stay in Lasher's apartment. He bought it, or he settled for it. He wasn't interested any longer in pursuing it, he said; he wasn't going to wait around in the dorm until I found time to discuss it with him.

The only change in Creery I noticed was his absence most nights at dinner. He ate with Lowell Hunter—that was Mark Twain's last name, Hunter.

"Fell?" Nina said. "Thanks for this. I need to be around creative people." She liked to wear gear. She had on an old camouflage jacket several sizes too large for her, a sailor's blue knit cap pulled down around her long blond hair, and old corduroys that had been pegged so the cuffs slid into her lace-up leather boots.

"What's New Hope like? I hear it's a tourist trap."

Nina said, "Some people'd say it's a little artsy-fartsy, but in winter it's just another small town." She giggled. "With a lot of artsy-fartsy antique shops and restaurants. It's pretty, though."

"It's a reward for the A+ you got on your Browning paper."

"Thanks to you. You really improved it, Fell."

"I like your new stories"—most of them were fantasies about future worlds—"but I'd like to read your old ones, too."

She shook her head. "You never will. I burned them. They aren't me now. I'm not the same since Mom's death."

"You might want to remember what you were like, though."

"I *am* working on a story about my mother and father. Their last fight. You know what it was over? A croquet game."

"One was winning and one wasn't?"

"They weren't even playing," said Nina. "My father had this unpainted sample from DOT, our mail-order division. He was supposed to approve it. It was in his study when my mother found it. She was like a kid sometimes. She loved games! She wanted to put it out on the lawn immediately.

Dad said she couldn't do it. He actually wrestled it away from her. It was weird, Fell: these two grown people tugging at a croquet set. He was shouting at her for unpacking it, and she was laughing at first. My aunt Peggy was visiting, and Mom was teasing him: Don't be a party pooper, Dave! Wait until you see my sister swing a croquet mallet! . . . But Dad was dead serious. No way were they going to set up that game! . . . I figured out why he didn't want her to set it up."

"Why?"

"It'd ruin the lawn. You know how he is. He didn't want the lawn spoiled . . . It was a terrible fight, too. They'd never fought physically before. They used to make these conversational digs at each other, but this time he actually slapped her. Then she kicked him. Hard. My aunt Peggy tried to break it up, and she almost got hit, too . . . It's awful when parents fight, isn't it? I hated it!"

"My parents usually fought about my father's hours. He'd come through the door after a night's work, and Mom would say, 'Who are you? What are you doing in this house?'"

Nina said, "And right after the fight over the croquet set, she broke her neck doing a swan dive. Hit the shallow end of our pool because she'd overreached. If it wasn't so sad, I'd say it was how she'd have wanted to go. Doing something beautiful and wild."

"I'm sorry, Nina."

"Me too. . . . My aunt never forgave him. She thinks my mother was in shock from his slapping her . . . and over what? The fact my mother wanted to play a game on the lawn."

"It must be rough on him, too. Still."

"I know. I think of that a lot, because he truly did love her. She was such a passionate woman. He was always trying to curb her, not maliciously. He's not mean. But he just wants to be in control. . . . She loved romantic stories. She was always talking about famous lovers, reading us love poems at the dinner table. I think she was rubbing it in."

"What would he do?"

"Oh, Dad tolerated it. I think that was her way of getting back at him. He'd forget birthdays, anniversaries, and when he did remember them, he'd come home with something like a new microwave oven . . . Emotion embarrasses him. She'd read us Keats, Shelley, some Frenchwoman named Duras . . . My shrink says Vell, dot is a form of hostile displacement ven you do dot." She looked across at me and laughed, but I didn't. I suddenly remembered the lady in the long black mink coat at Lasher's funeral.

"What's your shrink's name?"

"Inge Lasher. You knew her son, didn't you? He was a Sevens before he took a dive off The Tower. Or am I not supposed to mention that?"

"I didn't know you knew about it."

"Dad didn't tell me. It wasn't in the newspaper, either. They always hush up bad stuff that happens on The Hill."

"Then how did you find out?"

"She told me. She said it vas not a disgrace so she vould not hide it. According to her, he secreted less growth hormone. Only she pronounces it groat hormone. Gawd, Fell!"

"What?"

"If your own shrink's son does himself in, how are you supposed to be helped by her?"

"You've probably got enough groat hormone."

"She hated having to tell me. She told all her patients. Clients, she calls us. She told everyone. It must have killed her! She tries to keep her personal life so secret. They all do. You're not supposed to focus on them. But I'd see her daughter sometimes. Right after Mom died, her daughter was living in their town house. During my session I'd see her out the window coming up the walk with her schoolbooks."

"Lauren," I said.

"Is that her name? I didn't even know her son was on The Hill until he died. What's Lauren like?"

"Sort of sophisticated."

"More than me?"

"You're not the same type."

"How is she different. Is she prettier?"

"No. You can't compare you two."

"Why not?"

"Why do you care?" I said.

"She's my shrink's daughter, Fell. You've never been shrunk, have you?"

"No."

"Well, we basket cases care about things like that."

"You should concentrate on yourself."

"I bet you're sorry you said that. That's all I do." Nina laughed. "I know Lauren's got inky-black hair. I remember that."

"And she wears Obsession, like an old girl-friend of mine." Sometimes I'd say things like that thinking Nina'd ask me questions about myself, but she didn't. She'd go right past the remark.

She said, "I like White Shoulders better. Would you date her, Fell?"

"She's too opaque for me."

"Opaque. Oh, I like that word." I'd just tossed out whatever'd come into my head, but Nina looked like I'd told her the combination for a safe full of gold. "Then she's exactly like her mother! I think Dr. Inge is the most mysterious person I've ever known! . . . And she's sophisticated, too. European. On the elegant side. But Fell, she's married to this little potbellied shrimp with a bald head. *You* should see *him*! He's nothing!"

"I have seen them. They were both at the memorial service."

"Of course! Then you know! Was it a sad memorial service?"

"There're not a lot of happy ones. But it was short." I decided not to mention that her shrink had addressed the gathering. It would save me having to go into all that. "No one from Sevens spoke—that was a little strange. Rinaldo, one of our houseboys, read a poem he'd written."

"I know Rinaldo! Rinaldo Velez?"

"Yes."

"He was a senior when I was a sophomore. I didn't know he wrote. I thought he only worried about things like not carrying stuff in his back pocket so he wouldn't ruin his bun line."

"I never noticed his bun line."

"When he dances? He looks just like Patrick Swayze in that old movie *Dirty Dancing!* Someday I'll show you his write-up in my yearbook."

"I'd like to see it."

She hurried back to her own priorities. "Well? Can you imagine those two shrinks married to one another?"

"Love is mysterious, Nina."

"I don't think marriage has anything to do with love, Fell. I think people settle."

"My parents were in love."

She did her usual bypass on the subject of me. "I'll never settle!" she said. "I'll never do what my mother did! I'll never let the man I marry control me. In fact, Fell, I may never *get* married! That story I wrote about a future world where marriage is for inferiors with low I.Q.'s? I believe that! You don't have to get married to have children! Who says so? The law? Who cares about the law? You make your own laws, I believe!"

"Fine!" I said. "Now can we please talk about something I'm interested in?"

She looked surprised. "Okay. . . . Like what?"

"Like Spinoza's determinism," I said. "Or Descartes' dualism."

She gave my arm a hard punch. "Oh, Fell! You're good for me!"

I hoped so. There were times when we'd be talking about the future, about writing and Kenyon College over someplace like the University of Missouri's journalism school, and suddenly Nina would be out to lunch. Her eyes wouldn't move and her face lost its expression. I'd have to snap my fingers and say, "Hey, come back."

But she was behaving less and less that way, and I liked to agree with her father, who'd always get me aside when he could do it tactfully and tell me I was helping her; he could see she was improving, forgetting Eddie Dragon.

Once she even said that herself, actually implying that I was better for her than Eddie. "It's good to get to know someone, isn't it, Fell?" She'd spoken up one afternoon. "I never really got to know a male except Dad, not really. I was always too nervous and self-conscious. God! After Eddie and I were together, I'd go over and over what we said, how I looked, play by play, like my whole life depended on some dumb little interlude with him. But this is just us: easy, relaxed. It's good like this. It's better."

She'd even stopped saying "really" in every sentence.

We rode in silence for a while, following the Delaware River, which had chunks of ice floating in it, and Nina leaned over and snapped on the radio. She pushed the button to find music that suited her. She was sort of jumping around in the seat, taking her cap off to shake her hair free, putting it back on. She seemed to be acting out everything I was feeling: It was a great day, good to be away from Cottersville, pretty out there with the sun inching over to sink down in the sky, neat that the radio was playing old Elvis stuff.

When we got to the coffee shop where the Friday-afternoon poetry readings were held, there was a sign on the door:

"Didn't you *call*, Nina?"

"Would we be here if I had? Don't get mad at me. How do you think *I* feel?"

"Sorry," I said. "What'll we do now? Is anything open?"

We stood there hugging ourselves and stamping our feet in the cold, and Nina said unless I wanted to look at sleigh beds or weather vanes circa 1800, we were out of luck.

"I'm not hungry, either," she added.

"I guess we'll just drive back. No movies?"

"No movies." She was heading toward the car. "It's too cold to walk around."

"Didn't you know they closed in winter?"

"Fell, quit nagging me. Let's try to look at the doughnut and not at the hole."

I opened the car door for her and said I wouldn't mind looking at a doughnut, either—I hadn't eaten since lunch.

When I got back behind the wheel, she said to drive up near Point Pleasant. She thought there was a hamburger place that way.

She directed me while I tried to get myself back in a good mood. I knew the reason I was sounding cranky was that I was disappointed. I rated poetry readings about the same as guided tours through flower gardens, but at least it would have been special to Nina, something she'd remember us doing together . . . It'd been a long time since I'd cared about pleasing a girl. I wasn't sure how much of it had to do with my wanting her to get her bearings again, or how much it had to do with me being ready to crank up my own broken motor. Something was in the wind . . . and it was a relief from thoughts of a body falling, a voice shrieking, and unanswered questions that had caused a rift between Dib and me.

We listened to the radio for a while: golden oldies—The Beatles and Steppenwolf, Jimi Hendrix and Buffalo Springfield.

Finally she glanced my way and said she had an idea.

"What?"

"You're still mad, aren't you, Fell?"

"I'm over that. I wasn't really mad. . . . What's your idea?"

"I want to see something."

"*What?*"

"Something up ahead here."

"Food, I hope."

"Not food. . . . He's got a shop somewhere right near here," she said. "His sister runs it. He won't be there, so don't worry."

She waited for it to sink in.

It hit my stomach first, then traveled around in my gut for a while and settled in my windpipe.

When my voice returned, it said, "You planned this all along, didn't you, Nina?"

"And don't say my name in there," she said. "I promised him I'd never come here." She touched my leg with her hand. "Oh, Fell, this won't hurt anything. I'm just curious. Aren't you ever curious?"

I was staring straight ahead, mad as hell, when I saw it come into view.

A gigantic black dragon with gold wings and green eyes, breathing out fake fire.

Dragonland was an old, gray, cold, musty-smelling barn at the bottom of a hill. It was one of those hodgepodge places that sold everything from Pennsylvania Dutch hex signs to leather coats with fringe on the sleeves. They specialized in twenty-four-hour film service, "Award-Winning Wedding and Graduation Photography," "Furniture: Bought and Sold," and rental tools.

The giant dragon perched on the roof wasn't the only one. Dragons were everywhere, in every color, made of rubber, iron, tin, wood, and papier-mâché. There were dragonflies, too. If Eddie Dragon didn't run the place himself, his spirit certainly dominated the decor.

At one end of the barn there was a mural of a waterfall, an old mill, and a willow tree, an iron bench in front of it. A sign to the left saying:

DRESS UP IN OLD CLOTHES
TAKE HOME A SOUVENIR.

I'd seen the scenery before, in the photograph of Eddie Dragon that Schwartz had given me.

To the right there was a rack with assorted clothes, feather boas and hats with veils, canes, top hats, derbies, old furs, and mustaches and wigs.

There was a woman behind the counter with the kind of great, warm smile that could make you forget anything, including the fact you shouldn't have stopped the car to go inside that place with Nina.

She didn't look like someone who belonged in a Pennsylvania winter. I could see her out under the sun in some Kansas field with a piece of straw stuck playfully between her teeth and the wind blowing back her thick, curly, brown hair. She had magnificent white teeth; big everything: hands, feet, bosoms, the gypsy type loaded with beads and bracelets jangling on her wrists. She had on a long, red dress with a full skirt and some kind of Mexican-looking red-and-white shawl over her shoulders. You'd imagine her stirring pots of fabulous-tasting stews, or tending a garden, or mending something. She might as well have had one of those cartoon balloons over her head with "I'll take care of you" inside.

It was hard for me to guess women's ages. All the while I was with Delia, I thought she was maybe nineteen—she'd never tell me. She was really twenty-five. This woman looked older. I figured she was Dragon's big sister.

"You lost?" she said. "You look lost." She was laughing, picking up a Siamese cat who'd run to her with his ruff up the moment the bell jingled to announce our arrival.

I'd seen the cat before, too. I let Nina do the talking.

"We were really looking for someplace to get a hamburger."

"Not around here, I'm afraid. Try New Hope down the road. Or Doylestown up the road."

"You have a lot of interesting things."

"We try. . . . Are you visiting?"

"We came from New Jersey," Nina said. She wasn't one to worry that there was a Pennsylvania license plate on the BMW.

The cat was hanging on to the woman like we were going to bag it and toss it in the river. She got its claws out of her shawl and put it down on the floor. "Go find your mousie," she said to it, as though the thing would answer Okay! Good idea! and the dark-brown tail disappeared into a room behind her. No door, just a curtain of beads.

"Would you like me to show you anything?"

"I just *love* this place!" Nina sounded naive and girlish, instead of dark-hearted and possessed.

The woman gave us that great big white smile again and said, "I'm Ann."

Nina jumped right in. "I'm Lauren," she said, "and that's John Fell."

"Lauren, John," Ann said. "If you want to know the price of anything, there's a tag on the bottom."

"Fell, let's have our picture taken!" Nina said.

Ann said, "Just pick out your costumes. Anything over on the rack."

Nina headed that way, babbling about how we'd have a souvenir of the day, and soon she'd found herself a little green hat with an orange feather on it, a black velvet cape, and a white silk parasol.

"Ready!" she said.

I walked over, put on the top hat and a long black coat with a fur collar, grabbed a black cane to complete the costume.

Ann was standing there with her hand on her hip, laughing and *oh*ing and *ah*ing. As soon as we moved toward the iron bench in front of the mural with the mill, and the waterfall and the willow tree, she picked up a camera.

"I'm doing all the hard work now," she said, "while the boss is on assignment."

"Who's the dragon collector?" Nina asked.

"My husband. Eddie," Ann said. "That's our last name. Dragon."

I gave Nina a long, long look she refused to return, so I figured she was handling it Nina style: no show of the punch that must have just landed hard to her insides.

She was busy acting as though this was one of the best times she'd ever had, twirling her parasol, and affecting a haughty expression. "Let's try and look très, très superior," she said to me, something I would have expected from Lauren Lasher, never Nina.

I tried my best: tilting my top hat over my eye, resting my weight on the cane, my arm around Nina.

"That's jaunty, not superior," said Nina.

Ann just kept laughing.

Nina fixed the top hat so it sat squarely on my head, and she told me to stare straight ahead and hook the cane over my free arm.

"Good, Lauren!" Ann said. "That's fun!"

"Now don't smile and don't put your arm around me. I'll hook mine in yours," Nina directed me.

"Perfect!" Ann said. "It'll be ready in no time."

The cross-eyed Siamese was watching us behind the beads in the doorway.

Nina walked around looking at things I didn't want to look at, like rugs made out of animal skin and carvings made from elephant tusks.

I said, "You've really got a lot of variety."

"My husband's a pack rat. I never know what he'll walk in with, but it's always different." She laughed again. She was a hard laugher, tossing back her head, showing her love of life . . . and of Eddie Dragon, too, I thought.

I asked her what we owed her, and as soon as she'd given me five dollars change from a twenty, the picture was ready. It came in a small metal frame, with REMEMBER POINT PLEASANT written in gold at the top.

It wasn't good of me. I looked the way I'd begun to feel: like someone getting used to a bad smell.

Nina was a better actress. She came off looking haughty, superficial, insane.

"This has been fun!" Nina said, but the air was seeping out of the balloon: I could see it in her tired little smile, the kind that began to hurt the corners of your mouth because of all the effort that was going into it.

While Ann walked us to the door, she said, "Good-bye, Lauren, John. Thanks for stopping by. It gets lonely here this time of year."

chapter 15

We were driving along the river's edge. I put the fog lights on.

"He told me not to go there," she said softly.

"I can see why."

"Fell? I never, *ever* want to see him again!"

It was easy to ignore that one.

I snapped, "What's this crap about him being on assignment? She made him sound like a foreign correspondent or something."

"He takes pictures. Weddings and stuff."

"How come you knew he wouldn't be there today?" She didn't answer for a minute. Then she said, "I called there yesterday. I pretended I wanted him to take some baby pictures, and she said he was on assignment until next Monday."

"You've been calling him all along, then?"

"No. I never dared call him there. I wouldn't have known about that place, except when he got framed the address was in the newspaper."

"When he got framed. Sure."

"He got framed, Fell."

"And his *sister* runs the place. Sure."

"How do you think *I* feel, Fell? Believe me, I am *fin*ished with Edward Gilbert Dragon!"

"*Believe* you," I laughed.

"Don't you have any feelings for me?"

"Yeah. I have the feeling you've just forced me to become an informer."

"You're not going to tell Dad?"

"I'm not? Why aren't I? Dad's paying me."

"I didn't try to *see* Eddie, Fell. I didn't even want to see him. I just wanted to see Dragonland . . . He'd never take me there."

"I'm not surprised."

"Fell, *please* don't tell Dad! I can promise you I'll never have anything to do with Eddie Dragon again!" She turned to face me, pulling her knees up under her, slinging an arm across the seat. "Listen to me, Fell! I feel *horrible!* She's so . . . earnest."

"She's a lot more than earnest!"

"Do you think she's pretty?"

"Yes, I think she's pretty, and if the next question is do I think she's prettier than you, yes! And smarter, too!"

She touched my shoulder with her hand. "Oh, Fell, don't be mad. I'm trying to handle this thing, and I can't deal with it when you're mad at me."

"Tough!" I said. "Damn! Everything was going so well, I thought, and all the while you've got these snakes in your head!"

"That's a good name for them, snakes. Dr. Inge calls them compulsions, but they're snakes all right. They *were*, anyway."

She touched the bare skin at my neck with her

finger. "Fell? Please? I'm sorry."

"And don't try stuff like that!" I said.

"I'm just touching you, friend to friend."

"Don't!" I said. I leaned over and pushed on the radio. "I don't want to talk, okay?"

When we got to Cottersville, the black Lincoln was in the drive. The porch light was on. The downstairs lights, and a light where David Deem had his study.

I locked the BMW and handed the key to Nina. She gave me the souvenir photograph. "I don't want this thing—do you?"

I stuffed it inside my jacket.

We were standing in the driveway. Meatloaf was barking. She pulled off her stocking cap and shook her hair loose so the moon caught its shine.

"It was really good that we went there, Fell. Now I know the truth . . . Can't you at least think about not telling Dad? Sleep on it or something? I'm in little pieces right now."

"I'm not going to tell him tonight," I said. "I'm too hungry.'"

"You're always hungry." She was starting to cry.

"Nina," I began, not knowing where it would end, not having to worry because the front door opened and her father stepped out on the porch. "Come in, Fell! Mrs. Whipple made you both corned beef sandwiches."

"Please don't tell him, Fell," Nina said.

I said I couldn't stay, I'd take my sandwich with me, and David Deem picked up Meatloaf and told me what he had to say wouldn't take long.

"You go into the kitchen and wrap Fell's sandwich, honey," he told Nina. "Fell? Come in and sit down for a minute."

Then he said, "Do those boots come off?"

I was in my smelly stockinged feet again, my jacket over my lap, sitting forward on the couch.

"You've never told me how you like being a Sevens," said Mr. Deem, straightening his tie, leaning back in an armchair he was sharing with Meatloaf.

"Who wouldn't like it?" I said.

"Take me. I was this raw-eared kid from Pennsylvania Dutch country, father a farmer. I went to The Hill on a scholarship. I'd always made my own bed, didn't know what a soup spoon was, never, never had anyone wait on me . . . and suddenly . . ." He spread his arms out.

"That was all changed by mere chance," I said.

He laughed hard at that. "Yes . . . yes . . . it changed my life, Fell. It gave me my first taste of being somebody."

I let him talk. I didn't think it was the right

time to tell him "somebody's" daughter was still sneaking around after a pusher who suddenly had a wife in the bargain.

"I feel badly about what happened at The Tower." He lowered his voice to a whisper. "The suicide. I haven't told Nina. It just so happens that was her psychiatrist's son."

"Nina knows, Mr. Deem. Dr. Lasher told her."

He thought that one over. He said, "Nina's so interior. She calls *me* secretive because I lock my study. But look at her. You think she'd have told me she knew."

I resisted saying No, I wouldn't think that. I would think Nina wouldn't tell anything . . . and here's why, Mr. Deem.

"Her doctor overdoes the confidentiality rule, if you ask me. Here I've been so careful about keeping all that business to myself. Is Nina taking it all right?"

"Your daughter seems to handle things," I said.

"Yes. That's her mother's independent streak . . . Well, then, this clears the way for what I'm about to suggest. I'd like Nina to meet some nice young men now that the dragon's been slain." A pleased little haw-haw for punctuation.

I bit my lip. I'd hear him out first. I was thinking of the corned beef sandwich, too. I was hoping Mrs. Whipple knew enough to smear the bread with lots of Dijon mustard.

"The best young men are on The Hill, no doubt of that. And from what I see of you, Fell, Sevens is still instilling in its members the idea that you live up to privilege, and become more because of it."

How was I going to tell him I'd become less the second I saw Dragonland? I'd become Silly Putty in Nina's hands.

"One of the most amusing and memorable traditions of Sevens, of course, is The Charles Dance. What fun I had at those things!" He was stretching his legs out, letting Meatloaf wiggle onto his lap. "Do you know that at the first Charles Dance there were twelve boys dressed the same as me? Never go as Charlie Chaplin, Fell. You'll see yourself all over the place!"

"I was thinking of going as Damon Charles."

"Uh-oh, the founder himself, hmmm? That takes nerve. . . . I like that, Fell. I wonder if anyone's ever done that?"

"In his pictures he has a big handlebar mustache and a monocle . . . so it'll be easy."

Nina was back in the room, arms folded across her chest, an uncertain look in her eyes, directed at me.

"Mustard, Fell?" she said.

"Yes. Dijon?"

"Dijon. It's already on both sandwiches. I'd have had to make you another if you didn't like it . . . Well?" She shrugged. "Is this a private conversation?" She couldn't seem to look at her father.

"Not really, Nina, honey," he answered her, and his tone of voice told her I hadn't squealed . . . yet.

Then he said, "I checked with Sevens today and learned that Fell's signed up for a blind date for The Charles Dance."

He glanced across at me. "You don't have to take a *blind* date, Fell, if you'd prefer to take Nina. I'm ready for her to see how Sevens do things."

"Oh, Dad! Can I go?"

"Well, Fell?" said Mr. Deem.

Both of them were looking at me expectantly.

"Sure," I said. What was I supposed to say? "Would you go with me, Nina?"

"I'd like that, Fell."

"It'll be her very first time on The Hill," said Mr. Deem. "I wanted it to be for something Sevens was doing. This is perfect."

"Perfect!" Nina agreed. "Oh, I hope and pray nothing comes up to spoil this!"

Her father chuckled. "Such histrionics, Nina! You *hope* and pray? Nothing's going to spoil this. What could spoil it?"

Then he said, "I know you're hurrying, Fell,

and Nina's occupied a lot of your time today, so take the BMW. It's cold, too."

"I can hike it," I told him.

"Anyone can hike it, but what's being a Sevens all about? . . . Take advantage of your advantages, Fell. You can bring the car back tomorrow afternoon." Then, meticulous as always, he added, "I told you before, didn't I, that there's a spare key in the back ashtray?"

Nina walked me to the door. "I feel like a spare female. You don't have to take me to the dance if you don't want to," she said. "I know Dad sprang that on you in a way you almost couldn't refuse."

"He sprang it on you, too," I said. I was getting into my boots and thinking about buying myself some Odor-Eaters for the insides, if I kept visiting the Deems.

"He didn't spring it on me, exactly. I've been begging him to ask you to invite me."

I was glad, too glad, the kind of glad that leaps up the way Wordsworth's heart did when he beheld a rainbow in the sky.

"If today hadn't happened," I started to say, and she didn't let me finish. She put two fingers against my lips. "Today was the tag end of something. The Fates arranged for today to happen."

"You arranged for today to happen, Nina."

"It was like the final period at the end of the

sentence 'I don't care about him anymore.'"

"Just say the period. Never mind the final period."

"My tutor." She smiled at me, coming closer.

I moved back a step, remembering the dragonfly with the blue wings crawling out of her bra.

I said, "Why do I still have the feeling I can't trust you?"

"I'll make that go away. You'll see."

She was looking all over my face, and I could feel something shivering down my arms.

Her hands reached up, starting to rest on my shoulders, but I shrugged them away, trying to act the way someone would when he was still angry.

It wasn't easy.

Maybe my problem was I liked tricky females. I didn't have a history of elevated heartbeat except when I was confronted by the beautiful/sweet-talking/kinky ones who made chopped liver out of your heart.

She handed me the keys to the BMW, and I went outside where winter was waiting to cool me off.

chapter | 16

All I wanted to do that night was eat my sandwich in peace and study for the test on medieval history coming up Monday. I'd be expected to explain, in an hour, how a scruffy army of illiterate soldiers, chomping on hunks of raw meat between battles, could bring down the whole Roman Empire.

Sevens House was dead. It seemed as though everyone but Mrs. Violet, our housemother, was still over at The Tower. I looked at my watch. It was almost eight. They were finished with dessert by now, those who hadn't left for the weekend. Some were still hanging around over coffee, or starting to play chess and backgammon in the library. Others were on their way into Cottersville, to meet the bus from Miss Tyler's or to go to the movies, bowling, the play at the Civic Center.

I got my mail. That was when I noticed someone else abroad in Sevens House. Creery. Behind me in the phone booth. He wasn't dining at The Tower these nights. He looked like he'd just come in from the cold, too.

I could hear him telling someone, "I waited over an hour for you. Ask Lowell. Where were you?"

I opened a club bill for the gold 7 I'd already sent to Mom. OVERDUE was stamped across it.

"Then I'll come there tomorrow morning," Creery continued. . . . "Not too early because I'll be up late."

I didn't have any personal letters. I never opened my box that I didn't hope I'd see one from Delia. I was going to hear from Delia the day they discovered something that would rhyme with orange, but that never stopped me looking for the tiny handwriting with the long loops and the T bars flying off the handles.

I had the usual junk mail: Save the Seals and Support National Arbor Day. Your Christmas subscription to *Esquire* will be up next December so renew in March. A catalog from The Sharper Image promising that a Shotline Putter would release the pro golfer within me.

I tossed it all in the wastebasket while Creery told whoever he was talking to that he had to cram for the same history test. I decided to keep him in mind if we were called on to describe Alaric the Goth, the one who plundered Rome and got everyone eating each other instead of the parrots' tongues they were fond of baking into pies.

I did wonder who Creery'd have in his life to complain to, since it wasn't his stepbrother on the phone. And I thought about who he might be meeting "there" the next day . . . maybe the same one who arranged for Lowell Hunter to stay at number 6 Playwicky.

"How are you, Fell?" said Mrs. Violet. "Long time no see."

Our housemother was always in white, always gorgeous, usually stationed nights in the wing chair near the reception room.

"I'm fine, thanks. What are you reading tonight?"

She closed the book in her lap so I could see the cover. *Hunted Down* by Charles Dickens.

"You want to hear something extraordinary?" she said, not waiting for my answer. "Listen. *I have known a vast quantity of nonsense talked about bad men not looking you in the face. Don't trust that conventional idea. Dishonesty will stare honestly out of countenance, any day in the week.* She pushed a strand of blond hair away from her forehead and looked up at me. "And I always judge boys by whether or not they can look you in the eye."

"Maybe Dickens didn't mean boys," I said. "My dad used to say a really good con man always looks you in the eye."

So had Delia had that skill. So did Nina.

"I'll have to think about that," Mrs. Violet said.

Creery was going up the staircase in a long gabardine overcoat, the blue-and-white wool Sevens scarf wrapped around his neck, the tail behind his head.

It wasn't like him to greet Mrs. Violet. It wasn't like his eyes to see the people around him. His eyes saw La La Land, little blue and red pills, joints and smoke.

"Fell? That friend of yours from the dorm was in your room earlier this evening. He said he had permission."

"He does, ma'am."

"Sidney Dibble."

"Yes."

"And your mother called. She said it wasn't important. Just a hello."

Mom had probably received the gold 7 for her birthday.

I thanked Mrs. Violet and kept going. In a while her freshman groupies would come over from The Tower. A score of them. Healthy young boys who turned into groveling lackeys, eager to do any chore she could dream up. Or they simply sat at her feet while she read to them. It didn't matter what. She'd call them "darling" or "dear"—words most of them never heard from any lips but hers, unless they called home.

When I got up to my room, I saw that Dib

had left a red 7 hanging on my doorknob. All Sevens were issued one, which we could hang there when we didn't want to be disturbed. No one in Sevens House went through a door with one on it.

I pocketed it as I went inside.

The living room was dark, but I could see through to the bedroom, where there were green letters lit up on the face of the word processor.

I switched on a light and got out of my coat. I grabbed a Soho lemon spritzer from the refrigerator.

I supposed Dib had left me a message For My Eyes Only, probably something against Sevens . . . me and Sevens.

I wanted to relish the corned beef sandwich before I read it. I wanted to think a minute about Nina. Gather ye rosebuds while ye may, someone wrote. Not the same one who wrote Duty before pleasure.

There was just enough Dijon on the bread. I was too hungry to care that the bread was white and fell into the empty-carbohydrate category, too ravenous to regret it wasn't rye or pumpernickel. Too starved to miss a fat dill-and-garlic pickle.

I began demolishing it, still standing, which is the only honest position for rationalizing. All

I'd agreed to do was report back to David Deem if Nina tried to see Dragon. Technically, she hadn't tried to *see* him, only Dragonland . . . Chances were that what she'd found there *would* be enough to discourage her from ever wanting to see him again.

I played it back a few times and it didn't have a discordant note.

My dad would have said it was too pat.

But my dad hadn't arrived at his judgments when he was seventeen, horny, and far from Brooklyn.

I finished the sandwich and carried my bottle of lemon spritzer in toward the green letters.

Dear Lionel,

The enclosed copy of a letter from Cyril Creery to his stepbrother is self-explanatory.

I think you will agree that this is more serious than anything that has ever been handled in Twilight Truth, although ideally it should be done in that manner. However, it is unlikely, as you'll see in the fifth paragraph, that Creery would ever on his own allow it to be used in that ceremony.

The letter came into my hands because a concerned outside party knew the information in it was vital to Sevens. I make no apologies for passing it on to you, since the honor of Sevens has, for me, always had priority over any other principle.

*I've held on to this since Christmas, weighing
what course to take. Surely this calls for The
Sevens Revenge . . . and for the immediate ouster
of Cyril Creery from our organization.*

Sincerely,
Paul Lasher

Lasher's letter had been written three days
before his death.

I reached up and switched on my desk light.

Dib had left a note on my blotter.

*It wasn't a tutorial inside—it was a regular
microwafer I came upon when I pushed Microwafer
Directory and found LETTERS.*

*There are others there: complaints to stores,
and one to his father about the delivery of the
Porsche, but nothing pertinent.*

*They are all permanently stored, so just pull
the microwafer out, turn the two switches off,
and CALL ME.*

Dib

I called him.

"What do you think Creery's letter could have
said, Fell?"

"How would I know?"

"And what about The Sevens Revenge? You
said it was a myth."

"I thought it was. It's news to me, too."

"Sure. Surprise, surprise."

I couldn't convince him that I was as much in the dark as he was, but we made a date to meet in the morning.

I fell asleep reading about the Crusades and dreamed that Nina was handing me Creery's letter. Then her face turned into Delia's, and she said, "Surprise, surprise, Fell."

chapter 17

Saturday morning.

Nobody'd ever warned me about winters in Pennsylvania. The cold sky hung heavy above me, like some enormous net over a ballroom loaded with balloons waiting to be freed with the jerk of a rope, only snow would pour down. Everyone walking along the streets had little white clouds puffing out of them, their postures bent and huddled into benumbed bones. I had the heater going full blast; ditto the radio: warming up with INXS, Big Pig, and John Cougar Mellencamp.

I cruised up and down Playwicky Road. It was narrow and twisting, with few trees save for the oak I'd stood behind the night I'd seen Lowell Hunter come out of number 6.

Anyone on foot would be seen immediately in the daytime.

Most of the apartment houses had parking lots behind them. There were few cars. Those that parked out front were also too conspicuous for any serious surveillance.

I headed for the nearest supermarket, where you were most likely to find boxes of all shapes and sizes.

Dib was standing in front of the dorm when I

pulled up at eight. He hadn't expected me to arrive in a car. I had to beep the horn. He ran toward me layered in a turtleneck, a shirt, a crew-neck sweater, a parka. Levi's, boots, his old navy-striped Moriarty hat pulled down over his ears.

"Where'd you get the wheels?"

While I told him, and he interrupted to say he *had* to have something cold to drink, I got the first blast of a breath that could probably have killed little flying things as easily as anything Black Flag made.

"There's a store down on Main near the bus stop. You can get a Coke there."

"And aspirin," said Dib.

"How did you tie one on in the dorm?"

"I went out for an hour after your call."

"With your gang?"

"Just Little Jack. You don't mind if I have a little fun too, do you? . . . Where are we headed?"

"The only thing I can think to do is follow the one lead we have, while I have a car."

"Lasher's letter is the one lead we have."

"I'm talking about Playwicky Road now."

"Let's talk about why Lionel Schwartz didn't mention that letter to the police."

"Dib, we went over that last night. He might have mentioned it, and they might have their reason for keeping it quiet."

"I think Sevens is keeping it quiet."

"You told me what you think. Now let me take a look at number six Playwicky and see who's meeting Creery there."

"I'm not in any shape to sit around watching an apartment when we don't know what we're looking for."

"You don't have to watch it. You have to help set me up. Then you can go back to the dorm and sack out."

"I might even have to puke," he said.

He wasn't kidding. He looked pale. He was rubbing his stomach the way you'd soothe some frightened animal.

"What's the big box in back?" he asked.

"I'll explain that later. . . . Dib, you look and stink like something died in you."

"Cork it, Fell! I'm just hung over."

"What's going on with you? Do you drink a lot, or was last night a first?"

"We go out."

"Where do you go when you go out?"

"Around, Fell. What difference does it make to you? I have to have other friends."

"You can get yourself expelled—that's the difference it makes to me."

"Unlike you, hmmm?"

"Maybe I can't get expelled, but I can't get away with drinking either. We're self-regulatory, but the bottom line's the same."

"'Just a song at twilight.'" Dib sang off-key.

"Well, it's better than getting the boot. You're asking for it, Dib."

"You've swallowed Sevens hook, line, and sinker, Fell."

"I don't even hang out with them! I'm so busy tutoring a townie, it took *you* to bring that letter out of the machine."

"What about the gold 7 you got your mom?"

"I got it for *her*, not for me."

"My mom wouldn't wear one of those things, even if I was in Sevens. She doesn't buy designer clothes, either, and not because she can't afford to. She says she's not a walking advertisement for Calvin Klein or Gucci."

"Yours has been around more than mine. Mine's easily impressed, maybe."

"*You're* easily impressed, Fell."

"I'm not easily asphyxiated, or your breath would have killed me two blocks back."

We both began to laugh.

The tension that had started crowding us was broken. At Main Pharmacy he bought some Binaca for his breath and a couple of cans of cold Sprite.

A block before Playwicky Road, I pulled over to the curb.

"I learned this from my father," I said. "He'd do this when he was staking out some place they were dealing drugs. We're going to put that big box back there up where you're sitting, and I'm going to get inside it. See where I cut the holes?"

He gave a look. "What am I going to do?"

"After I get inside the box, you're going to drive up in front of the house. You're going to leave me under the box. You can catch a bus back near the pharmacy."

"So it'll just look like a car with a box in it."

"Right. . . . When my father'd be watching a crack house, sometimes he'd be stuck inside for a whole afternoon. He'd take along a wide-neck water bottle to piss into."

"Neat, Fell! And you'll be all right by yourself?"

"Why not? I'm just going to watch the place. Maybe I won't see anything important. But I want to try and find out who's there besides Creery and Lowell Hunter."

"It'll be a Sevens, for sure, and what'll that tell you?"

"I'll know when I know."

"And you're going to tell me when you know?"

"Yes. I'm going to tell you."

"Is that a promise?"

"It's a promise."

"Because it'd be easy for you to lie."

"I'm not going to. We're in this together."

Dib chugalugged a Sprite.

He said, "What happens when you've seen

what you came down here to see?"

"I slip out from under and drive off. I don't care so much about being seen *after* I find out who the third party is, I don't think. . . . But this way I can choose my time to exit the scene."

We got out of the BMW and began putting the plan into action.

Before I got up under the box, I said, "Anything you've got to say to me, say now. When you pull up and park, you get out fast and walk away."

"I'll meet you back at the dorm. What time?"

"Hard to say. I have to return the car."

"I'm going to sack out anyway, so I'll be in my room all afternoon."

"I'll call you when I'm back on The Hill."

It was twenty minutes to nine.

"You're going to freeze your ass," said Dib.

My father used to call that kind of surveillance B.S. He meant Box Surveillance, but he meant B.S., too, because that's what it was, a real crappy detail. You couldn't eat, glance at a newspaper, listen to tapes, or do anything but ache to scratch all the parts of you suddenly itching in violent protest at what you were doing. Your body also gave you two-minute spots of coming attractions if you kept it up: arthritis, headache, muscular aches and pains, constipation, urinary incontinence: the gamut.

Sometimes he'd come home from B.S. filled with ideas of how our lives were going to change. Mom wasn't going to work for a caterer anymore, she was going to become one. Since I loved cooking so much, I was going to apprentice myself to some famous chef in a fancy New York restaurant. Jazzy would go to day care. Dad would turn down any future assignments that might involve crack houses. We were going to shape up as a family. . . . Sure, because that's what you do under a box. You promise yourself you'll never be under another one. You begin making grandiose plans for yourself, and for everyone in your life.

By ten o'clock I'd enrolled in the hotel management program at Cornell University, where I'd work my way through in some kitchen. I'd canceled all Mom's credit cards, begun a savings plan for Jazzy's college, and gone through the 7s directory to see what alumni had connections with restaurants, inns, or resorts. . . . I'd talked Dib into going in on the venture with me (even though God knew he'd eat us into the poorhouse), and finally I'd found out Delia's address. For once and for all I'd see her again, one last time, the final period, as Nina'd put it, at the end of the sentence.

At ten–thirty I was cold enough to go into rigor mortis, and my normally reliable bladder was blaming me for the coffee I'd brewed back in my room at Sevens and swallowed down on the run.

At twenty minutes to eleven a red taxi from Cottersville Cab stopped in front of the BMW.

I watched while Creery got out. The same long gabardine coat, the Sevens scarf, Timberland boots, and the blue wraparound Gargoyle shades.

He said something to the driver, gave him money, and loped up to number 6. Mark Twain let him in. I saw him smile and clap his arm around Creery's shoulders as he shut the door.

The taxi driver cut the motor and lighted a cigarette.

I counted three more cigarettes smoked and tossed out the window before the driver turned his motor back on, still sitting there, waiting. It was not only freezing cold; there was a wind rising ominously, and I had no doubt that he was tuning in to local radio for the forecast. Snow and gales, followed by blinking digital clocks.

In minutes the snow began dropping in large wet, white flakes. Something dime sized on my back dared me not to itch it. My neck was threatening to lock itself in one position forever. I was starting to sweat, the kind that turns cold and clammy, when I saw the front door at number 6 open.

Creery first . . . then Lauren Lasher appeared.

She was hanging on to him, not because she needed to, not that way. Because she wanted to. It was all over her eyes.

He was carrying her Le Sac, a big beige thing he had over one arm. Her gloved hand was on the other arm.

She had on a short khaki storm coat with a fur collar, and wide-wale khaki corduroys tucked into boots with thick navy-blue socks tucked over the boot tops. Her long, black hair touched the red scarf tied around her neck.

She was looking up at him. He was looking straight ahead. He didn't look happy. She had the kind of look you have when you're worried about someone you're with. She was talking to him, her lips pursed as though she was saying soothing things.

Then they were telling each other good-bye. Not in words. She had her arms around him. Finally his went around her, too. I couldn't see his face at that moment. Only hers. Her chin nestled in his neck.

He opened the cab door and she got in. He passed the Le Sac to her and gave her a little two-fingered salute, unsmiling, then finally smiling as though she'd said, "Can't you at least smile?" as my mother'd asked me to, at Christmas, when I'd posed for pictures she was taking.

I waited for the cab to take off, and for Creery to go back inside number 6. Then I got out from under and over into the driver's seat.

On Saturdays the buses to Miss Tyler's, in Princeton, left from the Cottersville Inn every three or four hours.

I caught up with the red cab, heading down that way.

Out in front of the inn I caught up with Lauren, honking at her as I pulled over.

She came walking toward the car with a raised eyebrow, shaking her head as though she'd found me out.

I'd been trying to think how I was going to start the conversation, but she started it for me.

"So that was *your* car. Where were you, Fell?"

No way was I going to say under the box.

I said I was "around." I asked her if we could talk.

She said inside, it was too cold, and she had to make a phone call first. She'd meet me in the lobby.

I parked the BMW behind the inn, took care of my bladder in the men's, and waited for her in the lounge.

The Cottersville Inn was where Miss Tyler's girls stayed weekends they attended dances or dated on The Hill. They were always put on the fourth floor, off-limits to any males but uniformed waiters carrying trays.

In the lounge on the first floor the usual Saturday morning fare was being offered on TV. *Star Trek IV: The Voyage Home.*

A few Miss Tylerites were vaguely involved while they waited for their dates or the school bus back.

Lauren got her coat off and sat down. She had on a red sweater and the gold 7.

"I'm going back on the noon bus," she said, "so there isn't time for you to lie about how you happened to be up on Playwicky Road this morning."

"In time to see that tender farewell between

you and Creery," I said. "You're full of surprises, Lauren."

"So are you, Fell. Everyone will know at The Charles Dance anyway. We've been seeing each other. Is that all right with you?"

"If it's all right with you, it's all right with me."

"I hope so. I just talked with Cyr. He thinks Sevens is spying on him. On us. I told him that was your BMW outside. He wants to know what you're after."

"I'm not part of any Sevens team, Lauren."

"Are you the one who found out about us and told Paul?"

"Your brother knew? I didn't realize it was going on that long."

"Cyr and I sneaked around like thieves," she said. "No one over here knew, so we thought. We wrote each other more than we saw each other. Even Daddy didn't know, still doesn't. We met last October. Cyr was someone else's blind date. I took one look at him and that was it."

I tried to imagine what she could have seen in that one look that would make her fall for Creery. His skinhead? The two earrings in one ear? The stoned look in his eyes, like a chicken's staring back at you? Yet she was sitting there admitting it, and wearing his gold, I was sure. Fondling the 7.

"I know what you're thinking," she said, "but

Paul talked against Cyr so hatefully, I was expecting this slick con artist, not this shy—"

"*Shy?*"

"He is, Fell! He's shy and he's sweet. I know he looks goofy, but he's not. He reads Camus and Vonnegut."

"We all read Camus and Vonnegut. They're assigned."

She let that go by.

She said, "Paul and I were very close. Too close. Twins are. We told each other everything. All I used to hear about was Cyr, Paul's great hate. Hearing about someone's great hate is like hearing about someone's great love. You get involved yourself. And curious. When I heard he was coming to our Halloween Dance, I couldn't wait to see him."

Across the room Captain Kirk and Mr. Spock were visiting San Francisco. Behind them the snow was falling so thickly, it was all you could see from the windows.

She seemed to sense my concern about the weather. I was beginning to wonder if I could get the BMW back that afternoon.

"To make a long story short," she said, "at the end of Christmas vacation, Paul told me he knew about us. He said he'd been waiting to see if I'd tell him about it. He said there wasn't a meal he ate all the while we were home that he didn't throw up after. He waited right up until we both had to go back to school, and you know what he said?"

It was one of those questions you weren't expected to answer.

Her face was breaking like a baby's before it starts to cry. "He said . . . Paul said . . . Why didn't you just put a knife in me?"

I waited for her to get a hold of herself.

"So in a way you feel responsible," I murmured.

"Not in a way. I do. Of course I do. . . . We haven't even dared show up on The Hill together. Everyone will think, or *know*, we were the reason for his suicide . . . or they'll wonder how I can date Paul's worst enemy so soon. . . . Cyr's stepbrother says to just face it head-on. Go to The Charles Dance. Deal with it . . . He's the only one we've confided in until now . . . Fell? Why were you up on Playwicky today? Is Sevens up to something?"

"No, not Sevens."

I told her about Lasher's letter to Lionel, which had been stored in the word processor. I left out the part about The Sevens Revenge. I explained how Dib had come upon it . . . and how I'd simply gone to Playwicky out of curiosity, after I'd overheard Creery's phone conversation last night.

"I know about Cyr's letter to Lowell," she

said. "He wants to get off drugs, Fell. That's all. He wrote Lowell to tell him that, and to tell him about me. I'm helping him straighten out his life. Lowell is too. . . . Why wouldn't The Sevens be glad of that?"

"Maybe Schwartz expected him to do Twilight Truth."

"He might have. But Paul was trying to force it on him!"

"I think there was more in Creery's letter," I said.

"No. Cyr would have told me if there was. . . . And what does it all have to do with *you*, Fell?"

"I'm just nosy, I guess."

"Cyr doesn't believe that. Fell? Why? He's almost flunking out, he's so terrified. Last night he even forgot I was coming on the eight-twenty bus. He can't think straight anymore! And now he's really convinced there's this Sevens Revenge brewing . . . and you could be part of it."

"Tell him I'm not part of anything."

"We don't even know how Paul found out about us. Now you say Paul really did have a copy of Cyr's letter. How did he get it?"

I didn't have any answers for her.

Lauren took out a handkerchief and blew her nose.

She said, "Both Cyr and I are going down the tubes over this thing, Fell. I have to go back to

school now and try to study for midsemesters.
Cyr's thinking of quitting altogether, and he would,
too, if Lowell wasn't there to stop him. You don't
know how depressed he is! . . . Paul did this!"

"Creery did his share of baiting your brother,
too."

"No one is a match for Paul. You don't know
him!"

She realized she'd slipped into present
tense.

She said, "I mean you didn't know him . . . did
you?"

"Not really."

"What he was capable of?"

"I guess not."

Lauren pressed her fingers on my wrist. "I'm
going to tell you something that I've only told Cyr
and Lowell," she said. "I think Paul picked that
fight with Cyr deliberately right before he
jumped. He wanted everyone to think Cyr'd
pushed him."

There was nothing to say to that.

Lauren looked at her watch. "I have to go,
Fell."

I hadn't taken my coat off, only unbuttoned it.
I gave another glance out the window and started
buttoning it. Someone wrote something that said
when it snows hard, the whole world seems com-

posed of one thing and one thing only. That's what it looked like outside.

"There's something I don't understand, though, Lauren," I said. "Why does Creery think Sevens would want revenge?"

"Do you really want to know what I think? You're not to repeat this to *anyone*, Fell."

"Okay."

"I think trying to come off all the drugs has made Cyr paranoid. Lowell thinks so, too. . . . Things are bad enough, but they're not as bad as he's making them." She tapped her forehead. "Up here . . . he needs supervision while he's getting clean."

"Can't this Lowell get him in someplace?"

"Lowell's afraid that if he leaves school now, he'll never go back. His father's dying, too. If he can just hold out four more months!"

I helped her into her coat, and took her Le Sac.

"The lease on the Playwicky apartment is up the first of the month," Lauren said as we walked down the lobby. "Lowell's not going to move into a motel and live here until June."

"Was it just Paul's apartment?"

"Yes. I'd stay there sometimes."

"Because Rinaldo said some of the Sevens used it."

"Only to play cards in. . . . Rinaldo's such a know-it-all, isn't he? I hear he's selling everything we gave him."

"Well . . ." I shrugged.

"I don't care, really. I don't want anything of Paul's! I know right now his ghost is somewhere howling at what he's done to Cyr!"

"I have the material for the memorial book, by the way."

"I finally found a smiling picture of him, too. I'll get it to you, and then I wish you'd send it all to Daddy . . . I don't want to see his sick stories right now."

"Are you going to tell your father about Cyr?"

"I have to . . . and my mother."

Her fingers were back touching the gold 7.

"I'll get the blame for Paul's suicide. From him, not from her." Lauren stopped by the small bus line at the end of the lobby. "My mother would only blame me if it was one of her patients. She only cares about them. She's never even known our shoe sizes."

I handed her the Le Sac.

"I feel a little disloyal to Cyr right now, Fell," she said, "telling you he exaggerates his problems, and I don't believe they're that bad. It doesn't mean that I don't trust him. . . . I want to trust him."

"Yeah," I said. "I know how that works."

I looked through the glass doors at the thickening snow. It wasn't just the car I wanted to return—I wanted to return to Nina, too.

"Cyr's changing now. I think it's because of me. But you can't become someone new overnight."

"No, you can't," I agreed.

"He doesn't want to be punk anymore . . . or any of it."

"Yes," I said. "There's a time for departure even when there's no certain place to go."

"What an interesting thing to say, Fell."

"It's from *Camino Real*," I said. "Tennessee Williams wrote it. We had it in English last term."

"But you remembered it," she said. "That's nice."

chapter | 19

A mazing!" Nina said when she opened the door. "Dad's stuck at his office, says he's going across the street to the matinee until the snow stops . . . and Mrs. Whipple's son called to say the roads aren't negotiable."

"They aren't," I said. "What kept me going was the thought of your jar of Fox's U-Bet."

"I thought you were going to say me."

"Don't make me choose between you and an egg cream," I said.

While I took my boots off, Nina took my wet coat and put it on a hanger. Then she hung it on the back of the closet door and put a newspaper under it on the floor.

"If it was anything besides an egg cream, would I have a chance?" she asked me.

I looked up at her while I struggled with my left boot. She had on a black mock-turtle top, black pants, yellow socks, and black lace-up running shoes. Her yellow hair seemed just washed and still damp, no makeup. She was looking better and better to me.

"I'm still mad at you, Nina," I lied.

"Don't be, Fell. I'm a new person."

I made us some egg creams, and we sat in the living room talking. The snow clung to the tree branches winter-wonderland style, while she told me about the new person.

First, the new person was never going to say or think the name Eddie Dragon ever again.

Second, the new person was going to end her analysis.

Third, the new person was going to start shopping for a whole new wardrobe.

"Go back to two," I said. "What does your dad think about that?"

"He's been telling me I ought to take a rest from her. It costs him one hundred and twenty dollars a week. Just imagine all the Easter clothes I can buy! I want to start thinking about outside me for a change. I'm tired of inside me."

"Doesn't Dr. Lasher have a say in that?"

"She'll probably be glad, too. She used to complain that I used up her answering machine tapes with all my messages. I'd call and talk as long as I could to her machine, and then I'd just call again and talk, call again and talk . . . She'd say, Nina, vy can't you vait until de session for all dat?"

The new person was playing Tiffany softly in the background wearing the old person's White Shoulders. I was letting my head rest from thoughts of Lauren and Creery, the letters—all of it—while I watched the snow and her green eyes . . . and thought of Mom as Nina told me how long it had been since she'd gone to the mall.

"Why are you smiling?" she said. "That's part of being a female, caring what you wear, how you look."

"I know it is. But when I'm home, I live with a shopping junkie."

"Who? Your mother or your sister?"

"My sister's only five. It's my mother. My father'd say instead of a gun moll, she was a mall moll."

"What was he like, Fell?"

A personal question from Nina Deem.

I started talking the way someone from Maine basks in the warm sun of July, fearful that it won't last long, that a cold snap is right around the corner.

I think it was close to five o'clock when I was explaining how they "decop" a police officer before he becomes a narc. "Even the posture has to change," I was saying, "because a cop walks with one arm swinging. And another giveaway is not haggling over the price. If the doper says a quarter ounce of pot is fifty, the narc has to talk him down to forty, forty-five. Cops make the mistake of buying anything at any price."

The phone put a stop to my sudden diarrhea of the mouth.

Nina came back from the hall all smiles.

"Dad's met a friend and they're going down the

street for dinner. I guess you'll have to cook me mine, Fell. The new person can't think of anything interesting to do with a pair of chicken breasts."

"Where's Meatloaf today?"

"In Dad's office. He has a bed there, and his toys. He has office toys, home toys, and car toys . . . What happened to Tiffany?"

"My lecture on narcs happened to her," I said. "Do you have any Progresso bread crumbs?"

"You're a brand-name freak, Fell. Do you need them for the chicken?"

"And some Dijon mustard," I said. "They're *my* toys."

She sat on the stool in the kitchen while I slathered the chicken breasts with Dijon, dipped them in Italian Style Wonder bread crumbs, (not ideal, but okay in a pinch), and dotted them with butter.

"We put them in at four hundred for forty-five minutes," I said.

"That's all there is to it?"

"Wait till you taste them!"

While we waited, she said she had something to show me.

"It took me a long time to hunt this down," she said, "but the new me is determined to hear you, even if I'm a day late."

She handed me a thin white leather book with THE COTTERSVILLE CLARION written in gold across the front.

"Rinaldo's at the end, in the V's."

I found him immediately. You couldn't miss him. He had the same big, toothy smile, and a certain cock-of-the-walk expression maybe inspired by having good buns and hips that could do things *blancos'* couldn't.

Our Rinaldo on his own turf. He didn't look like somebody you'd send back to the kitchen for a clean fork.

VELEZ, RINALDO A.

"Velly"
Activities: vice-pres class 2; cheerleader 2, 4;
class treasurer 3; drama 3, 4.
Sports: tennis, golf, 1, 2, 3, 4

At the bottom of the page there was one of those quotes you found in yearbooks, supposed to sum up someone's personality.

I am
indeed
a king, because I know how to rule myself.
Pietro Aretino

In addition to the formal portrait there was a snapshot of each graduate. Rinaldo's featured him in a magician's cape, pulling a rabbit out of a hat.

The camera angle was bad. Rinaldo was all hands.

I remembered those hands reaching in somewhere else . . . to pull out mail. The blue CORRESPONDENCE box in Deem Library.

I thought of my conversation hours ago with Lauren: *We wrote each other more than we saw each other.* And, of course, I thought of the letter Creery had written to his stepbrother.

What would it have been worth to Lasher to have his own hands on Creery's mail? A pen? A watch? A VCR? Lasher had always believed Creery was involved with drugs and dealing on The Hill.

I handed the book back to Nina.

"There's one other thing about him under Class Prophecy," she said. "They did it in rhyme that year. Here it is."

She read it to me.

> *"Someday he'll show them on The Hill,*
> *He will!*
> *That he's a match for all of them,*
> *A gem!*
> *Velez, Rinaldo A.*
> *Hooray!"*

I wasn't great company at dinner. As soon as the snow stopped, I got ready to hike back.

"Fell," Nina said as she walked me to the door, "when I go to The Charles Dance with you, can I stay in Sevens House overnight like the girls from Miss Tyler's?"

"Your dad won't agree to that."

"Yes, he will. *He* told *me* about it, that they clear a whole floor, and it's the only night girls stay there."

"You'd be stuck in with a lot of other girls, three and four to a room."

"That's what I want, Fell. I want to be like everyone else. I want to have someone say about me what they said about Rinaldo. I want to rule myself."

"If your dad agrees, it's fine with me."

We kissed good-night right before I left.

I wished we hadn't. Either my mind was too much on Rinaldo or my memories were always going to spoil the present. I didn't feel the way I had a summer ago on a beach on Long Island after kissing Delia. I felt more like a preppy on a first date.

I was definitely down by the time I'd climbed my way through unplowed streets up to The Hill.

I wasn't in the mood for Mrs. Violet and her groupies clustered in the reception room, along with Sevens members and their dates.

It was only around nine o'clock, too early for everyone to be milling around, but I supposed the snow had kept them all from movies and coffeehouses and places they went on Saturday nights.

I knew I should have stopped by the dorm, that by now Dib would be steamed because I hadn't reported back to him anything that had happened on Playwicky Road.

I also knew I'd earned a Sevens fine of seven dollars for not calling The Tower to say I was skipping dinner.

I tried to make it to the stairs without answering to anyone, when I suddenly saw the familiar blue uniforms.

There were two of them. There are always two.

Then I saw Dr. Skinner, the snow still melting down his bald head, standing in front of the front-hall bulletin board where there seemed to be a space cleared just for him. He had on his mackinaw with a wet scarf, overshoes, standing arms akimbo, reading a sheet of paper thumbtacked there.

There was a semicircle of kids watching him, whispering together.

After he stepped away and walked over toward the policemen, I took his place.

The mystery of the missing letter was solved. There was the copy, for anyone to read.

Dear Lowell,

You will laugh, but can you send me somewhere I can kick this thing?

I mean it, Lowell! I gave myself an early Christmas gift, a new girlfriend. I think the pills are taking over, too. I take more and more and get back less and less.

I know it is my fault you have to work so hard, and I intend to make that up to you. I don't need college. I can learn the business.

This girl, by the way, is the sister of my old enemy, Lasher. Maybe you remember that name. Dad would! She's no dog, either, and I found out I like getting laid better than getting laid back. Did you ever think you'd live to hear me say that?

I don't know how much Dad understands anymore, but tell him not to worry about a Christmas gift for me. He gave me the best when he gave me Sevens. Nothing can top that!

There is Easter break after The Charles Dance, and that would be a good time for me to get clean. It will be the last time you have to pay out for me, Lowell. I promise. There is a place called Oxford Farm outside of Philadelphia. I'll find out

*more details. It's not just this girl making me
determined to get off these pills. She's okay, but
the novelty there is she's Lasher's twin and we
use his apartment, which would kill him! No,
it's more that I've finally grown up. You'll see,
Lowell. I know you'll find it hard to believe, but
wait! Oxford is supposed to do miracles very fast,
too, and I think I could kick this thing in about
a week. Come back, graduate, then get my tail
down to Miami to become your right-hand man!*

*Think this over and we'll talk when I'm home.
Please save some time.*

Yours,
Cyr

Scribbled across the bottom in fresh ink were
the words *Self-explanatory . . . Lasher paid for
what he found out. Now it's my turn. You'll never
see me again, either.*

CC

And we didn't. Not alive, anyway.

His body was found in a snowdrift at the bottom of The Tower. His frozen neck was broken
from the fall.

I am a Sevens. Sevens is part of me as twilight is part of the day, connected and vital to me as the heart to the bloodstream, always and forever.

I am a Sevens, brother to any Sevens, there for him as the sun and moon are for the tides, always and forever.

"Be seated," said Lionel Schwartz after we recited the oath.

We were in the Sevens House reception room, summoned there through the intercom.

Everyone on The Hill that Sunday morning was dorm or house campused until chapel at eleven.

"At this very moment Dr. Skinner is telling the dorm boys most of what I am going to tell you," Schwartz began, "except for this preamble.

"Before I begin, I call on Fisher to swear us."

Ozzie Fisher stood up. He was the only black Seven that year. A senior, an ardent political activist when I arrived on The Hill as a junior, he had named his tree for a black hero of South Africa, Mandela.

Some of us were still in our bathrobes. I was. Ozzie was. He stood in front of his chair and waited until The Lion said, "Sevens."

"Richard Wright, Toni Morrison, James Baldwin, Langston Hughes, LeRoi Jones, Gloria Naylor, Counte Cullen."

"Seven black writers, so be it," Schwartz said.

Normally, Schwartz would have given him an argument. The rule of this Sevens ritual was to name seven things that went together, not seven that were alike, but this was not normally, not the occasion to rev up Ozzie's motor. He knew it, and sat down with a glimmer of triumph in his dark eyes.

"This is for Sevens cars only," said Schwartz. "Late Friday evening Cyril Creery came to me and told me he was ready for Twilight Truth, but he hoped meanwhile word would get out that what he had to confess was an accident, and not a deliberate action. As a brother, he would not place me in conflict or jeopardy by giving me information I would be honor bound by Sevens to withhold from the authorities, at the same time legally bound to report to them." Schwartz's voice thundered suddenly: "WHY do you think he felt obliged to say that?"

Silence.

"Because," said Schwartz, "of The Sevens Revenge! He was terrified that we would get to him before he got to us!"

Schwartz peered around the room at all of us

through his John Lennon glasses.

"I believe it caused his suicide! . . . I believe he hoped I could prevent this alleged revenge . . . then feared that no one could. The legend of The Sevens Revenge is too overpowering! It overwhelms reason and in the long run it overwhelms justice! That is what it did to Cyril Creery.

"You may say he had no right to be a Sevens, because of his apparent admission that his father told him of the significance of the tree-naming ceremony. BUT . . . he did have a right to Twilight Truth, to speak his piece . . . and where his conflict with Lasher at the top of The Tower is concerned, Cyril Creery had a right to a trial!

"We cannot be anything but ashamed, this morning, that the ugly gossip of The Sevens Revenge forced him to kill himself.

"For once and for all, then, I tell you in this preamble, there is no such thing as The Sevens Revenge! It is a fantasy, a myth, a very dangerous one. Any Sevens who perpetuates it is ultimately destroying Sevens. Remember that."

Then The Lion told us what every boy on The Hill would hear that morning.

1. There would be no memorial service for Cyril Creery. Dr. Skinner opted to deny him such an honor due to his part in Lasher's death.

2. No one on The Hill was to talk with reporters.

3. The police would be investigating. Anyone approached by them was to tell the truth. Sevens would not be expected to explain the Sevens selection process to them, since it was not pertinent to an investigation.

4. The Grief Counselor would be back on campus Monday for individual and group consultation.

5. Everyone on The Hill was to bear in mind that the Gardner Board of Trustees would meet after Easter vacation to vote on the proposal for Gardner to go coed, an idea the student body was resisting. The sooner Gardner was back to normal, the better the chances for Gardner to remain as it was and had been for 123 years.

6. The Charles Dance, a tradition at Gardner for 101 of those years, would take place as scheduled next Saturday evening.

Schwartz took off his spectacles and wiped them clean as he concluded. "This morning, of all mornings, every Sevens member should be present in chapel. . . . We are Sevens . . ."

"Always and forever" came our answer.

The phone call from Lauren Lasher was announced over my intercom just as I had finished knotting my tie.

I put on my suit jacket and went down to the phone booth at the end of the hall, pushing the button that signaled I had picked up.

"Have you sent Paul's writings to my father, Fell?" She started right in, without a hello or any other comment.

"No. We only talked about that yesterday."

"Good! Don't! Daddy doesn't want it mixed in with his other mail. Hang on to it all."

"Lauren, how are you feeling?" I wasn't even sure she knew about Creery's suicide, or the letter he'd posted.

But she knew.

"I'm feeling the same way my family feels," she said. "Very litigious."

"Very *what*?"

"We're going to sue, Fell. That's why I'm calling."

"Are *you* all right?"

"Of course I'm not all right! Someone murders my brother, then tells the world he's screwing me because he hated Paul so much—migawd!"

"It wasn't put exactly that way."

"It's close enough. I read it, Fell."

"Who did you that big favor?"

"It might not sound like a favor, but it was. I have to know, since all of you do. Lowell wasn't in any shape to tell me. He could barely get out the words 'Cyr's dead.' Lionel drove over here last night, and we talked way past lock-in. Miss Tyler's allowed a man downstairs after one A.M. for the first time in its history, I guess. . . . I'm a mess, so don't smart mouth me, Fell."

"I had no intentions of—"

She cut me off. She wasn't in any mood for small talk.

"We figured out Cyr probably found a way to let Paul know about us, since that was his main interest: getting even with Paul."

"And how did your brother get Cyr's letter?"

"The way Cyr suspected, probably: went into his room, found the copy."

"I'm not so sure."

"Fell? Do me a favor, hmmm? Stop being boy detective. I don't care, at this point, how Paul got the letter. I don't care about any of the little cow pies you might come upon. It's enough for me to know about the cow. Do you get my meaning?"

"Yes. I'll cork it."

"Thanks. . . . I'm going to The Charles Dance with Schwartz."

"How come?"

"He said Paul would have wanted Sevens to give me support. He said the sooner I faced people, the better it would be for me."

"Well, that's probably true, Lauren."

"Or maybe he just suspects my family will hold Gardner *and* Sevens liable for Paul's murder . . . Maybe he's trying to soften me up."

"No. It sounds like something Schwartz

would think to do. He's very conscientious and thoughtful."

"I don't trust anyone at this point."

"That's understandable."

"Stop being so agreeable! I hate all of you right now!"

"Okay."

"Maybe not you. Sorry, Fell. . . . Something else. I hope you saved the microwafer with Paul's letter to Schwartz on it."

"Yeah."

"Naturally Schwartz claims he never got the letters, didn't know anything about them, doubts Paul put them in his box. We need Paul's as evidence."

"Evidence for what, Lauren?"

"It proves Cyr really had reason to kill Paul, and that Sevens knew he did . . . or Schwartz knew it, anyway."

"Maybe your brother never printed it out. He'd been stalling since Christmas."

"You don't believe that, and neither do I!"

"Why would Schwartz lie?"

"Because he's protecting Sevens, Fell! He puts Sevens before any other consideration! He was probably conferring with other Sevens to try and decide what to do, how to handle it! . . . Daddy says that little delay is going to cost them!"

Where had the simple life gone? Days I'd only have to worry about Keats playing around behind my back, my mother loose with her credit card in some shopping center, Delia's soft smile lying lovingly into my naive eyes, small, everyday occurrences in the life of a growing boy? Not homicide, suicide, and now litigiousness in preppydom.

I could hear the chapel bells tolling.

"Lauren? I have to go now, but before I do—I'm sorry all this had to happen."

"Some of it didn't *have* to happen. Cyr didn't have to put that letter up on the bulletin board for the whole world to see! Damn him! If he wasn't dead, I'd—"

I could hear the sob.

"Yeah," I said. "I'm sorry, Lauren."

"We're still going to do the memorial book, grim as Paul's writings were. Mother thinks it's like Jungian synchronicity, that he probably had a premonition of his early death. . . . We'll talk at The Charles Dance, Fell. You'll have time, won't you?"

"I'll make time."

"Because we want to go ahead as soon as possible. Paul would have wanted vindication. Nobody at that school cared but you and that Dibble kid! You and he and Daddy were the only ones who gave Paul the benefit of the doubt!"

"There're still some unanswered questions," I said.

"FELL?" she said threateningly.

"Okay," I said. "Okay."

But after chapel *I did* take care of one last loose end.

First, I tried to get Dib inside and make a date to talk. I hurried out of chapel after him. He waved me away and jumped into the old Mustang with Little Jack at the wheel. It was parked just a few cars behind Dr. Skinner's long, black limousine.

I walked down to The Tower by myself then, the cold winter sun warming me. I couldn't help think of Creery, seeing his face in my memory ways I'd never viewed it before. Sad ways of seeing the vacant eyes and silly punk paraphernalia. Alive, he'd angered me, reminding me of an old self maybe still around somewhere inside me . . . but dead, no longer any kind of threat to me, he made me think only of the waste, and how he wrote his stepbrother: *I think I can kick this thing.* . . . I thought of the dumb idea he had that he could be clean in just a week . . . and the stupid bravado bragging about having Lauren, getting laid . . . all the very personal things a guy could write, *I* could have written, never thinking it would get into someone's hands it wasn't meant for.

Rinaldo was in the kitchen, and the smell of rib roast wafted from inside as I called through the door.

While I waited for him in the empty library, I thought of the fear of The Sevens Revenge that Schwartz had spoken about that morning.

Maybe Lasher had delayed giving Schwartz those letters purposely, to feed that fear in Creery. Maybe Lasher had known The Revenge was fictitious but counted on the idea Creery would be left to wait for Sevens to act. . . . and the longer the wait, the worse the imagining of what would be done to him.

I could still picture Creery with the little rat tail behind his head, running around in his long gabardine coat and his Timberland boots.

Death brought it all back and colored it in softer hues, so even Creery seemed more human dead, and I felt differently about him. Sorry or something. But I felt for him, and it surprised me.

So did Rinaldo surprise me, coming up suddenly behind me, his hand over my eyes.

"Guess who?"

I took a chance while he was grinning down at me. "Lasher left something in the word processor about how he got Creery's letter to his stepbrother."

Rinaldo pulled out a chair. "Can I sit?"

I shook my head.

"And how he found out about Creery and Lauren."

"What do you want, Fell?" He wasn't grinning any longer.

"You took the mail from the CORRESPONDENCE box every night," I said. "One of Creery's letters for a watch? That was a fair price."

"Now you're going to try and do blackmail, Fell?"

"No blackmail. . . . Another letter, a pen. Right, Rinaldo?"

"I don't play the twilight game. That's for you guys."

"Just tell me about the mail game. I promise you it's just for my information."

"I gave him nothing, and if he wrote I did, he's lying."

"But he got into the mail."

"I turned my back and he got into the mail. He was looking for a way to connect Creery with dope, and he found a different connection. The sister. That ate at him until just before Christmas. Then the letter to the stepbrother was like butter on a burn. I knew from his reaction he'd struck gold. But I never saw any one of the letters, not one. He copied them on the Xerox machine over there. I never touched a letter, never handed one to him. . . . He showed up the last thing at night when I came here to unlock the box. I turned my back."

"And accepted payment."

"No money."

"I'm not saying you took money."

"I made an error in judgment, yes I did. He knew my weakness: nice things I could never afford. I learned to like those things from Sevens. Everything but your taste in clothes. I live surrounded by the good life."

"How many Sevens have Gstaad watches and apartments in town?"

"You know what I mean, Fell. You all live like you have them. I am part of Sevens, and I'm not. I have my steak on Wednesday nights, but I eat it in the kitchen on a stool. You get a chance to eat at the table for once, you take it."

We could hear other Sevens arriving at The Tower for Sunday lunch.

"I know Creery suspected me, too. Maybe he didn't know I let Lasher see the mail, but he believed Lasher told me things that Lasher never would. So-o-o—" He turned up his palms. "I was afraid too, for a while. I thought always that Creery killed him. We were the only ones here that day. I was sure of that. . . . Can you erase this thing in that machine?"

"There isn't anything about it in there. It was just my hunch, Rinaldo."

Outside, in the hall, Outerbridge was singing the hymn he'd sung in chapel.

> *"Ride on! ride on in majesty!*
> *In lowly pomp ride on to die."*

Rinaldo stood up. "I don't fear you, Fell. Warn me if I should . . . I have always feared your curiosity, but not you. You have not been in Sevens long enough for that."

He didn't wait for reassurance.

And I was thinking back to a day on Long Island when a stranger offered to pay my way to go to Gardner, posing as his son. It was how I'd gotten there. My own chance to eat at the table. Never mind all the foul-ups that had come as a result—I'd made quite a trade, too, for a better life.

The afternoon of The Charles Dance, I felt as though I was carrying Nina's entire closet when I lugged her garment bag into Sevens House. She said I wasn't that far wrong. She'd brought a lot of changes, because she wanted options in case things she tried on looked awful.

"At home I always change at least three times before I go anywhere important. Do boys?"

"Not boys going to The Charles Dance. One costume is enough."

I'd already rounded up a handlebar mustache and a monocle, to go as Damon Charles. The rest was easy: a rented tux and a pair of evening shoes borrowed from Dib.

He wasn't going. He was dorm campused. Last Sunday Little Jack had been pulled over for drunken driving. He and Dib had spent Sunday afternoon in Cottersville Tavern. Dib wasn't charged with anything, claimed he hadn't been drinking. But the place was off-limits to Hill boys, so Dr. Skinner decided, finally, to suspend Dib's privileges.

We were on the kind of speaking terms that just barely spoke. When he got the dusty pumps out of the bottom of his closet, he threw them at me. I wanted to apologize for not calling him from

Nina's, after I'd left Playwicky that morning, but he gave me the finger.

"Cork it, Fell! You got what you came for! Take them and get back to your Sevens!"

"We've got to talk sometime, Dib."

"About what? How wonderful you are?"

"Let's talk about how wonderful Little Jack is!" I said. I could see a Charlie Chaplin costume in the rental box on his desk, the cane and derby on top.

He saw me look that way, and he snapped, "Little Jack did me a favor! I'm not into kids' parties. You guys ought to grow up!"

I took the damn shoes. Then I was out of there.

I'd managed to get Nina assigned to my room, with Outerbridge's sister and Kidder's date, while I bunked downstairs, dorm style, with six other Sevens.

When I met Nina in the reception room that night, I was glad girls couldn't wear costumes. She was a knockout in an ankle-length white silk dress, hiding the blue-winged dragonfly but leaving her arms and back bare.

She had on white sling-back shoes that made winter seem like June, and made her look like a bride.

She was nervous and excited. I helped her into her coat.

"Let's not say anything on the way there, Fell. I'm too hyper."

I said okay with me, slipped the monocle into my pocket, and put on the blue half mask all Sevens wore until intermission.

It was about fourteen degrees out, but we didn't have far to go. The walk to the gym was clear; so was the weather. There was a slipper moon rising. I wished Mom could see us. I'd called her that morning. She had a job as hostess in a restaurant at the World Trade Center; she wasn't due there until noon.

"You never told me if you liked the gold 7," I'd said.

"I called you and got Mrs. Violet. You never called back."

"You don't like it, hmmmm?"

"I like it well enough, Johnny. Of course, our apartment number's seven, and I feel like some old lady who's wearing something that'll tell the neighbors where she lives if she's found running around the neighborhood babbling."

"I thought you'd like it."

"I do. I'm going to get some head charms to hang on it—a boy's head for you and a girl's for Jazzy. Macy's will engrave names on them."

Mom never wore one of anything except her wedding ring.

She said, "People are always asking me what's 7 mean."

"Well? Do you tell them?"

"What can I tell them? I've got a son in some club I don't even know how he got into?" She laughed. "I tell them it's in case I forget how many days there are in the week."

Jazzy got on the phone to tell me her favorite doll, Georgette, was in love with a doll named Mr. Mysterious, who wore a mask, cost $32.75, and could be purchased at most shopping malls.

In the background I could hear the fashion channel on television. A woman's voice was describing a polka-dot sundress with a bolero top and spaghetti straps underneath.

"Johnny?" Mom said when she got back on. "Are you meeting any nice girls?"

"I've met one named Nina."

"I hope she's not your usual type."

"What's my usual type, Mom?"

"Someone who can run circles around you. Someone who's older and wiser, like that Keats person."

Even Mom knew better than to mention Delia.

"This Nina person isn't like that Keats person," I said.

"Watch out, Johnny! You're a cream puff when it comes to the ladies!"

At the dance I'd nab the photographer and have a picture taken for Mom. One look at Nina in all white, and Mom would start fantasizing the wedding, the house we'd all move into, and the grandchildren she could buy more head charms for at Macy's.

I spared Mom the news about Creery, just as I had the Lasher story. The *Cottersville Compass* was already hinting that a suicide on The Hill was purportedly tied into the death earlier of another student. I didn't know how long it would take the news services to pick it up, or if Mom would even see it when they did. She probably wouldn't unless it was on the same page announcing a white sale or 50% Off Everything.

On the phone that week, I'd told Nina what I knew.

"Boy, does my shrink have egg on her face!" she'd said, the moment we'd sped away from her house in the BMW Mr. Deem had lent me. "Her groat-hormone theory was shot all to pieces!"

"Did she say anything Thursday?"

"I told you, Fell. I quit. Dad calls it a hiatus, but it's over. From now on I'm on my own."

She was, too. Or *I* was. As soon as we started dancing, the stag line began descending on us.

I lost her to Charlie Chan, Charles Dickens, Charles Bronson, three or four of the Charlie Chaplins who were there in force, and Charlie Chan again.

I began to feel as though I was ready for grief counseling with **HEADOC**, whose red Maserati had been in the faculty parking lot all week.

There was a seven-piece band playing, blue-and-white 7's hanging from the ceiling, where seven golden angels swung from fluffy clouds in Seventh Heaven. (It had seemed like a good idea when we were planning the decorations, but there was something slightly macabre about it in view of Creery's death . . . or maybe I'd just spent too much time reading Lasher's writings about heaven.)

The seven chaperones wore white dresses or blue suits.

"Fell?" Nina said at one point, when I'd wrenched Charlie Chan's white-gloved hands from her shoulder a third time. "If I don't remember to thank you for this, thank you now."

She put her fingers up on my cheek lightly, and we looked at one another for maybe six seconds. That was all it took for me to see the wisdom and the heartbreak of chaperones and separate quarters for overnight visitors.

Some of Charlie Chan's greasepaint had come off on Nina's dress.

"Thank heavens I brought a change, Fell!" she said to me at intermission. "Look at me!"

We were heading to Sevens House for the intermission ceremony. Mrs. Violet presided over the punch bowl there, while dorm boys served their dates from the bowl in the gym.

This was the time when the Sevens unmasked. The lights went off in the reception room, and our faces were illuminated by tiny gold flashlights shaped like 7's, **CHARLES** engraved down their sides. Each girl was given a corsage of white roses and blue ribbons, and most kept their dates' flashlights as souvenirs.

For the first time I saw Lauren and The Lion. He was in seventeenth-century costume as Charles II of England.

"That's my shrink's daughter, isn't it?" said Nina. "She looks enough like her to make me shake! . . . Let me go up and change before I meet her!"

"Nina *who?*" Lauren asked me after I explained my date was "freshening up," and as The Lion strutted down to the john.

"Deem. Nina Deem."

"Oh, *Fell*! How did you get roped into that?"

She passed me an envelope marked *Photograph. Paul, sometime last autumn.*

"Wait till you see her!" I said.

Lauren was in a red wool dress, her hair pulled up on her head, pearls dangling down the front. Red shoes. The smell of Obsession.

"That's the smiling picture of Paul," she said.

I was getting it out of the envelope.

"I know Nina Deem," said Lauren. "She was

mother's client. Past tense, so I can tell you watch out for her, Fell. She's needy. And that's a *nice* way to put it."

"I like her. You will, too."

"Fell, she'd get on my mother's answering machine and use up all the tape whining about this married dope pusher she had a crush on. Of course, *she* claimed he'd been framed. She was obsessed with what his wife was like, *convinced* he didn't love her. She'd go on and on about him, on the tape! Paul and I called her Screaming Nina. When we were home, we'd tune in to her and howl!"

I pulled Lauren to one side, away from the punch and the girls in the gowns with their Charleses.

"Tell me more, Lauren. She *knew* he was married?"

"She knew, all right. She was dying to get a look at his wife. I hope you're not involved, Fell!"

"What else?"

I was holding the photograph of Lasher in my hands while I listened.

"*Are* you involved with Screaming Nina?"

I hardly heard the question. I was looking at the picture of her brother. Lasher was dressed up in a gay nineties costume, sitting on a bench, the waterfall, the old mill, the weeping willow behind him.

"This was taken at Dragonland," I said.

"I don't know where it was taken. It was in a thingamajig and I pulled it out, because look at him smile! Paul never smiled unless he was up to something."

"Then he knew Eddie Dragon," I said.

Lauren looked at me. "That's the name of Screaming Nina's boyfriend," she said. "How would Paul have known him?"

I didn't answer Lauren, not only because I didn't have an answer but also because of what I saw suddenly across the room.

Charlie Chan was leaving Sevens House, putting on his coat over his costume, his gloves off, and there was something on his wrist I'd seen before. A dragonfly.

I started running, down the hall and up the stairs, the voice of the Sevens shouting after me "Off-limits to males tonight!"

Someone grabbed my coattails to stop me.

Kidder.

"Your date's not up there, Fell. She just went out the side door."

got out in the parking lot in time to see them take off in a white Isuzu jeep.

Nina hadn't changed clothes. I could see her pulling her coat around the white dress. She must have used the time to lug her garment bag down to his car.

I didn't have the BMW keys with me, but I remembered Mr. Deem telling me about the spare in the ashtray.

I got in fast and went after them, picking the jeep up in my headlights near the traffic light at the top of the hill.

They made a left, heading into Cottersville, and I followed a few car lengths behind them.

My mind was spinning like the BMW's wheels: recalling how Nina'd said she'd begged her father to let her go to The Charles Dance ... then how she'd come up soon after with the idea to stay overnight. I thought of Nina telling me she'd brought a lot of changes in her garment bag, and I remembered the way she'd thanked me for the evening right before intermission.

And of course I was remembering the afternoon at Dragonland, the way she'd pretended to be shocked by the idea Eddie was married. She'd known that all along, used me to satisfy her curiosity about Ann Dragon.

Lauren had laughed at the idea Nina'd claimed Eddie didn't love his wife. But my money was on Nina.

I was learning the hard way: Nina didn't *get* surprised as much as she surprised. And calculated. Nina went after what she wanted, even if it involved flirting her way along and giving little innocent-sounding speeches about how she was going to learn to take control of her life.

She didn't need any lessons in that.

What had Nina said to her father that first night I'd had dinner there? Something about the word "elope," after Mr. Deem said it was a word we didn't hear much anymore. Those who have a reason to use it do, Nina had said.

In Cottersville I inched up until I was right behind them.

Dragon wasn't doing any fancy driving. He was keeping to the forty-mile limit, heading out toward the shopping center.

What I couldn't figure out was how Lasher fit into the puzzle, what he was doing at Dragonland last fall.

I pushed the heat up all the way. They had coats, I didn't. I had an idea I wouldn't be getting out of the BMW for a long time, anyway . . . and that as soon as we hit the highway past the mall, I'd be in a race.

That was where I was wrong.

The Isuzu pulled into the shopping center's large lot, almost empty at that hour.

I followed.

Dragon headed toward the only parked car down in front of the Food Basket. It was a black Pontiac, its lights beaming up suddenly as the jeep came near it.

Then Dragon stopped.

When I pulled up, Dragon got out and stood there waiting for me. He'd ripped off his mustache and the rubber skin from his head. His hair was blowing in the wind, face streaked with grease-paint.

As I cut my motor, I saw the gun pointed at me.

That was when the driver of the Pontiac got out too, crossing to the jeep, reaching to help Nina with the garment bag she'd pulled out onto the asphalt.

It was Ann Dragon.

I could see Nina's face, tears streaming down it, while Ann led her toward the Pontiac.

"Get in the jeep!" said Eddie Dragon.

He waited while Ann Dragon got Nina into the front seat of the Pontiac and the garment bag into the back.

I could see the dragonfly tattoo very clearly now as his left hand gripped the steering wheel, while his right one kept the gun trained on me.

"Have you moved from dope into kidnapping, now?" I said.

"Just shut up!"

The Pontiac took off.

He turned back to me, swiveling his shoulders so he could look me in the eyes.

"My name is Ted Draggart. I'm an FBI undercover man. You're who? Somebody Fell?"

"John Fell. And I don't believe you. FBI men don't have tattoos."

"I'm doing the talking right now, John! . . . Nina is not being kidnapped, and you don't know shit about FBI men! . . . Nina is with my partner. We've been undercover here for almost a year. Ann will take Nina someplace safe, while you come with me. Do you understand?"

"Why doesn't Ann just take Nina home?"

"Because that's where *we're* going. I didn't count on you, but now that you're here, I'm going to have to! You're going to have to count on me if you want to save your ass, so start trusting me."

I didn't say anything, just watched while he stuck the gun in the top of his pants.

He started the jeep.

"I'll fill you in as much as I can, so you'll understand the action. For God's sake get rid of the handlebars!"

I'd forgotten my mustache, and I tore it off.

"You paid a visit to the base we set up. Dragonland." He started the jeep. "Everyone paid a visit there but the ones we expected."

"Nina. Me. . . Paul Lasher."

He snorted. "Yeah. Paul Lasher. When you're dredging, you get the dregs. But he was a bonus, it turned out. Let me tell you a few more things before we come to Lasher."

We were heading back to Cottersville.

He said, "Ann and I were given a name."

"She's your wife."

"She's my partner. Let *me* talk, John. . . . The name was David Deem. We got it from a fairly reliable source, if you want to call someone with dope connections and convictions reliable. But he wanted to make a deal, get himself out of serving twenty years. Deem was the bite. Our informer knew there was a sporting-goods setup involved too, but nothing else. . . . Ann and I set ourselves up in Point Pleasant after we got a read on Deem. Our case agent had nothing to incriminate Deem, so we came in blind."

We were making all the right turns that would take us to Jericho Road.

"I angled to meet Nina," Dragon said. "We'd found out she was the only one he had left to care about. She was my 'in' to Deem. I met him, and I found out all I could, which wasn't much. . . . Later we fixed my arrest for selling cocaine and arranged to get me off, with the newspapers picking up the story. . . . We didn't figure Deem himself would come after me. Everything we knew about him was clouded over, anyway, but we figured him as a guy who wouldn't want anyone muscling in on his territory . . . and particularly his daughter. We thought he'd send someone to Dragonland to threaten me, someone who'd lead us to his operation by some zigzag route."

"Deem sells drugs?"

"Not exactly. Not at all what we thought. Deem doesn't have a territory. He's a facilitator. He doesn't sell anything; he helps it get sold. He has this mail-order deal called DOT. Short for Deem Out There. Advertises: Out There You'll Need Us. All-weather equipment. Let me finish, John," he said, as I started to tell him I'd heard Nina mention DOT. "There isn't time now." He looked at his watch and picked up some speed.

"Your friend Lasher—"

"He wasn't my friend."

"This Lasher came to Dragonland last fall. He'd read the newspaper write-up of my arrest. He was sniffing around, trying to see if I knew this Creery. There was a point when I even thought he was trying to frame Creery, or get him killed. I didn't have time for it, didn't want him around, but while he was there he said he knew a lot about my girlfriend, Nina Deem.

"I paid attention suddenly. I asked him how the hell he knew her name. He told me his mother was her shrink. Then he began playing the bigshot, telling me a lot of stuff about Nina, like the fact I'd told her I was married. I finally told her that after my arrest. She'd gotten herself a tattoo like mine over in Lambertville. That's the first I realized she'd made this thing into a big romance."

"She fell in love with you. Didn't you *angle* for that?"

"She was a kid! I thought she had a crush on me, sure, but I never encouraged it, never even held her hand—nothing! I didn't count on this flood of emotion. She'd call Dragonland even after I told her not to, to let *me* get in touch with *her.* Then she appeared with you. And after that she called to apologize for bringing you there. I couldn't discourage the contact with her altogether, because I needed that."

We were passing Main Pharmacy and Play-wicky Road.

Dragon said, "You see, Lasher let something drop that got my ears pricking. He said his mother told him Nina was going away at Easter. It was going to be a surprise. Her father was planning to take her to Europe. . . . Lasher said maybe I could use that information . . . and maybe he could get me more if I'd help him get this Creery. . . . I wanted him to go because he was just in the way. I told him I didn't want to run off with Nina, thanks anyway, I was happily married. I had a hell of a time getting him out of there that day. He hung around, had his picture taken. . . . But he'd given me the tip: Deem was going to run in March. We had to work fast!"

We were a block from Jericho.

Dragon was slowing up. He said, "A few months later Lasher was killed. . . . I sent in for information on this Creery. Routine, not my province, but Lasher'd said Creery used drugs, so you never know. . . . I asked for anything the computer had on Creery, and lo and behold, we found a connection to DOT. It was there all along, but we hadn't been looking for it, and it still isn't too clear. I tried to get a court order to tap Deem's phone. It never came through, and we found out Deem was booked to go this Sunday. . . . We're going to park a few doors away. My backup's there somewhere. John, I don't want you to leave this car, okay?"

"Yes." It was beginning to fit, all of it. I knew then why Mr. Deem was so eager to get Nina to The Charles Dance that weekend, and why he'd allowed her to stay overnight. He was making all the arrangements in the house, packing up, preparing to close it and clear out.

I said, "And I suppose Nina thought you were eloping with her tonight!"

"She probably did, but there was no other way. When she told me she could stay overnight on The Hill, I was afraid Deem might take off solo. . . . Maybe not, but we couldn't take that chance, so we moved. We put a man on Jericho while Ann and I went for Nina. I wanted her out of there, and I wanted her prepared for what she's going to have to find out about her father. Ann's taking her in, and telling her everything. She'll be good with her, John."

"*Fell*," I said.

"Fell. I care a lot about Nina, too."

We went down Jericho and parked two doors away from the house.

We weren't there long before a man rapped on my window.

Eddie Dragon said, "You sit tight, Fell."

He got out.

I heard him say he had a Hill boy with him who'd stay in the jeep. I watched him stop and drop something. Then he turned around and came back to the passenger side.

The man was right behind him.

I rolled down my window.

"I didn't count on this, Fell. Sorry," Dragon said.

"No conversations!" a voice barked. "Just get him out and in the house!"

It wasn't a voice I'd ever heard before, but I knew the face when I saw it.

Mark Twain from Miami.

He was stopping to pick up Dragon's gun from the street. Then he had two.

The phone wires were cut, Deem told me, and there was a naked man locked in the crawl space. Deem said he had no idea who the man was, that Meatloaf had been let out to do his business and routed him out of the bushes. Then Hunter had taken his clothes, to go through them and to limit his action.

We were locked in, too, Deem and I, in Deem's study. If we tried anything, Hunter'd warned us, he'd kill us both.

From the sounds below, Dragon was being put in with the backup.

"At least Nina's safe," I said.

"No she isn't. Hunter made me call the school and say she was to come home immediately, alone. He sent a taxi for her."

I explained that she was with Ann, that Dragon had seen to that. Then I told him who Dragon was, or what he was . . . that Ann was his partner, and the naked man part of their team.

He looked too frightened to understand what I'd told him. "Don't try anything, Fell," he said. "Hunter means it when he says he'll kill us."

He was sitting in his big Eames chair hugging Meatloaf.

"What could I try? There're bars on those windows."

I was still absorbing the idea this man was involved with dope. He looked the same to me, right down to the suit, the necktie, and the shine on his shoes. It was hard for me to imagine him jaywalking, much less "facilitating" drug sales.

He knew I'd been told something by Dragon. He was having trouble looking at me, though I was right there on his footstool. It was the first time we'd ever been face-to-face when I'd had shoes on.

"Hunter killed his own stepbrother," he said finally. "Now he's going to kill me, too."

"How do you know he killed Creery, sir?" I didn't mean to call him "sir," but habit won out. He seemed to respond to the respect I'd given him unintentionally, and he met my eyes for the first time.

"I suspected as much," he said, "and when I accused him of it tonight, he told me he'd kill Nina, too, if I didn't cooperate with him. . . . What have I done, Fell?" he sighed. "What *have* I done?"

"How did you ever get involved with someone like Hunter?" I said. He had a handkerchief out and was mopping his brow.

He said, "You might as well hear it from me, Fell. Tell Nina, too; otherwise she'll never learn the truth. I won't live to tell her."

He lifted Meatloaf up to his chest and held him hard. "A long time ago, Bob Creery and I had dinner one night in Miami. We'd been friends in Sevens. My business was bad. He said he could help me out." He leaned down and brushed his lips against the top of the dog's head. "Bob was sort of an entrepreneur. That's a polite name for it. He had his paint business in Miami, a couple of warehouses. He was sometimes legitimate, mostly not. Bootleg stuff. We formed DOT together. I sold stolen goods. . . . It wasn't right, of course, but no one got hurt. Insurance covered the losses. . . . That was the way I rationalized it. DOT thrived. So did I. . . . Oh, Fell, Sevens did something to me. It gave me a taste for certain comforts, small luxuries. I'd never been as happy as when I lived as a Sevens. . . . I got spoiled for any kind of life that wouldn't be easy."

Meatloaf jumped out of his lap and down to my feet to sniff me.

Deem said, "Everything turned sour right before Barbara died. Bob had his stroke, and his stepson couldn't wait to take over! Next thing I knew we were in the cocaine business. It was being shipped from South America to the paint factory inside croquet mallets, the handles of tennis rackets, anything wooden. It holds up well in wood and doesn't add that much extra weight. . . .

He sent me samples to show me until I said, 'I don't want to know about it—stop it.' He'd empty out the cocaine, paint the stuff, and ship it on. My equipment and DOT gave him another outlet. He's got outlets all over the country."

"Did Creery's father know, or Creery?"

"Bob wouldn't have allowed it, not Bob. He wasn't a man of any integrity, but he wouldn't have okayed drug trafficking. . . . It's too dirty . . . and it's too risky. I wouldn't have either, if Hunter hadn't known all about DOT. Bob was paralyzed all down one side, and that left me at Hunter's mercy." Deem folded his handkerchief neatly and placed it carefully back in his breast pocket. "The boy didn't know, I'm sure. Hunter pretended to get the kid off pot by substituting pills. That's why there were rumors that Cyril was selling, because he could get all he wanted. Of course the kid got hooked. Hunter wanted him addicted. But that boy thought it was his own fault he couldn't stop. . . . And he was being bullied by that Lasher boy."

"Well . . . they bullied each other."

"I think he taunted him once too often. Didn't Nina say he had proof of some kind that Bob told him how to get into Sevens?"

"Yes. There was a letter."

"I believe the story going around The Hill is that Cyril killed Lasher. An associate of Hunter's told me, just last fall, that the boy was on a combination of amphetamines and Quaaludes. There was plenty of Miami gossip regarding young Cyril, speculation about how Hunter'd deal with him after Bob's death. . . . And drugs change your whole personality. You live a nightmare. You love the drug more than you love anything. Well"—he gave a strange little choked cough—"that's how we got rich. Cocaine made us rich. Richer than we'd ever been. . . . Hunter is a greedy man, Fell. He wanted that little empire for himself. Bob's near death. Cyril would have inherited everything from Bob . . . and there'd be a lot of explaining to do. So Hunter saw his chance."

"But if he knew Creery'd killed Lasher, why didn't he just turn him in?"

Deem shook his head. "No. In our business we know too well how elastic the law is. Hunter didn't want Cyril alive. The law wouldn't kill him, so Hunter did. . . . I didn't even know he was up north until Cyril was found dead. We never made phone calls to each other. We met in Florida, always. We never wanted any record of rapport . . . Even after young Cyril's death, I never expected him to walk through that door the way he did tonight. . . . Walked in here and caught me red-handed, said, You're not going anywhere. . . . Poor Nina. My poor, poor Nina."

I picked Meatloaf up and handed him to Deem.

He needed to hold on to something, do something with his hands, which he'd begun to wring. I'd never make a good policeman. I felt too sorry for people I knew who got themselves into trouble. I could see myself in them, maybe, see how easy it was to start heading down the wrong road.

"They say it's a small world." Deem was talking into Meatloaf's neck. "And it is indeed. Do you know how Hunter learned I was planning to bolt?"

He didn't wait for my answer.

He said, "Hunter spent some time with Inge Lasher's daughter these past few weeks. She told him her brother thought a man named Eddie Dragon was supplying Cyril with the pills. Cyril'd never told her the truth. . . . Then she told Hunter about Nina being mixed up with Dragon: She'd heard her on the answering machine. . . . One day Dr. Inge told her, Don't worry, she won't be calling here after Easter, Mr. Deem is taking her away. . . . Well. That was all Hunter needed to hear. He did a little investigating on his own, called the travel bureau, and found out I was leaving tomorrow morning."

"Thank God for Eddie Dragon," I said. "Or whatever his real name is. He got Nina out, anyway."

"He started it all," Deem said bitterly.

I noticed Deem blamed everyone but himself.

Sevens. Hunter. Eddie Dragon.

"By now Hunter knows he's trapped, too. He can't lock up the whole Cottersville police force in the dry cellar, can he? They'll be along, won't they?" He seemed ready to cry. "I hope you'll be kind enough to take care of Meatloaf, Fell. And to tell Nina I truly love her. . . . Hunter won't hurt you. Just me. I never should have put bars on those windows."

I was praying that he was right about the police coming, that by then Ann had gotten to them. But I was also remembering my father telling me of times local police didn't interfere with federal arrests.

We didn't say any more for a while. Deem sat there cradling Meatloaf in his arms like a baby. Then we heard a door slam.

Meatloaf began barking. "Don't, darling," Deem told the dog. "Hush and don't make trouble." He put his thumb and finger over Meatloaf's nose like a muzzle.

Hunter unlocked the study door and appeared with an armful of clothes, a gun peeking out from under trousers and shirts, underpants, coats, and shoes.

"I'll take your car keys, David," he said.

I petted Meatloaf with trembling hands. He was making low sounds close to growling. The gun in Hunter's hand was aimed at me and the dachshund.

The dog jumped down as Deem reached into his pocket.

Hunter looked at me and said, "You're coming!"

"Why take the boy?" Deem asked.

"For a shield," Hunter said.

Deem dropped the keys into Hunter's palm.

At first when I heard the noise, I thought there was a radio on in the house.

Then, as it became louder, I knew what it was.

"What the hell is that?" Hunter snapped.

He walked over to the window.

I could see the look on his face, and I knew I'd always remember it. The flesh caved in, and the eyes got wide.

"Get over here!" he said to me. "What the hell is this?"

They were in the yard with their gold flashlights shining on their faces. Singing.

I could see Charles Dickens and Charles II, Charles Bronson and two Charlie Chaplins.

There were about a dozen Sevens there. Kidder I recognized, and Fisher. Schwartz next to Fisher.

They were in good voice and I'd never felt more like joining in.

The time will come as the years go by,
When my heart will thrill
At the thought of The Hill,
And the Sevens who came
With their bold cry,
WELCOME TO SEVENS!

Then they began to shout our names, seven times apiece.

"DEEM! DEEM! DEEM! DEEM! DEEM! DEEM! DEEM!"

Behind me Meatloaf was dancing to the door and barking.

"Shut that damn dog up!" Hunter cried out.

There were tears rolling down Deem's cheeks as he realized they'd come to rescue him, however they had gotten word he needed them.

I might have bawled myself, but I had gone to quiet Meatloaf, near the door, telling him to be still, a moment before my hand reached for the knob and my legs did the rest.

I had my own cheering section to spur me on.

"FELL! FELL! FELL! FELL! FELL!"—and I was out of there for the last two.

When the Cottersville police arrived in their car, Dr. Skinner pulled up in the Gardner limo.

I told one cop about the naked man in the crawl space while another began calling to Deem and Lowell Hunter through a bullhorn, advising them that the house was surrounded, to come out hands up.

"I want you and Schwartz to come with me, Fell," Skinner said to me.

"Can't we wait to see them come out?"

"No. We're going back to The Hill with Lieutenant Hatch. He's going to ask some questions, and I hope he's going to answer some. . . . Schwartz had better answer some, too—about how Sevens got dragged into this!"

Skinner went over and tapped Schwartz on the shoulder.

I could hear Schwartz tell him he'd go back in Kidder's van with the other Sevens. But Skinner shook his head no. He pointed to the limo.

"Right now?" Schwartz said.

"Right this minute!" said Skinner. Then he walked over to The Sevens and said that they were to leave. Immediately.

Even though we were coatless in the bitter cold, we dragged our heels getting down to the limo. We were looking over our shoulders at the red brick house, the front porch illuminated by mobile spotlights.

In his brown flannel suit, striped cotton shirt, and silk tie, with the square cotton pocket hand-kerchief, Deem appeared there like someone yanked out of a PBS–TV play and pushed into the set of a cops-and-robbers sitcom. He had his hands up. He was smiling grimly.

"Is his daughter in there, too?" Schwartz asked me.

"No. But she's all right."

"What in the hell was going on, Fell? Did Dragon try to run off with her?"

Dr. Skinner said, "Get in back, boys! You'll have ample opportunity to discuss this on The Hill! Ready, Lieutenant?"

Hatch was looking over his shoulder too, in time to see Lowell Hunter follow Deem. All four of us were standing by the limo gawking.

Then Skinner said to the lieutenant, "I don't have a driver. You sit up front with me."

We got in, reluctantly.

Skinner leaned around to say, "I'm going to put up this window, but I advise you boys not to try collaborating on any story to shield Sevens!

I've had my fill of Sevens skulduggery! . . . I'll put the heat on. Fell, you're shivering."

He didn't have to tell me that. My teeth were chattering.

The glass partition between the front and the backseats went up, and soon after we began gliding down Jericho, I felt the warm air.

Schwartz said, "Lauren and I couldn't figure out what happened to you. Kidder said you took off after the Deem girl like a bat out of hell."

"I did." I was beginning to feel all the fear I hadn't dared feel for my own poor ass. Fear, then the fatigue coming in with the relief that it was over.

"Skinner doesn't know it, but *I* called the police," Schwartz said. "I told them to call Deem. They said the phones were out here, that something was going on down here, but they didn't know what. And Saturday night—most of their cars are out looking for impaired drivers. . . . They said they were going to radio them over to Jericho, where you were, probably. . . . How did they know that, Fell?"

The yawn came moaning out of me. I couldn't help it. It was the delayed sound of panic or relief, all that was left from a frustrated scream, probably.

Schwartz gave me a look. "You're a cool one, Fell."

"Far from it."

Schwartz continued, "We figured you two Sevens could use some help maybe. We were warned not to go into the house, so I said we'd do a little street theater outside and see what happened."

"I was never so glad to see you all! Thanks, Lion!"

"How did Creery's stepbrother get in on the act, Fell? And where's Eddie Dragon?"

I held one hand up. "Later. Not right now."

Schwartz gave my leg a punch. "See? I told you Fate arranges exits and entrances. . . . But I have to admit I never really thought Dragon would pull something like this!"

Another punch, that time to my arm. "We came through for you, though, Fell!"

Whatever Schwartz imagined had been going on at the Deems', it had him bubbling over. "That Deem!" He laughed. "Did you see him come out? Nothing ruffles our boy, does it? He looked like he was coming out of church on a Sunday morning."

"Since when do you come out of church with your hands up?" I said.

"The police didn't mean for Deem to do it. And I think they got Hunter confused with Dragon. . . . But I never liked the looks of Lowell Hunter. Guys in their thirties with white hair make me nervous."

"How about guys seventeen with white hair?" I

said. "I think mine's turning white after tonight."

"Not you, Fell. You're too nervy."

I put my head back against the leather seat and shut my eyes. I didn't want to think about Nina, but it was hard not to. Not to imagine her face when she found out about her dad. Not to wonder how she'd deal with that, and with the stunt Dragon had played on her: making her think her dreams had come true, he was whisking her away with him . . . and she'd worn that white dress, the kind a bride would choose.

Schwartz was humming a familiar tune.

What was it . . . Something about your voice calling . . . something right on the tip of my tongue.

Then he was whistling it softly.

> *Heavenly shades of night are falling—*
> *it's Twilight Time,*
> *Out of the mist your voice is calling—*
> *it's Twilight Time.*

I opened my eyes and turned my head to see his face. "Yes, Fell, that's for you," he said. "You owe Sevens a Twilight Truth."

"*I* do?"

"You do. Because you *are* nervy, Fell. . . . You never should have attended The Charles Dance as

Damon Charles. That's disrespectful, Fell. We don't make fun of our founder!"

"You're not kidding, either," I said.

"I don't kid about Sevens," said The Lion.

~

He wasn't the only Sevens who felt that way. Until I went home for Easter vacation, that song was whistled at me through my door, on campus, in the dining room at The Tower—wherever I passed another Sevens.

By the time I got back from Brooklyn, no one was whistling anymore. Maybe because of what happened at the end of those nine days.

I spent them cooking for Mom and Jazzy, and walking around God's country. Down to the Brooklyn Bridge, and across to the Promenade with its great view of the New York skyline. Up to the Botanical Gardens, where the Japanese cherry trees were in bloom, and over to the Brooklyn Museum.

In Carroll Gardens I dropped in to see my grandfather in the nursing home and listen to him tell me again why he was named after Theodore Roosevelt.

One night I made a lot of telephone calls until I connected with Nina. She was staying with her aunt Peggy up in Hartford, Connecticut.

"I'm glad you called, Fell," she said. "I thought

you'd be mad at me. He's called too, Eddie has. We're friends now. Just good friends."

We didn't talk about her father. She didn't seem to want to, and neither did I.

At the end of our conversation I said I hoped we'd be good friends too, and Nina said she'd like that.

"Am I a good friend?" Jazzy asked me after I'd hung up.

"Yes."

"Then do I get Mr. Mysterious if I'm a good friend?" I sat her down and talked about gift giving with her for a while. "Sometimes the best gifts are ones you don't ask for," I told her.

"But I like to know what I'm getting Johnny. I always know what I want."

"Don't you ever want something money can't buy?"

"Like what?"

"Well, what we were just talking about. Friends."

"Girlfriends or boyfriends?"

"You can't buy either kind. You can't buy a true friend."

"What's a true friend?"

How did I answer her? I don't remember. But whatever I said only reminded me of Dib. What had happened between us was all my fault. I'd left him out. I'd become too full of myself and Sevens. Dib had been right that morning he'd told me that I was the one impressed by the gold 7. Mom hardly ever wore it, even with the head charms hanging beside it.

~

Going back to The Hill on the train, I came upon the newspaper story about David Deem's death. Out on bail, he was found in his Lincoln shot seven times through the heart. Neighbors heard the gun go off at five in the afternoon . . . At twilight, I thought.

Police have not determined yet if the dead rat found between his teeth has some tie-in with underworld ritual. Purportedly he had no Mafia connections.

Lowell Hunter, alleged to be kingpin behind the DOT operation, has been held without bail charged with the murder of his stepbrother, Cyril Creery.

The Hill was buzzing with rumors about the three murders, Deem's in particular, because of The Sevens Revenge.

Since everyone in Sevens House had been on Easter vacation, far from Cottersville, it was being whispered that an alumnus had caught up with David Deem.

But Schwartz insisted it was someone with

connections to Hunter. Someone who wanted Deem silenced, and chose to make it look like The Revenge.

There were stern notices posted everywhere on bulletin boards, insisting that more than ever now, Gardner had to put the past behind it.

> GOSSIP, INNUENDO, REHASHING OF OUR CRISES
> CAN ONLY DO GRAVE INJURY TO THE FUTURE
> OF THE SCHOOL! DO NOT LOOK BACK.
> GO FORWARD.

That was my intention when I went down to the dorm late in the afternoon, after I'd unpacked.

Dib was coming out as I was heading up the walk.

"I want to talk, Dib."

"Not now, Fell. I'm going out to dinner."

I walked along with him, toward the familiar green Mustang parked at the curb.

"How come Little Jack's driving? I thought he was pulled over on a DWI?"

"You know, Fell, I'd worry more about your crowd than mine. You could end up with a big mouse in your mouth."

I let that go. "Let's get together tomorrow," I said.

"Maybe. If there's time."

Little Jack rolled down the window and gave me a salute. "Aye, aye, sir!" he said.

I walked up closer. "What's that supposed to mean?"

"Aren't you giving my boy some orders, Fell?"

Dib said, "He doesn't give me orders." He went around to get in the passenger seat.

"I thought he did," said Little Jack.

He smelled of beer or whiskey; maybe both.

"You're in great condition to drive," I said.

"Cork it, Fell!" Dib shouted at me.

"Dib, he's *drunk*!"

"Dib"—Little Jack made what I'd said into a high whine—"he's drunk!"

I should have gone around, opened the door, and yanked Dib out.

That was what I told myself as I stood there while Little Jack took off, waving at me. "Bye-bye, Felly!"

Dib was staring straight ahead.

I watched the car weave down the street toward the hill.

Little Jack Horner
Sat in a corner.

I couldn't remember the rest of the nursery rhyme that began humming in my head, not then and there. Just those two lines.

But later on it came back to me. All that long, sad spring it did.

Then, when summer came, I went looking for Little Jack.

Oh, yes. *He* was still around.

fell down

chapter | 1

ell, you're a mess," Keats said, "and you're wal-
lowing in it."

"I don't want to talk about it now."

"Then when?"

The waiter asked if he could tell us the specials.

It wouldn't have surprised me if Keats had
made him stand there while I explained all the
deep trouble my mind was in, but instead she
listened to him. Then she said she'd have the
fettuccine with seafood.

I ordered the Long Island duck.

"You look awful, too," Keats said while the

waiter was taking the menus from our hands.

"Thanks for pointing that out," I said.

"I should have suggested someplace tacky for dinner. Not here," she continued.

We were in the Edwardian Room, in the Plaza Hotel. She'd come all the way into New York City to take me out. I knew that it was really Daddy who would pay the charge: Lawrence O. Keating, an architect whose dreams for his only daughter did not include John Fell.

He didn't have to worry about it anymore. We were just friends, though he'd never believe it.

"Promise me one thing before you tell me what this is all about," she said.

"Okay. One thing."

"When your food comes, don't tell me what's wrong with it. Don't taste mine and tell me what's wrong with mine. If something's overpowered by its sauce or underseasoned, keep it a secret, okay? I like to think everything's wonderful."

"At these prices, I don't blame you."

"Even if we were eating at McDonald's, I'd feel the same way, Fell. Who wants to hear a whole critique? Just eat, drink, and be merry."

"Give me a break," I said. "I don't complain that much."

"Yes, you do. If you don't, you've changed."

"Well, yeah. That I've done."

"Talk!" she said.

"What do you want to know?"

"Why you're a jet crash."

"I wrote you about it."

"You said a close friend died in an automobile accident. But since when do you go to pieces over a friend's death? You didn't crack up when your dad died."

"No, I didn't."

"Maybe if you started back at the beginning," said Keats.

So I did. I told her Dib was my first friend at Gardner School, and maybe my only real friend there. I told her how we grew apart when I got into Sevens, the elite club on The Hill, with its own residence and clubhouse.

I told her how Dib took up with Jack Horner, known as Little Jack. I took the story up to the last time I saw Dib. He was getting into Little Jack's green Mustang. Little Jack had been drinking. Little Jack was driving.

My voice always played tricks on me at this point in the story, and I'd feel breathless, and a sting behind my eyes.

Keats said, "So you just left school—walked out and the heck with your final exams and everything."

"Yeah. I just walked out and the heck with my final exams and everything."

"So now you don't even have a high school diploma."

"*Nada,*" I agreed.

"Fell, it's not like you. You stayed together when your father died."

"Don't keep saying that. . . . Maybe that's *why* I let go this time."

"Oh?"

She looked across at me. She smelled of Obsession and she had on something silky and green, to match her eyes. I was glad I was in this phony place with her, because I needed things to be familiar. I needed to believe the world hadn't changed.

She looked like she belonged in that roomy armchair she was sitting in, under the colossal chandelier.

I was out of place. I had on some old seer-sucker suit of my dad's that'd looked great in the '70s, and my bow tie was a clip-on. I didn't have the clothes or the energy to try and look like someone who belonged with the beautiful people. Keats didn't need any extra push to look that way. She was part of that scene. When we went someplace like that, the maitre d' always addressed all his remarks to her.

Keats thought a few seconds about what I'd said.

She said, "Are you saying that you're having a delayed reaction to your father's death?"

"I don't know what I'm having," I said.

"I think you're experiencing a displacement,"

Keats said. "That means you might let something big go by, and then later on, without knowing it, react the way you should have earlier over something much less important."

"My shrink would love you," I said.

"Fell! You're seeing a shrink? I can't believe this!"

"I was seeing one for a while. Mom insisted I at least talk to one. I didn't go more than three times. . . . Do you know what they cost?"

"Of course I know! I'm a graduate! I went for five years!"

"I remember."

"You must be hurting, Fell."

"Not anymore. Not *hurting*."

"What then?"

"I'm mad as hell, Keats. That's all."

"At yourself?"

"No, I'm over the self-blame, finally. I'm not over the feeling I'd like to get my hands on Little Jack."

"What would that solve, Fell?"

"It wouldn't solve anything. It'd satisfy something."

"Diogenes said forgiveness is better than revenge."

"You just made that up."

"No, he said it. I did a paper on him."

"I've never believed what *The Cottersville*

Compass wrote about that accident. They claimed it was the guy who hit Dib and Little Jack who was drunk. . . . I *saw* Little Jack get behind the wheel drunk."

"Maybe they were both drunk. Who was the other guy?"

"Some stand-up comedian from Las Vegas."

The sommelier was circling. I always thought I looked twenty-one and not seventeen, but he wasn't fooled and passed on by with the wine list.

While we ate, I told Keats what little I knew about this man named Lenny Last. I only had one write-up in *The Compass* to go by. I'd read that on the train when I was leaving Gardner. Last had driven his old white Cadillac through a red light just as Little Jack turned the corner. Dib and Last were both killed.

Keats thought she might have heard the name . . . maybe from *The Tonight Show.* . . . I didn't push it. I wanted Keats to talk about herself, too. Mom had pointed out that I was so wrapped up in myself lately, I didn't show any interest in other people. I hadn't even realized Mom was dating the guy across the hall.

"Mom," I'd said, "you're *dating* that tailor?"

"What did you think I was doing with him?"

"Going to the movies with him, I don't know."

"That's *dating,* Johnny."

Keats told me she was going to become a

psychoanalyst. Maybe not a psychoanalyst, she said, maybe just a therapist because she didn't think she could go through medical school.

"It's too hard," she said, "and it takes too long. . . . How's your duck?"

"It's good," I said. I didn't say that there wasn't enough sour cherry sauce on it, remembering my promise.

Keats said anything from Long Island had to be good.

She was most partial to her hometown, Seaville, in The Hamptons.

For a short time it'd been my hometown, too. Brooklyn would always be my real home, but sometimes I remembered the ocean and the beaches, the roads winding through potato fields down to ponds with swans nesting there. The clean air and the blue sky and the smell of summer.

Keats glanced across the table at me and said suddenly, "Let me drive you back there."

The restaurant where I worked was open seven days, so we took turns getting weekends off. It wasn't my turn. But I wouldn't have minded heading out to The Hamptons, where so far there weren't people without homes sleeping in doorways and drug addicts stalking you. . . . All of that was hard enough to take when you were in good shape, but if you were on shaky ground, you had to wonder how long before *you'd* be out there, with everything you owned in a shopping cart you'd stolen from a supermarket.

"What would Daddy say if you showed up with me?" I asked her.

"I didn't mean Seaville, Fell. I meant let me drive you back to Gardner School. I've never seen the place."

"I could get my clothes, finally."

"And you could look up Little Jack. . . . He's a townie, right? So he'd be there."

"I'm sure he would."

"I think you need to tell him off."

"I need to wipe up a dirty floor with him, more."

"Whatever. . . . You haven't been back at all, have you?"

I shook my head. "If I want to graduate, I have to go back this fall."

"I thought Sevens was so powerful you could get away with anything."

"Sevens can't do anything about academics. I didn't take my finals." I shrugged. I wished I'd taken them. I must have been getting better, because I couldn't imagine myself just walking out on everything.

"I'd love to see Sevens House," she said.

"You're just being nice, Keats. Thanks, but you don't need to change your whole personality just because I'm having a nervous breakdown."

We both laughed. I figured that she couldn't

care less about seeing some prep-school clubhouse now that she was a college girl. In the fall she'd be a sophomore at Sweetbriar, in Virginia.

Then she smiled at me. I'd always loved her smile. It made her look more sophisticated than she was, and gentler than she was, too, though I couldn't fault her in that regard this night.

"I need to get out of The Hamptons," she said. "August is two weeks away, and you know what August is like. What we never dreamed would ever find their way out to the South Fork arrives in August, along with all the shrinks who take the month off, and all their nut cases."

"You should definitely be a psychoanalyst," I said. "You have all the sensitivity one needs for that profession."

"Only if you'll be my first patient and listen to me."

"I thought you were supposed to listen to me."

"Fell, be serious for a minute. Do you think you'll repeat the year so you can get your diploma? You should. It's a very fancy school."

"I might get a job as a cook's apprentice and forget my high school diploma. All I want is to own a restaurant someday."

Keats nodded. "I know that. But it'd only be one more year out of your life."

I was working at a French place on the waterfront, over in Brooklyn Heights. It was called Le Rêve. The Dream.

One night my boss had told me if I stuck with him, I could end up owning the place. He didn't have a child to pass it on to.

But you can't step into someone else's dream.

I can't, anyway.

"You know what's wrong with me, Fell?" said Keats, who had just set an all-time record for Keats, by going for over an hour without mentioning what was wrong with her.

"What's wrong with you?"

"I'm not in love. . . . Do you know how pointless everything is when you're not in love?"

I nodded. I knew.

"I don't even know why I'm shopping anymore."

"You still want to look great, and you do."

"Why do I want to look great?" she said. "Who for?"

"For whom," I said.

"Exactly! But I'm not sure you're sympathetic. Sometimes I think you hang on to that old romance with Delia so you don't have to deal with reality."

"I'm over Delia," I said. Do you know what an oxymoron is? It's the official name for something combining contradictory expressions. If that sounds complicated, just think of cold fire, or hot snow, or over Delia.

But I would never admit to anyone that she was

still there. I'd rather agree to the idea that Little Jack didn't kill Dib, Lenny Last did.

"Keats," I said, "you're right. We need to get away."

THE MOUTH

Of course Lenny Last was not his real name.

In 1961, he was enrolled in Gardner School as Leonard Tralastski.

Until he'd won the scholarship to The Hill, his life had not amounted to a hill of beans.

I yawn and snore to think of it!

Get out the violins until we're past the part where little Lenny's daddy goes down flying a torpedo bomber in World War II.

On the very day the Japs surrendered, September 1, 1945, Baby Leonard was born.

Happy Birthday, Tralastski!

Just when the Japs were crying in their saki as their emperor surrendered in Tokyo Bay, Mommy's little sweetums was at Lenox Hill Hospital bawling in his crib.

I know, I know: We don't say Japs anymore. But when we did, back when we did, there was no sign that Leonard Tralastski would have anything but a very ordinary fate.

His long-suffering mother raised him in a tiny two-room apartment on the West Side in New York City.

He was never poor.

His long-suffering mother worked in Hosiery at Macy's six days a week, and several nights sold tickets at a nearby Loew's.

But in a way our boy was a poor thing: poor in spirit and in poor health. He was, for an eternity, this too-tall, too-skinny kid who suffered from severe asthma, from mild acne, and from growing up without a dad.

He had no friends, no knack for making any.

He spent most of his time talking to his own hand.

He had a white glove that he pulled over his right hand, then closed the hand to a fist. On the back of the glove he painted a face, a lipstick mouth where the thumb and forefinger met. The thing's mouth moved when Lenny moved his thumb.

He called it Handy.

Sometimes he'd entertain his mother with Handy.

LENNY:	Good morning, Handy.
HANDY:	What's good about it?
LENNY:	Well, the sun's out.
HANDY:	Whose son?
LENNY:	*S-u-n!* Not s-o-n. The *s-u-n* is out.
HANDY:	Who let it out?

Only a mother would have clapped after, and cheered an encore out of him.

She was his only cheerleader, until the day he got off the train in Trenton, New Jersey, and got on the Gardner School bus, bound for Cottersville, Pennsylvania.

He was going to prep school.

He was going to be a junior.

They say in this life you have a very narrow chance of meeting the one person who is your other: your double, your *doppelgänger*. It is not a romantic meeting but a meeting of the minds. Some say the souls. And it is agreed that had you two never found each other, as most do not, then neither one would rise to the heights or sink to the depths such a coupling often inspires or propels.

Folie à deux.

That's the official name for it.

Would Gilbert have written without Sullivan? Would Lewis have discovered anything without Clark?. . . Would Loeb have murdered without Leopold?

On that bus, on that autumn day in Bucks County, when the leaves were being torn from the trees by a bitter wind in an early snap, Lenny Tralastski met *his* other.

"Is this seat taken?" said he.

I am not going to introduce myself.

I will tell you the story of Lenny Last with as few asides as possible.

You'll notice that I take some liberties, the privilege of any storyteller. . . . Maybe the dialogue isn't verbatim; maybe this one wasn't smiling, that one wasn't frowning when I said he was.

It'll all come out in the wash.

Aside:

Folie à deux means simultaneous insanity.

It takes two to tango . . . to tangle, too.

chapter | 2

Keats, this is Mrs. Violet, the Sevens' house-mother."

"Keats?" she said, raising one eyebrow the way she did when we'd do something she wasn't sure we should do.

"Helen Keating," Keats said.

"Keats. That's a nice nickname. I like that."

I thought of the fact I didn't even know Mrs. Violet's first name. I'd never seen her out of Sevens House, and I'd never imagined her having any other life.

"I didn't think you'd be here," I said. "Don't you ever take a vacation?"

She was all in white. When wasn't she? These thin-legged silk pants that grabbed her ankles, high heels, pearls under a flimsy blouse, and the blond hair loose, not held back in the bun as usual.

"I always go somewhere in summer," she said, "but now I have to help prepare for the girls."

"What girls?"

"The *girls*, Fell," she said. "The girls! Surely you know about it, or were you gone by the time it was announced?"

"We didn't go coed, I trust." I laughed a bit smugly.

"As a matter of fact, we did. . . . When I saw you two coming up the walk, I thought Keats was one of our prospective students, looking over the campus."

I was in shock.

Keats said, "Will the girls be able to come here?"

"When one gets into Sevens, yes, or as a visitor of a Sevens."

"Oh no!" I groaned. "Girls in Sevens!"

Keats gave me a look. "And what's wrong with that?"

"I just can't imagine it."

"I thought you were a little brighter than that."

Mrs. Violet said, "So did I, Fell. You are, too."

"Some sexist pigs are bright," said Keats, "but they lack emotional maturity."

"Don't gang up on me," I said.

"Oh, poor baby," said Keats.

Mrs. Violet was laughing. "You'll get used to the idea, Fell," she said.

She just assumed I was coming back. If I didn't, I supposed there'd be those who'd imagine it was because females were finally going to be a part of life at The Hill. Gardner'd gone coed. I tried to picture them there, but nothing would come through in focus.

I finally got around to showing Keats my suite, which was what had brought us to Sevens House.

If you've made a decision not to return, we must know immediately, Fell, the headmaster'd written just last week. *And, of course, you must alert Sevens.*

The place had the eerie look of some dead person's rooms whose loved ones had decided to keep just as he left them.

There was the Smith-Corona word processor Dib and I had bought together. There was a photograph on my desk of me dressed up as Sevens' founder, Damon Charles. I'd gone to The Charles Dance that way—every male attended as someone named Charles. I'd caught a lot of flak because it was disrespectful to dare to pose as him.

There were a few bottles of Soho lemon spritzer on the windowsill, and the jacket to my tan gabardine suit on the back of the desk chair.

And there, between a history of the downfall of the Roman empire and a Paul Zindel novel, was the little black folder, with the fleur-de-lys stamped on it in gold. Inside, Delia's letters with the Switzerland postmark, a paper napkin from The Surf Club in The Hamptons, a newspaper photo of her in Zurich, in a raincoat, a scarf around her long black hair, a cigarette burning. . . . Delia: the antidote to Keats, the one who'd "pulled me out in time," as Paul McCartney used to sing in one song. . . . A year later what I needed was the antidote to Delia.

I wondered where she was and if she ever thought about me. And I thought then what I couldn't get out of my head all summer: Dib had never even been with a girl, except that first time at Willing Wanda's. He hadn't had a clue to what it was all about.

Behind me, Keats said, "You guys are really spoiled! I live in one room half the size of this one."

"I wonder if I could ever come back here."

"You mean because it's coed?"

"I don't know what I mean," I said. But I did. I meant could I ever be the old John Fell again? I'd lied when I'd told Keats I was through blaming myself for what happened to Dib. That was like saying you'd gotten the mildew off something . . . and maybe you had. But it'd be back.

I couldn't shake the idea that if only I'd spent a little more time with him, he wouldn't have turned to Little Jack . . . and after he finally did, I was still too busy being a Sevens, and being me: self-absorbed, and self-important.

"It's too hot up here," Keats said. "I think I should go and check into that Howard Johnson's we saw coming into Cottersville. Obviously, you can stay here after all."

We hadn't been certain that Sevens House would be open.

I could remember the day when, given this situation, I'd be scheming to be in the same place she was that night.

Instead, I told her, "Most girls stay at The Cottersville Inn right in town."

"Then I'll check in there. You should pack some of your stuff up . . . and maybe call Little Jack, hmmm?"

She was standing in front of the window. I could see The Tower in the distance, where the Sevens clubhouse was. I remembered standing at the top of that thing that night I was asked to join. I remembered the Sevens serenading me down below:

> *The time will come as the years go by,*
> *When my heart will thrill*
> *At the thought of The Hill,*
> *And the Sevens who came*
> *With their bold cry,*
> *WELCOME TO SEVENS, I*
> *Remember the cry.*
> *WELCOME TO SEVENS!*

"What'll you do this afternoon?" I asked Keats.

"Shop," she said.

I had a sudden vision of girls streaming down from The Hill after classes, on their way into Cottersville to shop.

I walked Keats out the door, but she held up

her hand as I tried to see her down the stairs and out the front.

"No, Fell, you get as much done as you can. I'll be back for you around six."

"Don't snack," I said. "I know a great place we can get some lobsters. My treat."

"This is funny, isn't it, Fell?" Keats said.

"What do you mean?"

"Remember us? Can you imagine lobster being the highlight of our evening back then?"

"Was it escargots? Shrimp? I don't recall."

She gave my arm a punch. Then she leaned into me and kissed me. "Remember now?" she said.

"Of course! It was sautéed eel."

She blew me another kiss as she walked away from me. I smiled at the idea both of us were thinking the same thing about the night ahead of us: how far we'd come from the time we couldn't keep our hands off each other . . . when we'd named the backseat of my car "The Magnet" . . . and when we kept making our dates earlier because we couldn't wait.

"Fell?" Keats called at me from downstairs. "It'll be more like seven. I want to shop for shoes out at the mall."

As it turned out, she was waiting outside in her little baby-blue Benz at quarter after six, top down.

It wasn't my treat, either . . . wasn't fish, but ribs charcoaled on an outside grill.

We dined at a long redwood picnic table, covered with a blue-and-white-checked cloth.

We were in the backyard of 11 Acquetong Road, home of the Horners, Tom and Lucy and Little Jack.

We'd been invited to Little Jack's birthday party, but it seemed we were to celebrate without him.

THE MOUTH

Oh, the excitement (the rapture, really) of meeting your other! Can you imagine what that would be like?

Neither could they, of course, because neither one knew he was meeting someone on that bus who would change him forever.

Life is mysterious, you know, or we'd have some clue as to what we're all doing here.

"Is this seat taken?" he asked.

"Help yourself."

"I'm Nels Plummer."

"Leonard Tralastski. Hi!"

He sat beside Lenny on the aisle seat of the

Gardner bus. Everything about him seemed to be the opposite of Lenny.

Lenny was tall, dark, black haired, and brown eyed behind the thick glasses he could not see without. He had a plain, average sixteen-year-old face, regular features, no ethnic imprint.

Nels, same age, was short, light skinned, and blue eyed. He had one of those round, angelic faces, and angel hair, too, golden and curled. He wore a little slanted grin most of the time, but it wasn't particularly warm or friendly.

Lenny's clothes were picked out and bought at Macy's with an employee's discount, by his mother.

Nels's came from Brooks Brothers after he deliberated over them for a long time.

Lenny had on a brown suit and a wool tie.

Nels would not have worn either thing, not ever!

As they began talking, they discovered three things immediately.

1. About the same time Lenny's father was dying a World War II hero, Nels's mother was dying in childbirth. Then that summer past, Nels's father died, too. Poor little tyke was alone in the world . . . almost . . . almost. (Presque, as they say in Paris; and in Madrid they say casi. See how many languages you can say "almost" in.)

"All I have is this older sister, but she's too busy working," said Nels.

"All I have is my mother, and she's too busy working, too," said Lenny.

2. Lenny was the big reader, but the smart one was Nels, who claimed he read only Swinburne.

"Who?" said Lenny.

"He's a poet."

"I must have missed him," said Lenny, who never read poetry except for kinky stuff: *HOWL!* or Leonard Cohen.

3. Neither boy had a big collection of friends back home . . . "or even one," Nels admitted.

If Nels was comfortable being friendless, Lenny wasn't. He made excuses for himself. He said how sick he'd been as a kid, how he'd invented Handy as a result and become fascinated by ventriloquism.

Nels groaned. "Remember I told you I had a sister?"

"Yes. Annette."

"She's adopted. They adopted her because they didn't think they could have children. . . . Then guess what."

"You came along."

"Right, Lenny. Out of the blue, a mortal surprise to my mother. . . . But before I made my appearance, Annette was spending most of her time in bed. She was always sick with something. That's how Celeste came into the picture."

"Who's Celeste?"

"My sister's dummy. My father had it made for her. She was this big deal in our house when I was growing up."

"Is she wooden?"

"Wooden. Red wig. She's like another sister, Lenny. You see, Annette is a *real* ventriloquist. A professional. She's considered very good, I guess."

"I'd love to see her."

"She works for Star Cruises aboard the *Seastar*."

"Neat!"

"Except for the fact that I hate that little tree stump of hers!"

Lenny looked at him to see if there was a possibility he was serious. He was.

He said, "Celeste had her own room when I was growing up, and more toys than I had. . . . Now my sister's a fat pig because of her. You should have seen Annette when I was little, Lenny. She could have been a movie star!"

"How could Celeste make her fat?"

"She wanted her that way."

"Are you kidding?"

"She'd open this ugly little red mouth and whine: *Tick tock tickers! Where's my Snickers?* That's her favorite food. Snickers bars."

"I suppose Annette had nothing to do with it."

"Oh, sure, Annette's partly to blame."

Lenny said to himself: Partly.

Nels said, "My sister is always on this seafood diet."

"You can't get that fat eating seafood."

"On my sister's seafood diet she sees food and eats it."

Lenny laughed, but he was thinking, He's not kidding about the dummy doing that to his sister, is he?

The school was coming into view.

It was at the top of a big hill.

Lenny said once that it "loomed" at you just as you rounded a bend and saw the city sign: COTTERSVILLE.

The bus was met by a dozen boys in light-blue blazers and navy-blue pants.

All the blazers had gold 7's over the blue-and-white Gardner insignias.

Nels raised an eyebrow in a cynical expression as he looked out the window at them and back at Lenny.

The group began to form a seven, all the while singing:

> Others will fill our places,
> Dressed in the old light blue.
> We'll recollect our races.
> We'll to the flag be true.

And . . . da da dee da da dee—I can never remember the words, but Lenny got to know them by heart. He loved that song as much as Nels didn't.

Nels made up some vile verses of his own, so irreverent only he'd sing them.

Anyway, as they walked down the aisle of the bus, Nels asked, "What's the seven supposed to mean?"

"Search me," Lenny said.

"Well, it must mean *something*," said Nels.

(You better believe it, Big Guy.)

———

Lucy Horner made spareribs that fell off the bone when you touched them with a fork. She made fresh applesauce from the apple trees in the yard. Potato salad with hard-boiled eggs in it.

After she'd served us this double-layer fudge cake with a butter icing, I was mellowed out on home cooking and into a soaring chocolate high.

They could have convinced me of anything, even that Little Jack was innocent.

Innocent . . . heartsick . . . and don't forget: eager to contact me.

I told Mr. Horner that if his son had been all that eager, it would have been as simple as picking up the phone.

"He wanted to. He couldn't."

"I tried to stop him from driving that day," I said, "but he laughed and called me Felly."

"He wanted very badly to see you. He still does."

"What for? To say he's sorry he was bombed?" I wanted to rub it in that Little Jack had been drinking. Somebody had to admit that. The police must have known. Maybe the Horners didn't.

But they did. Mr. Horner's eyes looked past me to some safer place in the distance.

He said, "I think the two of them had a fight in that car, and I wouldn't be surprised if it had been about Jack's drinking."

"He hasn't touched a drop since," said Mrs. Horner. She was taking the candles out of the birthday cake to save, same as my mother'd save them for the next cake. When she'd come out with the cake inscribed HAPPY SEVENTEENTH BIRTHDAY, JACK! she'd made some apologetic noises about it being his favorite cake, and even though he wasn't there it wouldn't seem like his birthday if she didn't bake it.

She had these big brown eyes, and a cherubic face framed by mounds of tangled hair.

I felt sorry for her, not sorry enough to join her in singing "Happy Birthday," as Keats did . . . but sorry a woman like that had to be stuck with such a son.

"Says he'll never drink again," Mr. Horner said.

I don't know why they both sounded as though that was some kind of major accomplishment. He was several years away from the legal drinking age.

I wanted to get back to the alleged fight. I asked Mr. Horner why he thought there'd been one.

"Jack was crying one night and—"

"Crying his eyes out," Mrs. Horner interrupted. "I've never seen our son weep that way."

"He could hardly talk, but he did manage to get out that the last words he said to Dib were *Shut up!*"

"Dib must have been reminding him he had one DWI and if he got another he'd be in big trouble. That's what I think," said Mrs. Horner.

I jumped right in at that point. "But apparently he *didn't* get in big trouble."

"Fell, Jack was run into. That old Cadillac crossed the line and rammed into Jack."

I couldn't really give either one of them a hard time. It was as though Central Casting had picked them to be The Nice Parents. . . . He even smoked a pipe, which gave him a sort of philosophical air: the thoughtful type. A pharmacist by profession, you could imagine him ministering to people, wearing one of those short white coats people wear who can't have the long one that means MD.

"We're not proud of what happened," Mrs. Horner said.

"We're not ashamed of it, either," her husband said defensively. "Jack didn't murder anyone, by design or by accident. Jack's a victim, too."

"Well . . ." said Mrs. Horner.

"Well *what?* He is!"

"Well, he didn't get charged for driving while drinking. We should be very grateful for that."

He shot her a look.

Then he sighed, and by his posture seemed to cave in with relief that someone was finally saying what had been unspoken all evening. He stretched his legs out in front of him, ran his hand through his thinning hair, and sighed again.

"In a small town, people are family," he said.

She said, "If Mrs. Greenwald, across the street, has a migraine and late at night needs something strong to get her out of pain, Tom's not going to tell her sorry, you have no prescription."

Keats was nodding in agreement and sympathy.

"The authorities knew Jackie had that one DWI, and his license was suspended. . . . He could have been in real trouble."

"He's never going to drive again, either. Never! That's what he says," Mrs. Horner said.

"That's what he says now," said Mr. Horner.

"I'm glad he's not driving this weekend, with all the drinking that'll be going on there."

"I doubt there'll be drinking," he said.

"What kind of a convention doesn't have plenty of drinking?" she said.

He said, "Jack's at a ventriloquists' convention."

"The fellow driving the car? Ever hear of Lenny Last?" Mrs. Horner said.

Keats snapped a finger. "Of course! Now I remember! Lenny Last and Plumsie!"

"He was a ventriloquist," Mr. Horner said. "I never heard of him."

"I heard of him and I saw him!" Mrs. Horner said. "He was on *The Tonight Show* once, and I saw him on an afternoon show, too."

"Anyway, that's where Jack's heading tonight. He's going to a convention and selling the dummy," said Mr. Horner.

"How did he get the dummy?" Keats asked before I could.

"It seems Lenny Last was alive for a while," Mrs. Horner said. "He spoke to my son. He said, 'Please take care of the dummy for me.' That's why I feel so bad about what Jack's doing."

I helped myself to another piece of the cake. It was the real thing, made from scratch, not the airy fluff that you opened a box, added an egg to, and then baked.

"He's doing the only sensible thing," said Tom Horner. "How do you take care of a dummy? You turn it over to someone who knows how to pull its strings."

"Tom, it doesn't have strings. It's not a puppet."

He ignored the correction and turned back to me. "This fellow Last had only one relative: his mother. She's in a home in upstate New York. I called her to offer my help, and she asked me to place a death notice in *The New York Times*. She put everything but his hat size in it, said she didn't care that it'd cost an arm and a leg. And I helped her get the body up there, too. Who was going to do it all if I didn't?"

"Tom did everything he could for the old lady."

"She had no quarrel with the idea that Jack keeps the dummy. She seemed relieved, if you ask me."

"Then our telephone began to ring off the hook," said Mrs. Horner. "This fellow was eager to buy the dummy."

"Are you too young to remember Charlie McCarthy?"

"I've seen him in old movies," I said. "He always wore a tux and a top hat, and the ventriloquist's lips moved."

"Edgar Bergen and Charlie McCarthy," Keats said. "Sure. Edgar Bergen was Candy Bergen's father."

"The same men who made Charlie made Plumsie," said Mr. Horner.

"They were brothers," she said. "The McElroy brothers. I remember the name because we've got McElroys for neighbors."

"This fellow trying to buy the dummy is up to a thousand dollars now. One thousand dollars!"

"That's why Jack went out to The Hamptons. He thinks the dummy's probably worth a lot more."

I was waiting for Keats to squeal, *The Hamptons!*

Mrs. Horner said, "But he did the dumbest

thing of all. He forgot Plumsie's suitcase. Called us last night—"

Then it came. "The *Hamptons*? That's where I live!"

"You're kidding, Kates!" Mrs. Horner just couldn't get the name right.

"Keats will be heading there tomorrow," I said.

"There's a God in heaven!" said Mrs. Horner. "Do you know a place called Kingdom By The Sea?"

"Cap Marr's place, sure," said Keats. "Everything there is named after a poem by Edgar Allan Poe."

"And the rooms don't have numbers, they have names. Jack's in one called 'The Raven.'" Mr. Horner's face was wrinkled up suspiciously. I didn't figure him for a poetry lover.

Keats laughed. "Yes, that's the place, all right. It's very romantic. There's a big fountain in the courtyard. Cap Marr's dead wife was supposed to be related to Poe. . . . Last year they had a convention of numerologists."

I'd never heard any of it. I'd only lived in Seaville under two years. But I remembered the place. It was outside of Amagansett, a huge structure that rambled on behind the ocean dunes. Last time I'd seen it, it looked like an old, abandoned amusement park.

"Would you take the suitcase to Jack?" Mrs.

Horner asked Keats. "It's got a whole wardrobe for the dummy inside. The convention begins tomorrow and runs to Monday."

"Fell?" Keats looked at me. "Will you be finished by tomorrow? Would you come with me?"

"It sounds good to me, sure." It sounded better than work. It sounded better than responsibility.

"Jack thinks he can get a better price if he's got all Plumsie's clothes. They're very fancy duds, Jack says."

"I would love to peek in on a ventriloquists' convention," said Keats. "I can't think of anything more bizarre."

"And that'll give Jack the chance to talk with you, Fell," Mr. Horner said. "I think he wants you to know exactly how the accident happened."

And how it went unreported that Jack was drunk, with a suspended license for one DWI already—sure. Jack wanted to fill me in on all that.

But I was full of good food and pleasant summer-night-backyard vibes. It wasn't the Horners' fault they loved their son.

Keats and Mrs. Horner rambled on as they went in to get Plumsie's things. I watched some bumblebees duck inside a red rose, leaned back, shut my eyes, and almost forgot Mr. Horner was across from me.

I sat up and glanced over at him.

He'd been watching me, I think. He looked

away and back, shaking his head. Then he said, "I thought you'd be a lot more interested in all of this than you are, Fell."

"Why is that, sir?"

"Oh, never mind the sir. . . . I wish my boy had picked up some of that Hill polish. I guess being a day student is different."

"Yes, it's hard to be a townie at Gardner."

"And of course you're in the famous Sevens club."

"How did you know that?"

"I remember Jack telling me that Dib's best friend was a Sevens. That's you, isn't it?"

"That's me."

"It's why I thought you'd be more enthusiastic about all this involvement my boy's had with Lenny Last. He was the last one to speak to him . . . and now he's got the dummy."

"I don't get it, Mr. Horner. What's the connection with Sevens?"

"Why, he was a Sevens, Fell!"

"Are you sure, Mr. Horner?"

"He was staying at your residence."

"That wasn't mentioned in *The Compass*."

"I noticed. We protect our own. You protect your own. It wasn't even mentioned that he was visiting Gardner. I guess Sevens *and* the school just can't take any more bad publicity . . . But I sent some drugs to him there. Asthma medicine, and a little Valium. A Mrs. Violet signed for them."

"During Easter vacation?"

"That's right, Fell. And when he left . . . there was the accident. That same day."

"I didn't know," I said.

"I've always been curious about the club. . . . The things you hear, sometimes it's hard to believe."

"Like what?"

"Oh, you know the things. That you take care of your own throughout a lifetime. That you live all over the world, and you keep in touch . . . the rewards . . . The Revenge."

I knew he was going to get around to that.

"I think The Sevens Revenge is more myth than reality," I said.

"Oh, Fell, I'm not trying to pin you down. . . . You should be proud of yourself. You must have done something good to get in with that group."

That's what everybody thought. If they only knew I hadn't done anything but name a tree something with seven letters in it.

It was the great secret of Sevens, known only to its members.

We'd gotten in by mere chance.

Keats was carrying the suitcase when she came back with Mrs. Horner. It looked like the little cowhide carry-on my mom had ordered from the Sharper Image catalog for me.

I reached for the bag, and we thanked them for dinner.

"Fell?" said Mr. Horner. "Will you do me a favor? Will you let Jack talk to you before you say anything to him? He's just a kid. He doesn't have that Sevens polish."

Keats gave me a poke in the ribs, grinning. "Not like Fell, hmmm?" she said to them.

The one sure thing to break Keats up was the idea I was cool. She'd known me from way back when I was wrestling wheels of cheese after school, in Plain and Fancy, then tooling up the long drive to her palatial home, my old 1977 Dodge Dart backfiring to announce me.

We stuck Plumsie's suitcase in the trunk of the Benz and waved good-bye to the Horners.

Keats asked me to drive. She was tired.

"I'm so excited, Fell! To think you're going to be upstairs in Adieu again . . . this time with Daddy's permission."

Her father had named their house Adieu, because it was the last one he would ever design before his retirement.

I could see her father's face very clearly, the grimace after he'd asked me what *my* father did for a living and I'd said he was a detective.

"Was?" he said. "Is he dead?" He made it sound very déclassé to be fatherless.

I didn't have the right stuff for Keats's crowd,

only for Keats herself, and that was enough to blackball me forever.

"I think I'd better sleep on the beach," I said.

"No. I think Daddy likes you now that he knows we're not involved that way anymore."

"To me, that's more bizarre than a ventriloquists' convention: keeping Daddy posted when you're not involved that way anymore."

"We're a very close family," she said.

I said, "Don't."

"Don't what?"

"Remind me of close families," I said. "My mother's starting to date and I hate it!"

She reached over and messed up my hair. "Fell," she said, "you're so available when you're down. . . . It's nice."

THE MOUTH

Nels said, "What's the seven supposed to mean?"

"Search me," Lenny said.

"Well, it must mean *something*," said Nels.

"I wonder if they assign roommates or what," said Lenny.

"If not, I'm your man," said Nels.

In no time at all Plummer/Tralastski was on the nameplate in 2B, South Dormitory. (Or was it 3B? I never can remember.)

No one at Gardner could help being impressed by the Sevens, except Nels. Lenny wanted to think that his new best friend was just putting on an act. They couldn't be that far apart in what they liked and what they didn't, and Lenny admired the Sevens. They had such style.

"If you're after style," Nels told him, "throw out that orlon sweater. Never wear any clothes made out of petroleum—only fibers made by sheep, plants, or worms."

"You can afford that. I can't," Lenny complained.

Nels had shoes that cost five hundred dollars each. Not each pair. Each foot.

They were John Loeb handmade reversed waxed calf.

"But that's not style," said Nels. "That's extravagance. That's what I learned at my father's knee."

"What did he do for a living?" Lenny asked him.

"What I'm going to do, probably. Inherit."

One November day, near twilight, seven of the Sevens cornered Nels as he was coming from track.

He was in shorts and an old T-shirt, the sweat on his body just beginning to turn cold.

Nels thought he was in for some kind of new-boy

harassment from Sevens. Apparently they were in charge of whatever hazing there was at Gardner. New boys had been warned that they were to have memorized as many seven things that went together as they could.

Nels liked to stroll around their room while Lenny was studying, pretending to practice for this very moment. He'd say, "Let's see: ca-ca, shit, merde, poop, feces, turd, number two.

"And, let's see: pee-pee, tinkle, wee-wee—"

"SHUT UP!" Lenny would holler.

"Sevens!" a senior shouted at him.

Nels named the seven wonders of the world.

But in between the Pyramids of Egypt, and the Tomb of Mausolus, as he faced the steely-eyed, self-assured Sevens who'd barked the order, Nels thought, Dog-Breath, you stink! And after the Pharos of Alexandria, before the Hanging Gardens of Babylon, Nels thought, When you go home, throw your mother a bone.

He told Lenny that was how he got through it.

Once he was one of them, he said to the same senior, "I hope this isn't going to conflict with my membership in the Book-of-the-Month club."

The senior roared with laughter.

What a joker!. . . Right?

Across campus, the lights were just going on.

There, on a pathway near the library, another confrontation was taking place.

"Sevens!" a senior shouted at Leonard Tralastski.

Lenny named the seven hills on which Rome was built.

Soon, members of Sevens in both locations appeared with lighted candles, singing.

Singing Plummer and Tralastski into the most privileged organization there . . . and, some thought, *anywhere*.

For a while the reason was not clear to them, particularly since their backgrounds were so different, and particularly because they were the only two new members admitted that year. Why just the two of them?

It was weeks before they were told the truth, the same day they were moved into suites across the hall from each other, in Sevens House.

They had both almost forgotten all about a tree-planting ceremony after they got off the bus that first afternoon.

But they did remember how they laughed, later, when they found out each one unbeknownst to the other had chosen to name the tree after one of its relatives: Celeste.

chapter | 4

Packing up, Fell?"

"Just a few suits, Mrs. Violet. I'll be back for the rest if I decide not to stay on."

"I hope you decide to stay."

"Thanks. I'm glad you're still up. I wanted to ask you something."

It was ten thirty when I dropped off Keats at the inn. She was too tired to take me back to The Hill, so I'd borrowed the Benz. I'd seen only one dim light on in Mrs. Violet's suite. I figured she was probably tucked in with the TV on.

But no—she was bright-eyed and high-heeled, and she said she'd just gotten in herself. She thought she'd see how I was coming along. I had an idea she thought she'd see if I'd invited Keats back for the night, which was against the rules. Even though we were supposed to be self-governing, Mrs. Violet always seemed to know everything that was going on.

"What did you want to ask me, Fell?"

While I told her about the evening at the Horners', and asked her what she could tell me about Lenny Last, she came all the way into the suite and sat down on the couch.

"Yes, he was here," she said. "He stayed in the

guest suite for a few days."

"Did you talk with him?"

"Far more than I cared to. Every time I came out of my door, there he sat in the reception area, chain-smoking his Kent cigarettes and wheezing. He had very bad asthma."

"And the dummy?"

"Was locked in the car. Plumsie he called him, sometimes just Plum . . . and he never called him a dummy. He said Plumsie insisted on being called a figure. That's when I knew I had very little to say to the man. . . . Do you have any instant coffee, Fell?"

"Sure!" I got up and went across to plug in the hot plate. "No milk, though," I said.

"I take it black."

"Did he just hang around here by himself?"

"Here and in the video stores. He was looking for an old film called *I Love Las Vegas*. He said it'd inspired him to become a professional ventrilo-quist. He said Elvis had a cameo role in it."

"I'd like to see it myself. I'm curious now."

"*Now?* You're always curious, Fell."

"So you never saw the dummy?"

"I began to think it was alive. He bought candy for it! Can you believe that? A certain candy bar—the name skips my mind right now."

"Are you kidding me?"

"No, Fell, I'm not."

I was jabbing a fork inside a jar of Taster's Choice to try and chip away a teaspoon of the stuff. The coffee'd been sitting in the sun on my windowsill.

"Never mind," she said.

"I'm getting some, just be patient."

"I don't feel like it anymore. It's too hot up here."

I put down the jar and unplugged the hot plate.

Mrs. Violet uncrossed her long legs and stretched. "I'm tired, too. . . . You know, he wasn't called Lenny Last when he was on The Hill. He was Leonard Tralastski. And he was best friends with the mysterious Nels Plummer."

Nels Plummer was sort of a minor legend at Gardner, and particularly in Sevens. He was like James Hoffa, or Judge Crater, or Etan Patz. One day he'd just disappeared.

She said, "There's a writer named Tobias who's fascinated with missing people. He calls here sometimes, still. He called after Lenny Last's death notice appeared in *The Times*. He thought I was the old housemother and he started in saying Mrs. Kropper, you know what I want: I want to hear the account of the accident in *The Cottersville Compass*."

Mrs. Violet was standing, ready to leave. She said, "Apparently Lenny Last made a habit of coming back here from time to time. He told me everything started here for him. I said you mean being a ventriloquist? He said no, the whole *miesse meshina*. I didn't know what that meant and he said it's Yiddish; it rhymes with Lisa Farina, and it means wretched Fate. I liked that, and I wrote it down. . . . Then he laughed and said he was exaggerating. He said what he meant was he came into his own here. I'll never forget what he said next."

"What?"

"He said that the best was right here, that after this nothing could ever measure up."

That had a familiar ring. I'd heard a few old grads say the same thing.

"I guess he went downhill after he graduated," said Mrs. Violet. "He didn't look too successful. He had nice clothes but he was driving that old boat of a white Cadillac."

"Some people prize those old cars."

"He was wheezing and coughing so much and he smelled of liquor. I bet Mrs. Kropper liked that a lot," she said sarcastically. "She was such an old biddy. . . . But he said they got along famously. He said she'd known them both: Plummer and him."

"Plumsie must have been named for Plummer."

"You know, I never thought of that, Fell."

"Didn't this Tobias write a book about Nels Plummer?"

"He wrote a book about four famous missing

people. Plummer was one of the four."

"Famous, I guess, because he was rich."

Mrs. Violet nodded. "Tobias claims the two boys were fast friends and may have had a fight right before Plummer's disappearance. Do you know anything about all of that?"

"I wasn't even born," I said.

"Don't be cruel," Mrs. Violet said.

She walked over to the door. "There was something else, too. He couldn't get over my first name."

"Which is?"

"Laura."

"Laura Violet. Nice."

"But Laura isn't all that rare a name, Fell. He said he'd known someone named Laura, and wasn't that odd that it was my name, too? I didn't think it was so odd."

"I don't either."

"But he went on and on about it, as though it was some kind of omen. 'Really?' he said. 'How extraordinary! A dear, dear friend of mine was named Laura. Now she's a shrink in Philadelphia. I haven't seen her for years!' . . . He made so much of it, Fell. Perhaps he was just very lonely. He said my name took him on a little trip down Memory Lane."

"He talked that way?"

"There's nothing wrong with that."

"It's pretty corny."

"As you get older, the corn gets dearer." She gave me a little farewell salute. "Come back this fall, Fell."

I said, "We'll see."

As soon as she left, I finished packing.

What did I care about Last or Plummer? One was History, the other Ancient History. I had the clothes I'd come for, and Fate had arranged a meeting for me with Little Jack.

Laura Violet poked her head back inside the door. "The candy bars Plumsie likes are Snickers, Fell. . . . Maybe you should take him some," and she snickered herself.

THE MOUTH

In tennis love means zero and in Sanskrit it means trembling elbows.

It surprised Lenny how fast and how much Nels liked him.

Adored him, truly. Zero . . . Trembling elbows.

Lenny had never been adored by anyone but his mother, who was so busy working so he could have things, that he never had enough of her.

Now there was someone always there for him.

And that someone was not ordinary, nor was the time they spent together ever predictable or dull.

Nels taught Lenny about sex and psychoanalysis. His father had hired people to introduce him to both, said Nels.

Nels liked Republicans, and Lenny Democrats. They pushed their politics at each other ardently, both night owls who liked to stay up to study and argue and eat.

While Lenny went out for the drama club, Nels threw himself into debating, and made the Gardner team. . . . When Lenny danced and sang a lead role in *The Sound of Music*, Nels's argument for invading Cuba "now!" put his team over the top against Groton.

Of the pair, it was Nels who could express affection, and Lenny who didn't know how.

Lenny wished he could be more relaxed and accepting.

Instead, he would cringe down the school hall when Nels called out, "Hey, Lover-Boy, wait up!"

He would jump when Nels took his arm under an umbrella.

He would suffer, get red, and then ask Nels, "What's this thing you have about acting like a fairy when people are watching us?"

"A fairy wouldn't dare act as I do, Lenny."

"I guess not. . . . You have to realize that my mother

and I only kiss at birthdays or at bus and train stations."

"My father always said he'd die young, so we'd better get our hugs in. Plummer males don't live long. I won't, either!. . . Annette learned from Daddy. She hugged me and kissed me and told me she loved me every day. Of course, she told Celeste the same damn thing. I'd hear her in Celeste's room cooing at her, promising her this and that, and that little witch would make fun of it."

"Yeah, yeah," said Lenny, who had no patience with his crazy talk about Celeste.

Sometimes Nels would come running quietly from a long distance and hop on Lenny's back, hook his legs and arms around Lenny, and say playfully, "Giddyap, horsie! Your master wants a ride!"

Lenny was miserable if it was in Sevens House and others saw. He'd try to look as though he wasn't miserable, but he blushed so easily, and then as his face got hot, so did his temper, and it showed in his features he hated Nels doing that. Any minute he'd expect someone to crack the wrong kind of joke, but the Sevens loved Nels.

His aweless approach to their sacred club was unique.

They'd ask themselves, What would impress a Nels Plummer?

No. Wait. They wouldn't say "a Nels Plummer" as though there was more than one.

They'd ask themselves, What would impress Nels Plummer?

There was only one Nels.

I'll tell you someone who impressed our boy. Algernon Charles Swinburne. (Never heard of him, right?)

This twisted poet of yore (a lush, yes; none of them are ever happy) inspired Nels to underline so many passages!

One afternoon Lenny took a good look at what it was that captured his pal's attention.

> I wished we were dead together today,
> Lost sight of, hidden away out of sight,
> Clasped and clothed in the cloven clay,
> Out of the world's way, out of the light.

Oh, yes . . . and how about this one?

> At the door of life, by the gate of breath,
> There are worse things waiting for men than death.

Sick, sick sick . . . and he was all Lenny's.

chapter | 5

My five-year-old sister answered the phone and told the operator she'd accept the charges.

I thought the operator'd tell her to ask an adult if it was all right, but the operator didn't pay the phone bills.

"Mommy's across the hall with Mr. Lopez," Jazzy said.

"You don't sound happy about it."

"You know what he's doing to her?"

I held my breath. "What?"

"He's taking up the hems on all her skirts!"

I had to laugh or I'd cry. "Well, that's good isn't it? What are boyfriends for, anyway?"

"They're not for that!"

"How do *you* know?"

"Because boys don't sew!"

"But honey, Mr. Lopez is a tailor."

"I know what he is! I hate it!"

"Oh, come on. Boys sew, girls sew—who's to say who's supposed to sew and who isn't?"

"Daddy wouldn't sew. He wouldn't never sew!"

"He *would* never sew."

"That's what I just said, Johnny. When are you coming home?"

"Soon, sweetheart. Go get Mommy."

"Tell her Daddy wouldn't want her going to the movies with Mr. Lopez, Johnny!"

"Jazzy, I know it's hard to get used to, but Mommy has a right to go out. Daddy's in heaven."

"Daddy's not. He's rolling over in his grave."

"What?"

"That's what Aunt Clara said. She said Daddy's probably rolling over in his grave."

Jazzy let the phone drop on the table with a clunk, and I stood waiting, in the phone booth just outside The Tower. It was another hot July morning, and in Bucks County it always felt hotter than anyplace else.

It was ten o'clock on a Saturday. Keats was picking me up in another hour. She liked to sleep in and she liked to take her time dressing.

At least I was back in my clothes—had on a pair of my favorite khakis and an old Depeche Mode T-shirt Jazzy'd picked out for me for Christmas one year. My Sperry topsiders, with my left toe coming through the hole.

When Mom took the phone, she asked me what was so urgent.

"I'm going out to The Hamptons."

"Couldn't you have told Jazzy that?"

"I thought you might want to know the reason."

"I know the reason," Mom said. "You're with *her* and she leads you around like a dog on a leash."

"Mom, Keats and I are just friends now."

Mom made some deprecating noises. She'd never forgive Keats for the time she stood me up on the night of her Senior Prom. Forget the fact it was long gone where I was concerned.

"Well, I guess I'll see you when I get back," I said. I was expecting her to ask me some questions: What *was* the reason? How long would I be away? What about my job? (I figured she could call Le Rêve and tell them I was sick; I'd be back Monday night.)

"Next time don't make me stop everything for something Jazzy could have told me."

"Why, because your seamstress is waiting with a beating heart?"

"He's a *tailor*, Johnny, and his beating heart is my business, not yours."

"At least Dad did man's work." I couldn't believe I was saying those things.

"Mr. Lopez does man's work, too—and he doesn't call up his mother to get her to call the place he works and say he's sick. . . . That's what you really want, isn't it?"

"No, that's not what I really want!" My voice croaked in midsentence, so that I even sounded like a liar. "I didn't even think about that. I had something important to tell you, but you'd rather get back across the hall and have your skirts pinned up!"

There was a pause.

My heart was pounding.

"Oh, Johnny," my mother finally said softly. "What's the matter with us? Oh, honey, I'm sorry."

"I'm sorry, too, Mom."

"Let's start all over, hmmm? Where are you calling from?"

I told her, and I told her all about where I was going and why. But it wasn't an easy conversation. Once you've spit out a lot of venom at each other, it's hard to just get past it.

"Lenny Last, sure," Mom said. "I saw him on *The Tonight Show,* I think. Lenny Last and Plumsie . . . I remember Plumsie called him Tra La, and Lenny got so mad!"

"Why Tra La?"

"How do I know? At first I thought he was singing. You know: Tra la la la. But no. He was calling Lenny that."

"See, Mom, all those years of staying up late waiting for Dad have paid off. You know everything about show business."

I suppose I should have left Dad out of it. I didn't know what was right anymore.

Mom skipped by it and said, "I thought you didn't like this Horner kid. Why go out of your way to see him then?"

"I don't like *him.* I like his folks. I want to face up to him. . . . I don't even know what I'll say. But I want to put him behind me."

"And you have to go to The Hamptons to do that?" Mom asked. "I hope you're not just running, Johnny. You've got your job now, and it's a good job. They like you there."

"I'm not running," I lied.

I said, "It's better than sitting on a park bench all day, isn't it?"

For a long time I'd done that. I'd gone to the Esplanade in Brooklyn Heights and stared across the river at the New York skyline and out at the Statue of Liberty. I'd thought about jumping in and swimming out until I wouldn't have the breath to make it back.

"Johnny, I love you," Mom said.

"I love you, too," I said. "Will you call Le Rêve for me and tell them I have a very bad case of flu, that I won't be in tonight or tomorrow?"

When I got off the phone, I walked into The Tower. Deem Library was there. The infamous Sevens alumnus David Deem had donated it to the Sevens clubhouse. Before he'd died a mysterious death last spring, he'd fooled everyone. He was your all-around good citizen, owner of a sporting goods store, dutiful father to one daughter and one dachshund. All of Cottersville and Gardner were shocked when he was indicted for dealing drugs.

While he was out on bail, he was shot in his car one afternoon at twilight, seven times through the heart. There was a dead rat in his mouth, said to be the signature of The Sevens Revenge, the deadly punishment Little Jack's father'd mentioned. It was rumored to be meted out by a Sevens on a member who had disgraced Sevens.

Twilight was a special time for Sevens. No one really knew why that was, but there were many rituals at twilight and songs with "twilight" in the verse.

I'd known Deem and trusted him. All of that was part of my breakdown, too, and I wasn't eager to hang around in there. What I wanted was to glance at something I knew would be in the library.

It didn't take me long to find his name in the directory, along with the years he'd attended Gardner.

Then from the collection I pulled out the light-blue leather-bound volume with *The Hill Book, 1963* stamped across it in white.

I opened to the P's and there he was: some male version of the old child star Shirley Temple: all curls and dimples, and a big grin.

NELSON PERCY PLUMMER III

New York, New York
Nels . . . Nelly
The Sevens Club, '62, '63.   Debating, '62, '63.
Ambition: To continue as is.
Remembered for: His ego and his alter ego, Tra La.

Slogan: Here's to Swinburne et moi!
Future Occupation: Leader

I flipped a few pages to find Tralastski, who was a serious young man with dark frames on his eyeglasses and his dark hair parted down the middle, lending him an old-fashioned, somewhat scholarly appearance.

LEONARD JOSEPH TRALASTSKI
New York, New York
Lenny . . . Tra La
The Sevens Club, '62, '63.   Drama Club, '62, '63.
Tennis, '63.   Gardner Follies, '63.
Ambition: To be an actor.
Remembered for: Being buddies with Plummer.
Slogan: We three: My echo, my shadow, and Laura.
Future Occupation: Show Biz.

THE MOUTH

Not knowing one tiny thing about Sanskrit, I can't promise you that love means trembling elbows, so you may feel let down by me. Or question my reliability.

Nels made Lenny feel the same way sometimes.

For example:

One summer day when Lenny was little, his mother took him to Central Park, to escape the heat.

There was a lake in the park. His mother rowed one of the boats out to the middle of it.

"Just think, Leonard," said she, "we wouldn't be here right now if it wasn't for an awful murder."

That was her way of starting the same lesson over again, which she would teach Lenny as long as she drew breath: that if he thought for one minute the rich were happy, *listen!*

Then she told him of two young men: one filthy rich named Loeb, the other Leopold. Of how they snatched this small boy and murdered him. (It left Lenny terrified of being kidnapped.)

"Why wouldn't we be here if it wasn't for them?" Lenny asked her.

"Because the Loeb family didn't want everyone to remember them for that awful crime a relative committed, so they gave this boathouse to the community."

~

It was one of the stories Lenny told Nels Plummer, to give him an example of what his mother was like.

Nels used it when he wrote his New Boy's Composition, something required of all entering students.

The theme was "History in Our Daily Lives."

One morning, Sister and I took a boat out on the little lake in Central Park.

"Just think, Nels," said Sister, "we wouldn't be here

if there hadn't been a certain violent crime some years ago."

As Nels was reading this to Lenny, Lenny stopped him.

"Very funny!" said Lenny.

"It's not supposed to be funny."

"I ought to know that, since it's my story."

"*Your* story?"

"I told you my mother took me to the park and told me that! Come on, Nels!"

"Did you, Lenny? I don't remember that."

"Well, where do you think it came from? Your sister never took you there and said that."

Nels thought about it. "She could have. We lived right across the street."

"But she *didn't*, Nels!"

"Sometimes I get us all mixed up, Lenny. I don't know where you stop and I begin and vice versa."

"I think you mean it."

"I do! I swear I don't remember you telling me that. Don't be mad at Nelly, okay?"

"Do you have to call yourself that?" Lenny asked him.

"My father was called that and his father was, too. It's a proud old name in our family."

"It sounds faggy."

"Not to us. . . . But Celeste always said that Captain Stir-Crazy thought it was faggy, too."

Stir-Crazy was Nels's nickname for the Captain of the *Seastar*. Captain Ian Stirman. Nels didn't like him. Nels didn't like anyone his sister admired.

Jealousy, they say in Hong Kong, comes into the eye as a little yellow freckle.

Nels said, "Stir-Crazy claims that Nelly is what Englishmen call the old ones. Nellies. Why should I care what the English do? Why should he?. . . Unless he's a fag himself."

Lenny wanted to get back to the subject. "Are you going to hand in that essay?"

"I don't have another, Lenny, and it's awfully good. Do you mind?"

"Be my guest, I guess."

"Well, you weren't making use of the incident, were you, in yours?"

Lenny'd written a very dull essay about a trip to the Statue of Liberty. The only people in it were "the French" and "the Americans."

From time to time, Lenny'd catch Nels doing more things like that. He'd made Lenny teach him chess because it was Lenny's favorite game. In no time he played it as though he had for years. Eventually he could beat Lenny, though Lenny knew at times he let Lenny win.

He took on all of Lenny's enthusiasms, forgetting (so he claimed) that they were Lenny's. He'd never even heard of Lenny's favorite poet, Leonard Cohen, never read science-fiction writers like Harlan Ellison, Richard Matheson, or Alfred Bester. He glommed onto them and began finding things in them Lenny hadn't found . . . and of course sometimes he'd recommend something to Lenny that Lenny had told him about.

Sometimes, after one of their bull sessions in Lenny's suite, when they sneaked in a bottle of chianti, Nels would cry, "Toodle-oo to boo-hoo-hoo," which was something Celeste said sometimes in her act, and he'd cross the hall singing Annette's old song to him when he was little: "Seeing Nelly Home."

It was her sign-off, and Celeste would add remarks like "Who *wants* him home?" or "Get *yourself* home next time, jerk!"

Celeste always called Nels "Big Guy."

Nels had a nickname for Lenny, too, but Lenny loathed being called it. Tra La. From Tralastski.

"What's this thing you have against nicknames?" Nels asked him. (Even the expression *What's this thing you have* . . . was Lenny's.)

"I just don't like Tra La," Lenny insisted.

The only other nickname Lenny had ever had he had hated more. It was Wheezy . . . because of his asthma.

Since he had arrived on The Hill, he had not had a single asthma attack.

He attributed that to the clean country air of Cottersville, although there was a tire factory just outside town. Nels claimed it was Nels; Nels said no one ever gave a damn about you before, that's all.

"Tra La and Nelly," said Lenny. "That sounds awful!"

"Agreed," said Nels. "It would sound much better if it were Nelly and Tra La."

A lot of things Nels thought were funny Lenny didn't, at least not right away.

Sometimes not ever.

Tra La not ever.

chapter 6

H ow can someone disappear into thin air?" Keats
said.

"Someone murders him, or kidnaps him . . . or
he decides to begin a new identity."

"He could have amnesia, too," Keats said.

"Maybe we could look the case up on microfilm when we get to East Hampton?"

"No, don't, Fell! Who cares? We're on vacation!"

I didn't feel like heading indoors to stare at
microfilm, anyway, that morning. It was the perfect summer day: blue skies and sun above, the
green hills rolling by as we left Pennsylvania, top
down. Keats was driving.

"I called home and Mummy says she's almost
positive Daddy'd want you to spend the week
with us."

"Not a week, Keats. A night, two. That's all."

"Fell, you need more time away!"

"What did your mother mean she's 'almost
positive'?"

"It means he's not there to ask, but it'll be fine."

"I've got a job, remember?"

"You'd make better tips in Seaville, or in
Bridgehampton."

"Wanna bet? I do very well at Le Rêve."

"Good! Because you owe me dinner out somewhere wonderful!" Keats said. "Somewhere they serve enormous lobsters. You whetted my appetite when you promised me that yesterday."

"We'll go to Gosman's in Montauk," I said.

"Let's go early, too, so we can see the sunset and get a table down by the water."

"What if something interesting's going on at the convention tonight?"

"They have to eat dinner, too. We can go there after dinner."

We were making our plans.

Every time I caught myself doing anything fun and familiar, I marked it, telling myself I was back and okay. But I was suspicious of the idea at the same time. If I really was back and okay, how come I was so conscious of it?

Then I'd dip down again for a few seconds. I'd have this picture of myself opening the car door and becoming a big red splatter on the highway.

Keats shoved in an old tape of Tracy Chapman singing her songs of social conscience.

I mumbled something about wondering if a Mercedes Benz convertible was the ideal place to listen to lyrics about homeless people and police brutality.

"Don't ruin everything, Fell," she said.

"Remember that old Billy Joel song—'We Didn't Start the Fire'?"

"We don't have to fan the flame, though," I said, but she turned up the volume.

Why couldn't I just let her be happy?

It was late afternoon by the time we hit Seaville. No matter that Brooklyn was my real home, I'd always feel as though I was coming home when I made that right turn at the traffic light and saw the long pond by the road and the graveyard up on the slope. Then the rows of Dutch elm trees and Main Street, with its old white houses and green lawns.

"When I lived here, Kingdom By The Sea was a real dump," I said.

"When you lived here, only the bar was open anymore. But they've remodeled it. Now it's very gothic and spooky. And tacky."

"Mom used to call it The Eyesore, and Jazzy made that into The Ice Store."

There wasn't a lot of traffic as we followed Route 27. It was a perfect beach day. It was the kind of day shopkeepers took chairs out to the sidewalk and sat there reading.

"I'm going to drop you off," Keats said. "I'll give you a few hours and then we'll head for Gosman's."

"I thought you were dying to see a ventriloquists' convention?"

"I am, but I'm also dying to take a bath and change. They'll still be there later tonight, and tomorrow. . . . And you should see Little Jack alone, I think."

"You're the boss."

"No, that's Daddy, who should be home right about now." She took a look at her watch.

I knew then what she was going to do. Beg Daddy to let me stay there.

I said, "I'm not that anxious to be under the same roof with him, either."

"Hush, Fell. Our guest room has a private bath with a sauna, a view of the ocean, and a waterbed."

"I wouldn't mind being under the same roof with him," I said.

"He'll like you, too. Just don't tell him you're suicidal."

"What if he asks?"

She laughed.

She said, "Should I stop at Seaville Video and see if I can find a great film to watch later tonight?"

"See if you can find one called *I Love Las Vegas.*"

"You're kidding, I hope."

"No, I'm not. Lenny Last was hunting for it right before he died. I just wonder why, what's in it."

"You always do this, Fell."

"I always do what?"

"You get too involved . . . in everything."

"Aren't you curious?"

"I'm mildly curious about a lot of things. I'm not consumed with curiosity over every little thing."

"I'm not either."

"Yes, you are. You're like Gras, our new dachshund. If he knows there's anything even remotely resembling food in the room, even an old wadded-up candy wrapper someone's got in his pocket, he roots around and roots around until he finds it."

"Better than your old poodle, Foster. He was a real stuck-up dog."

"He was really Daddy's dog. That's why he didn't take to you."

"Try and get the movie," I said. "Elvis has a cameo role in it."

"I'm not an Elvis fan, either. I think Bruce Springsteen has it all over Elvis."

"Sure, he copied him."

Just when I was beginning to think we'd spent too much time together, and were getting on each other's nerves, Keats said, "Look! There it is!"

It was up on the dunes, a great gold-and-white castle complete with drawbridge, towers, and domed roof.

"I love what they've done to it," said Keats. "It's the tackiest thing I've ever seen in all my life."

"Sure you don't want to come in with me?"

We were crossing the drawbridge.

"No, I've got to get home."

"Don't feel bad if Daddy says no. I can find an old turret in this place to curl up in."

Kingdom By The Sea was right on the dunes, the sea just a short walk away. As we drove up to the entrance, I could feel the wind become cooler and smell the salt air.

Keats stopped the car under an enormous banner flapping in the breeze.

WELCOME TO THE
10TH CONVENTION
OF AMERICAN VENTRILOQUISTS!
WELCOME TO KINGDOM BY THE SEA!
CAPTAIN MICHAEL MARR, PROPRIETOR

A kid dressed up in sailor's whites came down the steps and asked if we had any luggage.

"A bellboy! I don't believe it," I said.

"A bellperson," said Keats. She handed the sailor the key to the trunk and told him which bag to take.

The sailor hustled inside with it.

"Check out the room situation here," Keats said. "There's a million-in-one chance Daddy'd not be in the mood for company of any kind, nothing to do with you."

"Sweetheart," I said, doing my old Humphrey Bogart imitation, "don't sweat it."

THE MOUTH

Ah, The Charles Dance. Of all the events at Gardner School, this was the biggie.

In honor of the Sevens founder, Damon Charles, all males attended the annual Charles Dance as someone named Charles.

Nels was putting together a pilot's outfit to go as Charles Lindbergh, famed aviator and father of a kidnapped child.

"If I was ever going to kidnap," said Nels to Lenny, "I'd do exactly what the Lindbergh kidnapper did—take someone who couldn't talk."

"The Lindbergh kidnapper killed the baby anyway," Lenny said, "so it didn't matter if it could talk or not."

"If I was to suggest kidnapping to you, Tra La, what would you say?"

"I'd say don't call me Tra La."

"Seriously! What would you say?"

"I'd say get some aviator goggles, a silk scarf, or something! You don't look like a flyer, Nels!"

Lenny didn't see any point in talking about kidnapping.

But he remembered the conversation.

One day he would think back to it, and he would remember it very clearly: Yeah, there *was* mention of kidnapping . . . way back that first year.

Nels changed his mind about the Charles he wanted to be, and went to the dance as Charles Ryder, a character out of a novel called *Brideshead Revisited*.

Of course Lenny was going as Charlie McCarthy, of the famous ventriloquist team Edgar Bergen and Charlie McCarthy.

There was another member of Sevens dressed up like the dummy, too.

Nels told Lenny, "Before I'd appear anywhere dressed the same as Carl Delacourt, I'd step into the men's and strip down until I was bare-assed."

Carl Delacourt's head came to a point. His ears stuck out like the handles on a jug. He had mean little feral eyes.

He was a scholarship student like Lenny. The dense and sullen son of an evangelical minister. Diamond, he had named his tree. Diamond? the Sevens asked. He said it was for his idol, for Neil Diamond.

It was well known that Delacourt got furious if anyone brought up the old rumor that Diamond's famous song "Longfellow Serenade" was written to his penis.

Almost anybody would rather put his name on the blind-date list than bring his sister to a dance as his date.

Not Carl Delacourt.

Right after his name on the Sevens list of Members & Ladies was Delacourt, Laura (Sister).

"She's probably a major wallflower," Nels said while they eyed the list. "Carl says they're both going to be shrinks."

He and Lenny were going stag. You could. It was more fun. It was cheaper, which appealed to Lenny: no corsage to buy. You could play the field, too.

Just as soon as the pair noted that Carl was dressed up as a dummy, and right after their little repartee about it, Laura Delacourt came into view.

"She's not so bad after all," said Nels.

Lenny didn't say anything.

"They couldn't be *blood* relatives," Nels said.

Lenny didn't say anything.

Delacourt and his sister began to dance.

"She moves like an angel and she looks like one," said Angel-Face himself. "I wouldn't mind being shrunk by her."

Silence from Lenny.

"Beauty and the Beast," said Nels.

Lenny didn't say anything.

"Or isn't she your type?" said Nels.

Silence.

"She'd be mine if I liked blonds," said Nels, who would just about come to her shoulder. She was tall and long-legged.

Then Nels finally turned to Lenny, looked up at him, and said, "Where are you, Tra La?"

For the first time, he saw Lenny's face.

He saw the look in Lenny's eyes as they followed Laura Delacourt in a fox-trot with her ugly brother.

He saw the end of something and he saw the beginning of something.

He felt what he saw like a sock to his insides, but he never showed it.

The old shrug. What would he do without that old shrug to his shoulders?

"Why don't you cut in, Tra La?"

He nudged Lenny with one hand in a halfhearted way.

Still, Lenny couldn't talk. Couldn't move.

Nels didn't push it. Nels wasn't in any hurry to speed this thing along.

A thing like this could change history.

Already had, many times over.

It didn't matter if it was your little destiny it interfered with or the fate of an entire nation.

It left its mark . . . if it ever left.

Lenny finally said something.

"So that's Laura Delacourt."

The sailor gave the suitcase to a heavyset fellow at the registration counter. Attached to his dark-blue blazer was a plastic name tag: *Toledo*.

I asked him how I could get in touch with Jack Horner, in The Raven, and he pushed some phone buttons and talked to me while the number rang.

"Is Horner a vent?"

"A what?"

"A ventriloquist?"

"He's here for the convention, yes. You call them vents?"

"They call themselves that," he said. "There's no answer in The Raven."

"Thanks for trying, Mr. Toledo. Would you check the bag, please?"

"Just plain Toledo. . . . Your friend could be at the Gospel Vents' workshop on the mezzanine, or at Beginners' Tricks down the hall. They're almost over now."

I chose Beginners' Tricks. I went around a corner to French doors opening on a courtyard packed with folding chairs and people sitting in them. . . . People weren't the only occupants, either. There were dummies sitting in some seats. The first thing that struck me was how alike most of the dummies looked, as though they'd all come out of the same mold. Some had different colored wigs, and they were dressed in everything from tuxedos to sailor suits, but they all had those big dark eyes with the wide red mouth and a certain wild-and-crazy-guy expression.

Latecomers were standing in the back.

A skinny, bald guy in a bow tie was pointing to a blackboard where there were four giant letters in white chalk: p, b, m, and f. He called them "the bane of our existence, and the reason for most flapping."

I asked a white-haired man standing next to me what flapping meant.

"Moving your lips," he whispered.

Next the speaker held his hand to his face. It was made up to resemble a tiny head. From the mouth of lipsticked fingers came a shrill little voice saying, "P. B. M. F. . . . Please be my friend."

Everyone clapped.

I tried saying the same words softly to myself, without moving my lips.

Out came *lease e eye wend*.

"How does he do that?" I said.

The man beside me said, "You missed the best part. This is almost over."

While everyone was trying to say the same sentence, I looked at the others. There were a few kids around six or seven and a few my age. There were about a dozen females. The majority were men, all ages. Some had their dummies on their laps.

Jack Horner did.

Little Jack wasn't holding Plumsie as the others held theirs. Plumsie was stretched out on his back, on Jack's bare knees, his eyes staring up at the sky.

Little Jack didn't see me. (I remembered the day he'd called me Felly.)

He had on a black T-shirt and denim shorts, in contrast to Plumsie, who was in a tux with a white shirt, red tie, and red cummerbund. ("Bye-bye, Felly.". . . And Dib's last words to me had been "Cork it, Fell!")

Little Jack was chewing gum, straining to see the speaker past the people in front of him. The sun had bleached his hair the shade of beach sand. He wore it straight, and very long in the back. His tan made his eyes all the more blue.

The speaker's lipsticked fingers opened and the same voice that had begged please be my friend announced the session was over. Part II would begin the next morning at nine.

The man next to me was watching me stare at Little Jack. He didn't look like an Easterner. He had on white pleated pants with a silver buckle on a black belt, a white short-sleeved shirt with silver pocket buttons, and a bolo tie with a turquoise stone.

"So that's how Plumsie ends up," he said. "My, how the mighty have fallen."

I turned to face him. "Did you know Lenny Last?"

"Most of us old-timers did. That's why there was that moment of silence for him at the banquet last night."

"I just got here," I said. "I'm not a vent."

"Your questions told me that." He stuck out his hand. "I'm Guy Lamb," he said. "What are you doing at a vents' convention? Selling something, or buying something?"

"An acquaintance of mine is selling something."

He looked in the direction I was looking. "How'd he get his hands on old Plum?"

"He inherited him from Lenny Last."

"Who is he to Len? Len had only his mother, and she was getting along in years."

I explained that Little Jack had pulled Lenny Last out of the wreck and that Last's dying words were "Please take good care of my dummy."

"That's a lot of bull merde, son."

"That's the story, Mr. Lamb."

"You can call me Guy. . . . That's quite a story. Whoever dreamed up that one didn't know Lenny Last."

"Why do you say that?"

"Len would have never said 'dummy.' That word wasn't in his vocabulary. Particularly when it came to Plum. And he'd never give Plumsie to a stranger. . . . We're all attached to our figures, but Lenny was overtaken by Plum. Some figures do that. They bewitch their owners."

"Maybe Little Jack misheard him." I had my eye on Little Jack. Now he was standing with Plumsie caught between his legs, its face squashed against his calves.

He was lighting up a cigarette, talking to a fellow who was Asian, tall and twentyish, with a string mustache.

Guy Lamb's mouth was tipped. "Did your friend mishear Len or did he put words in his mouth?"

"Why would he want a dummy?"

Guy Lamb put his hand on my arm. "Please. Don't say dummy. Say figure. Say Plumsie. Anything but dummy."

"A figure," I said. "Why would he want it enough to lie about it?"

"Why does *anyone* want something enough to lie? Money, my boy, *dinero.*"

"I don't think Little Jack was thinking about money. He'd just survived an accident and he was drunk, too."

"I'd heard *Lenny* was, that it was Lenny's

fault," said Guy Lamb.

"Was he always a drinker?"

"A big one near the end. Some say it was the gambling debts he was carrying. Others say it was something in his past. Plumsie began remarking about it, too, as he took over the act, about the drinking *and* the asthma. That was around the same time he decided he didn't like the name Plumsie."

"What did he want to be called?"

"He never said. What he said was he didn't want a name with seven letters in it, so Lenny started calling him Plum. I think he just liked to irritate Lenny."

I must have made a face without realizing it.

Guy Lamb said, "Sounds farfetched, hmmm? But you should have seen them near the end. Lenny'd wheeze but Plum wouldn't. Lenny'd drink until he slurred before a performance, but Plum never slurred. Then there was this high little voice that would come out of Plum. He'd scold Lenny in it. He'd called Lenny 'Big Guy.' If Lenny fluffed a line, Plum would trill, 'Nice try, Big Guy.' Sometimes with an Italian accent. 'Nice-ah try, Big Guy.' Sometimes it'd be a French accent or German.

"The audience picked up on it, and they'd call out 'Nice-ah try, Big Guy!' Or 'Nice twy, Beeg Guy,'—always in falsetto, like Plum. Some folks

thought it wasn't funny, if you know what I mean."
He pointed to his ear with one finger, turning it in
circles. "Some folks thought Lenny was headed
around the bend."

"What was his personal life like?"

"He didn't have one. Lenny was like me, a
loner. Now, what went on before I knew him, or
inside him—that I can't tell you. Plumsie probably told us more than Len wanted us to know.
Some figures will do that, will bring out your
devils. My Earl never did, thank the good Lord."
He looked over at Little Jack, who was holding
Plumsie between his knees while he wrote something down. "Yes," he said, "Lenny was like me.
He wanted Plum to end up in The Vent Haven
Museum . . . not like that."

"Do you know who Little Jack's talking to?" I
asked him.

"Your friend is talking to Fen. He's only been
on the scene a few years now, but he's climbing
the ladder fast. He played The White House last
Christmas."

"Is he Japanese?"

"Vietnamese. Now *he* might be interested in
buying Plumsie. He's not too happy with the figure
he's got. That's her in the chair behind him. Most
vents have figures their same sex, and I expect Fen
would be better off with a male himself."

I could see only the back of something about

three feet long, all in black with a white wig.

"That's Star," said Guy. "She's got more clothes than a movie star."

"Why do these figures all look alike?" I said.

"They don't. You just don't look carefully. Some look like a lot of others because they're cheapos. Plywood and plastic, stuffed with cotton."

"How much is a cheap one?"

"About five hundred dollars."

"And an expensive one?"

"My Earl upstairs is worth fifteen thousand. Crestadoro made him."

"And Plumsie, what would he go for?"

"Hard to tell. There aren't many like Plumsie anymore. He was made by the McElroys years ago. He probably had a few owners before Len bought him."

"Give a guess," I said.

"Twenty, twenty-five thousand, maybe more. *But* there're not that many collectors interested in figures that expensive, and a professional performer would hesitate to work with him. Plum was too much Lenny's, and he was too strong for Lenny. So he has this undertone. That's what we call it."

"Sort of like a jinx or a curse, hmmm?"

"We call it an undertone," he said emphatically. "Now that Fen fellow wouldn't know enough to be wary of Plum, wouldn't know his history."

"I don't think Little Jack does either, or his worth."

"The blind leading the blind."

"Yeah."

"Of course you're going to enlighten your friend, hmm?"

"I think I'll stay out of it," I said.

Guy Lamb chuckled. "So he's not that close a friend. . . . Good, because I don't like his story about how he got Plum. And it'll be interesting to see if Plum acts up on this Fen."

"How can he, if Fen knows nothing about him?"

"He can, he can. . . . You're a civilian, my boy. That's what we call people who aren't a part of the show-business family. You'd probably whistle in the theater, say the name Macbeth aloud, and wish some poor actor luck, none of which is done. We have our traditions and our customs. We're on the superstitious side. We favor fancy over fact."

My father used to say the mark of the ignoramus was to poo-poo something just because *you* couldn't imagine it.

"Old Plum will take care of himself," said Guy Lamb. "I'll bet on old Plum any day."

We stood watching while Little Jack picked Plumsie up. He rested it against him face to shoulder, the way someone might hold a small child.

"That's better," Guy Lamb said. "I don't like to see Plum carried around like some stuffed animal won at a carnival for shooting ducks down. He deserves some respect."

That was when Little Jack looked back and spotted me.

It wasn't really a wave he gave me. It was more like a resigned salute.

THE MOUTH

And now we come to Laura, or Laura comes to us . . . and it is summer: *Sommer*, they say in mad Berlin, in gay Paree *été*. Now Venice, where it's *estate* . . . and in Sanskrit (truly this time) trembling elbows.

"Poor Nels!" said Laura.

"That's one adjective you can't use in the same sentence with Nels Plummer," Lenny said.

"But you like him, don't you?"

"You know I more than like him, Laura."

"I worry about him . . . spending the summer alone."

"He could go anywhere, Laura, do anything."

"But who'd he go with, who'd he do it with?"

Good question!

The three of them that summer!

They decided to take jobs at a plush inn in Lake Placid, New York—the boys waiters, and Laura a waitress.

They knew while they were doing it how sweet it was, that not much up ahead of them would match the lazy, crazy days from June through August 1962.

One little song like "The Wanderer" or "Ramblin' Rose" would start them off years hence, they all bet on it!

They'd remember the three of them chomping into egg-and-olive sandwiches Laura made on mushy white Buttercup bread, while they floated around on their days off in a Placid Palace rowboat surrounded by the mountain, their skins glistening bronze in the sun while they slathered each other with Coppertone.

Laura could do a good imitation of Barbra Streisand, and she'd sing old revival hymns for them. "Throw Out the Life Line" (*There is a brother whom someone should save*) . . . "Bring Them In" (*Bring them in from the fields of sin*) . . . And "I'll Stand by You 'Til Morning."

She said the way to turn a gospel hymn into blues was to substitute "baby" for "Jesus," and she'd try out her theory with hymns like "Jesus, I Come," and "All for You, Jesus."

They'd skinny-dip by moonlight and at sunrise.

Nels never spent more than he made, and he never once complained about the work. He'd get as excited by a big tip as they would.

The only extravagant thing Nels did all summer was to buy a secondhand white Cadillac for them to get around in. After work, they'd take it across the lake to Smitty's, where they could dance until the stars were fading in the morning sky.

Lenny was in love with his life that summer. In love with Laura, and basking in his loving friend's company.

Nels kept them laughing. He could even make Laura laugh the time a party of ten ordered lobster dinners and walked out without tipping her. It was called "getting stiffed."

Nels's remedy was applied as they sat around a campfire on the beach. He'd made up his hand like a face.

NELS: Good evening, Handsome.
HANDSOME: What's good about it?
NELS: Not much. I miss the sun.
HANDSOME: Whose son do you miss?
NELS: S-u-n! Not s-o-n!

Laura was laughing.

"Wait a damn minute, Nels!" Lenny said.

"I know. I know. Some of it is your idea."

"Not some! All!"

"I never saw you do ventriloquism!" Laura said to Lenny. "You just talked about how you used to do it."

"At Sevens House I do. Where do you think Nels got it?"

"I changed the name from Handy to Handsome!" said Nels.

"Big deal!"

"Who cares, Lenny?" Laura said.

Somehow Lenny came off the bad guy for caring.

Laura moved closer to Nels. "What's your sign, Handsome?"

"Sagittarius."

"Like Nels."

"Just like him."

"That's a fire sign."

Lenny pretended to snore. (He had hated astrology ever since Laura had told him Leo, her sign, and Virgo, his, were not a good combination. Leo would be beaten down by Virgo's tendency to criticize.)

Laura talked above the snoring. "I'm a fire sign, too. We're filled with passion, Handsome, not like that earthbound character over there."

"When's your birthday, Beautiful?"

"Tomorrow."

"*Tomorrow?*" Nels put down his hand, his face suddenly filled with alarm and disbelief. "Why didn't someone tell me?" He was looking straight at Lenny.

Lenny shrugged. "We would have. Tomorrow."

"Too late for me to run out and get Laura the Seven of Diamonds," Nels joked. Of all the jewelry the

Sevens purchased for their women, that was the best.

"It's always going to be too late for that," said Lenny sarcastically. "At least where you're concerned."

And Nels looked miffed. "I was just kidding, Tra La. . . . But I do wish someone had said *something*. Aren't we going to have a big birthday party?"

Lenny grabbed Laura's hand. "We're going to have a little one."

Later, Laura said that Lenny was petty sometimes.

"Poor Nels," she said. "You never let him get out front."

"You're doing it again: calling him *poor* Nels."

"There's something very defenseless about him," Laura said. "He's probably not original enough to dream up his own ventriloquism act."

"I didn't like what he said about it being too late to run out and get you the Seven of Diamonds."

"He was kidding. He said so, Lenny."

"The Seven of Diamonds is only given to fiancées or wives. Where does he get off even kidding about it?"

"First we invite him along with us *all* the time. Then you pull the rug out from under him when he takes anything for granted."

She made Lenny feel bad about how he'd treated Nels. . . . After all, the two of them had a big advantage over Nels that summer. They were the couple.

Lenny encouraged Nels to do Handsome again,

but in honor of Laura's birthday, Nels said he wanted to present something original . . . Dr. Fraudulent. His hand had a German accent and a beard made out of fresh corn silk.

"Und zo, Fräulein Laura, vat I hear iss you vant to be a doctor like me?"

"Ja, Herr Doktor, ja!"

"Tell me den, vat iss your darkest secret?"

"I like nice things," said Laura, "beautiful things! But I hate to admit it."

"Vell, I hav here something beaudeefill for you."

It was a thin, 14-karat-gold chain, perfect he said, for a gold 7, someday.

Coincidentally (and because Laura was determined to be a shrink), Lenny had given her the collected works of Sigmund Freud. He felt like a jackass for being so unromantic.

Some nights Lenny would see Nels standing by himself at the edge of the dance floor, watching. He would see him ask a girl to dance, only to find that when she stood up, she was even taller than Laura. Nels looked like a little squirt leading her around. He looked like some twelve-year-old kid at a wedding party having to dance with a grown-up.

Lenny's heart broke for his buddy then.

He hated seeing Nels embarrassed, or awkward.

At times, Nels would go off on his own after they

came off their shifts. All there really was to do was dance. Nels would wander into town, hang out at the soda shop or the Laundromat, watching for short girls.

Lenny'd lend him a hand, tell him the new young clerk at The Outdoor Store was just about five foot one . . . some other female he'd spotted not an inch over five two. He'd keep a shortie watch out for Nels. So would Laura.

It really didn't matter that much that Nels usually did not have anyone.

They'd sing until they were hoarse and dance in a triangle until the soles of their feet burned.

Maybe times it was just the three of them were the best times, because that was most of the time, and most of the time was better than good.

"Promise that we'll never forget this summer!" Laura was fond of exclaiming, and they would: They'd promise.

At its end Nels gave Lenny the white Cadillac to take back to Gardner.

"We'll have that to remember the summer by," he said, "and Tra La can make some money renting it out."

Weekends Laura'd come to see Lenny, they'd zip around Cottersville in it, the three of them squeezed into the front seat.

little Jack was lighting up.

He smoked Camels. He carried a silver Zippo. He was the only one around in shorts. His baby face, his height, and the shorts made him look even younger than seventeen—more like twelve. People probably wanted to take him over their knees and spank him for smoking.

Even I had to remind myself he wasn't a little kid.

"Hello there, Fell. I hear you've been busy snooping around while I've been away."

"Your suitcase is at the desk," I said.

He didn't say thanks or anything else.

We started walking along together, toward the door that led from the courtyard back to the lobby. He had Plumsie tossed over his shoulder.

He said, "My mother said you wanted to ask me something."

"Your father said you wanted to go first."

"You go first."

"I'm having a lot of trouble with the idea the accident wasn't your fault, Little Jack."

"*Jack*," he corrected me, without any sign in his face that I'd say anything he didn't expect to hear. "That big old Caddy came right at us. It was like a suicide mission if you ask me. We couldn't have gotten out of the way if we'd wanted to."

"What about if you'd been sober and you wanted to?"

"Cork it, Fell. I wasn't that bad off."

"I remember you that day."

"I remember you, too. You finally decided you had a few minutes to spare Dib, and you thought he'd be so thrilled at the prospect, he'd drop everything."

"I should never have let Dib get in that car with you."

"What the hell were you in Dib's life? See you around, Kid, when I'm not busy being a kiss-ass Sevens!. . . Dib was the only friend I ever had."

"What about all those scruffy-looking characters you always had in your car?"

"I'm talking about having a friend. One who comes first."

I said, "He came first with me, too."

"Sevens came first with you. Dib told me that."

We were walking down the long hall toward the registration desk when he shot that zinger at me.

I didn't have an answer for it. It came like a punch to my guts.

"He should have just chucked you, but Sevens fascinated him. That's why he let you treat him like a doormat. He was curious about that club. That's the reason I wanted to get in touch with you. Let's sit over here a minute. This dummy's heavy."

He pointed to two captain's chairs. As we headed toward them, he got off a few remarks about Sevens that were more obscene than they were anything else. And naturally he said we were all faggots because it always comes down to that with Neanderthal types.

"If you were such a big friend of his, why didn't you get him in?" he asked.

"It doesn't work that way, and you know it."

"I don't pay any attention to Sevens. What I'm planning to do for Dib is something he'd want, not something I'd ever want."

"Well?" I looked at him while I waited for him to light another Camel from the old one. He was an insecure Neanderthal. He needed a prop when he talked.

"I want you to arrange to get him on The Seventh Step," he said.

On The Seventh Step outside Gardner Chapel there are gold footsteps with names on them. They're in memory of any Sevens who died while he was enrolled at school. A few were from World War I, more from World War II, when kids enlisted because they couldn't wait. . . . None from Korea or Vietnam. One was in a plane crash. One had had cancer.

In Sevens we joke about ending up on The

Seventh Step, or seeing to it that someone else does. It's part of our slang.

I said, "Only Sevens get on that step."

Plumsie was stretched out at our feet, staring up at me. He had a little smile, like he was listening, amused.

Little Jack said, "So change the rule."

"The Sevens would never allow it, much less go to the expense for a nonmember."

"I'll pay for it."

"No, they won't let you do it!"

"I'm going to have some money soon. In a few hours, in fact."

"They're not going to make any exceptions. It doesn't matter if you have money."

"Don't say *they*. You're part of them."

"So I am. Thanks for reminding me."

"Gardner didn't use to take girls. Now they are. Things can change."

"Some things can, but this is a waste of time."

"I'm selling the dummy. The damn thing gives me nightmares."

"Maybe it's not the dummy; maybe it's your conscience."

The atmosphere in the place was getting to me, I think. I could swear Plumsie was laughing, that his chest was moving and his lips were stretching wider.

"Get off my case! I told you what happened.

It's your *own* conscience bugging *you,* Fell!"

"I have a date," I said. "Forget The Seventh Step."

"I'm getting good money for this block of wood. I'm getting a couple thou. . . . Tell that to Sevens."

Either Fen was taking him or they were both stupid. It wasn't my business. I wouldn't mind being around the day Little Jack found out he could have gotten a lot more thou than a couple, but that was that.

I didn't really have any more business with Little Jack. I realized that, finally. What was I going to do, hit someone who looked twelve years old?

I said, "I'm going." I stood up. He did, too, stubbed his cigarette out in one of those silver sand buckets, and picked up Plumsie.

"Not a bad price for something I dragged out of a car wreck."

I looked to see his face. The expression was wise-guy smug.

He said, swaggering a little now, "Sure, I swiped the dummy. Lenny Last was dead."

"So you made up the story he asked you to take care of Plumsie."

"Yeah, I made it up. I had a right to the dummy, considering what he did to my best friend and my dad's car. If this wood chip here can pay for one of those gold footsteps, then it's worth it. I'm not going to take your no for an answer."

"Do what you want," I said.

"Thanks, I will," he said.

He was still keeping up with me. He wasn't finished.

"The guy that's buying him? Fen? He says the damn thing's cursed anyway. I've heard others say the same thing. . . . He says that might have caused the accident."

"Then why's he buying him?"

"He's from Vietnam. He's from a culture that doesn't believe in our myths. He says the dummy he's got doesn't like her clothes." He guffawed, and looked up at me for my reaction.

I couldn't give him anything. I shrugged and said, "That's the way they talk."

"He wants the dummy right away because he's got a job tonight, so I'm going to take the money and run."

We were in front of the registration desk.

"You're John Fell?" the fellow named Toledo asked me.

I nodded, and he pushed a piece of paper across the desk, and said I was to call that number.

It was Keats's.

I'd probably need a room somewhere that night. I knew what the price of a room on the ocean was in summer, even in a place like

Kingdom By The Sea. There'd be no lobster dinner at Gosman's unless I took myself down to the beach and konked out under the stars.

I told Toledo to give Little Jack the bag, and I left him without saying any more.

I escaped into a phone booth across the way.

Keats answered and began wailing that the cook had quit and her folks were having sixteen people for late supper after theater that night.

"I can't go anywhere, Fell," she said. "I have to help Mummy somehow. Don't ask me how."

"What was the cook planning to do?"

"We're up to our necks in shrimp. That's all I know. I'd say come here, but I wouldn't even have time to talk to you."

I was watching Little Jack come toward the phone booth carrying a suitcase.

Keats said, "Did you see Little Jack?"

He was carrying *my* suitcase.

"Keats," I said, "you gave the bellperson here *my* suitcase. You've got the one with all the dummy's stuff."

"I wondered if you'd shrunk," she said, laughing. "I peeked inside and saw this teensy tiny pair of jockey shorts." Then the wailing began again. "I could kill Cook! She ruined everything!"

"Keats," I said, "tell Mummy I do fantastic things with shrimp. When I worked at Plain and

Fancy, shrimp was on the menu of most of our buffet dinners."

"That's right! *You* cook! That's right!"

"Tell her that if she doesn't mind having the cook spend the night in the room with the waterbed, the ocean view, and the private bath with the sauna, I'd be happy to do her party."

"Can you do it all by yourself, Fell?"

"No, not all by myself. You'll put on an apron and assist me."

Keats giggled.

THE MOUTH

Christmas 1962.

Over Sheep's Meadow and through the park to Grandmother's house we go.

"Do you really live here?" Lenny's question was answered for him by the doorman.

"Good evening, Mr. Nels. Miss Annette said to tell you she and Celeste went out for dinner."

The Fifth Avenue apartment that had once been Nels's grandparents' place was one full floor, the front windows facing the Central Park Zoo.

It was all dark wood and thick rugs, embroidered

pillows on silk sofas, leather-bound books, and paintings in rich, gilded frames.

A butler named Lark had let them in and repeated the doorman's message. He'd been smirking as he did.

Nels said, "They're usually not even here for the holidays, but the *Seastar* decided to bring in outside entertainers this Christmas. . . . Lark hates it when they're home."

"Then you both live here?"

"The three of us live here: Annette, Celeste, and me."

"Wow, Nels! A whole floor to yourselves! What a way to live!"

"It would be if Celeste wasn't around. We even have room for more, but Celeste won't allow anyone else to live here. She doesn't care a fig for Father's wishes."

The hall they were walking down had walls adorned with old masters, each with its own light.

Nels continued. "My father'd tell Annette never to thank him for adopting her, but to remember it by adopting her own child one day. Do you think Celeste would ever let that happen?" He gave a snort.

He stopped in front of a door at the end of the hall. "Wait 'til you see this, Tra La."

It was a girl's room with everything in miniature. The canopied bed, dresser, desk, chair, and velvet-covered chaise longue. Tiny closets all the way around the room were open, exposing frilly little dresses on hangers, and elaborate shoe trees all filled with minuscule high heels.

There were several red wigs on stands.

The room was a mess, clothes strewn about, makeup left open atop a small vanity in the corner, various coats on the backs of chairs, and one white fur thrown to the floor.

"As you can see," said Nels, "Celeste isn't very neat."

Lenny was used to that kind of talk by then. He just let remarks about Celeste's personality and habits go by.

"A dressmaker does her wardrobe," said Nels. "If my sister's been invited someplace formal tonight, Celeste will be in a gown, complete with evening slippers, evening bag, real pearls, real diamonds, and probably the mink, since there's the ermine on the floor."

"I'm dying to meet her," Lenny said. "And your sister, too, of course."

"One of these days you will."

"Not this vacation?. . . I was counting on it."

"Not yet, Lenny. It isn't time yet."

Then he changed the subject. "You should see all the jewelry Celeste has! Laura would turn green with envy."

"You've got Laura all wrong. She doesn't care that much about all that."

"She cares, though. She *does* care about it, Lenny. You should have let me pay for that Seven of Diamonds for her Christmas present."

Lenny couldn't get it through Nels's head that he and Laura weren't even engaged yet, and that when the time came for something that expensive, Lenny'd want to pay for it himself. For Christmas, Lenny had barely been able to afford the gold 7 to go with the gold chain Nels had given her. In the winter there were fewer rentals of the white Cadillac.

"You have too much false pride, Tra La."

"Pride, maybe. But not false pride."

"I'd *loan* you the money, if that'd make you feel better."

"Laura would know where I got it."

"So what! The time to get her something beautiful is when she's young and beautiful. She'll be old and wrinkled when *you* can afford it, *if* you ever can." Nels laughed. "An actor spends a lot of time in the unemployment line."

"I'll take care of Laura."

"Someone like Laura ought to find trinkets from Cartier under her pillow at night and baubles from Tiffany in her coat pockets."

"I think I know her better, Nels."

"You haven't got any romance in you, Tra La. How sad for Laura."

Then suddenly he said, "Let's get out of here!"

"We just got here," Lenny said.

Lenny kept mumbling protests all the while they went back down the hall, got their coats from Lark, and found themselves in the polished wood and brass of the little elevator, descending.

Hailing a cab, Lenny said he'd have liked to see the rest of the apartment, at least, and Nels snarled, "I feel like getting plastered!"

Then he pounded Lenny's back good-naturedly and flashed him a smile.

"Let's go, Lenny. I know a place they don't check ID's."

They headed downtown in a taxi. Soon they were standing at the bar in Joe's Rathskeller, holding schooners of suds, singing "God Rest Ye Merry, Gentlemen" and "Roll Me Over."

After Nels spotted a redhead who was not many inches over five foot, he told Lenny he was going to concentrate on her. "Toodle-oo, Tra La. Leave if you want."

"I probably will." He was starting to feel his drinks.

"Give my love to Laura when you call her later."

"Okay."

"We must make a plan, Tra La. It's time to start making a plan."

He was standing on tiptoe, cupping his mouth with his hand, funneling what he had to say into Lenny's ear.

"A plan for what?" Lenny could tell Nels's beers had hit him hard. He only said "Toodle-oo" when he was bombed. It was part of Celeste's sign-off, and his sister ended her letters that way.

Lenny had trained himself not to get angry when Nels tried to tell him how to treat Laura, as he had back at his apartment.

He knew it wasn't easy for Nels, suspected Nels was half in love with Laura.

"We have to plan the kidnapping," Nels said. "Start thinking about where we'll dump our victim, what ransom we'll demand, that sort of thing."

"Oh, are we kidnapping somebody?"

"Shhhh. Don't talk too loud."

"Who are we kidnapping?" Lenny was amused at the idea that Nels was so plastered. Nels never lost control, never rambled. But here he was back on the old kidnapping theme.

"We're not kidnapping anyone right away," he said.

"When are we going to do it?"

"A little under a year from now. We'll be on a trip."

"I think you're traveling in outer space right now."

"No, I'm not. But I am planning our trip."

"And we're going to kidnap someone on it?"

"Yes, Tra La."

"Who's the lucky fella?"

"It's not a fella," said Nels. "It's Celeste."

chapter | 9

A dieu was on Dune Road, at the top of a hill overlooking Seaville and the Atlantic Ocean.

I expected Eaton, their butler, to answer the door, but he wasn't on duty.

Keats's father did the honors instead.

"Hello, John." He was in a dark suit, always.

"How do you do, sir?"

Gras, the two-ton dachshund, was growling at my pants cuffs, while Lawrence Keating eyed the suitcase I was carrying, his mouth turned down.

"So!" he said. "I'm told you're here to rescue the supper party."

"I think I can," I said modestly. I knew I could.

"We want to pay you too, John."

"Oh, no, sir. I'm doing this as a favor to Keats."

"She tells me you do this sort of thing professionally," said Himself, sticking a hand down his pocket and rattling his change. "I never designed a house for anyone free of charge."

I felt like saying, Try it, you'll like it.

But he wasn't the type.

I said, "I like to cook."

"I liked what I did too, John, but I expected recompense."

Mrs. Keating came rushing out then like a little

bird running down a lawn. She was thin and tiny, always very tan and quick to smile. She had on a long, red dress.

"Hello, dear. My my, you didn't waste any time getting here."

I was still carrying my suitcase, but I stuck out my left hand and we shook.

"Speaking of time," Mr. Keating said, "if we're going to the Stewarts' before theater, we'd best get started."

"Sweetheart, I have to show John the kitchen and see what he can make of all that shrimp."

"Do you have bread and salad greens?" I asked her as we went down the hall.

"Yes, plenty of both. And luscious tomatoes!"

"Then don't worry . . . Dessert?"

"We have cookies. We have peaches."

"Peaches, good! I'll do peaches with bourbon. You have bourbon?"

"Of course. . . . The help have the afternoon off, but they'll be on duty again at seven. This is awfully nice of you, John."

"Everyone calls me Fell."

"I know, but I can't call someone by his last name," she said. "And at ten o'clock, for enter-tainment, we're having one of those ventrilo-quists from the convention."

"Was that Keats's idea?"

"No, we didn't even think our daughter would

be here this weekend. Someone from the club told me about this young Vietnamese. He's performed at The White House!"

"Fen," I said. Fen trying out Plumsie!

"Yes, that's his name, dear. I wish there was someone to put your suitcase up in the guest room."

"I'll do that, Mother," said Keats, rounding a corner wearing an apron and a maid's cap.

"Darling, what *have* you got on? I thought you were cooking the shrimp."

"It's cooked," she said. "All Fell has to do is shell it." She took my bag and blew me a kiss.

"Did Mr. Keating speak to you about payment, John?"

"He did, ma'am. And I told him I didn't want any."

"Oh, dear, dear, dear. He'd be more impressed if you took something, you know."

"I'm not trying to impress him," I said.

"Anymore," she said.

After I shelled the shrimp, I made layers of shrimp, onion, lemon, and parsley in a casserole.

Keats was assisting me by sitting on a stool waiting to show me something she said was a surprise.

I'd asked her to let me get things under control first.

"Shall I preheat the oven, Fell?"

"This isn't going in the oven," I said. I added more lemon and parsley, also tabasco. Dripped some olive oil over that, and topped it with bay leaves. "This will marinate for four hours, then it's ready to serve."

"Men are sexy when they cook."

"So are women," I said.

"I think I've lost it, Fell."

"Lost what?"

"My sexual feelings and my sex appeal."

I was cutting little red new potatoes in half, dunking them in olive oil, ready to pop into the oven in a few hours.

"You're still sexy," I said.

"Don't be flippant. I'm discussing something sincerely with you, or trying to."

"I'm sorry," I said. "I'm trying to get dinner ready for sixteen people."

"Eighteen counting Daddy and Mummy. . . . I really mean it, Fell. I'm bored with sex. The whole idea of it bores me. It even repels me."

I sighed.

"You don't want to hear about it, is that it?" she said.

"No, that isn't it. . . . I feel the same way sometimes."

"You do?"

"I just can't get interested in anyone."

"Ever again?"

"I hope it isn't permanent."

"I have a sneaking suspicion I'll never again be really interested *that way* in anyone. I'll probably marry someone I like but I hate going to bed with. It'll be awful, too, because you don't like to turn down someone you really like, and yet there's no way you can stand sex night after night when you're not horny yourself."

I recognized a true Keats tirade gaining momentum. Her theme hadn't changed much. It always centered on her own worthlessness, how she would never amount to anything, blah blah, blah blah. It was the kind of anxiety rich girls suffered from before they jumped into their sports cars and broke the speed limit hurrying somewhere wonderful to shop.

My own mother, who wasn't rich, got on the subway and headed to Macy's when she was upset over anything, too.

Keats and my mother just didn't get upset over the same kind of thing.

"Where is the corn?" I asked.

"Are you listening to me?. . . It's right by your feet, under the table."

"Keats, let's not worry about ourselves tonight. We're doing good things here. We're saving your folks' supper party. Later we'll see Fen and the famous Plumsie!"

There were about fifty ears of corn in a box.

"I've had this feeling for a year," Keats continued. "I haven't been horny for a year! I don't even have good dreams anymore. I dream in clichés. I'm flying or I'm falling or I'm shopping in my underwear."

Thank God for the now-and-then nights that brought me dreams of Delia.

Keats said, "Corn is a terrible idea for old people at a party! It gets caught up in their crowns."

"Your mom and dad are only in their forties."

"Only? Who wants to be almost fifty, Fell?"

"At least when you're fifty, this man you've married who you like but can't stand in bed won't be after you night after night."

"There's that," she said.

"Help me husk the corn," I said.

"No, I've got a surprise, remember?"

"It's going to keep you from husking corn?"

"From doing anything but reading to you."

"I thought you were going to assist me?"

"I put the maid's apron and cap on. I was all set to. Then I thought I'd better lie down and put my feet up for a few minutes, just to rest . . . and I opened something to read. It's a journal I found in the suitcase with the dummy's things. It was under a shelf in his makeup kit."

"I wonder if Little Jack knows about it."

"I bet he doesn't. The Horners didn't mention it."

"It must have been Lenny Last's."

"It's more like a story, Fell."

"It's more like an excuse not to husk corn."

"A story about Lenny Last *and* Nels Plummer."

I made a grab for it. "Let me see that thing!"

"No. I want to read it to you."

"Who wrote it? Is there a name inside?"

"No name. It sounds like some third party telling about Lenny Last meeting Nels Plummer. It starts at Gardner school, or on the bus going there. I've been skipping around a lot. The handwriting's horrible."

"Read it," I said.

"Please."

"Please."

Outside on a chaise, Gras was sleeping on his back, all four paws and long dachshund nose sticking straight up.

Beyond him were a dazzling emerald-green pool, rosebushes, a croquet game waiting on the lawn for someone to play it, and, just over the dunes, the Atlantic Ocean lapping at the beach.

I promised myself before the summer was over I'd get Mom and Jazzy out to Coney Island or Riis Park for a picnic.

Keats began to read.

～

"'Ruby is my birthstone,' Laura said. "'Someday I want a real ruby. . . . Do they cost . . .'"

"Wait a minute," I said. "Who's Laura?"

I remembered Mrs. Violet saying how Lenny Last had carried on about her name being Laura, that he'd told her he'd known someone named that, and she was a shrink now.

"Just listen," Keats said. "They're at one of the Sevens' Sunday tea dances: Lenny, this Laura, and Nelson Plummer himself! I'll start at the beginning of the entry.

"It took Sevens to turn the worst part of any weekend into the best."

THE MOUTH

It took Sevens to turn the worst part of any weekend into the best.

The Sevens' Sunday tea dance got under way around four in the afternoon. It went until nine or ten, when the boarding-school girls had to catch the last trains and buses out of Cottersville.

The basement of Sevens House was transformed

into a grotto. The girls were given blue caps with 3+4 in white letters on the peaks, or 6+1, or 2+5.

Stevie Wonder and The Beach Boys came through the speakers, Bobby Vinton and The Four Seasons, and a new group called The Beatles, singing "Love Me Do."

It was at the last Sevens' Sunday tea, the day before graduation, when Nels got Lenny and Laura to go out back, to the white Cadillac, for a surprise.

Lenny had worked hard to keep it running well and looking even better. He rented it out for proms and Saturday-night trips to Philadelphia. In winter it had been protected by a shed Lenny'd made for it in the Sevens parking lot.

After they piled into it, Nels said, "Guess what Celeste gave me for graduation. . . . Psychoanalysis!"

"That'll cost a fortune!" Laura said.

"She's the moneymaker of the family," said Nels.

The late-afternoon sun was starting down in a pink sky. The campus smelled of honeysuckle and roses.

"I thought you were supposed to pay for your own analysis or it wouldn't work," said Lenny.

"You are," Laura said.

"Psychoanalysis is just the care of the id by the odd," said Nels.

"Oh, Gawd, I've got to write that down!" Laura laughed.

"That's all it is," said Nels. "The care of the id by the odd."

"We heard you the first time," Lenny said.

Laura said, "Lenny? What's bugging you?"

"Tra La doesn't have my golden tongue," said Nels. "It's hard to be average when your best buddy is superior."

But both boys knew what was bugging Lenny.

It was Nels's crazy idea to kidnap Celeste and ask for a $50,000 ransom.

Lenny could have the money. The money didn't matter to Nels. What he wanted was to destroy Celeste.

He said what he wanted was to have his sister back.

"How do you know she won't just get another dummy?"

"She won't. There isn't another Celeste—and she'd never settle for less. No. Without her, she'll retire."

"Is that what you want? You want her home with you?"

"Home. Back. Yes."

"Does she have that much money, Nels?"

"Don't worry about my sister. She's still got every cent she inherited from my father, and she's my heir, too. Fifty thousand is peanuts to Annette!"

"But what if she won't pay it?"

"She will."

"She could go to the police!"

"The ransom note will warn her that going to the police means the end of Celeste."

"But Nels, how are you going to—"

Nels would cut him off. "Let me take care of the details, Lenny. I'll come to you when I'm ready."

Both boys knew how much $50,000 would mean to Lenny at that point in his life.

He could marry Laura and put her through medical school, the one thing she wanted most.

Otherwise she'd be shipped off to Oral Roberts's new university. Since she was a pastor's daughter as well as an A student, she'd been offered a scholarship there.

Lenny would be stuck in New York City, trying to get a job doing anything, waiting for the lucky break that'd head him toward Broadway. Some actors never got there.

Nels was planning to take some courses at Columbia, nothing strenuous, and live at home. He'd be around to remind Lenny he'd had his chance once and he'd let it slip through his fingers. Too bad, hmmm?

The scheme made Lenny nervous, angry, hopeful, afraid, and not too sure Nels's love for his older sister was all that brotherly. . . . Was that any business of Lenny's?

Lenny had crawled into the backseat of the Cadillac while Laura sat in front with Nels. Even though Nels never drove a car, he liked to be in the driver's seat.

Nels snapped on the radio, and the Drifters came through it singing "Ruby Baby."

"Ruby is my birthstone," said Laura. "Someday I want a real ruby. . . . Do they cost much, Nels?"

Notice who she asked.

She knew Lenny wouldn't have a clue.

"They're not as expensive as diamonds," said Nels. "You should have both."

Laura laughed. "Hear that, Lenny? When your rich Aunt Martha dies, I want a ruby and a diamond!"

Months ago, Lenny had started mentioning an Aunt Martha, saying he hoped she'd live through her heart bypass, that the money she'd leave him would never be worth the loss.

Nels had told him he couldn't just wake up one morning $50,000 richer without some explanation to Laura.

Next to Lenny on the backseat were three boxes, wrapped in white paper and tied with gold ribbons.

"After tomorrow," said Nels, "we have to stop wearing things with Sevens on them. School's out."

Laura covered the gold 7 around her neck protectively. "I'll never stop wearing this. It'll always remind me of the first time I ever came to The Hill."

"Laura, take off your cap," Nels said. "Tra La? Would you pass around those packages on the backseat?"

"I hope these aren't graduation presents," Laura said. "I don't have anything for you, Nels."

"You're not rich and I am."

Lenny was taking Laura to her school prom and the party after, in a Philadelphia hotel suite. He had saved enough to pay for the satin gown she had wanted and her father had told her was "the devil's creation."

Lenny was renting a tux for himself and buying a white-orchid corsage for Laura.

Already his expenses were close to $500.

When he had told Nels that, Nels had answered, "Chicken feed for someone like Laura, Tra La."

Any chance he got, Nels had begun reminding Lenny how much $50,000 could change his life. And hers, too. Mostly hers, he'd admitted. Laura had more dreams.

"Besides," he'd added, "the best schools are in the East. I'd have my two best buddies close by. That way I don't have to go to college myself. I'll get my education through you guys, vicariously."

The three of them unwrapped the packages.

Inside each was a white cap and a white sweatshirt.

Written across them in red: THE TRIP TO NOWHERE.

There were tickets inside the caps, and announcements of the sailing, on the *Seastar*, five months away.

PASSENGERS LEAVE FROM NEW YORK AT MIDNIGHT ON

NOVEMBER 21ST, AND TRAVEL WITH NO SIGHT OF LAND AND NO DESTINATION UNTIL THE MORNING OF NOVEMBER 24TH, WHEN THEY FIND THEMSELVES BACK IN NEW YORK CITY.

EAT, DRINK, AND BE MYSTERIOUS.

BE PREPARED TO ATTEND A COSTUME BALL ON THE LAST NIGHT OUT. TAKE ADVANTAGE OF OUR THIRTY-FOOT LAP POOL WITH A SWIM-UP BAR. . . . FOR GOLF BUFFS A NINE-HOLE PUTTING GREEN, AND ON BRIDGE DECK A SIX-WICKET CROQUET COURT.

ASK THE SHIP'S MASSEUSE TO RELAX YOU AND THE SHIP'S ASTROLOGER TO TELL YOU WHAT'S AHEAD FOR YOU. PLAY BACKGAMMON WITH THE SHIP'S CHAMPION, AND LEARN THE LATEST DANCE STEPS WITH THE SHIP'S INSTRUCTOR.

DANCING NIGHTLY IN THE BALLROOM TO PETER PORTER'S ORCHESTRA.

IN THE LOUNGE, CELESTE—WITH ANNETTE, OF COURSE.

EACH DELUXE STATEROOM HAS A PRIVATE VERANDA.

—THE SEASTAR, MARTIN STIRMAN, CAPTAIN.

"It's something to really look forward to!" Laura said. "Now I don't feel so badly about going away with Daddy this summer!"

In July she was bound for Africa, part of a missionary conference her father'd arranged for her to attend.

Reverend Delacourt had his eye on Lenny. He was

on his knees nightly praying against him, and in his study a good part of every day plotting for ways to get Laura out of reach.

"We'll have one bang-up reunion!" said Nels. He glanced back at Lenny and gave him a wink. "And you'll get to meet Celeste, at last!. . . Celeste, my sister, and Captain Stir-Crazy. Of course we'll be in deluxe staterooms. Tra La and me in one and you in the other, Laura: *muy* proper."

After Lenny'd put Laura on the bus back to Philadelphia, he went to Nels's suite in Sevens House.

"I don't know if I can do this to your sister," he said.

"You don't have to do very much at all, Tra La."

"But it's major *tsuris* for her," he said, suddenly remembering his mother's Yiddish for woe. The Yiddish always came back when anything troubled Lenny deeply. "Why should I do it to her?"

"*I'm* doing it to her. I'm doing it *for* her. . . . Tra La, she's playing some tacky lounge on a ship with all these guys tossing back drinks, you can imagine the crapola she takes!"

He was packing.

He was piling his Brooks Brothers suits on the bed, and his Turnbull & Asser shirts on the dresser.

Two large steamer trunks were open on the floor, waiting to receive his wardrobe.

Lenny sat down in the big, soft leather Eames chair Nels had ordered for himself and was now leaving behind for the next occupant of his suite in Sevens.

"You're the only person I've ever trusted, Lenny."

"I trust you, too. But this is different."

"Yes. It's different. A once-in-a-lifetime opportunity, Tra La . . . and it'll be the easiest fifty thousand dollars you'll make."

"If we can pull it off."

"Oh, we will."

"Not many kidnappers get away with it."

"But we're dummynapping, Tra La," said Nels. "And our little victim can't tell on us or die. She'll just disappear into the deep blue sea. Deep-sixed."

Lenny stretched his long legs out in front of him and stared at his old, scuffed Thom McAn loafers.

He shook a Kent out of a pack and lit it. He'd been smoking cigarettes ever since January, when Nels had finally convinced him he was serious about this thing.

"Your sister must like being on the *Seastar*, though. Maybe she doesn't think she takes crapola."

"I purposely never introduced you to Annette," said Nels. "I didn't want you to get fond of her, or you'd never want to do this. . . . So put her out of your mind. My sister is too complicated. Our relationship is too unusual to explain."

Lenny grinned finally. "You'll have to shell out for your own analysis after it's done, Nels."

"No. Because then I won't need it. Celeste has always been my only problem."

chapter | 10

I made Keats go back and start the journal from the beginning. I'd long since finished the corn, and I was sitting opposite her on a stool, fascinated.

When the front-door chimes rang, I wished we could just ignore them so she could keep reading. But Gras flew off the chaise outside and came running in, barking nonstop, dachshund style.

"Whoever that is, tell him we don't want any," said Keats.

I headed down the long hall as Gras raced ahead of me.

Fen spoke first, introducing himself, starting to say something about wanting to see where he'd be working that night.

"I like to check the acoustics, the space, and—"

Then Plum spoke up. "Oh, shut up! Just zip it!" and perched on Fen's arm like a big bird, he turned to face me. "And who are you?"

"John Fell," I said. "I brought your clothes with me from Pennsylvania."

"You can take those clothes and shove—"

"Plum! Is that any way to talk to someone who did you a favor?"

"Then tell him Finders keepers, losers weepers."

"Finders keepers," said Fen. "We don't want anything from Plum's past. You'll see why tonight."

THE MOUTH

Tick tock tickers! Where's my Snickers? Tick tock tickers! Where's my Snickers?"

Celeste's voice was drowned out by the shriek of the *Seastar*'s whistle, and the moan from its horn.

Midnight. Time to sail off into the dark, friends.

"Tick tock tickers! Where's my Snickers?" A white gardenia was pinned to her red wig.

Annette smiled at Lenny and Laura. "No matter how many times we've sailed, it still makes Celeste a little nervous to leave land, and she needs her Snickers."

"At your service," said Nels, putting one of the candy bars into the dummy's coat pocket.

"No, no, Big Guy. Put it in my evening purse!"

Annette said, "Put it in my evening purse, *please!*"

"He knows where he can put it!"

"Celeste!" Annette said.

She looked embarrassed for the dummy and she said to the others, "I have to apologize for Celeste.

Don't judge her by this performance."

"No, please don't," the dummy agreed. "This performance is a little wooden, wouldn't you say?"

The five of them were on deck. Behind them an oompah band had just finished playing "76 Trombones."

There was a full moon. The big ship pulled out while visitors from bon-voyage parties waved and blew kisses.

Laura spotted her brother, Carl, in the crowd and called out to him, "Don't tell Daddy!"

Lenny tried not to stare at Celeste. Nels had told him not to show any interest in ventriloquism, so he would not be suspect when the dummy was taken.

Lenny tried hard not to stare at Annette, too. She was not at all what he'd expected. Lenny wouldn't describe her as "fat." Big, yes, nearly six foot. Overweight and quite handsome, dark eyed, swarthy, short black hair she slicked back. She was clearly no relation to Nels. With her Amazon build, she looked like Wonder Woman in a Dior gown and high-heeled slippers.

Around her neck was a purple silk scarf, and a small nosegay of violets was pinned to her ankle-length mink coat.

The flowers were from Captain Stirman, she'd explained. She'd bought herself the mink. She'd bought one for Celeste, too. Of course. What did you think?

Lenny was racking his brain for an excuse for

what he was going to help Nels do to her. The minks would do it! He'd never liked women who wore furs. What kind of a person lets little animals be killed so she can parade around in their skins? His mother'd taught him to think about that. She could always turn their inability to afford luxuries into something noble.

A ventriloquist's dummy in mink! Oy! His mother would have held her head in pain. *Oy vay iz mir!*

Annette and Celeste were having late supper in Captain Stirman's cabin shortly. Lenny had met the Captain only briefly, but he had recognized the possessive gestures: the hand at her elbow, on her back, up on her shoulder . . . the eyes waiting for hers, the mouth soft, the face besotted.

The next morning Lenny put his greatcoat over his pajamas and stepped out on the private veranda.

It was nine thirty. In four hours he would be in the service room behind the dining hall. After lunch Annette performed. At the finish she came behind the curtains to set Celeste down in a chair.

Then, as Annette took a bow alone, received a bouquet from the Captain, and spoke briefly to her fans, Lenny would pounce.

He would grab Celeste, put her into a garment bag, and go into the ship's health spa, a door away.

Through the spa to the other entrance, out the door, and up a flight of stairs to this cabin.

The garment bag would be hung in the closet until nightfall.

Then bricks would be added to its bottom, and Lenny would step out on the veranda again.

So long, Celeste.

There were contingency plans, of course.

But that was the main one. Quick and simple.

Lenny went back inside the cabin, his cheeks wet with sea spray.

Nels said, "You want to hear the ransom note?"

He was sitting on his bed in white silk pajamas, shivering from the blast of cold air Lenny'd just sent his way. He was sipping coffee and finishing toast.

Lenny said, "I ought to check on Laura."

"Don't you know by now she likes to sleep in?"

Lenny felt like punching him.

It was nerves, not Nels, he reasoned with himself. Nels was always telling him what Laura liked, what Laura was like. Lenny and Laura had even joked about it together, calling Nels "The Big L.A." secretly. The Big Laura Authority.

"Listen, Tra La!" Nels said.

The note read as follows:

Celeste will be all right if you follow directions.

If you don't, Celeste will be destroyed.

1. See to it that your butler has $50,000 in cash, in a pillowcase, in $100 bills.

2. He drops it from your back bathroom window into the alley at 11:00 A.M. Sunday morning.

3. He answers the phone at 11:15 A.M. He will be told where Celeste is on the *Seastar*.

4. He will call the *Seastar* no later than 11:20 A.M. to tell Miss Plummer where Celeste is.

ANY ATTEMPT TO MARK BILLS, TRAP RETRIEVER, SEARCH SHIP, OR IN ANY WAY HINDER THIS OPERATION WILL BE MET BY DESTRUCTION OF DUMMY.

DO NOT FOOL WITH US AND YOU WILL NOT BE SORRY.

FOLLOW DIRECTIONS FAITHFULLY.

"I hope we can trust Lark," said Lenny.

"Lark loves me like a son," Nels said, "and he doesn't have to do very much. Annette will call our lawyer and the cash will be sent over to Lark. He keeps a thousand for himself—that makes him more than an accessory—and then he claims he lowered the rest from the window. . . . He says he waited for the call saying where Celeste was and it never came."

"Won't they want to know where Celeste

is *before* they hand over the fifty thousand dollars?"

"If it was a kid, they might. But they'll figure no one would gain anything by destroying a dummy . . . and a dummy can't tell on the dummynapper. They'll go along with it. After you hang Celeste up and leave here, you slip the ransom note under Annette's door, right?"

"Right. Then I come looking for you."

"And Lenny, if you're going to miss lunch because you feel slightly seasick, start acting sick."

"I plan to."

"But before you do . . ." Nels reached under the pillow on his bed and took out a small blue box. He was grinning.

"This isn't for you, Tra La. It's for Laura. It's a premature wedding gift."

"I haven't even proposed to her."

"You're going to tell her your aunt died, right?"

"Yeah."

"Tonight. Right?"

"Shouldn't we wait until we have the cash in hand?"

"Tonight is the time," said Nels. "And this is from Uncle Nels."

He handed the box to Lenny.

"Remember I said she should have diamonds *and* a ruby?"

Inside the Tiffany box was a small Seven of Diamonds.

Where the horizontal bar joined the vertical, there

was a ruby instead of another diamond.

"The ruby's for her birthstone, remember?" Nels said. "I can't wait to see her face!"

He gestured for Lenny to return it, and while Lenny was saying whatever it was he said at that point (Lenny could never remember), Nels put it in the inside pocket of his tweed sports coat, next to him on the bed.

"For now it stays with me," said Nels. "I'm keeping it with me until we surprise her with it! I figure a good time is after dinner, when the dancing's started. That's the time to pop the question."

Lenny did remember he asked Nels, "Do you want to do it for me?"

But Nels only laughed.

Nels didn't notice the anger in Lenny's tone.

chapter | 11

As soon as she saw Fen, Keats decided she'd be the one to show him where he was performing that night.

I thought she'd let out a squeal or a holler when he introduced Plum to her, but she behaved as though nothing could faze her.

When she finally got around to seeing how I was coming in the kitchen, she could hardly talk.

"What's the matter?" I asked her.

She leaned against the counter, holding her head with one hand, breathing in deeply, then letting it out.

"Are you all right, Keats?"

"I will be."

"Where's Fen?"

"I made him put the dummy in the car. Plum's so mean, Fell. Was he mean to you?"

"Plum is a stick of wood. *Fen* told me to take the suitcase full of clothes and shove it."

"That's not Fen at all. Fen would never say that. That's Plum."

"Never mind."

"Fen says Plum won't need his old things at all."

"Did you tell him about the journal?"

"No."

"Don't."

"Is he out in the garden? Can you see him?"

I could. Gras at his heels, Gras's tail wagging acceptance as they strolled down a stone walk near the rosebeds.

"He's there. . . . Did you ask him why he wanted to buy Plum so badly?"

"I didn't ask him anything about the dummy. I hardly said anything. . . . Fell, my heart is coming through my blouse."

"*Why?*"

"Because of him."

"*Him?*" I looked again. He was very tall and very skinny. Silky, straight black hair like Gras's, and the mustache . . . "What's so great about him?"

"I don't know."

"I mean he's probably a nice guy, but—"

"Never mind, Fell. Something's already started."

"Well, before something is almost over, try to find out how he heard about Plum, and why he wanted to own him."

"I think he's Japanese. He looks rich, doesn't he? And he's driving a new Porsche."

"He's Vietnamese," I said.

"That's right. Mummy said he was Vietnamese. Oh Gawd, Fell, I don't know anything about Vietnam, even where it is exactly." She grabbed her head then. "And my hair!"

"It's fine."

"I've got to fix it! I've got to put on some lipstick. . . . Fell? I have another surprise besides the journal. It's upstairs in the VCR in the guest room."

"*I Love Las Vegas?*"

"Right."

"Thanks, Keats." But she was gone.

Later, I watched them walk along together. Keats had changed to white shorts and a purple T-shirt. I could remember when she'd teased me about having purple eyes, and how one whiff of Obsession (which the downstairs reeked of suddenly) could make me go weak.

They stood down by the fountain in the rose garden for a while. He was all in white, except for a light-blue shirt and a dark blue-and-white-polka-dot tie.

Everything he had on fit him so well, he had to have a Mr. Lopez in his life.

I started fixing the peaches, glancing out at them from time to time.

Their eyes never left each other's face, and every time I looked, they were grinning together or laughing aloud.

I began to feel tired . . . not just of what I was doing, but of what I wasn't doing, feeling, having in my life.

I cleaned up after myself, took the journal with

me, and headed up the back stairs to the guest room.

I remembered the times I used to sneak down those stairs, nights I wasn't supposed to see Keats, on orders from her old man.

I flopped down on the bed and it gurgled. I turned on the VCR, and *I Love Las Vegas* began with that old early-sixties music sound when Tina Turner was still with Ike, and my mom was in high school learning all the dance steps from the Mashed Potato to the Watusi.

She could still remember most of them.

All you'd have to say is Mom? Do the Funky Chicken.

Mom? Do the Hully Gully.

The windows in the guest room were very tall and wide, so you could lie on the bed and look out at the ocean. Its color was early-evening green; the sky was still pale blue.

I kept thinking about Jazzy, for some reason . . . about maybe taking her someplace for fun . . . so she could get away, say she'd been someplace that summer when she got back to school.

I didn't feel like fast-forwarding to Celeste. I just let the movie play, and I picked up the journal.

Elvis was singing "She Thinks I Still Care."

The handwriting was tiny and not easy to

read, but I finally found the place where Keats had stopped.

If you're ever curious to see Annette and Celeste in action, catch the movie I Love Las Vegas.

THE MOUTH

If you're ever curious to see Annette and Celeste in action, catch the movie *I Love Las Vegas*.

Elvis is in it, so it's still around, mostly on late-night TV.

It's all there:

Dr. Fraudulent telling Annette that psychoanalysis is just the care of the id by the odd.

Annette asking Celeste if she'd like to join her secret sorority and Celeste saying she hoped it wouldn't interfere with her membership in the Book-of-the-Month Club.

Celeste announcing that Annette was on a seafood diet. She sees food and eats it.

And of course, her trademark:

CELESTE: For sunburn or windburn, I turn to my Swinburne.

ANNETTE: Oh, no, Celeste.

CELESTE: Mr. Swinburne, you know me so.

ANNETTE: Honey, we don't want to hear those gloomy poems again. We want to be cheerful. There are young lovers in the audience.

CELESTE: Hello, young lovers! . . . "I wish we were dead together today/Lost sight of—"

On and on. (You'd think Nels'd never had an original thought!)

Ending with . . . the old song Annette used to sing to Nels when he was little.

"Seeing Nelly Home."

And Celeste would interrupt and say . . .

"Who *wants* him home? He is a horse's *derriere!*"

The audience aboard the *Seastar* loved it.

Some of them who'd seen the act before had Snickers bars with them for Celeste.

Laura had to laugh despite herself. She whispered to Nels, "Does it make you furious when Celeste says that?"

"I could kill her," Nels smiled back.

It was one twenty-six, close to her finale.

Lenny was ready.

He was trying not to think about Nels or Laura while he waited for Celeste to be placed in the chair.

He was trying not to think about marriage, too.

When it had been a kind of faraway dream, it had seemed idyllic, but now that Nels was forcing it to happen way ahead of time, Lenny had cold feet.

He imagined all the *tsuris* he'd get from his mother because Laura wasn't Jewish.

And he'd have to face Reverend Delacourt's threats of vengeance, if not in this life then in the next.

Nels loved to orchestrate other people's lives, didn't he? Not other people's, either . . . just theirs: Laura's and Lenny's. He'd probably arrange to be along on their honeymoon.

And if Nels had his way, and Lenny did propose right away, what would Laura remember about the night?

Six diamonds and a ruby.

Still . . . $50,000 was such an unbelievable amount to come Lenny's way when he was only eighteen.

If he'd never met Nels, he'd probably be in some chorus line, or waiting tables as he'd been doing for months, hoping for a break . . . even a walk-on in an off-Broadway play.

Laura would probably have drifted away from him.

Suddenly Lenny heard the *Seastar* audience singing:

I was see-ing Nel-ly ho-oh-ome . . .

I was see-ing Nel-ly—

The next thing Lenny knew, the dummy was in the chair.

Everything went without a hitch.

Lenny hung up the garment bag with Celeste

inside and shut the closet door. He sat on the bed and lit a Kent.

He wouldn't have minded taking the dummy out to look at her closely, but he'd promised Nels he would not do one thing that was not in their game plan.

Maybe later, before she was deep-sixed, he could admire the handiwork that had gone into creating her.

He sat there smoking, just beginning to feel the thrill of what was going to be possible now.

He put out the cigarette, walked across to the mirror, and watched his reflection give him a smile and a wink.

He'd pulled it off. No small thanks to Nels, and to the anger he'd felt toward Nels when he was back in the service room waiting to grab Celeste. That had helped defuse the fear.

His face glowed. He could have everything now. Let Nels give her the stupid Seven of Diamonds!

He gave his hair a swipe with the comb, then had second thoughts: mussed it, stopped smiling, made his eyes seem sad. After all, when he caught up with Laura and Nels, he was supposed to be still a little sea-sick.

Lenny squared his shoulders and set off for the next step: the ransom note he'd leave under Annette's stateroom door.

She lived one deck above, near the Captain's quarters.

Lenny went up there and in one quick motion bent down and gave the envelope a push.

When he stood up straight and started toward the stairs, he saw the Captain.

The Captain wasn't supposed to be there. Nels said the Captain never missed one of Annette's performances.

The Captain was coming out of his door with another *Seastar* officer.

From the looks on their faces, there was something wrong.

Part of the contingency plan was for Lenny to ask a silly question if he was seen someplace where he seemed out of place.

Make a point of it. If you were guilty of anything, you wouldn't.

So Lenny said, "Oh, Captain, is the Jacuzzi nearby?"

The Captain looked at him.

There was something very, very wrong.

"*What?*" Lenny asked, because he had never seen a man just let tears roll down his cheeks.

"President Kennedy's been shot in Dallas," he said.

The other officer said, "He's dead."

chapter | 12

I was stretched out on the waterbed, holding the phone on my stomach, waiting for *I Love Las Vegas* to rewind.

"Of all the missing people, Nels Plummer's the one I remember best," Mom was saying, "because he disappeared the day the President was killed."

"What do you remember about him?"

"That he was from the food-chain Plummers. They're very rich, Johnny. I remember wondering why his sister had a job on a boat, when they had all that money."

"Do you remember that he went to Gardner and that he was a Sevens?"

"*Really?* That wouldn't have meant anything to me back then. So he was in your fancy club? Well, that figures."

Mom would never believe you didn't have to have money or pull or something special to be a Sevens. Since I couldn't tell her how you became one, I'd never convince her that wasn't it.

Now there was a new threat to the Sevens' secret. Keats had stumbled upon it in the journal. Even though she swore on her eyesight and her ability to feel emotion that she would never, *never* speak of it again, to me or to anyone else, I'm not so sure I would have sworn on those two essentials that she could be trusted.

The moon was rising over the ocean. The sun had set on any dinner plans I might have worked out with Keats.

Fen's blue Porsche was still in the driveway. No sign of them in the garden, but Gras was on the grass destroying a rawhide chew stick, which meant someone wanted him out of the way.

Mom was still talking about Nels Plummer. "I remember one theory was that he fell overboard upchucking. There was talk of all the drinking on that ship once the news was announced."

I still hadn't finished the journal, although I'd been trying hard to read it at the same time I watched *I Love Las Vegas*.

Thoughts of Jazzy'd kept intruding. I was thinking of what a lousy summer she was probably having.

"It's funny that you called right now," said Mom. "I've always thought we had ESP. Has Jazzy been on your mind?"

"I was thinking tonight that I ought to take her someplace like Jones Beach or Fire Island, before summer's over."

"She couldn't wait. She's taken off by herself."

"What do you mean?"

"What I said. She's been missing two hours. Then you call up and ask me about a missing person. . . . Maybe she's at Aunt Clara's, up on the roof over there. They've got it planted. Clara maybe thinks I know Jazzy's with her."

"Sure. Where else would she be?"

"Bernard's walking over there now to see, and if she's not there, then we call the police."

"Bernard?"

"Mr. Lopez," said Mom.

"She'll be there," I said, "don't you think?"

"I don't think," Mom said. "It's wasted effort when it comes to your kids. I just react."

"Yeah," I said. "That's what I do, too."

"You, you don't know," said Mom. "You take off when anything gets you. You don't react. You take off."

"Do you want me to come home?"

"You're out there now. She's just at Aunt Clara's."

"She's there," I agreed.

"She'll be all right," Mom said. "Don't worry."

"Okay. I won't," I said.

"I'm glad you called, Johnny."

"Me too," I said. "I'll check with you later."

I looked at my watch. It was twenty past eight. Where was a five-year-old at twenty past eight in the evening if she wasn't at her aunt's?

I supposed Mr. Lopez would take care of it.

He was practically family, wasn't he?

Dear Lord, I hoped he wasn't. . . . There was

something about Mr. Lopez I was never going to like—maybe the fact that most times I'd talked to him he had pins in his mouth.

There'd be this little hole in his lips words would come out of, and there'd be three or four pins.

That's how I remembered him.

The house was quiet except for the sound of music. It wasn't the Von Trapp family trudging down the Alps with Julie Andrews leading them in "Do-Re-Mi"—more like an old Madonna album, more like "Like a Prayer."

I supposed Keats was playing things for Fen. They were probably sitting on that great, soft, white couch in the living room with the French doors opening onto the garden.

No doubt in a little while Bernard would arrive back at our place with Jazzy in tow, and they'd put her to bed, then sit around in front of the TV the way they did, drinking homemade wine and eating Fritos.

To each his own, hmmm?

At such times I often found myself on the verge of trying to imagine what Delia was doing, who she was doing it with, and where. Rome? Hong Kong? Paris?

Then very quickly, before the stinging behind my eyes turned into salt water, I refocused my thinking.

I turned to something far away from me and my experience.

I turned on the little Tensor lamp and picked up the black leather book.

Of course, the only one on the Seastar *not upset about Kennedy was Nels.*

THE MOUTH

Of course, the only one on the *Seastar* not upset about Kennedy was Nels.

He refused the Captain's invitation for all passengers to assemble in Main Dining for prayers. Many were settled in there, watching the large TV flash the latest news bulletins from Dallas and Washington. Laura was among them.

Captain Stirman had announced that the *Seastar* was heading back to port. The ship would arrive in New York harbor at midnight. Two days ahead of schedule.

"This screws up everything, Tra La!" Nels complained in their cabin. "I've got to think! Go stay with Laura."

"Do you think your sister's read the ransom note already?"

"Has to have! I can't stop it now. When she was

taking her solo bow? Someone opened the door and shouted, 'Kennedy's been shot!' People started crying, screaming—Annette didn't get out of the room for about twenty minutes. That's when I should have moved: found you, put Celeste back, and gotten the note from Annette's stateroom. Why didn't I think faster? This is such lousy luck, Tra La!"

"We can't pull this off now, Nels."

Nels was pacing, hitting his fist with his palm.

He said to Lenny, "I need to make new arrangements, that's all. We'll smuggle Celeste out somehow."

"I don't feel up to this, Nels."

"What's the matter with you?"

"The President's dead, Nels!"

"Don't pull any crap on me, Tra La!"

"Don't you know what's going on aboard this ship? Everyone's in a daze."

"That could work for us."

"Let's just give her back the dummy, Nels, and forget it. It's all different now."

"No way. We've set things in motion. Lark is prepared and we are. We just have to rearrange the schedule, push it up. I'll figure it out."

"Won't the banks close down?"

"Not yet, and I bet my sister's already been on the phone and arranged to get the money."

"We can't count on anything running normally, even your sister, Nels. Laura can't even talk."

Nels opened his jacket and patted the bulge in the

inside pocket. "She'll have plenty to say when she sees this tonight."

"No, Nels. Everything's changed now."

"They'll still have dinner and dancing."

"No one's going to want to dance."

"You'll see. The show must go on. Their show must, and so must ours. Celeste is about five hours away from her watery grave . . . just as soon as it turns dark."

Lenny said, "Did Jackie Kennedy get shot, too?"

"Damn you, Tra La, pay attention to *us!*"

"We're stopped. At least for now."

"We're not stopped. You know, I didn't plan this for myself, Lenny."

"Didn't you?"

"This is all for you and Laura."

"For Laura, anyway."

"I don't have time for this. Go and be with Laura."

"Don't do us any more favors, Nels."

He stopped pacing and faced Lenny. "What does that mean?"

"I'm going to quit while I'm ahead."

"Don't be a fool!"

"The President's shot and you're pacing around planning how to do your sister in!"

"You're a mush head, Tra La. You've got mashed potatoes for brains!"

His eyes were narrowed and his hands were balled to fists. "You don't deserve Laura!"

"I thought that was it, all along. You wish you had

her, Nels, but you don't and you won't and you can't!" Lenny laughed in his face, even though his stomach was turning over.

Lenny was almost crying then. His voice sounded younger and sillier and shrill. "You've always wanted what was mine, from my childhood stories to my Handy act to my girl. You can't make it on your own! That's why you want your sister home, and it's why you want Laura and me in New York."

"I don't deserve this from you, Tra La." Nels's voice was very calm.

For a moment Lenny thought Nels was going to talk to him, make things okay again somehow, take back the ugliness between them.

Instead he socked Lenny, hard.

Lenny lit into him as though all he'd ever been waiting for was an excuse to beat up Nels.

No holds barred.

When Nels finally fell to the floor, there was blood trickling from his mouth. His right eye was already swelling to a slit.

Lenny looked down at him, amazed at what he'd done.

He leaned over, put his hand out, ready to pull Nels up.

"I'm sorry, Nels."

But Nels shook his head and pushed Lenny's hand away as he propped himself up on one elbow.

"Get the hell out of my sight," Nels said quietly.

~

When Nels didn't join them all evening, Lenny figured he was angry, and probably resigned to the fact there was no way they could follow through on their plan. He hoped Nels was with his sister, as Laura thought he might be.

Laura was frightened by the assassination. She had put in a ship-to-shore call to her brother, although Lenny had tried to discourage it. Twice she sent Lenny back to the stateroom to find Nels, but he wasn't there. The garment bag was. Still.

Laura kept saying she bet Nels was taking it hard.

Lenny finally snapped back. "Nels doesn't give a damn about Jack Kennedy or anybody but Nels! Don't you know that?"

"You've never really liked Nels," Laura said. "He loves you and you just use him."

"He uses us, too."

"How?"

"I'm not going to analyze it now."

"You can't. Because he doesn't."

Lenny decided not to continue the argument. They made a halfhearted effort to eat dinner. No one in the dining room was finishing. Few were even talking.

"I didn't mean anything I said a while ago," Laura finally ventured. "I just feel very insecure."

"Same here," said Lenny.

"When we get to New York, I'm going on home

with my brother, Lenny. Do you mind?"

Lenny lied and said he didn't. He knew he was losing her.

He wished that suddenly Nels would come around the corner with just the right thing to say, and the perfect thing for the three of them to do ... because Nels could always do that.

If anyone was looking for Celeste, Lenny wasn't aware of it. Nearly everyone was glued to the television. Some were praying; a small group was singing songs like "God Bless America." The bar was doing a good business.

After the *Seastar* docked, Reverend Delacourt, with Carl, came aboard to take Laura back to Philadelphia.

Neither one would speak to Lenny, or believe that Laura had occupied a separate cabin.

"Well, good-bye," Laura said.

Lenny had to turn away. His eyes were full.

When Lenny went to get his things, there was still no sign of Nels. His luggage was there. And Celeste was still hanging in the closet, in the garment bag.

Lenny slung it over his shoulder and carried it off the ship with his own luggage.

He didn't know why he did it.

People, that day, were not thinking about why they did what they did.

Lenny took a cab to his mother's. All through the

early-morning hours, Celeste sat in a chair across the room from them while they watched replays of Johnson taking the oath of office, and of Jackie Kennedy coming home in her blood-stained pink suit with her husband's coffin.

chapter | 13

No, Plum would not need his old clothes.

Fen sat in a flood of light, on a stool in the garden of Adieu. Star, in black satin and pearls, was on one knee.

And on the other?

Celeste, in white satin . . . looking exactly as she had in *I Love Las Vegas*.

The only difference was around her neck.

The Seven of Diamonds . . . and where the horizontal bar joined the vertical, there was a single ruby.

But how could it be?

In the journal Nels Plummer had it in his jacket pocket the day he disappeared.

The show began:

CELESTE: Tick tock tickers! Where's my Snickers?

STAR: I ate them, dear. It seems I was always coming across them in the pockets of the tacky clothes I had to wear.

CELESTE: Even my hand-me-downs are too classy for you, love. You don't understand class or Swinburne, or—

STAR: *My* favorite poet is Billy Idol.

CELESTE: That will never do, love, if you're to perform with *moi*. You have to change.

STAR: The way *you* changed? Folks, she changed from a male into a female. She's one of your transsexuals.

CELESTE: It's time for a songfest!

STAR: To drown out the truth, Plumsie?

CELESTE: *I was see-ing Nel-ly ho-oh-ome, I was—*

Join in everyone!

"And now what do you think of poor old Plum?" a voice asked.

I turned to face Guy Lamb. He had on a cowboy hat and boots, the same bolo tie with the turquoise stone, the black belt with the silver buckle. At that party he stood out like a Froot Loop in a china bowl filled with bonbons.

He didn't wait for an answer to his question.

He said, "At last I know what became of Celeste. She was turned into Plumsie. I should have figured that out long ago. There aren't that many McElroy figures still performing." He popped a shrimp into his mouth as a uniformed maid passed with a tray. "Very tasty!" he said. He wiped his mouth with a paper napkin that said Adieu.

I figured it'd be *adieu* to him as soon as one of the Keatings spotted him. He'd obviously crashed the party. Not another soul there looked like him; no one looked as if they even knew someone like him.

"How did you get here?" I asked him.

"I was just going to ask you the same question."

I told him how I had. He said he'd come there to sell Fen an alligator figure case Fen'd wanted to buy. When he couldn't find Fen all afternoon, he found out Fen had a date at Adieu. "I'm leaving early tomorrow morning. I'm glad it worked out this way. I wouldn't have missed this for anything."

"What do you think? Did Fen know he was buying Celeste when he bought Plum?" I decided to get as many questions in as possible, before he got the boot. I knew the Keatings. They wouldn't tolerate a gate crasher.

I didn't have time to tell him anything about the journal. Where I'd left off, Lenny had taken Celeste from the boat the night of Kennedy's assassination.

Guy Lamb shrugged. "I don't know what to think. Celeste was way before Fen's time. She was from the early sixties . . . and Lenny Last came along with Plumsie near the end of the sixties. But Fen knows her pretty good, I'd say. That's Celeste, if I ever heard her. That's how she looks, too, and that's how she dresses." He shook his head sadly. "Maybe that lady who owned Celeste sold her to Lenny and then Lenny did the worst thing."

"What's that?"

"Changed her sex. You don't do that. It's very

bad luck. . . . No wonder Lenny went downhill."

The Keatings' guests were joining in singing "Seeing Nelly Home."

We had to shout to hear each other.

I asked him if he remembered that something had happened to Annette Plummer's brother.

"Yes," he said. "He was a missing person. You think that's why she sold Celeste? Too broken up to perform after?"

I shook my head as though I didn't have a clue.

He said, "What's your connection in all this, Fell?"

"None."

"It doesn't sound that way." He grabbed another shrimp from another maid's tray.

It was around eleven o'clock, with a cool ocean breeze and a full moon overhead.

I could see Keats way down in front, her chair as close as she could get to Fen.

After the song, Celeste started doing Dr. Fraudulent.

I was as amazed as Guy Lamb, who hit his head with his fist and said, "Golly darn! She's the real thing!"

"What about the necklace?" I asked him. "That's new, isn't it?"

"It's a fake. Star was wearing that same seven yesterday by the pool. I asked Fen if it was insured. He said it was just a copy. . . . So that surprises me. Celeste would never have worn a fake in the old days."

"Did Fen say who had the original?"

"I didn't ask him. You sound like a claims adjuster, Fell."

Just at that moment I saw Mrs. Keating heading our way.

I figured Guy Lamb was going to be pointed toward the garden gate.

It was me Mrs. Keating wanted.

"I'm sorry to tell you this, John," she said. "Your mother called. Your sister is missing. The police are looking for her."

Whatever Eaton's official title was (Caretaker? Butler? Estate Manager?), he became my chauffeur that night.

While I waited for him down in the driveway, I stood beside Fen's Porsche.

When my mother's in a strange house, she likes to take a peek in the bathroom cabinet. She says you can tell a lot about someone by seeing the bottles and tubes lined up on the shelves.

The closest I could come to discovering anything about this fellow was by reaching into his car for a look in his glove compartment.

Eaton caught me at it.

He said in his sourest tone, "Of course you know that's not the car we're going in."

He was carrying my bag over to the black Lincoln, after giving me one of his looks. I used to suffer them when I was dating Keats.

"I don't know why Mr. Keating is being so generous to you," Eaton said. "Perhaps he's just glad to get rid of you."

I kept my big mouth shut.

I didn't feel like a skirmish with Eaton. It never pays to get the driver ruffled when you're going a long distance.

We were about two and a half hours from Brooklyn.

And I was too worried about Jazzy.

I wasn't so rattled that I didn't notice that the bag Eaton was putting into the back with me was not mine. I was about to make off with the little clothes and the journal again, but this time it suited me just fine.

On my excursion into Fen's glove compartment I'd discovered his address and his last name on his automobile registration and his driver's license.

I had an excuse now to pay a call there, pretending that I thought Fen would want what was inside the suitcase.

You see, Fen lived on Fifth Avenue.

His last name was Plummer.

THE MOUTH

Lenny'd fallen asleep in front of the TV. It'd been on all night. He didn't even hear his mother leave for her job at Macy's next morning. He woke up in time to see Lee Harvey Oswald shot dead.

Then the phone rang.

"I'm glad I got ahold of you, Leonard. This is Captain Stirman."

Stir-Crazy . . . probably hunting down Celeste.

Lenny had to turn down the sound to hear him. He wondered if he should tell him Oswald had been killed.

"Is Nels with you, Leonard?"

"No. Didn't he go home?"

"We haven't seen him. His sister and I are very, very concerned. When did you last see him?"

"Just after Celeste and Annette performed. Around two."

He could have sworn Celeste was smiling at him from the rocking chair. "He wanted me to be sure Laura was okay, so I went down to Main Dining to be with her."

"I saw him about an hour later. Did you and Nels have a fight, Leonard?"

"No. Why?"

"Someone had worked him over. He *said* a kidnapper did it, and Celeste *is* missing. There's even a ransom note. What do you know about it, Leonard?"

"Nothing! I'm sitting here watching what's going on in Dallas. Did you know someone just shot the guy who shot Kennedy?"

Lenny needed time to think. Was this a trick of Nels'? Was Nels trying to pin something on Lenny?

Stirman said, "I'm taking care of my own before I start worrying about Kennedy and the rest of it. . . . Nels told me he tried to stop a masked man from taking Celeste."

"I told you. I know nothing about it."

"Nels said he thought Celeste was thrown into the sea in all the assassination confusion."

"It's news to me."

"Would your girlfriend know anything about it?"

"Of course not!"

"May I talk to her, please?"

"She went home with her family."

Lenny gave him the number. Lenny hadn't spoken to Laura since they'd said good-bye aboard the *Seastar*. He had the feeling it was good-bye forever. He had the feeling he would not fight for her left to his own devices. But Nels would make him do it. Nels would never let her go.

On television they were replaying the most recent shooting. Lee Harvey Oswald was grimacing, holding his stomach in pain.

Suddenly the world seemed to have gone mad.

Lenny imagined that Celeste was winking at him.

"Nels will show up soon enough." Lenny told the Captain what he had been telling himself over and over. Nels was either hiding somewhere to punish Lenny or he was working on the kidnapping. Lenny doubted Nels was doing that, or he'd be frantic about Celeste's whereabouts. He'd have called Lenny long ago.

The Captain began asking him about girls in Nels's life, saying there had to be some.

Lenny said, "Why? He was always bashful."

"Did you ever know him to buy jewelry for a girlfriend?" the Captain asked.

"No. Did you?" It was a strange question. Had Nels shown him the Seven of Diamonds for some reason?

The Captain said, "I don't know him as well as you do. Would he buy jewelry for his sister?"

"I doubt that. Why?" Somehow the Captain *must* have seen the gift for Laura. Next Lenny imagined the Seven around Laura's neck, the three of them together again, this all forgotten.

He could still see Nels's bloody face, one eye closing.

He could still hear Nels telling Lenny, I don't deserve this from you, Tra La.

That was right. Nels hadn't deserved it.

The Captain dropped the subject of the jewelry. Lenny had crossed the room and picked up

Celeste. He had never seen a figure so beautifully made. The head was molded in plastic wood; the eyelids and retractable lips were fashioned from leather, and skillfully grafted onto the head.

There was a plate behind her ears, which opened to a spaghetti network that made her moves and expressions possible. There were levers inside that looked like typewriter keys.

The Captain said, "When Nels gets in touch with you, tell him we're calling the police. I only waited because I didn't believe that whole story he told me, and because our problems seem so minuscule compared to what the country's suffering. But now we have to take steps. Celeste is very much a part of our concern, too. She is extremely valuable. I'm not speaking now just of sentimental value. She is unique."

Yes . . . Lenny could see that. He was fondling Celeste's headstick. . . . Valuable . . . complex.

"Take this number down, Leonard. It's my private phone. If you hear one word from Nels, call me. I'll make it worth your while. . . . Dear God, where *is* he?"

It was a question that would obsess Leonard Tralastski long after he'd submitted to the police inquiry . . . long after he'd become Lenny Last.

He would never stop wondering about Nels.

Sober, he would think of all the possible accidents Nels could have had (ill from the punches to his gut, Nels had leaned too far over the ship's railing). He would toy with the idea Nels had amnesia from the blows to his head. (Nels had just walked off the ship in a daze.)

Drunk, he would suspect everyone of murdering Nels, including himself. Could he have blacked it out? Hadn't he, deep down, wished Nels dead sometimes?

Nels would haunt him forever.

But that Saturday afternoon, on the 23rd of November, it was Celeste he became fascinated and obsessed by.

He hung up the phone and bounced her on his knee like a proud father.

"Well, well, well, well," said he, "how's the little lady doing?"

He typed inside her head until she tilted a little to the right. She grinned into his eyes.

"What makes you think I'm a lady, Mac?"

"What makes you think I'm Mac? I'm Lenny."

"How do you do? You can call me Plumsie."

"I thought your name was Celeste."

"My *old* name was. I'm Plumsie now."

"How do you do?"

"Get me out of this drag, will you?"

Lenny's fingers typed some more and the figure put its hands on its hips and looked back at Lenny and rolled its eyes.

"Wipe off my lipstick, would you, Big Guy? And lend me a snappy necktie."

That night Lenny threw the red wig down the incinerator in the hall of the apartment building.

He'd get him a new wig when the weekend was over. It was Lenny's idea to rig Plumsie up so that even Nels would be fooled when he saw him.

chapter | 14

Back in Brooklyn, home sweet home.

"You must promise me never to do that again."

"I was only downstairs," said Jazzy. "Make Mom give Georgette back to me."

"Mom's trying to teach you something. You know how upset you feel now without your doll? That's how she felt."

"She didn't even know I was gone for a long time. She was down the hall at Bernard's."

"Mr. Lopez to you. Not Bernard," I said.

"Mr. Stinkmouth to me! I want my doll back and I want *him* dead!"

"I'll get Georgette for you, but don't run away anymore. Not even down to the laundry room. Okay?"

"*You* run away, Johnny. You've done it twice times. From school once, and once from the restaurant."

"Two times, not twice times. I'm not going to run away anymore," I said. "Neither are you, kiddo!"

I went down the hall and knocked on Mom's door. It was half open. The light from the television was still on.

"Are you awake, Mom?"

"She can't have Georgette. Not until tomorrow."

"Mom, it's already tomorrow. It's three A.M. She can't sleep without Georgette."

"Tough, Johnny! Do you know what it's been like around here tonight? No, of course you don't. You were off in The Hamptons with your rich girl-friend."

"May I come in a second?"

"Don't talk. This is almost the end."

How many times had she seen Ingrid Bergman walk away from Humphrey Bogart at the end of *Casablanca?*

I sat on the edge of her bed.

It was my second or third time. It was one of the few movies my dad had liked watching on TV. We used to tease him that it was only because he bore a slight resemblance to Claude Raines, the actor who played the dapper police chief.

I spotted Georgette leaning against a Kleenex box on the shelf behind Mom.

Jazzy used to dress her as a ragged, poor person, then change her into fancy costumes: ball gowns, silk dresses with sequins, queen's robes.

I waited until the music's swell and the credits. Then I picked up Georgette. She had on jodh-purs and a riding jacket.

"My kingdom for a horse," I said.

Mom sighed. "All right, take it to her."

"He's the one upsetting her," I said. "Bernard."

"Would you kids be happy if I'd set fire to myself the way widows used to do in India?"

"You know how Jazzy felt about Daddy. . . . If there was ever a daddy's girl—"

"Talk to her, Johnny."

"I did. I will some more."

"I shouldn't pass this information on to you, since you think Mr. Lopez is only fit to darn and stitch, but we were talking after Jazzy got home and we could think straight again. Mr. Lopez happens to be fascinated by the Bermuda Triangle. He knows all about your Nels Plummer."

"How does Mr. Lopez think Nels Plummer got anywhere near the Bermuda Triangle?" I said in the same tone Eaton had used on me.

"Never mind. You're too superior to talk to, I can see that."

"Mom, the *Seastar* wasn't anywhere near that part of the Atlantic where all the planes and ships disappeared!"

"Bernard knows that. But Nelson Plummer disappeared in 1963, and in 1963 a tanker with its entire crew disappeared in the Bermuda Triangle, and so did two Air Force tankers. Bernard buys anything to do with it, and he has a book across the hall about missing people. Your Nels Plummer is in it."

I said, "Thanks, Mom."

"Bernard's not your dad, but he's not what you're making him out to be."

"I know. But Jazzy and I think even Mr. Rogers wouldn't be good enough for you."

"You're right about that."

When I dropped Georgette on Jazzy's bed, she said, "Have you got a doll, Johnny? Where'd you get all the neat clothes?"

"I told you," I said. "They belong to a ventriloquist's dummy."

"I wasn't listening to all that stuff about ventrilquims. I was missing Georgette."

She was hugging the doll, settling down under the covers. I put a sweater of Plumsie's back inside next to the journal.

Then I changed my mind and picked the journal up to take out to the Hide-a-Bed where I sleep in the living room. There was a lot I hadn't read, and a lot I never would. But if I could make out the handwriting, I was game for one last read . . . the few pages at the very end.

"Do you promise to hang around from now on?" I asked Jazzy.

"Do you?"

"I'll be around until I go back to school," I said.

"Okay, me too," she said.

THE MOUTH

And now, of course, it's time for me.

I'm not really a writer, you know, even though more and more I have had to rescue the act with my own material.

Sample:

If Leonard feels a little wheezy,
(Asthma does that) . . . well, it's easy,
For then the act becomes old Plum's,
And in the darkness someone comes,
Someone wet and someone hissing,
"Would you leave me down there?
Missing?

Oh, it would get him very, very crabby, that would. "Leave Nels out of it!. . . You're no writer, Plum!"

I never reminded him that it's me writing this thing so it looks like a story—and why? So Tra La De Da doesn't have to face that it's his very own autobiography.

He likes to distance himself from himself, you see. From himself, from everybody. That began way back when he said toodle-oo to Laura. He gave her up, or she gave him up. We'll never know, since he didn't call her again. I take a little credit for that—Old Plum is on the selfish side, doesn't like to share . . . doesn't even like the word unless you're talking about a piece of cake.

Maybe I'm not a writer, but who cares? I don't even read writers. I read nothing.

I'm a boob-tube geek.

Ask Tra La. When he's out drinking and gambling away our hard-earned money, I sit and watch the big picture.

When he drags his behind home, broke, he sits beside me watching, too, and he says, "What a pair we are, old buddy."

I know how to get him.

Say I, "Who do you mean, you and Nels?"

Once he cried.

He said, "When are you going to leave Nels out of it?"

"What if he comes back and he finds out we left him out of it? He won't like that one bit, will he?"

But back to me.

I like what's hot!

Writing in this journal is not hot, so I told him ce soir (that's Spanish, dear hearts. It means this evening)— I told him no more scribble scribble, Leonard.

Your life history is over, say I.

Finito . . . (that's French for finished).

Do you get it YET, amicos and amicas? (That's Russian for friends.) Ha! Ha! Get the picture?. . . I lie for enjoyment. Others golf, shoot pool, jog, and you know what, but I like prevaricating. . . . Doesn't that sound filthy?

Say I, "No more scribble scribble, Tra La."

Say I, "What your future holds now can never be recorded, and you know it, Tra La. Nothing about this can be put down in writing."

(There were times when he'd cry out, "Don't call me Tra La!" but he doesn't fight me anymore.)

Say I, "Lovely to be back in Cottersville, is it not?"

Says he, "It's not."

Say I, "You're at Sevens House again, eh? And you're on another of your little trips down Memory Lane, hmmm?"

Pause.

Say I, "You may answer, Tra La."

"Knock it off, Plum. This is different. I've never killed anyone."

"That you remember, Tra La. Your mind is shot. I doubt sincerely (don't you love me using that word?) that you'll remember anything about this visit to your old alma mater either . . . but it will get us out of debt, Tra La."

He has no reaction. Sits there like a lump.

Say I, "They couldn't have made it any easier for you, and what a cute little gun they got you, Tra La."

Say I, "Revenge is sweet, too, isn't it? Particularly when Sevens set it up. . . . Answer me, Tra La De Da."

Says he, "There's no such thing as The Sevens Revenge."

Because, you know, he was *taught* to say that. They teach them all to deny there's any such thing.

Say I, "At least they knew who'd welcome *any* kind of work, even dirty work."

Says he (speaking without permission—*tsk! tsk!*), "I didn't need to buy a rat for the job, either, since I have you."

Which is *why*, Ladies and Gentlemen, Boys and Girls, Fans and Foes, I refuse to leave this lovely old white Cadillac, even to go inside Sevens House for a minute.

Leave me out of it is my new motto, and I told Tra La I was parking my carcass in the car.

Where I will wait . . . and wait.

Old Plum is good at waiting.

And I like old cars.

Lately I have longings for old things . . . things like Snickers bars, which Tra La brings me.

Say I, "Thank you, Big Guy."

Makes him wheeze to hear me call him that.

Wheeze wheeze, Louise: His asthma is worse than ever now.

It's why I took over the act in the first place, you know.

Nobody wants to pay to hear someone gasping for air in the middle of a joke. Toodle-oo to boo-hoo-hoo.

Lately I have longings for old things.

Said I that?

Easter is in the air, that's why—Easter vacation.

Easter always reminds me of when I was Celeste.

I was known for my Easter hats.

Is that a song I feel coming on?. . . Oh, *In my Eas-ter bon-net . . . with blah blah blah upon it . . .* Who wrote that, pet, do you know?. . . A box of Snickers to the lady in the front row who answered Ozzy Osbourne.

We always have to credit the author, don't we?

Pictured here is Nels Plummer, 18, of New York City, scion of a wealthy food family, who vanished on board the luxury liner *Seastar* in 1963.

He was last seen in his cabin by the Captain at 3 P.M. on the afternoon Kennedy was shot in Dallas. The ship was nine hours north of New York.

Annette Plummer, the sister of the missing man, rules out suicide. The skipper of the 16,567-ton vessel states that the heir to a fortune could not have accidentally fallen from the ship, which was constantly in serene waters. "Those railings are four feet high, even on the private outdoor verandas. I defy anyone to fall off my ship, unless a person climbs up on a railing and jumps."

Investigators declare that leaves only one conclusion: murder.

—from *Still Missing* by George Tobias.

chapter | 15

I had the feeling that Bernard Lopez had bought the Tobias book only to get me over to his apartment.

The book was so new, some of the pages were still stuck together. I think his interest in the Bermuda Triangle was zilch, too. He had nothing to say about it when I asked him.

This is what he wanted to say.

"Johnny, I'm no brain, but any problem you might have taken to your dad, feel free to come to me about. I'll do my humble best."

I felt like telling him to shove it, felt like saying I'll look you up when I want to know what's the best thread to use on a coat hem, or how to fit a hammer foot attachment to a sewing machine.

But I felt sorry for the guy. Did he *really* think my mother'd get serious with *him?* Or that he'd turn out to be just like a father to me and Jazzy?

He kept rubbing his long, skinny fingers together and whining that he hadn't had time to "pick up" because Jazzy'd run off.

His apartment looked like the back room of a tailor shop, one of those places where the guy watches TV while he works. He was watching a Sunday-morning news program, chain-smoking

Benson & Hedges and sipping something he called coffee/I called rotgut.

I was glad to get out of there, even though it meant getting on a subway next. It was shaking from side to side, stinking of garbage and don't-say-it, rushing me under the East River and into Manhattan: God's country, next to Brooklyn . . . or was it anymore?

Now New York looked like some ex-lover whose beauty was still showing, even though she was homeless, and standing in the gutter with a needle in her arm. You wondered if it was too late for her to go back to what she used to be.

I'd called Annette Plummer, so she was expecting me.

chapter | 16

I could hear the church bells ringing down the street at St. Patrick's, and over on Park at St. Bartholomew's.

Lark must have been sneaking up on eighty, a wizened, white-haired old man in a navy suit that had seen better days, too. Going up to the third floor, Lark told me that he operated the elevator for the Plummers himself now that the building had gone self-service.

He said Captain Stirman was at church, but Miss Plummer only went on holidays, or when her son was home.

"I didn't know she had a child."

"She adopted this little boy, Fen, from Vietnam, right after her brother disappeared. You know about the brother?"

"Yes."

"Is this about him?"

"No. Not really."

"But Nels has something to do with why you're here?"

I nodded.

I was tempted to ask him if he'd ever received his $1000 from the ransom money for Celeste, but he looked so frail I couldn't.

He said, "There's a writer name of Tobias comes here every so often. Lark, he says, anything new?. . . What could be new after all these years, am I right?"

He was fishing.

"You're right," I said. "What could be new?"

As he let me into the apartment, he said, "She likes to talk about Mr. Nels, though, so don't worry about bringing up the subject. . . . And she's very happy this morning. Very, very happy. Fen found something for her we all thought was gone forever."

She looked very happy. All smiles as I came off the elevator directly into her apartment foyer.

"Come in," she said. "I just spoke with Fen."

"And he said he didn't want the clothes."

"No, we want them." She led me down a marble hall, carrying a cigarette in a long gold holder, continuing, "Fen said maybe our dressmaker can do something with those tiny suits and sweaters and shirts. Put lace on the cuffs or change the buttons to pretty little pearl ones. . . . Of course Celeste is such a snob she won't agree to wearing hand-me-downs, but the other one will."

She laughed. It was a strangely thin and lilting laugh for one so enormous. Her hair may have been as white as Lark's behind the Clairol, but it was raven black, slicked back in a wet look, her eyes a vivid green, the sort that watched yours to see what she could learn about you.

And she did like to talk about "Mr. Nels," particularly after I told her I was attending Gardner, and I was in Sevens. She said "Nelly" was crazy about that club.

She was drinking black coffee, letting me refill her cup from a silver pot. I was having orange juice, served by Lark in a long-stemmed glass.

On the coffee table was the photograph she'd hunted down to show me when I told her that the night before, I'd watched Fen work with Celeste on one arm and Star on the other.

In the photograph there was a curly-haired young boy in one of those old-fashioned-looking sailor suits with short pants and knee socks, and a big bow tie in the front.

While I studied the picture, she talked.

"Celeste won't tolerate Star in the act for long. She's always been the whole show, except for when she was younger. Then I'd make her share with Nelly. See him there on the right?"

He was sitting on one of her knees, and the dummy was on the other. Celeste had on a matching sailor suit, except hers had a skirt instead of pants.

Annette Plummer grinned down at the photo. "Those were happy days. Little Nelly'd pretend he was like Celeste. I taught him a whole routine to go with hers. He got it in his little head it was better to be made of wood than flesh and blood. . . . He wanted a room like Celeste's, too, with everything scaled down to size, but Daddy said no. Daddy said, He's going to grow up thinking he needs you to talk or smile or walk or think!"

In the picture, little Nels was leaning forward to get a look past Annette to Celeste.

The two females were both smiling at the camera, but Nelly was staring at the dummy, as though he was checking to see what she was up to.

"Was Fen good?" Annette Plummer asked me.

"Very!"

"I taught him everything I know, and of course Celeste is everything I know. . . . Even when I thought I'd never see her again, I taught Fen her routines. From the time he was just a little tyke. . . . He was five when I adopted him. I was keeping a promise to my father to adopt a child."

"You and the Captain?"

"No. Fen is mine alone. The Captain and I aren't married. One day he'll talk me into it, I suppose, but for now we just live together."

She smiled at me, lighting a cigarette for herself. She seemed in a mood to talk: not really lonely, but not sorry that I'd dropped by, either.

"This is a big place," she said. "Room enough for everyone." She waved her hand toward the large room with all its antique furnishings and works of art. Thick rugs. Old vases. Flowers everywhere. Through the long windows, I could see the treetops across the street at the Central Park Zoo.

She blew out a few smoke rings, as though she was clearly satisfied with herself that Sunday morning in July.

I decided to jump in.

I said, "Celeste was wearing a Seven of Diamonds around her neck."

"Of course, you'd know that. Yes. It's a copy. The original is in my safe. I'm very surprised Celeste wore the copy. Star would, of course, but *Celeste?*"

I didn't bat an eye.

I said, "I've never seen one quite like that. Who gave it to you?"

"Nelly, of course," she said. "It was his last gift to me. He told the Captain he'd ordered it especially for me."

She shook her head. "Here he was in pain from being beaten up. You know my brother's case, don't you?"

"Yes, I know it."

"I guess everybody does, no matter what age. Nelly's become like Judge Crater or James Hoffa. Legendary."

"Yes, you could say that."

"The person who took Celeste beat him up. May have gone back and killed him later, but the Captain saw him in the meanwhile. Nelly wanted to be sure that I got the Seven of Diamonds immediately. He told the Captain it might cheer me up, so he wasn't going to wait until journey's end to give it to me. He knew how I loved John Kennedy. I was the only Democrat in the family."

I remembered the journal: the description of Nels with the jeweler's box inside his sports coat, just before the fight with Lenny.

"It's the first one I've ever seen with a ruby," I said.

"Nelly didn't get a chance to tell me about that, but I guessed," said Annette Plummer. "A piece of bright-red color in a row of diamonds. It could only stand for Celeste in my life, with her red wig. It was terribly original, which surprised me because Nelly wasn't all that original. He always copied from other people. Daddy said I'd done that to him by making him play dummy all the time. It wasn't like him to think symbolically: He was so direct. But what else could the ruby stand for?"

For Laura Delacourt's birthstone, I thought.

Annette Plummer said, "Of course Nelly loved drama! He loved doing dramatic things, and he could afford to. What Nelly wanted, Nelly got. I'm afraid Daddy led him to believe there were no limits for him."

She stopped smiling and looked off toward a vase of long-stemmed white roses, shaking her head.

"Maybe that's why I went off to sea," she said in a sudden, merry voice, as though she was mocking herself. "I ran off to sea like some young boy. I skipped college, said toodle-oo, and took off. For years I wrote Nelly every day. Much as I adored him, I had to get away."

"Was he controlling, was that it?"

"Not controlling, really. No. He was beginning to turn into me. It's hard to explain, but if Nelly truly admired you, he became you. It was as though you'd absorbed him. He was there but he was you. It was rather frightening. Whatever it was, he had no way of his own. . . . It's hard to explain, Fell."

Thanks to the journal, it wasn't hard to understand, though. Leonard Tralastski had made the same complaint about Nels.

Or Plum had . . . if you wanted to believe they weren't one and the same.

"Celeste never trusted him, you know," she said.

I had no response to that remark, and she went on.

"Nelly knew it, of course. A part of me used to think Nelly'd destroyed Celeste himself, then changed his identity. But how could Nelly just walk out on his inheritance? He could never have afforded himself. He bought several new suits a month . . . and shirts, shoes. He was a world-class shopper."

"My mother's one of those."

"The Captain isn't chopped liver when it comes to shopping, either—only what *he* likes you can't bring home on the bus in bags. You steer home the things he likes."

She lighted yet another cigarette, in a mood to talk.

"A few years ago the Captain learned there was this broken-down ventriloquist who played the casinos and sang 'Seeing Nelly Home' in his act. The Captain began to suspect Celeste had not been thrown overboard after all. When he found out that Lenny Last was Nelly's old school pal, he was sure. But he didn't want to say anything to me. I had almost put the whole tragic affair behind me. And how could he ever prove it?"

I had an idea I knew why the Captain didn't want to say anything.

He didn't want her coming face-to-face with Lenny Last and finding out what the ruby really stood for, and whose necklace it was to be before the Captain took it.

Took it and then did what to Nels Plummer?

Had the Captain sent Plummer to a watery grave, just as Nels had wanted to do to Celeste?

Had the Captain found Nels injured from the fight with Lenny, and then finished the job himself?

But why?

Annette Plummer had more coffee.

Then she began to answer the questions I would have liked to ask her . . . the very ones I was sitting across from her asking myself.

She said, "The Captain always felt threatened by Nelly. My brother and I were like some kind of nightclub act when we were together: playing straight man for each other, doing one-liners that cracked each other up—oh, you know how it is when you're very, very *simpatico* with someone. . . . The Captain was jealous of Nelly. Celeste spotted it almost immediately, and as the Captain would come toward us, she'd say, 'Here comes jelly belly, jelly of Nelly belly, jelly of Nelly.' I'd have to hush her."

Maybe all vents were space cadets when it came to their dummies. So far I hadn't met one who wasn't.

I said, "When did *you* find out that Celeste wasn't destroyed—that she was really Plumsie?"

She looked insulted suddenly, and her eyes narrowed. "Celeste was never Plumsie! Plumsie tried to take her over, yes, but Celeste was too strong for him!"

I said, "Sorry."

Her face softened. "I am, too, Fell. I shouldn't be cross when you only came here to do us a favor . . . And here I've been blabbing away selfishly about myself and Nelly and Celeste. Forgive me!"

"I'm having a good time."

"I think I miss having a young man to talk to. Fen's such a good listener."

"Please go right on with the story," I said.

Another smoke ring. She admired it for a moment, and then got back on the subject. "As soon as Lenny Last was dead, the Captain told me his suspicion. They were more than suspicions by then. He'd actually had Fen sneak off to a performance of Plumsie's out in Las Vegas. Both of them vowed to get her back for me. And for Fen, as well. . . . Fen knows Celeste's entire act, but he can't make it work with Star. She's clearly inferior."

"Not a McElroy," I said, straight-faced.

"Far from it!" said Annette Plummer, looking pleased that I understood.

She said, "You see, the Captain would like to have Celeste back on the *Seastar.* Fen would like living on shipboard, too, I think. And I am happiest at sea. We could all four be together. It'll be enormous fun!" Her face was radiant then. "Celeste will *love* hearing what we've planned for her!"

She rose finally and said it was so very nice to meet someone from her brother's school . . . and club.

"Although," she said, "there are some very ominous things about Sevens, aren't there? Some kind of Sevens Revenge?"

"I never heard of that," I said loyally.

Celeste, Plumsie, Lenny, whichever one it was, was right, of course: We're taught to say that.

But it was the very first time I'd ever said it and known better. For when Deem was convicted of drug dealing, and then killed mysteriously during our Easter vacation, I'd believed the rumors that the drug lords had copied descriptions of The Sevens Revenge to take suspicion off themselves.

Thanks to the journal, I finally knew better.

Thanks to the journal, I knew better, I knew more, I knew then that in a world so full of cunning and concealment, I needed all the help I could get . . . whether I owned a restaurant, had a chain of them, or worked as a chef in one.

No matter what I did, or where I did it. I'd best get my butt back to the books, to The Hill, to the Sevens.

Before I left, Annette Plummer showed me Celeste's room, exactly as it had always been, still waiting for her . . . across the hall from a smaller room where Star lived.

I asked her if she wanted me to put the suitcase in Fen's room, and she answered that she'd like that.

That was when I slipped the journal into my pocket. I must have always known I would not leave it for Fen to read, for I had never mentioned it.

Lark took me back down in the elevator.

"Did you talk a lot about Mr. Nels?" he asked me.

"Enough to make me suspicious," I said.

He laughed as though I'd said something funny. He said "That Mr. Tobias? He's full of suspicions. At one time he even suspected Miss Annette. And he's always snooping around in the Captain's life. He could be right about the Captain."

"Why do you say that?"

"The Captain's a man who likes what money can buy. A man who drives an Avanti around likes what money can buy. Her money bought it, of course. And the boat. Imagine wanting a boat when you work on one? But it's quite a boat, and she bought it."

"What were Nels and she like together?"

"When he was small she called him Little King Tut, and he was, too. The master spoiled him rotten. Remember, it wasn't her brother. Not a blood relative at all. . . . She was always jealous of Mr. Nels. He came along so unexpectedly, and he was a real Plummer—and a male in the bargain. The master focused all his attention on the boy, see, because the Mrs. passed away. But Mr. Nels adored Miss Annette. He tried his best to please her, always. Poor Mr. Nels."

"And how did he feel about Celeste?"

"She's an itch with a b in front of it, Mr. Fell."

I laughed and so did he.

Then I said, "What do you really think happened to him, Lark?"

"Someone murdered him, Mr. Fell. . . . That school friend of his, maybe . . . or someone closer." He looked around him in the small elevator, as though the culprit could be riding down with us. "Someone very close, maybe."

When we hit the first floor, he hung on to me. Someone should have been taking *him* up and down in the elevator, not the other way around.

He said, "That day Jack Kennedy was shot is like a bad dream. It wasn't real and yet it was. And I don't think we'll ever know the whole truth about that or this."

The next day before I checked in at Le Rêve,

I tore a few pages out of the journal: the ones that described how Lenny and Nels named their trees Celeste, winning admission to Sevens . . . and at the very end, the pages about Lenny Last going to Cottersville to perform The Sevens Revenge on Deem.

Both Lenny Last and Deem were dead. The score was even.

I made some phone calls next and found out the address of George Tobias. Then I wrapped the journal up and mailed it to him.

It was his case, after all; he should be the one to solve it.

As for any immediate punishment due the Captain, I was betting on Celeste.

I was betting that with Celeste back aboard the *Seastar, The Ancient Mariner* would read like the story of Little Bo Peep.

chapter 18

That September I returned to Gardner and to Sevens House.

Not everyone on The Hill had resigned himself to the fact we were now a coed institution.

There were pickets out with signs reading BETTER DEAD THAN COED, and WOE, MEN! WOMEN!

There was only one new member of Sevens, a junior named Parson Stalker.

He told the Sevens he was assigned to that he had named his tree Dazzler, after his horse.

He moved in right across the hall from me.

I'd walked over to introduce myself and tell him whatever he might want to know about life on campus as a Sevens.

He was sitting in a leather chair with his back to the door. He was smoking. The view in front of him was of The Tower, where the Sevens had sung him into the club . . . and where we ate evenings, separate from and better than the others at Gardner School.

"Hello there!" I called out to him. "If you have permission to smoke, do it down in the smoker, first floor."

There was no response. He didn't move a muscle.

He was reading a book by James Tiptree, Jr.

"I'm John Fell from across the hall!" I said.

He actually blew a few smoke rings, reminding me of Annette Plummer that Sunday morning I'd gone to see her.

The book he was holding up was called *Her Smoke Rose Up Forever.* His did, too; maybe he couldn't see me through it. I went closer until I was right in front of him and then finally he looked up at me and said, "Who're you?"

"Fell!" I said. "No smoking!" I was teed off.

Then I saw the cord coming down behind his ear and inside his shirt collar.

He put his fingers to his lips making a shhh gesture. He pointed to his cigarette.

I shook my head. "No way. Put it out!"

He laughed and gave me a beseeching look as though he was saying "Please?"

"Stalker, butt it!"

"Parson," he said. "Parr. Who're you?"

I told him again.

He was a turn-head, kind of good-looking; male or female, you'd want to be sure you were seeing right. He belonged in movies, on the slick pages of magazines, and up on billboards. He had dark eyes and black hair and he was tanned. White, perfect teeth. A mole just to the left of a dimple. Forget Tom Cruise!

He put out his cigarette, shrugging. "Okay,"

he said. Then he pointed to the hearing aid and said, "I'm deaf. This alerts you more than it helps me hear. I read lips."

"You speak good."

"I do everything good." He laughed.

"Yeah, you even brag good."

He laughed again and nodded. "I brag good."

"Welcome to Sevens." I grinned at him.

He said, "You're all lucky to have me," and he grinned back.

He said what?

I was late for Science. I was up to explain Lamarckism that morning, so my mind was on acquired characteristics . . . but he said *what?*

I told myself probably Stalker was just a wiseacre, but you know the feeling you have when something says what you see is what you're getting?

There was that feeling.

There was that feeling, there was my forthcoming discussion of the French naturalist Jean Baptiste de Lamarck, and there was a September rain that added whole new dimensions to the meaning of the word wet.

I was running through it when I saw her.

And she is somebody I am always seeing, even though it is never her. She is at bus stops as I go by in a car, in crowds I see from buses, at the backs of restaurants until I get closer, and again and again flying with me in dreams.

But that September day in the pouring rain I swore that I saw Delia on that campus.

By the time classes were finished, the rain was too.

The late-afternoon sun brought my sanity back, I believed, and the beginnings of autumn colored the campus.

In my mailbox was a letter from George Tobias and one from Keats.

Keats's first.

Yes, I'm in love and that's why you haven't heard from me! My life would be perfect if it were not for her. She calls me Bleeps, because she says what she wants to call me would be bleeped out. And DON'T tell me it's really Fen, because it really isn't. Maybe she isn't real, but she is a force, Fell! I was almost glad to get back to school to be away from her! Fen is coming this weekend, without her.
Can't wait. He's my fella, Fell.

xxxxx Keats

P.S. He doesn't know anything about the journal and I'd just as soon keep it that way now that I've met Celeste. I don't want Fen swallowing

that mystique of hers. It's bad enough without
written confirmation of her power!. . . Do you
really think Tobias will take it to the police?

Tobias's letter answered her question. He
had already called me in August, to thank me for
sending the journal.

Dear Fell,

A detective who investigated the case years
ago is having a look at the diary, comparing it
with the Captain's testimony.
It'll take time, but I think we're onto some-
thing. Keep quiet about it.
The detective knew your dad. He also
wants to know about your mother. Seems he
dated her before your dad did. His name is
Tom Bernagozzi. Would your mother mind if
he called her? I'll keep in touch. Thanks!

G.T.

I was in a good mood, glad to be back.
I went up to my room in Sevens House to
drop off my raincoat and give Mom a buzz.
At the end of our conversation I told her that
the detective working on the Nels Plummer case
had known Dad.

"What's his name?" she said.

"Tom Bernagozzi," I said.

"You've got to be kidding!" she said.

"I'm not," I said.

"Tommy!" she said. "I didn't know he was still around."

I said, "Well, he is, and he's asking for you. I'm supposed to find out if he can call you."

"If he can *call* me?" She laughed. "He can do more than *call* me. Him with *his* eyes?"

"Yeah, but what about Mr. Lopez?" I said.

"What about him?" she said. "He's just a neighbor."

I changed into shorts and Keds. I felt like running. At least that kind of running had a purpose.

I was ready to go when I smelled cigarette smoke again. I heard the sound of female laughter.

Parson Stalker was breaking two rules at once this time: smoking above first floor, and entertaining a female in his room on a weekday.

I thought right: Woe Men, Women!

I went across to speak to them, to get her out of there . . . fast.

She was sitting on the windowsill facing Stalker, wearing something red, smoking a cigarette.

When she saw me, she stood up.

She looked at me, the same way she had always

looked at me . . . her eyes all over my face, the pitch-black hair spilling down her back.

I felt my knees almost give and my insides flip.

I said, "Delia?"

"No, her sister," she said. "April." She was coming toward me with her hand out. "April Tremble," she said. "And you must be Fell."